THE BLOOD FOUNTAIN

MARK OF VALLIATH
—BOOK THREE—

M. H. WOODSCOURT

True North Press

Edited by Sarah B.

Cover design by MiblArt

Published by True North Press

www.mhwoodscourt.com

Paperback ISBN: 978-1-959619-11-6

Hardback ISBN: 978-1-959619-12-3

For those who seek redemption—
You're not alone.

CONTENTS

NAKANIA

Neminar
KryTeer
Tivalt
Vylam
Clanslands
Keep Lunorr
Amantier
Bahadronn
Kavacos
Shing
Lilu River
Kyon Taro
Snowblinds
Tild
Frostfire Canton
Kilitheer
Keep Falcon
Snow Wastes
Drifting Sands

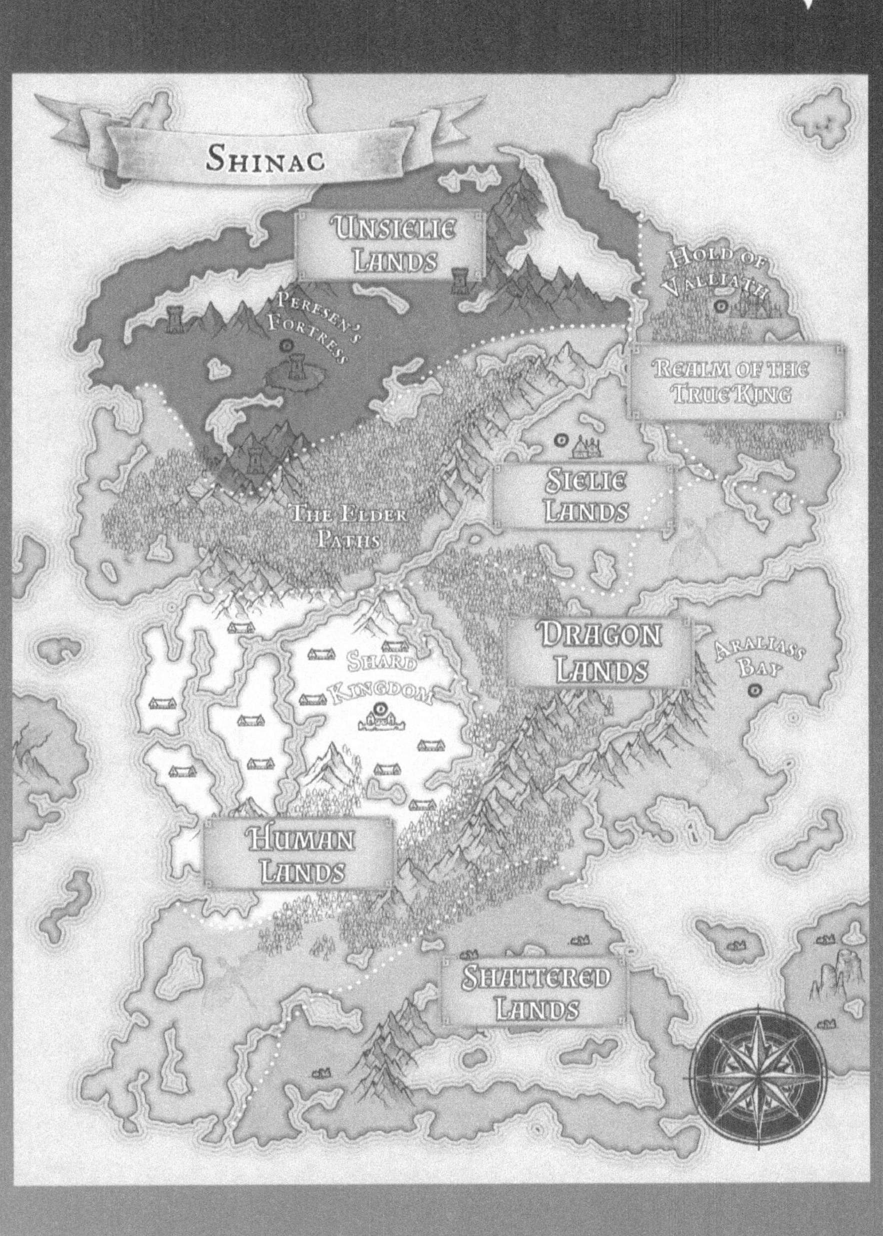
Shinac
Unsielie Lands
Hold of Valliath
Peresen's Fortress
Realm of the True King
Sielie Lands
The Elder Paths
Dragon Lands
Aralias Bay
Shard Kingdom
Human Lands
Shattered Lands

CONTENT WARNING

This book contains war violence, death, possession, and other strong themes commonly found in fantasy novels. Proceed at your own discretion.

— M. H. W.

CHAPTER 1
CLASHING WINGS

A deafening roar ripped over the damp night air.

Jetekesh clutched his dagger tighter and dragged his eyes heavenward, where an army of lace-winged *Unsielie* swelled. The dark force glowed in the starlight above the ruined fortress in the wetlands of Shinac. The hum of their wings was like a swarm of locusts, and Jetekesh shuddered at the magnitude of their number.

He expected them to descend upon the company standing among the stone debris, but instead, the army of fae flew northward.

The deafening roar sounded again.

Sharo whirled toward the noise. "That's—"

"Taregan!" Kethalas shouted. "Spirits be praised!"

A great silver dragon soared into view above the gnarled tree branches scratching at the black sky. Its mighty wings beat the air, gaining speed, until it rammed into a formation of *Unsielie*, a storm of claws and teeth and spiked tail. Dark fae scattered as fire wreathed the heavens, painting the world orange.

"I should help him." Kethalas started to move away from the company, but Dakarai caught his arm.

"Do not be foolish," the clansman said in his level tones. "We did not bring you back to Shinac for healing so that you could get yourself killed."

Jetekesh's stomach wrenched. *We didn't come to Shinac to break the ancient seals, either.*

He couldn't bring himself to say as much out loud. The implications churned in his mind. He'd longed to bring Shinac back to Nakania—but that had been under the hope that Nakania would become worthy of joining the fae kingdom once again. Not yet. Not this way.

Not at the expense of losing Nakania.

Fire bloomed overhead, drawing Jetekesh's gaze. The silver dragon wheeled and veered, tackling the *Unsielie* forces with brute power and shrewd maneuvers.

Movement tickled Jetekesh's instincts, warning him.

He whirled. "Look!"

Another force of *Unsielie* soared from the east, three times the number Taregan faced alone. The dragon wouldn't be able to outmatch so many.

Kethalas seemed to draw the same conclusion. "I'm going." He jerked free of Dakarai's hold and darted away from the company until he had room to transform. The ice blue scales rippled with light as he expanded himself into a beast a quarter Taregan's size—though still an impressive two-hundred-foot span from snout to claws.

"Hold fast!" called Emerin, but the ice dragon shot into the air, wings wide and glittering. Emerin swore under his breath, shoving back his tousled blond locks.

"Leave the dragons to it," commanded Prince Sharo. "Our problems are closer to the ground." He turned to spear Jetekesh with a look. "You've granted Lord Emerin forgiveness, and as your liegeman, 'tis your right to pardon him—but I should like a complete explanation for his behavior."

Jetekesh's eyes cut to the lord of the Keep of the Falls. "As would I. Is that possible to give, Lord Emerin?"

The man stared at the remains of the fallen *Unsielie* warriors who had tricked Jetekesh into breaking the seal between Nakania and Shinac. Their leader, Tavassed, had either vanished or been crushed beneath the shattered stones of the hold.

Emerin inhaled a long breath. "Even with my end of the bargain now fulfilled, I'm not certain what I can and can't say. I dare not."

"Because of your curse?" Jetekesh asked. "Or something else?"

"*My* fate isn't important," said Emerin.

Then, someone else's fate is tied up in his actions. A hostage, then?

Jetekesh nodded. "Surely, we can find someone to help you discover if you're still bound to silence."

"Yes," said Dakarai. "Perhaps yourself, Your Highness."

Jetekesh blinked. Though his gift was seeing the truth, he didn't know how to view it on command—or if it could be used in such a specific way. He rubbed at his jaw. "Well, I could try—"

"Please do," said Emerin.

"Do what you must," King Aredel cut in. "I need to locate Artassa if she still lives."

"But..." Jetekesh scanned the debris. He couldn't bring himself to state what appeared obvious.

"There is likely a dungeon. It may be intact." Aredel started off, picking his way between the cracked stone boulders.

"We should help," said Sharo. "Ashea?"

The fairy winked into sight, her lavender hair dancing in the breeze. Her iridescent wings beat the air. "I shall attend the Blood King and see what we may find." She flitted off with the noise of a hummingbird.

Dakarai slid his spear into the holster on his back. "Anenyasha and I will also search." His black eyes found Jetekesh. "Help Emerin. We will assist King Aredel." He glanced at Kajsa. "Stay near the Marked Prince."

The Norvian girl nodded, clutching her borrowed bow. Two arrows jutted from the quiver strapped to her back. Her cheeks were dirt-smudged, and her tunic was torn and bloodied.

Jetekesh returned his focus to Emerin—but a thundering scream pulled his eyes skyward.

The two dragons were encircled by the *Unsielie* forces. Lightning split the air around them. As Kethalas unleashed a stream of ice from his maw, flakes of snow sparkled down from the heavens. Did Jetekesh imagine the ice dragon struggling to beat his wings?

The tang of the storm rested on Jetekesh's lips. "They need help."

White smoke shot from the rubble before him. Jetekesh dropped his eyes toward the source. King Aredel stood atop a large obsidian stone, his hands held high, pouring forth a storm of white that stretched up to blind those in the heavens. The shrieks of *Unsielie* followed.

Jetekesh stared at the KryTeeran king. Aredel's entire body glowed. His brown eyes had taken on a golden cast, blazing with a fury that pulsed out from his aura. The gems on his clothes flashed. Dragon fire joined the torrent of white smoke, and Jetekesh flinched away, his eyes watering in the brilliance of the two attacks. Shadows stretched and pitched at his feet, twinkling with ice flakes.

Emerin shifted to block the light, using his body as a shield before Jetekesh. Seconds flew by. The light faded, shrinking the shadows.

The keep lord twisted to face the heavens, allowing Jetekesh a clear view. Ashes and snow fell like gray snowflakes, drifting in a slow waltz to the ground. The dragons wheeled in patterns, alone now. No sign of *Unsielie*.

Did Aredel burn away every dark fae?

Jetekesh sought the Blood King among the ashfall. The KryTeeran man remained upon the large boulder, his hands now at his sides, his head bowed. Sorrow cloaked his frame, but with it teemed a powerful rage that ate at the ground around him. Rock crumbled beneath his feet, rolling down the black rock to clatter below.

A hand fell on Jetekesh's shoulder, jolting him. He stared up into Emerin's face.

The keep lord winced. "Apologies, Your Highness. I didn't mean to startle you. You just seemed...lost."

Jetekesh started to open his mouth to protest, but snapped it shut. Weren't they all lost? He searched Emerin's eyes—the vivid green depths filled with secrets—probing. Hoping. He needed Emerin's reasons for betraying them to be profound and sympathetic. He needed Emerin to be an ally.

Something shifted. Like the faint dawn glow on a distant horizon, Jetekesh saw a thread of truth binding Emerin's lips. Similar strings wrapped around his heart, like fine spider threads, holding him to an oath he couldn't break.

Beyond that, Jetekesh saw nothing. No revelation about Emerin's loyalty.

His shoulders drooped, but he corrected his posture at once.

He sought out Sharo. The fae prince picked his way toward King Aredel on the boulder. A compulsion to join them lurched through Jetekesh, and he heeded the feeling while glancing toward the heavens. He expected another *Unsielie* contingent to wing into view at any second.

Sharo's voice reached Jetekesh's ears as the prince approached.

"It seems you were gifted with the Dawn Light of Valliath, Blood King," the fae prince said. "I knew you had been Touched when last you entered Shinac, but this is more than I could have fathomed."

Aredel turned away to stare into the gloom of the wetlands. "What good has it done me or any of us?"

"You just saved all our lives," Sharo said, his tones cradled in compassion. "That means a great deal of good." He angled his head to meet Jetekesh's eyes. "Join us, Marked Prince. Between the three of us, we may yet stand against what has come."

"How?" asked Jetekesh. "Nakania's overrun."

"Not quite yet," said Sharo. "Shinac is also reeling."

Jetekesh folded his arms. "Not the *Unsielie,* and they caused all this. Won't they fly off to destroy the royal cities of my world?"

"Not Bahadronn," said Aredel, twisting to face him, fury sparking in his deep brown eyes. "It was already crippled by *Erisyrdrel.* She burned half of it."

Jetekesh's heart twisted. If *Erisyrdrel* could wreak such devastation alone, what chance did any country stand against a fleet of dark fae? He whirled on Sharo. "What can we possibly hope to do? Your seals binding *Erisyrdrel* in the ocean depths all failed—and she was only one entity."

Sharo blew out a low breath. "Aye, so she was. But *Erisyrdrel* was a more powerful entity than most, for she was a demon. Few of her kind remain in Shinac. Fewer still could have survived outside its magical boundaries."

"Is Navolleth a demon?" asked Jetekesh. Shivers tracked down his arms, though his words thrummed like a discordant note, not quite the truth.

"No, he is not," Sharo said. "Demons such as *Erisyrdrel* tempt and taint, but their words are usually only compelling to those hungry for power. Navolleth, on the other hand, is something else. Something broken and gentle, yet vengeful." His blue eyes danced toward the heavens. "He and my father are *not* allies—

that much my heart tells me. Which means we have two enemies before us."

That did nothing to quiet Jetekesh's anxiety. He rubbed the fine hairs on his arms, willing the persistent chill to dispel.

Don't try to take on every burden at once. Face what lies before us now.

"What do we do first?" he asked.

"Seek Artassa," said Sharo, "as we planned before. Once her fate is known, we can chart our next course."

Aredel leapt from the boulder and started west, weaving between the debris.

Jetekesh followed, and Sharo fell into step beside him. The others in the company trailed at their backs.

Dakarai's voice drifted toward him. "I can see the ghost wolf now."

"You can?" asked Kajsa softly.

"Yes, ever since we entered Shinac I have seen Raum. But there wasn't time to mention it before now."

No, thought Jetekesh. *There wasn't.*

The prince's mind turned over all that had transpired leading up to the breaking of the seal between two worlds. His journey from Amantier to Shing, then from Shing into the Clanslands. And from there, a step through the Arch under a lake and into Shinac itself. The battle at the fortress gates. And then...the breaking.

"Navolleth seemed determined to keep me from finding the Arch," Jetekesh said in tones only Sharo could hear at his side. "He kept trying to stop me, even kill me."

Sharo nodded. "Proof that he and King Darint do not seek the same results—or, at least, they each employ vastly different methods. My father is a greedy man. His line has long believed themselves the rightful rulers of Shinac and Nakania alike. If carnage is required to achieve his ends, so much the better in his mind."

Aredel halted ahead of them and turned around, his eyebrows arched. "I thought you said he was a likable fellow."

"Certainly," said Sharo. "To those within his sphere. But he cares little for common folk. They are but riffraff and peasantry."

"The riffraff and peasantry are what makes him a king to begin with," Jetekesh muttered, disgust edging his tones. "He sounds like my mother. Utterly blind. Stubbornly so."

Sharo sighed as they moved forward again. "What can one expect of someone raised within the walls of a castle? We see little beyond the view of our courtyards, our moats, our gardens. Every other person is seen as lesser, always bowing and scraping. Yet royalty, perhaps, knows less of the world than the farmers and peddlers who walk the byways and fens. The common folk understand the soil, the water, the mountain herbs. They understand hearts and souls."

Lines appeared between Sharo's eyebrows. "Those of us raised in palaces only know what other people tell us. We experience so little unless we leave our finery behind and discover the world." A breeze caught his snowy ponytail and curled it around his shoulders.

Ahead, Aredel tensed. White smoke curled around his fists. The Blood King bolted forward, and Jetekesh squinted in the gloom until he spotted what might be a trapdoor smashed into splinters among the shattered fortress stones.

Jetekesh quickened his pace, causing the burns across his slinged arm to flare. He reached the remnants of the door just as Aredel dropped into the gaping hole. The stairs within led into blackness. Aredel descended with hasty strides, his outline glowing a faint white.

Jetekesh crouched to ease himself into the opening, but Kajsa caught his uninjured arm, halting him.

"You're too injured," she said without a trace of her Norvian accent. Entering Shinac had removed all language barriers for the company. "What if there are enemies?"

A jolt of annoyance charged through him, despite the good sense in her words. He wrestled against an impulse to shake her off.

Dakarai stepped forward. "I will aid the Blood King on your behalf, good prince."

Exhaling, Jetekesh nodded. "Very well."

"Let me come too," said Emerin. Silence followed his request. Every eye settled on the keep lord, but Emerin ignored all except Jetekesh. "Please." The single word was the faintest whisper. His eyes glinted with a desperate edge.

He thinks whoever he's protecting is down there.

Jetekesh nodded. "Go, my lord."

Dakarai descended first, followed by Emerin. The rest of the company stood at the lip of the gaping hole, waiting in silence, while a silver dragon wheeled in the sky. From the darkness to Jetekesh's left, a slender figure strode close. The prince turned to find Kethalas limping from the dense fog. The dragon-turned-man lifted a fanged grin to him, then winced.

"You pushed yourself too much," said Sharo, moving to the dragon's side. "Taregan will scold you heartily for that."

"He already did," said Kethalas with a faint chuckle. His slitted silver eyes scudded over the broken terrain. "We shouldn't linger here. The air is fouling."

"Agreed," said Sharo. "But give the Blood King a few moments. He thinks he may find—"

Above the fae's words, a harrowing cry sounded below the earth: A desperate, broken thing.

Jetekesh knew that sound all too well.

The agonizing pain of heartbreak.

CHAPTER 2
BRAVERY

Rille stood at the edge of Sharo's war camp, her amber eyes trained on the darkening sky. Mere moments ago, a massive pillar of golden light had struck the heavens far to the southwest, near where Aredel, Anadin, and Prince Sharo had aimed their steps.

Please be all right, she prayed, though her instincts hummed a warning.

Whatever that light had been, despite its warm, potent hues, it hadn't been a sign of gallant victory. The darkness seeping across the world confirmed her fears. Slate-colored clouds plumed like smoke, rolling over the sky to hide every shard of twilight. Thunder drummed and growled, like a deranged army closing in on every side. Horses screamed and galloped around the corral, desperate to escape, though there wasn't any place they might run to.

Rille turned and found Thrissa, Sharo's elven mother, racing toward her in silent, supple boots. The fae's clothes shimmered, their colors undefinable, their material foreign.

Thrissa stopped just shy of Rille. "The borders of Shinac have shattered. We must go into hiding before chaos ensues."

The words, spoken in almost icy calm tones, took a moment to seep into Rille's understanding. She stared at Thrissa. "Borders? The borders between Shinac and *what*?"

"Nakania," said Thrissa. "Darint has succeeded at last."

Rille stared on, unable to process the elf's pronouncement. It simply wasn't possible. She shook her head. "Why does King Darint want that? Why is this bad? I don't—"

"Not now," said Thrissa. "I shall explain once we are away." She reached for Rille's hand, but the girl pulled back.

"No. Hold on. Why are we running? Don't you have an army? Did Sharo say to dismantle his encampment?"

The elf's lips stretched into a thin line. "You do not understand, child. Nakania has no love of fae, light or dark. We will be slaughtered by the humans."

Rille caught the panic that flashed in Thrissa's eyes, and understanding dawned, settling like a blanket to snuff out a cold wind. "Oh. You're afraid." She shook her head again. "Don't retreat, not now. Nakania isn't what it once was. My uncle, King Jetekesh, is an honorable man. He would never march against the fae."

"I trust no human king."

Rille stepped forward, setting a palm to her chest. "Then trust me." She reached out her small hand. "Thrissa, Nakania isn't your enemy, just as Shinac isn't mine. If our borders have united, let it be in friendship. Isn't that what Prince Sharo would want?"

The elf curled her fingers tight at her sides. Her eyes shone bright with a feral fear. She stared at Rille's open palm. Her lips parted, and she whispered words too low for Rille to catch. Then Thrissa grasped Rille's hand. "You share Sharo's strong spirit, young seer. Long have my people fled the memory of Cavalin's fall and Shinac's ascent into a realm outside the true flow of time. We had hoped never to re-enter Mithrinn. Yet, it seems, the Meridian forces our hands."

Rille blinked at the unfamiliar terms, but now wasn't the time for questions. "Gather your forces close," she said. "We must prepare for *any* threat until we learn how and why the two worlds have been knitted back together."

Thrissa nodded, extracted her grip, and darted off with the nimble grace of a deer.

Rille tracked the fae queen's progress, ignoring the lump swelling in her throat, and the fear nipping at her core.

Anadin and Aredel were at the heart of that pillar, along with Sharo. Did they survive or did they perish in the struggle against Darint's goals?

She couldn't know, not unless a vision struck her. And she had no control over that.

All Rille could do was hold back her fears. It was what Yeshton and Anadin would do.

CHAPTER 3
THE BLOOD OF CAVALIN

Axel stood on a ledge above the village of Tuksa, near Ingrid's abandoned home, tracking the birds in flight. An arrow was balanced against his bow, trained on the fattest of the geese above. Tightening the bowstring near his cheek, he inhaled a deep breath. Aimed. Released.

The arrow sailed and struck the goose. The bird shrieked and tumbled from the sky.

Pebbles rattled and bounced at Axel's feet. The ground quaked. A rumble tore over the air.

Axel lost his footing. Flailing, he tipped over the ledge and plummeted into the thickets below. The drop was short, but he landed with a grunt. Thorns and twigs dug into his flesh like merciless teeth.

With a curse, he wrestled against the brambles until he broke loose of the thorns, and stood among the firs surrounding the village. One sleeve was torn, and he cast the thickets a withering glare. Not long ago, he could have asked Kajsa to mend his shirt, but she was long gone. She'd abandoned him to aid the detestable

Shingese swine who lived north of the Snowblinds. All because she was a coward.

He sneered, but a surge of guilt washed over him, tempering his rage. Hadn't *he* been the one to chase his friend away? He knew how timid she was, how prone to hiding in a thunderstorm. No wonder she'd run away at the first hint of war.

The ground trembled again, not as strong this time. Axel swayed but kept his feet and glanced at the craggy Snowblinds. Luckily, most of the snowpacks had melted, so the risk of an avalanche had passed.

Axel. The voice pooled into his mind, quiet, sorrowful.

He reeled around to face the village. The first few times Navolleth had spoken in his head, Axel had nearly leapt from his skin. The unexpected voice still startled him, but now he was much faster at responding to the call. Axel charged toward the lodge where Navolleth had taken up permanent residence at the insistence of the elders. The Archons across the Cantons of Norva had each tried to convince Navolleth to stay in their palaces with them, but he'd refused them all.

"The kindnesses of a humble village nestled under the Snowblinds have been innumerable," Navolleth had declared. "I will not betray them for palace poshness now."

Mud squished under Axel's boots as he careened around the first house along the main thoroughfare. He kept his footing. The ground seemed to have settled. A few lengthy bounds brought him to the lodge porch. He flung through the carved front door, glad of the heat that curled over his cheeks and seeped into his damp clothes. Only now did he recall the goose he'd shot down and left unclaimed somewhere—but that hardly mattered if Navolleth needed him.

Navolleth stood before the great hearth, wearing his usual midnight blue cloak, though a generous fire blazed to chase away the springtime chill. Usually, Navolleth was surrounded by a cluster of elders and other prominent members of the village—and recently, a handful of officials from the other Cantons—but he stood alone now, hands clasped at his back, white hair pulled back in a braid that reached his tailbone.

Navolleth's strange eyes stared into the flames, their molten gold depths flashing in the fire glow. His expression was pensive, as usual, though more lines than normal grooved his brow.

Axel slowed to catch his breath, glad Navolleth gave him a moment to collect himself and smooth his rumpled apparel. Navolleth liked cleanliness, order, and quiet.

"My lord?" said Axel as he neared the slender man.

Navolleth stirred, his pupils seeming to slit before he blinked. He turned his full attention on Axel, and his soft, broken smile appeared. "Ah, Axel. Thank you for coming so quickly. How was your hunt?"

Axel stifled a wince and told himself to find the fowl later. "Successful. I hope you enjoy goose."

"I do upon occasion," said Navolleth. His eyes drifted back to the fire. "Things have changed, Axel. The Marked Prince has been used by my enemy to thwart me."

Axel tensed. He didn't know much about the Marked Prince. Navolleth had only mentioned him a handful of times, usually with no context to understand who the man was beyond an enemy Navolleth hunted.

"Does this change our plans?" asked Axel.

Navolleth nodded. "Come." He moved to a table and a pair of plush chairs, but he didn't sit. Instead, he pushed aside several parchments until he uncovered a large map.

Axel blinked and leaned closer, his heart stuttering. He'd never seen such a detailed layout of the continent. Nakania's powerful nations were defined in broad ink strokes: KryTeer in the high northwest, and Amantier east of the channel that divided the two countries. Small islands above Amantier represented the lesser lands of Tivalt and Vilam, while due east of Amantier lay Shing.

Axel swallowed a lump. *Kajsa.* She traveled somewhere between Shing and the Clanslands, in company with enemy warriors.

Navolleth's lithe fingers brushed over the map, smoothing faint wrinkles. His fingertips caressed the borders of a southern land labeled simply DRIFTING SANDS. Axel stared at those letters. He knew the legends of Shinac, country of magic, beloved the world over until a tyrant had risen in KryTeer and marched against the rightful heirs of that fae realm. Cavalin the Great had stood against that evil...and fallen on the battlefield.

The legend claimed that after Shinac had vanished from Nakania, King Cavalin's second son Norvik broke away from Amantier, took his family and loyal followers, and traveled into the Snow Wastes to become the folk of Norva. The mountain winters hadn't been so merciless then, but in Shinac's absence, the weather of the world had changed, and the people of Norva had hardened with it.

"Do you believe in magic?" whispered Navolleth.

Axel wrenched his gaze from the desert scape depicted on the map, finding his leader's eyes. He stared into them, searching as he always found himself doing, though he didn't know what he sought. He recalled Navolleth's question after several seconds.

Shaking himself, Axel turned back to the map. "I...would've answered differently a few months ago, but with everything..." He drew a breath. "With the *vashalan* and Kajsa and you, I think the tales of Shinac are more than myth."

"Ah," said Navolleth in a soft tone. "The boy begins to see. Good." He stroked the desert lettering on the map again. "Then you are finally ready—and just in time. Come with me, Axel." He drifted away from the table, heading for the front door.

Axel followed him from the lodge, along the thoroughfare, and back up the hill that led to Ingrid's turf house. As they passed the structure where the old healer's body had been found— where Kajsa had usually stayed rather than in her parents' old house—a shiver tracked Axel's spine. He'd once taken Ingrid's presence in his life for granted.

Kajsa's, too.

They continued toward the pass that led eventually over and into Shing, though Axel had never seen the fair country with its rice fields and cherry blossom trees. He wasn't sure how much he could believe of the hearth-tales.

Navolleth didn't stop until he reached a ledge far above Ingrid's house, where he turned to overlook the village. Axel's eyes traced the familiar paths made of mud, from the large lodge to the turf roofs, to the circular prison housing spies from across the Snowblinds.

Then he sought the horizon as he had countless times, taking in the distant lines and dots that defined the Frostfire Canton.

His heart lurched into his stomach. *By the name of all the mountain gods!*

Jutting out of the tree-and-snow-smudged country, black towers rose like broken teeth. Dozens of them.

The sky buzzed with strange, winged things.

Axel whirled toward Navolleth. "What is this?"

"The Unsealing," answered the man in his quiet, sad voice. "Too soon. Much too soon. Now, all he fought for is undone." He set his knuckles against his lips, the lines reappearing around his eyes. "Axel, I must tell you a story."

That startled Axel. Navolleth's words always held a sort of bespellment—a kind of hypnotic compulsion—but he'd always spoken plain fact. Axel never thought of him as a storyteller.

Axel waited.

"Three hundred and twenty-four years ago by Nakania's reckoning," Navolleth said in a carrying whisper, "the world broke."

He shifted his stance, rustling the velvet of his deep blue cloak. His eyes strayed heavenward where swarms of winged creatures encircled the nearby canton. "Humankind betrayed its own, and Cavalin fell from his horse to lie in his own blood. The greed of humans had consumed and corrupted the land, and Shinac withdrew, claiming all magic, draining it out of Nakania. This, on the heels of a dark deception that had closed the borders of Valliath even to those made of magic. Cavalin's death...his sacrifice...all of it was for naught."

Axel's spine stiffened. He'd never found any reason to disagree with Navolleth before—but *this*... "Cavalin was a noble-hearted hero. His end *wasn't* meaningless."

Navolleth's lips pulled in a thoughtful frown. "Indeed? Why not, young Axel?" His tone was curiosity mingled with that usual thread of sorrow.

"He restored order and inspired many to defend against injustice. He fought all evil. I'm a descendant of his line through Prince Norvik—the *rightful* heir of Nakania." Axel tried to keep his voice level, but pride in his heritage ignited his passion. He'd let no one smear Cavalin's name. Not even Navolleth.

The quiet man studied Axel in a silence that was only broken by the wind rustling the pine boughs. "Do all Norvians feel as you do?"

"Too right," Axel said. "Our faith claims he rose to godhood after he fell on the field. He leads the mountain gods who guide us."

"Ah." Navolleth's eyes drifted toward the Snowblinds. "Faith."

Axel felt as if needles had riddled his flesh. "I'd venture to say even our northern enemies still pay homage to Cavalin's memory. Amantier's royal line also descends from him—or, well, that's how it was three centuries ago. Though they *stole* the throne."

Navolleth's hungry look fell away. He turned his back on Axel.

"I see." A plume of breath appeared before his hidden profile. "You are his kin."

Axel's cheeks warmed. "Yes. Distant, but..."

"Blood does not lie," whispered Navolleth. "Nor does magic." He lifted a hand to the darkening sky. "Shinac has returned to Nakania, Axel. I intended that much myself, but this is too soon. I have not finished my reckoning—it has barely begun. We can no longer wait to gather our forces." He inhaled. "Darint must be stopped."

"Who—or, or what—is that?"

Navolleth fell so still, he might have stopped breathing. "A devil in human skin."

Axel shuddered. He didn't dare ask more.

After a heartbeat or two, Navolleth turned around. "He is the ruler of Shard Kingdom, father of the noble Prince Sharo. Across the years, Darint has enlisted dark fae in his efforts to bring Shinac back to this world—but it is only so that he may rule over all things. His greed is unparalleled."

Axel shook his head. "Does he have the power to achieve such an end?"

"His allies are made of a darkness most foul. And by bringing Shinac back into the timestream—right now, during the Meridian —he will have access to the darkest of evil arts." Navolleth's pupils narrowed into cat-like slits. "But surely even the *Unsielie* are not foolish enough to call on our greatest enemy."

Cold pattered over Axel's flesh like the touch of a thousand spiders. "You mean...?"

Navolleth nodded. "The Obscure One. He who stole the True King of Shinac, yes."

Legends and myths—yet true, for if Navolleth claimed them as fact, surely, they must be.

"Short of that, there is still much Darint can do to harm Shinac through his utter blindness. He must be thwarted."

"What do we do?" asked Axel.

Navolleth's gaze landed on the circular prison housed behind the lodge among the tall evergreens. "We must change tactics if possible. Darint is a larger threat than our northern neighbors."

Axel bristled. "We're allying with Shing and Amantier?"

"For now," said Navolleth, "I think we must. Come." He started down the hill.

Axel followed with supreme reluctance.

CHAPTER 4

INFINITE COST

The bottom step of the *Unsielie* dungeon gave way to a wide, dank chamber. The walls held chains and rusted instruments of torture.

Jetekesh cradled his burned arm and rushed into the gloom. The only source of light was the white glow surrounding Aredel, who stood above Emerin. The keep lord knelt upon the ground, cradling a body to his chest.

It wasn't the only corpse.

At least a dozen others lay in a circle around the two men. The remnants of burnt-out candles circled the bodies. All were women. All were dead. One wore the colorful, layered apparel common among KryTeeran females. Queen Artassa.

Jetekesh staggered backward. Upon first entering Shinac, almost a year ago, he'd helped Sharo free a handful of captured maidens. They'd been gathered to use as a sacrifice in Lord Peresen's attempt to breach the barrier between two worlds. The dread lord had intended to bring an *Unsielie* army into Nakania.

The same magic had been invoked here. Successfully.

I caused their end. I used them as fuel.

Bile scored Jetekesh's throat, and he spun away to retch.

What have I done?

Artassa hadn't been a maiden. Had the *Unsielie* included her in the spell merely to spite Aredel? To punish him for disobedience?

Jetekesh slumped to his knees, landing in his vomit. Tears swam in his vision, blurring it. Voices rose around him, vicious and desperate in turns. The clash of blades rang through his ears. None of that mattered.

I killed them.

A hand seized his arm and dragged him to his feet. Aredel's eyes flamed, the brown of his irises ringed with white smoke. He slammed Jetekesh against the wall, his grip like a vise.

"You killed her." His voice was the soft rumble of death.

Jetekesh stared into those eyes and imagined Driodere, Death himself, staring back. Somehow, he didn't tremble under that gaze. "I didn't mean to," he said in a calm, detached tone, though his heart cracked as the king's accusation reverberated through him. "But I realize that I was used...and I—I'm so vehemently sorry."

Hollow, empty words. What did his regret matter against such pain?

Sharo slipped into view at Aredel's side. "The young prince could not know, Aredel. Please do not make this tragic hour even worse."

The Blood King pressed Jetekesh harder against the stone wall and unsheathed a curved ruby-studded dagger. The Amantieran prince refused to flinch. He wouldn't cower before his death.

"Give her back to me," said Aredel, ignoring Sharo. The king stared at Jetekesh. His eyes were almost inhuman, deadly cold, like a beast breaking free of every restraint, intent upon the kill.

"I can't," said Jetekesh.

Nothing of reason, nothing of the tentative friendship

between two royals, remained on Aredel's face. He was the dread hand of KryTeer, remote and unhinged.

"Aredel, release him," came Ashea's command.

The Blood King didn't move.

Jetekesh hung suspended somewhere beyond his frame, caught in the cocoon of his mind. His heart hammered from a great distance, and perhaps his legs trembled, but he observed from the outside, awaiting the killing blow.

"Your Majesty, please." Dakarai's voice, calm, quiet. "No one feels this tragedy as keenly as the boy."

Another voice spoke from across the room. Emerin's. Low. Soft. "They're trying to break you, Aredel."

Did the Blood King's hand tremble where it gripped Jetekesh, or did the prince only imagine it?

"They have succeeded," came Aredel's low reply. "I am bereft of all that mattered." His fingers tightened. "I will *not* be thwarted in my vengeance."

"And we will not stand in your way," said Sharo, "so long as your path lies toward those who are truly responsible. The *Unsielie* used you as a tool, just as they did Jetekesh. By that logic, are you any less to blame?"

Aredel's teeth ground. "No. I hate myself most of all. I will not exempt myself from the cost. But I must begin somewhere."

"Stand down, Aredel." The new voice was like wind, strong, unusually so—yet blessedly familiar.

Jetekesh's heart sang. He craned his neck to see past Aredel. The Blood King dropped the prince and wheeled around.

Near the stairs, glowing with light like a golden dawn, stood Jinji Wanderlust. The storyteller was thin and short, as he had been in life, but his hair had changed from black to snowy white. His eyes, a bright turquoise hue, shone with an anger Jetekesh had never seen in the man's countenance before.

Aredel's dagger clattered to the stone floor. The Blood King crashed to his knees with a sob. Jinji strode forward, golden light still outlining his frame. The storyteller knelt before Aredel and rested a hand on his half-brother's shoulder.

"Your wrath is understandable," whispered Jinji. "But do not destroy your allies. Jetekesh was ill-used, but he is not the enemy. He wields the sigil of the True King of Valliath, who has great need of him." Jinji lifted his gaze to meet Jetekesh's eyes, and the anger on his face softened until he wore a sorrowful smile. "Alas, Jetekesh must always live with the knowledge of what they made him do."

Bowing his head, Jetekesh didn't fight the searing tears that collected in his eyes. His lungs constricted, dimming his senses. His heart hung like a wilted flower under late autumn's frosted breath.

"Jinji." Aredel spoke in a despairing rumble that magnified Jetekesh's pain.

"Up, Aredel. Stand, please." Jinji rose and held out his hand to the broken king kneeling before him. "Fight for those who remain. It is your way. Any other path will destroy you."

"I...have nothing left to give."

"I do not believe that. You do not know how to fall." Jinji stooped until his hand hovered before Aredel's bowed head. "Come, my brother. The True King has called you to his cause. You must stand at Jetekesh's side—or the *Unsielie* will use you against us."

Aredel rose to his feet in a fluid motion. "And will you be standing there as well, my *shaqin*?"

"Yes," Jinji said. "Lord Ehrikai has sent me here to represent him in this crisis. I can do little of myself, but I will not let Shinac or Nakania fall if any means can be found to prevent such a calamity."

"Why doesn't the True King return?" Aredel asked. "Doesn't he have the power to restore the seal?"

"Not yet," said Jinji. "He fights on a different battlefield. He cannot return to Shinac at this time."

"Do we matter so little?" asked the Blood King.

"On the contrary, my dear Aredel, he risks all to protect us. There are many who would enter this world from beyond and drain Shinac of its magic, but his efforts prevent that." The storyteller caught Aredel's arm. "Don't despair. He has not forsaken our world."

Aredel shook his head. "Don't ask too much of me, Jinji. All I feel in this moment is anguish and rage. You alone hold me in check. I will stand beside the Amantieran prince if you need, but I will not forgive him—or myself—for what I've lost. Nor can I forgive your lost king for allowing any of this to transpire."

"An understandable position." Jinji squeezed Aredel's arm tighter. "You need time to heal. Alas, time is sparse, and we cannot remain here." He dropped his arm and turned toward Jetekesh and Sharo. "King Darint knows that the seal is broken, and he is free to march on Nakania. His forces will soon amass on the borders of Shinac from every dark region. We must answer or Nakania will fall."

"Do you know the numbers of his forces?" asked Sharo, stepping closer.

Jinji shook his head. "Not precisely. At last count, it was three-hundred thousand strong and growing."

"Well, then," said Dakarai, inching forward. "Let us move. Where are we to head?"

"To my war camp," said Sharo. "We can ride upon Taregan and reach the encampment by morning." His blue eyes landed on Aredel. "First, we should bury the dead."

Aredel shook his head. "I won't leave Anadin and Artassa in this fell realm."

"Then we will bring them," Sharo said gently.

"What of the others?" asked Dakarai.

"We cannot bring them all."

Jetekesh reluctantly scanned the room and found Emerin still kneeling on the stone floor, clutching a body to him with a desperate tenderness. When the keep lord looked up from the young woman's body, his green eyes were vivid, perhaps wet with unshed tears.

Jetekesh approached the circle of corpses, keeping his gaze on Emerin. "Who was she?" he whispered.

Emerin's throat bobbed as he swallowed. "My sister." His head bowed, and a shudder racked his frame. "They promised they would return her to me if I did all they required."

A throb pulsed through Jetekesh. He knelt before Emerin. "Forgive me."

The keep lord caught his arm. "Don't. *I'm* the one who brought you here. I should've known better. *Unsielie* can't be trusted to keep their word after all..." He brushed blonde curls from the dead girl's face, his hard features softening. The spider threads of his curse glistened, then fell to the floor, as though broken. "Her name was Saylia."

"I didn't know you had a sister." Jetekesh studied the girl's face. She was perhaps his age, or maybe as much as eighteen years. Her expression held peace, and for that he was grateful. Despite her soul being used as fuel, perhaps her end hadn't been painful.

"She was extremely shy, much like Kajsa." Emerin shifted her weight in his arms. She hung limply, dangling like a doll. "But she was a skilled huntress, and she insisted on joining me that day in Bard Pass. We came to Shinac together." Lines of pain gathered around his eyes and mouth. "She begged me not to heed the *Unsielie*, but I would do anything to save her. Yet in the end I failed."

What could Jetekesh possibly say? He sat with Emerin while voices spoke behind them. Sharo and Dakarai began carrying the women's bodies from the dungeon, and Aredel moved to claim his dead queen. He wouldn't meet Jetekesh's gaze as he scooped Artassa into his arms, then retreated toward the stairs.

Footsteps scraped close. Jetekesh twisted his head to find Kajsa standing beside him, still clutching her bow. At her side, the ghostly wolf Raum glowed in the gloom. The Norvian girl studied Emerin's sister with open sorrow, then lifted her gaze to the keep lord. She said nothing, but her eyes spoke with such kindness, Jetekesh could almost read her thoughts.

Emerin folded himself over his sister's body and wept.

Jetekesh turned away to give the man some semblance of privacy, heart quaking in his chest. No matter what he did going forward, the prince of Amantier could never escape his guilt.

He'd drained the life from twelve innocent women and set two worlds on fire.

CHAPTER 5
ONE YEAR

Ashea cast a spell around the dead women, preserving and protecting them where they lay in the swamp until they could be properly removed and returned to their noble families. Since Aredel and Emerin refused to leave their own dead behind, Sharo agreed to let them do as they wished.

Once the bodies were safeguarded, Sharo led Jetekesh up the leathery silver wing of the dragon elder, Taregan. The horses would remain behind, with Sharo's pledge that he would have the dead and the beasts brought to his war camp within the next day or two.

Jetekesh's guilt ebbed as he studied the gleaming scales of the giant beast. He knew the feeling would return, but he welcomed a moment's reprieve as he settled onto Taregan's back and grabbed a thread of black mane when Sharo directed him to.

The dragon craned his long neck and peered at the assembling company with fierce slitted eyes the color of fire. Those eyes impaled Jetekesh like a lance, as though the dragon could read every inch of his soul. With a nod of his great head, Taregan acknowledged Jetekesh. Words broke across the prince's mind like a torrential wind.

"Greetings, Your Highness. I am honored to meet you."

Jetekesh's bones rattled under the rumbling authority of this majestic being. He looked around, but no one else had reacted to the statement.

With a faint nod, he murmured, "Thank you, my lord. I too am honored."

Nearly everyone had arrived. Kethalas, Kajsa, and Anenyasha sat nearby, each clutching strands of mane. Behind them, Aredel and Dakarai kept the bodies of Artassa and Anadin grasped between them. In the rear, Emerin held his sister's corpse, a grimness lining his face and aging him by ten years.

Regret erupted in Jetekesh's stomach like a mass of heat, dulling his burns and bruises.

Jinji lighted the dragon last, Ashea flitting at his side. The storyteller smiled at Jetekesh and sat beside him while the fairy winged to Sharo's shoulder.

Taregan took to the sky. Despite the dragon's immensity, the lift was smooth and swift. Jetekesh leaned back under the force, gripping the mane in his hands to keep from tipping too far as the dragon gained height.

Once the ride leveled out, he straightened. Wind snatched at his long hair.

"This is the strangest sensation," Kethalas said. "I'm not usually a passenger."

Jetekesh glanced back, catching a flash of Kethalas's fangs in a grin. The prince tried a smile in reply, but his lips only quivered, then fell. He turned to study the dragon's long neck and the wisps of mane floating across the night sky. A shooting star streaked past, and he watched its descent with a plummeting heart to match.

Jinji had said Jetekesh would have to live with his mistake for the rest of his life.

How could he bear it?

Jetekesh bowed his head, letting silent tears scorch his cheeks. The flight fell away from his mind, leaving him in a private ocean of agony beyond sight, sound, or time. He swam in his misery, welcoming the growing discomfort of his burned arm. He deserved this pain.

"There," called Sharo, cutting into his reverie.

Sunlight spilled over the world. As reality settled back in around him, Jetekesh blinked in the growing light. The dragon tipped downward. Tightening his hold on the mane, Jetekesh leaned out to try to see the ground, but the dragon's girth prevented much of a view.

Beside him, Jinji rose and strode along the dragon's back, heading for Taregan's neck. His balance was perfect, despite the wind, despite the beat of massive leathery wings. His white hair whipped to and fro, flinging in his eyes, but that didn't faze the storyteller. Reaching Taregan's neck, Jinji caught several locks of mane, then spoke. Whatever he said to Taregan was lost in the wind noise.

The dragon twisted his neck and rumbled an answer. Sunlight flashed across his silver scales, blinding Jetekesh. The prince winced and turned away until a hand fell on his shoulder. Jerking upright, he found Jinji staring down at him. The storyteller still stood.

"You're in great pain," Jinji said.

Swallowing, Jetekesh tried to school his face. "It's nothing."

The storyteller lifted a brow. "Lady Thrissa will be able to help you with your arm at least."

Jetekesh hugged his useless arm closer to his chest. "What were you saying to Taregan just now?"

"He agreed to travel south to the dragon lands and raise an

army. He'll take Kethalas with him, so the poor fellow can be healed as well. That will be better than Thrissa's efforts. Dragons require special care for magical wounds."

A thread of hope weaved around Jetekesh's splintered heart. "How many dragons will come, do you think?"

"If Taregan summons them?" Jinji smiled. "All. He is the elder, his word is law."

Knots loosened in Jetekesh's stomach, but as the dragon swooped lower, they snarled again. The prince drew a few breaths, gripping the mane a little tighter. "Will we wait for them, or...?"

Jinji shook his head. "Sharo will gather his captains together once we land. We'll learn his plans there."

Taregan landed in a wide meadow dotted with purple and yellow flowers. A minty fragrance haunted the air, and a forest stood against the boundaries of the grassy field. Twisting around, Jetekesh found Prince Sharo's army.

A well-ordered encampment, complete with log palisades and wide corrals, spread out across the field. Pennants snapped above rows of tents. At least two dozen different provinces boasted support for Prince Sharo judging by the varied heraldry in attendance. Sharo's army was at least one hundred-thousand strong.

A decent showing, but not enough.

He followed Jinji down the dragon's sparkling wing, every step jarring his wounds. Kajsa and Anenyasha stayed close, both likely watching him to be sure he didn't trip or straight-up collapse.

Sharo had disembarked ahead of him, and the fae prince caught Jetekesh's eye to offer a sympathetic smile. Ashea was perched on his shoulder, her iridescent wings lazily batting the air. Sharo gestured toward the palisades and the tents beyond. "While the others see to their dead, Your Highness, let me bring you to Thrissa. She'll look at your burns."

Jetekesh trailed behind Sharo toward the camp gate, Kajsa at his side. Grass whispered at Jetekesh's feet until he reached the gate where sentries in polished armor stood at attention. They saluted Sharo, spines straight, heels clicking.

Sharo nodded to them and passed through the open gate. Jetekesh accidentally brushed up against Kajsa as they passed through together. When his hand bumped hers, he felt a flash of embarrassment and jerked it back. If she noticed, she didn't twitch. Inside the camp, he inched a little to his left to avoid connecting with her again.

Orderly rows of knights marched toward them, then halted where a wide opening gave them room to fan out. Sharo saluted the woman at their head and walked toward her.

Jetekesh's eyes widened. She was an *elven* woman, with long silver hair. Pointed ears framed her angular face. Her clothes shimmered—the strange material changing hues as she moved. They seemed to camouflage with her surroundings.

Sharo spoke to her in quiet tones, and the woman's silver-green eyes darted to Jetekesh. Her lips twisted down as her gaze landed on his wrapped bandages. The woman nodded, then approached in long, graceful strides. Sharo stayed on her heels.

"Welcome, Prince Jetekesh of Amantier," said the woman. "I am Thrissa. Sharo tells me you're badly burned. Please come with me." She pivoted, and the knights—all of them elven, Jetekesh realized with a jolt—parted in a flowing motion to let her through their ranks.

Jetekesh glanced at Sharo, who nodded.

"I'll summon you for the council when it's organized," Sharo promised.

Appeased, Jetekesh jogged after Thrissa, ignoring his protesting burns. Kajsa matched his pace. He glanced at her, and she offered him a shy smile.

"I'm still your healer," she said.

Thrissa guided Jetekesh to a tent made from the same material she wore. Colors shifted as he neared the flap, and as Thrissa pulled it aside, her hand seemed to vanish where it gripped the cloth.

A stream of sunlight flooded the entryway. Jetekesh bent slightly to enter. The scent of beeswax, mingled with lavender and other herbs, met his nose. It reminded him of Father's chamber during the king's years of illness.

A cot crouched at the rear of the tent, and a few chairs stood near shelves laden with bottles and tinctures. A mortar and pestle sat on a table strewn with herbs, some fresh, others dried. More bundles of herbs hung upside-down from loops sewn into the tent ceiling. Ornate lanterns lit up the interior, a dozen of them, leaving little room for shadows within. A wide rug served as a floor, its intricate pattern strange but beautiful.

"Please sit," said Thrissa, nodding toward the chairs. She moved to the table, then cast a glance at Kajsa. "You're a healer. I can smell it."

Kajsa tensed, then bobbed a hasty nod. "Yes. I—I mean, I was in training. I know some herb lore."

The elven woman smiled, and whatever shadows dared remain seemed to flee. She was radiant, ageless, with a solemn wisdom in her strange eyes. "Your soul is a healer's soul. Come." She motioned to the table. "I welcome your aid."

Kajsa tossed a startled look at Jetekesh who offered an encouraging nod before he seated himself on a delicately carved oak chair. The Norvian girl squared her shoulders and moved to Thrissa's side.

"What is your name?" asked the elf.

"Kajsa," she replied.

"It's beautiful." Thrissa handed the girl several herbs. "Crush these, please."

As Kajsa set to work, Thrissa turned from the table and drew near Jetekesh. "May I see your arm?"

As he gingerly pulled it from its sling, the skin pulled against the bandages and he winced.

With great care, Thrissa unwrapped the bandages, revealing the red, puckered flesh on his neck, arm, and part of his hand. Jetekesh shuddered. Somehow, he'd forgotten how bad the damage was.

Thrissa twisted his arm, flaring the pain higher, her eyes roving over every detail of the burns. She shifted to examine his thigh and calf, then nodded to herself. Retreating to the table, she sprinkled dried herbs into the concoction Kajsa mashed together in the mortar.

Jetekesh didn't dare ask for Thrissa's verdict. He wasn't prepared to hear the deafening truth: His life as a swordsman was finished.

Thrissa murmured to Kajsa. The girl slipped to Jetekesh's side with the herbal concoction and proffered it.

"Drink."

He eyed the mashed green substance. The overpowering scent of lavender, chamomile, and other, unfamiliar herbs caressed his face. Kajsa pressed the mortar to his lips, and he swallowed the concoction down with a grimace, gagging against the bitter taste.

Thrissa moved across the room, her hands cupped horizontally before her abdomen like she clutched a hidden ball. "The herbs will soften the pain."

As she stepped closer, Jetekesh glimpsed light leaking between her fingers. He lifted his gaze to meet hers. "What is that?"

Thrissa held his stare steadily. "Healing magic. But it comes at a high cost, Prince of Amantier. Should you accept my aid, you will lose one year of your life."

The fine hairs on his neck rose. "O-one year of..."

She held still, letting him absorb the price.

An entire year of his life, taken in payment. He swallowed. "You trade in lives?"

Thrissa blinked, then she shook her head. "Not I. 'Tis the cost your body must pay for such accelerated healing."

Jetekesh stared at his ruined flesh. His useless hand. He drew a breath, then nodded. "Better to live a full, short life, than a long half-life."

"That is one answer. Others may choose differently." Thrissa uncupped her hands to reveal an orb of pale green light the size of a pebble. It hovered between her fingers, pulsing with power, smelling of green, growing things. The pulsing light grew brighter, and the fragrance of a forest filled Jetekesh's senses until he imagined trees surrounding him.

Thrissa's voice came from far, far away. "Prepare for the pain, Your Highness."

The herbs were settling into his blood, dulling the pinching throb of his burns. He had difficulty concentrating on how to brace for what was to come—until fingers touched his chest, and the pulsing orb sank beneath his skin and bones. Magic poured into his soul, bursting with sound, color, taste—filling every sense until he nearly choked on the vitality of life.

Energy flowed into his core, churning there, mustering strength.

Thrissa spoke a single word: *Heal.*

The energy surged down his arm, seeping into bone, tissue, flesh. His skin burst into flame.

Jetekesh screamed. Agony crawled up his ruined flesh, heightening it until his vision bled white. He jerked backward, and the chair collapsed. He tumbled to the ground, but hardly felt his body's impact against the rug.

Time lost all meaning. He writhed in a den of flame, spasming. The energy crept along every damaged inch of skin, scraping, clawing, probing. He wept—he knew that much, though he couldn't feel the heat of his tears.

Why couldn't he lose consciousness? Why couldn't he escape this torture, even for a moment? It endured until, surely, everything he knew and loved had died and decayed .

At long last, the burning faded from his arm. The surge of energy snuffed out. He lay upon the cot, beneath a thin blanket, staring up into the guttering shadows of the tent created by one nearby lantern.

His cheeks were damp. His lips felt chapped.

"He appears to be awake." A female voice, low and soft. The sound filtered through one ear, not both.

I suppose the price to heal my hearing would have been steeper still.

Footsteps padded close, and Sharo drifted into view above him, his blue eyes bright in the lantern glow. "That must have been very painful. I'm sorry for that."

Jetekesh sucked in a shuddering breath. "H-how long...?" His voice cracked.

"It's been about an hour. I know it felt much longer."

Yes, it had felt interminable. Jetekesh swallowed and shifted to speak, but Sharo leaned out of sight, then returned holding a clay cup.

"Water?" Sharo's smile was as dazzling as sunlight on a lake. He leaned close, helped Jetekesh to sit up, and let him sip from the cup until every last drop had been drained dry. Then the fae prince eased Jetekesh back onto a stack of pillows.

"Thank you," Jetekesh said, glad his voice had recovered. He turned his neck to survey the tent's interior. Thrissa and Kajsa were both absent, but Sharo wasn't alone.

Seated in a chair beside the cot, Rille smiled at him. "Hello, Cousin." Her voice was its usual calm, prim tone. She wore a simple silver dress, and her pale blonde hair hung loose in soft curls, freshly washed.

A grin broke out across Jetekesh's lips. "Rille! How are you?"

She bobbed a demure shrug. "A sight better than you, though thankfully, your burns are mended."

He jolted, then lifted his arm, relieved when it obeyed with a fluid motion. His torn sleeve hung loose, revealing supple flesh, the same hue as his other arm. No hint, no ghost, of the burn remained. His thigh and calf also held no pain. Relief swelled in Jetekesh's chest, full and warm.

Skirts rustled, then Rille pressed against the cot's edge. "Sharo explained what happened at the fortress..."

The cresting emotions cracked, then bled away. Jetekesh dropped his arm and met Rille's amber eyes. He read grief there, plain as the spray of light freckles on her nose. She knew about Anadin. She likely knew about everything.

He tore his gaze away. "It's my fault."

"Nonsense." Her firm tone brooked no argument. Somehow that surprised him. He'd expected her beratement. He'd even hoped for it. No one could lecture him as well as Rille—but she didn't blame him?

A sigh escaped her lips. "The outcome wouldn't have changed, no matter if you'd served the *Unsielie* unwittingly or through brute force. Your companions would have been tortured, one by one, until you agreed to do what they wished. Do you think otherwise?"

Jetekesh turned his cousin's words over in his mind, weighing them, then he grimaced. "No." Somehow agreeing with the girl felt strange. They'd rarely seen eye to eye, even after they'd come to respect and even like each other.

But, deep down, Jetekesh acknowledged that Rille was usually right.

"Anyway," Rille went on, shaking out a wrinkle in her skirts, "what's done is done. We have a war to fight now, and—"

Prince Sharo turned from the bed, cutting the girl off. His eyes narrowed on the tent entrance, and a moment later, the flap flung aside. Thrissa entered with the Blood King at her back. While the elven woman stared straight at Sharo, Aredel's eyes roved the tent, landing last on Jetekesh. The darkness there sent chills down Jetekesh's arms.

"We have a visitor," said Thrissa. "Outside the gates."

Wind rippled over the air, and an image sprouted up in Jetekesh's mind: A man, tall, lean, draped in a dark blue velvet cloak.

Jetekesh sat up, chest tight. "It's Navolleth."

Sharo whirled toward him. "How do—" He cut himself off, blue eyes searching Jetekesh's face. "Very well." He turned back to Thrissa. "Invite him to my tent. I shall meet him there directly."

Thrissa tapped her collarbone, then flicked her hand away in what might be a salute. "As you will." She slipped from the tent on silent feet.

Aredel remained. His brown eyes speared Sharo. "What could that vile man want?"

The fae prince set a finger against his lower lip. "A fair question, and one I hope to learn the answer to very shortly." He turned to Jetekesh and Rille. "Will you both accompany me—if you can manage it, Your Highness?"

"I'll manage it," Jetekesh said. "I want to meet this man in person. He's tried too many times to kill me."

"You might be a lunatic, Cousin," Rille stated, then offered her hand. "Come. I'll be your crutch."

He grinned, accepted her hand, flung aside his blanket, and stood up. The weight of Aredel's eyes settled on him like the scales of justice. Jetekesh's grin died. He lifted his eyes to meet the Blood King's stare.

This man will remind me of my guilt all the days of our lives—however long that is.

That fact, indisputable, rested on Jetekesh's shoulders like the finality of death itself. He set his jaw and held Aredel's gaze steadily.

So be it.

Lips set in a grim line, he flexed his left hand. The fingers were nimble, the tendons responded well, the muscles didn't ache. All at the cost of one year of his life. It seemed a small price, compared to the lives he'd used as fuel for the *Unsielie.*

Rille took his arm, tucking it into hers. "We're ready," she announced to Sharo.

"Will you join us, King Aredel?" Sharo asked, twisting to face the KryTeeran shadow.

Aredel tensed. "That *man* is responsible for unleashing *Erisyrdrel* upon my homeland, thereby destroying much of Bahadronn. If I face him, it will not be to talk."

Sharo inclined his head. "I understand. In that case, please don't join us."

Aredel offered a clipped nod, then slipped from the tent.

"Shall we?" Sharo moved toward the flap.

Setting his jaw, Jetekesh strapped his sword belt to his hip, then Rille tightened her fingers around his arm, and drew him after Sharo.

They stepped out into the war camp to face the man who had been stalking Jetekesh for weeks.

CHAPTER 6
STRANGE ALLIANCES

Morning sunlight gleamed on the accoutrements of an army preparing for open warfare. The scent of iron and fire rose above the distant clang of smiths' hammers, while black smoke plumed into the sky. Shouts sprinkled the air: commands for last-minute arrangements before the army pulled out. Sharo hadn't held council yet, but no one doubted the inevitability of their march to the front lines. Jetekesh could taste their resolve like the spices of KryTeer on the air.

Sharo led Jetekesh and Rille between rows of fine tents. Clusters of armored men and women, some human, most elves, parted to let their royal commander pass. Curious glances skimmed past Jetekesh's face, then snapped back to study him.

Whispers chased them all the way to the middlemost tent.

"The Marked Prince."

"Did you see the beacon?"

"So, the Meridian is at hand."

Cheeks blazing, Jetekesh refused to glance back. Refused to acknowledge the voices at his heels. None sounded angry, only curious, and even reverent.

You'd change your tones if you knew what I've done.

They would likely learn that much at the council—unless Navolleth's arrival changed everything.

Sharo reached the large, peaked tent, and slipped inside. Jetekesh hesitated for a breath, then entered, blinking to adjust his vision to the relative dimness. The fragrance of lantern smoke lived within, just as the healer's tent, but rather than the odor of herbs, the interior smelled of ink, parchment, and leather.

A table sat near the center of the tent, strewn with sealing wax, scrolls, and quills—and on its far side stood a figure cloaked in midnight blue. The breath of cold winter surrounded the man, and the memory of his voice chilled Jetekesh's blood.

"Hello," said Sharo, stepping closer to the table. "Do I have the privilege of meeting the Sundered One in the flesh or a mere mirage of him?"

The figure lifted long fingers to his cowl and tossed back the cloth to reveal a face with an angular bone structure and a pale complexion. He had golden eyes and platinum hair. Navolleth looked more ghost than man, draped in sorrow heavier than his velvet cloak.

"I am come in the flesh," he answered in a faint whisper. His eyes slid to Jetekesh and halted, narrowing. "So, the Marked Prince yet stands." His words dripped with darkness. "I had hoped your fell deed would be your undoing. A pity, then, that you live while so many will die."

Jetekesh flinched, heart tight in his chest.

Sharo rested a hand on his shoulder reassuringly. "We were *all* used, Navolleth. Perhaps even you. Your actions drove Prince Jetekesh forth to thwart you, and so you sent him on his way. That you constantly dogged his steps made him all the more determined."

Navolleth's lips twisted down. "I see... We are all the prisoners of fate." His eyes drifted from Jetekesh, skimming over Rille—then backtracking to eye the girl again. "A seer, yet you did not foresee this outcome?"

Rille tensed. "No. I didn't."

The man sighed and turned his attention back to Sharo. "Darint's armies march toward the Nakanian borders. What will you do?"

"Answer with our might," said Sharo. "And you? Will you be our enemy?"

Navolleth shook his head.

"Why not?" demanded Jetekesh, his hands curling into fists. "You were bent on our destruction not days ago."

Navolleth kept his gaze on Sharo. "Not at the cost of King Darint tainting the land. I will stand with you against him first, and then we shall do battle." He turned a frigid stare on Jetekesh. "At that time, your kingdom will fall with the sound of deafening thunder."

"Why?" Jetekesh lurched forward a step. "Why do you despise humanity? What good does killing us do?"

Navolleth's pupils narrowed into slits. The shadows around him writhed. "I will not explain myself to he who is marked to destroy all that Shinac is. Silence, child of woe."

Each word struck like a hammer blow, and Jetekesh flinched back, chest tightening until he couldn't breathe.

Sharo stepped in front of him, holding out a hand to stave off Navolleth. "Hold fast, Sundered One. We do not know the meaning of the prophecy. That's merely an interpretation, and an ill one by my judgment."

Navolleth's voice was a faint rumble lined in cool silk. "The prince is born of tainted blood. See you not the mark?"

"I see the True King's sigil," Sharo answered. "That is enough for me."

"What are they talking about?" whispered Rille.

Jetekesh tried to shake his head, but he couldn't move.

Prince Liu's accusation tolled through his mind like the cathedral bells during Driodere's Wake, the bleak night before the Holy Nocturne began. *How do you even know you're the king's son?*

Father's face flitted across Jetekesh's memory, clear, bright. Those gentle eyes, that quick smile. An ache followed, a longing to know that Jetekesh *did* share the royal blood of Cavalin the Third. That he was the son of the good-hearted Jetekesh the Fourth.

But it doesn't matter.

Jetekesh straightened, caught by the truth of that phrase. It *didn't* matter. Jinji had been born of two self-indulgent, utterly greedy souls. Neither had cared a whit about the product of their illicit affair. Neither had claimed him. Both had discarded him.

Yet Jinji had grown into a strong, kind, wise man.

And Kajsa, born of waifs, was as noble in spirit as Mother ought to have been but never was.

Dakarai was illegitimate, yet he'd been raised by the chieftain as kin and became the leader of his tribe—because he had earned that title through more than his blood.

What does blood matter at all if it's not accompanied by love?

A hand caught his wrist. Jetekesh started, then twisted to find Rille's bright amber eyes.

She smiled at him. "I'm here."

His heart eased. They might not always see eye to eye, but they were kin, and she accepted that fully.

He returned her smile, then dragged his eyes back to Navolleth.

Sharo had taken another step toward the man. "If you wish to ally with me," the fae prince said, "you'll need to accept that Jetekesh is also my ally, as well as my friend."

Jetekesh clenched his fists tighter. "You can't trust Navolleth. He'll stab us in the back, Sharo."

The fae prince glanced over his shoulder. "I believe he won't."

He turned back to Navolleth. “Not if you give your word on the grave of Cavalin.”

“You ask too much, young fae.”

“No,” said Sharo. “I ask what is just. Surely, you do not begrudge me that.”

The man’s lips folded down more and he dipped his chin, casting shadows around his eyes. “Very well, Sharovyr. Upon Cavalin’s grave, I swear not to betray your cause until King Darint’s reign is over.”

Sharo’s eyes glittered, then he bowed his head. “I accept your oath, Navolleth Sundered’One. And I likewise will not break our alliance until that time, unless you first dishonor your oath.”

The air hummed with power, and Jetekesh felt chains of magic wrap around the two fae men. Something in his chest burned in answer.

“So witnessed,” he declared with a voice that wasn’t his own. He shuddered under the authority that blazed through him.

Navolleth’s eyes met his, hate-filled, dark—and maddened.

CHAPTER 7
WELL MET

Sir Yeshton of Amantier stood within a circular array of aquamarine-hued magic, in a meadow he'd never seen before. Beside him, Lady Song of Shing and the Blood Knights, Shevek and Ledonn of KryTeer in their full red armor, also waited for Navolleth's return.

Just beyond the glowing array, young Axel stood with bow and arrows, his eyes trained on the distant palisades of an army camp. Several soldiers stood outside the gate, watching Axel, but no one approached. If the soldiers could see into the array, they made no indication.

Song shifted, letting out a sigh. "He can't really mean to form an alliance."

Yeshton's mind shot back to Navolleth's visit this morning when he'd announced that plans had changed.

"*We will ally with Prince Sharo now that the border between Shinac and Nakania is broken.*" So he'd declared, and then he'd ushered Yeshton and Song from their prison and transported them to the meadow, alongside the others in company. He'd offered no other explanation for himself, for how Shinac had returned to the mundane world, or what purpose allying with the legendary Sharo served.

Still, this promised a means of escaping prison, albeit an unconventional one.

The soldiers at the gate stirred, then the gate pulled aside to let a stream of people through. Axel straightened, fingers twitching toward his quiver.

At the head of the column, Navolleth walked beside a tall, lean man with long white hair: Sharo himself. Yeshton recognized him from Emperor Gyath's court.

As a youth, Yeshton had pretended to be the fae prince, befriending dragons, rescuing stray fae, battling harpies and goblins. His stomach flipped. He was about to speak with that legend. It was almost like Cavalin of old rising from the dead.

As the train of people neared, Yeshton let his eyes stray from the two men at the fore, wondering what other legends walked with Sharo.

He blinked. At their backs, Prince Jetekesh marched, glowing with an inner radiance more brilliant than before. His eyes were bright with concern, lips set in a grim line.

And there. Yeshton drew a breath, and it caught in his lungs. Rille walked beside her royal cousin.

The knight lurched forward, but Song caught his arm.

"Don't be rash," she whispered. "The array is still there."

He almost didn't care. At last, he was reunited with Rille. She was safe. She looked well and whole and as stern as ever.

The girl spoke to Jetekesh, then lifted her eyes to study the meadow. She made no sign of recognition, proving that Navolleth had hidden their presence in the array.

Axel strode toward the stream of people and bowed to Navolleth. "My lord, we're staying?"

"The alliance is made," replied the man in his somber tones.

"We return to Norva to bring your countrymen here. They will understand once they see what we're fighting against."

Axel dipped his head, then straightened. "What of your guests?"

Navolleth's eyes skimmed the circle of magic, then he lifted his hand and swiped it across the air. A ripple pulsed through the ring, then Rille gasped.

"Yesh!" She darted forward, arms outstretched.

Song released Yeshton's arm. He leapt over the darkened runes encircling his companions. As Rille reached him, he dropped to one knee and swallowed her up in his embrace. Relief swept through him until he nearly choked.

"I'm so glad you're here," Rille whispered, burying her face in his shoulder. "I've been so worried." She was trembling.

No, she was crying.

He held her tighter. "I'm well, my lady. And so are you, thank the blessed saints."

She trembled more. "Yes... I'm well. But...Anadin is...dead."

He tensed, then bowed his head and rubbed her back, trying to instill what comfort he could. "I'm so sorry, my lady... I know how special he was to you." A lump formed in his throat. What would Kyella do? She'd fallen in love with Anadin. They'd planned to wed.

Rille sniffed, keeping her face hidden. "Why—why must I lose all that I love, Sir Knight?"

"You'll not lose me," he whispered, letting all his feelings pour into the reckless vow.

Footsteps rustled near, and Yeshton raised his eyes to meet Jetekesh's sober face.

The Amantieran prince inclined his head. "Sir Yeshton, how glad I am to see you, you'll never know. There's someone else you need to meet." He shifted aside, allowing Yeshton a view of the rest of the train.

Most faces were unfamiliar, but near the back, a memorable, beaming smile met him, banishing the chill of loss in the knight's blood.

"Jinji!" He didn't mean to shout, but the emotions that bubbled up burst forth.

Rille pulled back, a tattered smile on her lips. "Go to him, Sir Knight."

Yeshton rose, his heart panging. He strode toward the storyteller—the same lean, short man, no longer bone-thin, though his hair was entirely white now. Jinji slipped from the column and approached.

"Well met, Sir Yeshton," Jinji said. "Congratulations on your knighthood. It is well deserved."

Yeshton swallowed a lump down, then pulled Jinji into a fierce embrace. "You died..." His words hitched.

Jinji chuckled. "So I did, and so I remain. But the dead are not so far removed from the living as all that." He pulled back and looked up into Yeshton's face. "I return at my king's behest to aid this world in its time of distress."

"What's happened?" asked Yeshton, a flood of concern washing away some of his joy.

"A council has been called," Jinji said. "Join us, and all will be explained."

Navolleth's voice drifted toward them. "We will not join you at council. Axel and I shall return to Norva and bring our forces here. We will return well before nightfall."

"Then we will hold the council at that time," Sharo said.

"Do not delay for us," replied the pale man. "Make your strategies. I will comprehend them." Navolleth motioned to Axel. "Come. We depart at once." He caught the boy's arm, and a flash of light followed. As it faded, Yeshton searched the meadow. Navolleth and Axel had vanished.

CHAPTER 8
CONTROLLING DARKNESS

The crisp air billowing down from the Snowblinds slithered through Axel's fur-lined coat to nip at his bones. He stood beside Navolleth above Tuksa, eyeing the muddy tracks crisscrossing between village structures soggy from the drizzling rain.

After the vibrant meadow and warm sunlight farther west, returning here was a dagger in the ribs.

Axel spun toward Navolleth. "I don't understand, my lord."

"No. You do not." The man's face was drawn, his eyes unfocused, as though he stared into some other world. "Do you trust me, Axel?"

That gave the young man pause. Until today he had, implicitly. Navolleth spoke of a better future for Norva and all her people. For fertile lands and sweet revenge.

Now, though, Navolleth sided with Amantier, Shing, and even bloody KryTeer. The enemy.

Navolleth turned to face Axel, his golden eyes sharp. "You are proud of your lineage. Proud to belong to Cavalin's line."

Axel straightened up. "I am."

"So is the Marked Prince."

Axel's eyes widened. "He's of Amantier's royalty?"

"Yes." Navolleth's gaze drifted south to stare out over the cantons of Norva. "He will be sent away. He will not stay with the army."

A snort escaped Axel's nose. "Is he so fragile he can't even fight?"

"His will be a quest of utmost importance. Sharo will send no other." Navolleth's voice was faint as broken glass. "That quest must succeed, though not as they envision. I will send you with his company."

"I don't understand."

"No. Not yet." Navolleth turned toward Axel. "It is not your fault. Humans understand so little. If only we had more time..." His jaw set, and his gaze strayed, but he tensed and caught on Axel's eyes again. His pupils were distinct slits, more reptilian than feline. "You agreed with me before, Axel, that war is necessary to prevent future deaths. That some must bloody their hands to spare the whole. Ugly choices, made by a few, to preserve the innocent."

"Yes. Yes, definitely." Axel pressed a fist over his heart. "I feel that in my core."

"So you do." Navolleth inhaled. "I have made ugly choices, Axel. So many. All to preserve...to protect...to avenge..." He turned south again, toward the amassing winged things descending on the world. "I control darkness so that it cannot control me. Can you accept that?"

Axel turned the words over, then nodded gravely. "Better that such power is held by someone like you, than by some KryTeeran scum."

A feeble smile met Navolleth's lips. "Indeed? That I cannot judge." His fingers flexed at his sides. "Your confidence, your loyalty—these fill my heart with warmth. I feel I can trust you,

Axel." He lifted one hand. "I will show you my truth." He began to shift.

Somewhere in the trees, howls rose in a chilling chorus.

Heart in his throat, Axel stared at Navolleth's true form and trembled.

CHAPTER 9
THE SILENCE BEFORE COMBAT

Aredel watched the gathering in the meadow from atop the palisades. Beside him, Thrissa observed the proceedings with the same distant expression that marked his soul. After a moment, Navolleth vanished, and something coiled up inside the Blood King's soul.

"Well," she said. "Things are now in motion. The council will be held shortly." She turned away from the meadow. "Best prepare for that."

Aredel almost asked her what the point of it all was—but he knew the answer. Though he'd lost most of what he fought for, others hadn't. And Jinji had asked him to fight on. He moved mechanically, like he struggled against a tidal wave, making no progress but not holding still.

It was the best he could manage.

Thrissa brushed her fingers against his arm. "Come, Blood King. Your expertise will be needed."

He inhaled. "So it will." He could help. Through the haze of his grief, he would do all he could. All that was asked of him.

For Jinji. For Anadin. They wouldn't want Aredel to give in to his sorrow.

For you, and nothing else, I will stay standing, shaqel *and* shaqin.

The sun heaved itself into the sky, climbing toward noon, as the company beyond the walls made its way back into the camp. Among them, Jetekesh walked beside Yeshton and Rille, conversing in quiet tones.

Aredel looked away, unable to process the complex emotions that stirred when he observed the Amantieran prince. His gaze snagged on something glinting red in the crowd.

He froze. A faint pang of relief broke through his haze. He leaned over the palisades to be certain.

"Shevek, Ledonn!" His voice cracked over the air.

The two Blood Knights straightened, saluting before they'd even located their king. Then they grinned broadly.

"Your Majesty!" they called in unison.

Aredel grinned back, but it slipped away, leaving him as empty as before. The KryTeeran knights shuffled between the press of people, forcing their way through the gate ahead of Jetekesh and his companions.

Pivoting, Aredel spotted his knights below as they cleared the gate.

"Go to them," said Thrissa. "Find solace with your own."

He doubted solace would ever be his. It never had been. But he obeyed just the same, leaping from the logs to land lightly in the dirt. He straightened up in time to find Shevek and Ledonn barreling toward him with glints in their eyes. They caught him in a bear hug, crushing him, fierce and affectionate, all decorum forgotten.

Ignoring the soldiers looking on, Aredel let them have their moment of joy. A trickle of happiness stirred inside him, but he stomped it down. He deserved none. That, like solace, wasn't his to claim.

Ledonn extracted himself first, then tugged his half-brother away. "Get off. Let the man breathe, you slug."

Shevek elbowed Ledonn but heeded him. They moved back a step, then fell in unison to their knees, clapped fists to their plated chests, and bowed their heads low.

"Sire!" Their cry was heartfelt, and it broke through the numbness a bit more.

Aredel inched forward and brushed his fingers against their lowered helms. "Rise, my friends."

They moved as one, straightening to their full height, bloodred armor shining in the sunlight. Both wore smiles they couldn't stifle.

"It does me good to reunite with you," Aredel said. He scanned the common area surrounding them, but the soldiers had all moved on. No one hovered to watch, except Thrissa still upon the palisade.

"You must know," Aredel began. He paused, mustering strength to speak on. "Anadin and Artassa are dead."

Shock flashed over their faces, then wrath.

"Who is responsible, my lord?" growled Ledonn. "Has vengeance won?"

"Not yet." Aredel swallowed, wrestling to keep his expression stoic. "The *Unsielie* are to blame, and we will soon march to war against them."

"Good," said Shevek with fervor. "They will suffer."

"A council begins soon," said Aredel. "We're invited to join them. Let us prepare for battle."

The knights bowed their heads together, then parted to flank him as Aredel moved toward the heart of Sharo's camp. No one spoke. The voice of KryTeer was always silent before combat.

CHAPTER 10
THE WATERS OF TRUTH

Near the healer's tent, Kajsa hung back from the flow of people moving toward the center of camp. Jetekesh caught her eye, and she listed forward before she caught herself. She hadn't been invited to the council, and she couldn't find Thrissa to ask if she was allowed.

I'm not really qualified to attend anyway.

She didn't want to plan for war—she'd traveled past her homeland, across the Snowblinds, into Shing to prevent it. She'd met Jetekesh, traveled with his company to the Clanslands, and reached Shinac in an effort to stop Navolleth.

Yet now, according to every rumor across camp, Navolleth was an ally and the whispering threat of war had grown into a full-fledged storm.

At her side, the ghost of Raum sat on his haunches, his yellow eyes pinned on her. The silver and black wolf let out a whine that pitched into a question. Kajsa crouched beside him while the procession of people slipped around a corner between rows of tents. She ran her fingers through Raum's translucent fur and tried a smile.

"I'm all right. Merely..." She hesitated. "Well, useless."

"The only useless person is she who chooses not to act." Thrissa's voice was a quiet, musical sound.

Kajsa snapped upright. Recovering, she curtseyed before the elven woman standing in the quiet of the vanished procession. "My lady."

"Aren't you coming?" asked Thrissa, folding her arms. Her tunic caught the light of the sun and shimmered brighter. "Your companions are all going to be in attendance."

Kajsa dipped her head. "They're all warriors. I'm..."

"Blooded," said Thrissa. "You've fought at their sides. Do not discount yourself so." The elf tipped her head toward the vanished crowd. "Come along, Kajsa."

The girl started to protest, then stopped herself. Her chest fluttered. She straightened her spine, ran a hand across her stomach, and offered a nod. "Lead on, Lady Thrissa."

The elf's eyes glinted with approval, then she motioned. "This way."

They walked together, Kajsa trying to keep up with the tall woman's strides. Doubts cluttered her head, but she shoved them back. Thrissa was right; more than once, Kajsa had fought alongside Jetekesh, Emerin, and the rest. She'd journeyed into the Clansland jungle and found *traveria* to save a life. She'd earned her place outside of Norva.

Back home, the villagers of Tuksa had looked at her askance. Questioned her abilities. Shunned her as though she were cursed. All except Axel.

Will I see him again now that Norva is an ally?

At the end of a row of tents, Kajsa turned a last corner and faltered before the brimming pool of people. She tensed.

Don't be a coward.

She shook herself and tried to peer over the soldiers to find Jetekesh, but she wasn't tall enough.

Thrissa set a slender hand on her arm, then moved ahead through the crowd, pulling Kajsa with her. When the soldiers recognized Thrissa, they shifted out of the way and lowered their eyes in respect. Kajsa fought against a desire to duck her head and dart off. Instead, she kept her stare fastened on the elf's shoulder, letting the woman steer her through the crowd.

They broke free before a large stone table where Sharo stood, along with Jetekesh, Aredel, Dakarai, Anenyasha, Emerin, and several unfamiliar men and women dressed in armor. Three were elves, the rest looked human. Among them, a little girl stood beside a tall swordsman.

Maps were spread across the table's surface, held in place by several goblets along with a wine decanter whose crystal facets sparkled in the bright sunlight. As the light hit her eyes, Kajsa winced and turned back to those assembled at the table.

Sharo had been speaking to the crowd for a few minutes and was wrapping up an explanation of how the seal had broken, joining Nakania and Shinac together. Murmurs drifted through the crowds, and several soldiers motioned to Jetekesh.

The Marked Prince shifted his stance, then fell still, keeping his attention rooted on Sharo.

"Make no mistake," said Sharo in tones that cracked like ice. "Those responsible for this premature reintegration are King Darint and his council. *They* will feel the full weight of accountability, and no others. Do I speak plainly enough?"

Sounds of confirmation rippled through the assembled soldiers.

"Now." Sharo rested his knuckles on the table. "We plan for war. The Sundered One has agreed to ally with us."

Murmurs rose again until Sharo's sharp eyes cut over the crowd.

He spoke on. "He will return before nightfall, along with his forces, and he will be treated with every Shinacian courtesy."

Sharo smiled. “Taregan has gone to assemble his clans. I’ve given him two weeks to return with every able dragon.”

The faint noise pitched into hopeful tones.

“We have but one more task left to organize ahead of our march to Nakania.” Sharo’s eyes landed on Jetekesh. “I am hoping you might agree to undertake it.”

Jetekesh’s eyebrows shot up. “What task is that, my lord?”

Sharo angled toward the short, white-haired man called Jinji—the one Jetekesh looked up to. Kajsa studied the storyteller. In his mien, she read kindness tinged with sorrow, in that way all wise men and women looked. Ingrid had worn the same sort of mantle over her shoulders.

Jinji cleared his throat, and a silence fell over the crowd, muting even the faintest shuffles. Every eye rested on the storyteller true.

“Long ago, when Shinac and Nakania were one land, a human queen bore triplets: three healthy sons. As often happens, the sons grew up in strong rivalry for the throne. Determined to choose whichever of his sons was most worthy, the king refused to name his heir, awaiting a sign.”

Kajsa started. The imagery of the story unfolded around her, and she found herself standing among ancient royalty as they interacted. It was as though she’d been dropped onto a stage, invisible, and the solid players moved around her—oblivious to her presence.

Jinji’s voice filled the air, cradling the details, painting emotions. “The eldest son, feeling himself most worthy by divine right, was threatened by the king’s hesitancy, and he chose to secure his place on the throne through underhanded deeds. Those most loyal to him swore an oath to murder his younger brothers, and within the same month, the middle brother met with a horrible accident. He tumbled from a high castle turret and died against the stones of the courtyard below.”

Kajsa flinched at the gruesome sight before the story swept on to a new scene.

"The queen suspected foul play and warned her youngest son to flee lest he be killed soon after. He did indeed run away in the dead of night but not before he swore an oath to avenge his fallen brother.

"The king soon afterward declared his eldest son the rightful heir. Alas, within a fortnight, the king, too, met with an unfortunate accident. The elder brother—now the new king—was determined to leave his mark upon the kingdom. He increased taxes and encouraged slave labor to erect monuments of himself. As he waxed stronger and stronger, the people grew disgruntled.

"Far away from the kingdom, the younger brother found his way into the fae lands, where he was captured and brought to the Hold of Valliath, stronghold of the *Seelie*."

The brilliant exterior of the castle—made from crystal and granite—stretched before Kajsa, glittering, spired, standing atop a great hill covered in trees that flamed with autumnal colors. A road wended its way up the hill, and above the castle snapped a pennant depicting a golden tree against a white field.

Trumpets blared, and she witnessed the younger royal prince being escorted to the castle gates by a contingent of woodland elves.

The scene shifted, and she stood within the castle among the gentry in the grand throne room. On the two tall thrones sat a couple. The man had dark hair and piercing, pale blue eyes. The woman had pale blonde hair like all the Norvians, and she wore it in an intricate plait. Her eyes were dark and gentle. Both the king and queen were beautiful and fair, with kind smiles.

Jinji's voice fell like gentle rain, willing the scene into motion like the players on a stage answering their cues. "The Lord of Valliath and his Lady listened to the young prince's plight, and they offered him sanctuary—but the prince, tormented by thoughts of revenge, requested instead that justice be served.

"'True justice,' said the Fae King, 'is a weighty demand, for it leans upon truth without a modicum of compassion. Are you prepared to weigh your heart upon such austere scales?'

"'I am,' the prince replied, his voice ringing up to the high rafters.

"'So be it,' said the Lady of Valliath. 'Bring your brother to the blood fountain in the valley of Litwathe where truth cannot be hidden. There, you will face justice without mercy's hand, and what will be will be.'

"The prince bowed and took his leave. He sent out a challenge at once to his elder brother, and the new king—determined to end any threat to his rule—agreed to meet the prince in the Valley of Litwathe, where the blood fountain had stood since the dawn of Shinac.

"Both brothers reached the valley of Litwathe as the sun ringed the world in red at sunset, and the fountain seemed to flow with blood.

"Dragons are the justicers of all life," Jinji said, and a vision of a sapphire dragon wheeled in the crimson sky directly above the fountain. "When a trial is invoked, none can easily deceive their kind. So it was, that evening at Litwathe, that two brothers would face the truth of their hearts as the dragon tested them."

The dragon swooped down and transformed into a human shape as he landed before the fountain. He was draped in a sapphire cloak and wore a circlet of delicate twined silver.

"'Drink from the waters of truth,' the dragon commanded. 'Your worthiness to rule shall be judged here and now.' The dragon motioned to the fountain. 'If your desire to reign is purely selfish, you will die. If your desire is to aid and protect your people above yourself, then you have nothing to fear."

"The brothers each considered the waters flowing forth from

the fountain. Then, as though they had communed in their minds, they drew their swords as one and ran the dragon through."

Kajsa's heart wrenched. She threw a hand over her eyes, trying to block out the sight of the dragon-turned-man falling to the ground, pierced by two broadswords. In that moment, the grass across the wide, deep valley changed from lush green to crimson.

Jinji's next words flowed through her despite her efforts to block him out. "As the dragon lay dying, the two brothers turned on each other and fought viciously. The sun had long set before the elder brother fell to his younger brother's sword, and, victorious, the younger brother left Litwathe to claim his new crown.

"The sole surviving brother became king, as he had wished, and he reigned at first with a benevolent hand, proud to undo the damage his elder brother had dealt. Alas, his desire to be better than the former king soon fell away under the temptation of power, as so often happens, and by degrees, he grew into a harsher king than his brother had ever been.

"But the flames of justice do not dim, and the slaying of a dragon ends in a curse. This the king conveniently forgot until the day of his wedding. He had sent out a decree that the fairest women of the kingdom be sent to him, and he chose from among them. The young woman who was selected had no say, but she didn't argue. And when the ceremony was performed, she wordlessly offered up a goblet to the king. Pleased with her quiet obedience, the king accepted the goblet and drank deeply of the red liquid. It wasn't wine. The waters of truth from the blood fountain poured down his throat, and his heart stopped at once.

"In the shock that followed the king's collapse, the woman revealed herself to be a red dragon and the mate of he who had fallen to the brothers' swords. As the new queen, she decreed that no ruler should sit upon the throne unless they were first judged at the blood fountain and found worthy. To do otherwise would stir the dragon's death curse once more, this time against the land itself.

"After that, she vanished, and the kingdom found its new king from among the common folk, using the fountain's waters as their guide. He was hailed as Cavalin the First, also called Cavalin the Merciful."

The story faded away. Kajsa blinked and found herself back among the soldiers in Sharo's camp.

Jinji bowed his head. "So the tradition of selecting a ruler from the common folk continued until Cavalin the Third fell upon the field, and Shinac vanished from Nakania. The wars that have plagued Nakania are caused by the fountain's absence. The dragon's ancient curse has awakened."

Kajsa found Jetekesh near the storyteller. The prince's face had lost its color. By the law of the blood fountain, his line wasn't the rightful one. They'd sat upon Cavalin's throne without the fountain's consent.

She read his thoughts clearly: His family had cursed Nakania.

CHAPTER 11
TWO PROPHECIES

"Your Highness," said Sharo, cutting into Jetekesh's horror like a dagger.

Jetekesh tore his gaze from Jinji's profile to find Sharo's sky-blue eyes. His heart thudded against his ribs and drummed through his good ear.

"Will you seek out the blood fountain?" Sharo asked. "It once existed in the realm of the dragons, but one day the valley of Litwathe vanished. Thrissa believes it now dwells in Valliath."

A lump grew in Jetekesh's throat. "How can I—" He broke off. His voice sounded tight. Afraid. He swallowed hard and tried again. His voice still failed him. He didn't want to go—to be the one who found it. To admit his line was at fault for all the wars over the past three centuries. In the beginning, they'd surely known about the dragon's curse, and yet...

Sharo's smile slipped a little. "King Darint, and indeed, the Sundered One, believe that the throne of Amantier belongs to the ruler of all Nakania. They also believe, as do many, that the heirs of Cavalin's blood are unworthy of that throne. If we're to end this war before it's a massacre, we must find the rightful human ruler and put an end to the curse."

Jetekesh's limbs quaked. His heart thudded louder, drowning out the murmurs that filled the crowd. His insides writhed. Sharo's gaze remained pinned on him, waiting, expectant. Jetekesh wanted to scream in protest. To dismiss Jinji's story as absurd. The storyteller had lost his wits—he'd lied. Nothing of truth lived in his words.

But surely, Jetekesh knew better than anyone that Jinji spoke true. He'd felt the story's resonance in his blood. He'd seen the dragon fall before the blood fountain, and something in his newfound gift confirmed this was more than a mere story.

His vision blurred, but he wrestled back the tears and bowed to Sharo. "If that's how I can best serve Nakania." Jetekesh rose, swallowing past the lump lodged in his throat.

"I believe it is." Sharo's voice was kind. He understood what he was asking—yet he asked. "If the blood fountain chooses a high king or queen for Nakania, then the Shinacians will acknowledge their right to rule. It may stem some of the fear that is flooding our conjoined realms. Certainly, it will ease tensions and eliminate in-fighting. More importantly, my father won't be able to claim Nakania for himself if a worthy ruler is chosen first."

Never mind about the horrible curse.

Jetekesh swallowed harder, trying not to let bitterness root around in his churning stomach. Sharo was his friend; he cared. What he asked was *that* important. Jetekesh couldn't fool himself on that point.

The fae prince turned back to the crowd assembled around the table, and his words flowed out, distant, and unimportant. Jetekesh was being sent away—he would take no part in the war. Instead, he must seek out the means of dethroning his line.

Maybe the waters will choose you?

He shoved that thought down at once. What good could come of flimsy hopes?

Jetekesh let his gaze wander, ignoring Sharo's war strategies, determined not to heed what didn't matter to him.

He scowled at himself. *It still matters, Kesh.*

Kajsa's gaze struck him. She stood at the fore of the crowd near Thrissa, her pale blue eyes searching his face. Her lips parted to ask a silent question: 'Are you all right?'

He started to nod, then froze, and finally shook his head. He had no reason to lie to her—he'd never done so before, and he hated to start now.

Kajsa's eyes flicked to his immediate left, and he followed her gaze just as a dark hand fell on his shoulder. Dakarai. The clansman smiled down at him, wielding the same sympathy that adorned Sharo's and Kajsa's expressions.

The man stooped close to Jetekesh's good ear. "I will come with you."

A pang shot across Jetekesh's chest. He whirled to stare into Dakarai's face. "You will?" His voice was the faintest whisper.

"Certainly." The clansman's deep voice was a low rumble. "I am sworn to you until I can safely return you to your father in Kavacos."

Jetekesh blinked back the mist in his eyes. "Thank you, Dakarai. What of Anenyasha?"

"She will certainly come too."

Laughter climbed up Jetekesh's throat, but he stifled it. His relief filled him with a kind of hysterical elation, but he would stay composed. He'd been trained well enough to avoid making a scene.

As the meeting continued, a little of Jetekesh's relief bled away. The facts of his quest remained the same: He sought the means to end Cavalin's line of kings. But at least he wasn't going alone.

His gaze strayed to King Aredel standing at the edge of the crowd, sandwiched between his loyal Blood Knights.

What will you do, Aredel? Will you seek death on the battlefield, or live long enough to save Nakania?

Aredel found him. Their eyes locked. Nothing of fondness or tolerance remained in the Blood King's face. He was a stranger; a threat.

Jetekesh's lungs tightened until he could barely breathe. *Saints preserve and guide me.*

He tore away from Aredel's endless glower, seeking out Kajsa. She was still there, still watching him. The girl offered her timid, warm smile—a steady candle in the blizzard of the Marked Prince's soul.

When the war council ended, and soldiers marched off to break camp, Jetekesh stood still in the stream of bodies, waiting for the majority to clear away.

Sharo approached, carving a path from the table. His expression was apologetic. "Could you leave this evening, my friend?"

"Sooner," Jetekesh said, "if necessary."

Sharo glanced at Dakarai, then turned back to Jetekesh. "Take whomever you wish. I would join you myself if I could."

"I understand." The words came out in a frigid rush. Jetekesh grimaced. "I do understand, Your Highness. But I...I wish you'd given me some warning." He drew a breath. "And I wish you would explain whatever prophecy Navolleth referred to. What did he mean about my mark and the destruction of Shinac? Is it because of the dragon's curse?"

Sharo sighed. "It's an old prophecy, made on the heels of the true king's vanishing. The trouble is there are two prophecies, and many assume they reference the same person. I believe otherwise. One is certainly about you:

"'*After the Way is sundered, he who breaches two worlds shall stand as a beacon guiding the heir of Cavalin to his rightful place. You shall know him by his countenance, marked by the emblem of Valliath.*'"

Jetekesh rubbed his thumb against the healed flesh of his left wrist. "And the other prophecy?"

"It is more archaic, far less clear, and I have my doubts as to its prophetic nature. It says,

"'*Beware the sundered day, when two worlds collide, after which the broken heir shall spill blood like rain upon the fields of harvest. Shinac, O beloved land, now fallen. Wilt thou rise evermore?*'"

The fae prince offered a graceful shrug. "That's all of it. You can see how the common phrases, 'two worlds' and 'sundered,' would connect the prophecies in most minds."

Turning the words over in his head, Jetekesh weighed them against each other. He was no scholar, but the events felt related. "Navolleth assumes I'm the broken heir." He swallowed. "Because I must go to find the rightful ruler of Nakania."

"I think so, yes," said Sharo.

"But you don't believe I'm the broken heir?"

The prince's eyes flicked to one side, then back. "No. I believe it's referring to someone else."

The answer nearly choked Jetekesh. "You mean Aredel."

"It's a strong possibility. He is indeed broken."

"But he's also a king, not an heir," said Dakarai.

Jetekesh nearly jumped out of his skin. He'd forgotten the clansman stood beside him. Glancing at Dakarai, he read a grimness in the man's strong jaw and dark eyes.

"True, that," said Sharo, nodding. "Unless..." He hesitated, then shook his head. "Many have ventured guesses in the past, at other times no less unsettling than this. I might be as wrong in my assumptions as any man or woman before me."

"Or," said Jetekesh, "you might be right." He rested his hand against his sheathed sword hilt and fingered the gems sparkling there. "Sundered. Why do you call Navolleth that?"

"Ah. That." Sharo's gaze cast around like he sought an exit, but he didn't run. His boots remained firmly planted against the hard-packed earth. "Navolleth is a sad creature, known to all who belong to Valliath true."

"Sad." Jetekesh tasted the word. Yes, Navolleth exuded a sorrow that permeated the very air around him. "Then you know why he wants to destroy Nakania?"

"Yes," said Sharo. Shadows crossed his face, and he looked suddenly weary, far older than his youthful features implied. The fae prince turned his gaze skyward. "He was Cavalin's dragon."

CHAPTER 12
CHANGING PATHS

Jetekesh stared at Sharo. "Cavalin's…what?"

Sharo lowered his head, and his mournful gaze struck the Amantieran prince like a hammer blow. "Navolleth is a fallen dragon. He was bonded to Cavalin when that good hero fell to Tallat's blade. It…broke him."

The words penetrated Jetekesh's mind slowly. He shook his head. "But…why would he wish to destroy Nakania after everything Cavalin did to protect it?"

"Cavalin was protecting *Shinac* from Tallat's forces," Sharo said. "That is the simple truth. And then Shinac vanished from Nakania, whose people had been judged unworthy to cross into the land of magic. That is likely Navolleth's perspective. Humankind failed their king."

Nausea roiled in Jetekesh's stomach. His eyes lost their focus as his thoughts retreated inward, chasing Sharo's words, trying to change them. Navolleth blamed Amantier, KryTeer, Shing, and the Clanslands, perhaps even the island countries, for Cavalin's death. Why? Didn't he understand how dearly Cavalin had loved the realms of Nakania? How much he'd sacrificed?

If you were there, if you were bonded to him, how could you not see?

Jetekesh's lungs pinched. He struggled to breathe. *He was there, Kesh.* You *weren't. Are things different than we believe? Did the historians lie?*

Jinji had already cracked Jetekesh's world with a single story about the blood fountain and its waters of truth. Did Jetekesh know anything about anything, or was Amantier to blame for the great hero's death, like Bareene had lied about loving her child, like Emerin had lied about helping Jetekesh, like...like...

The world wobbled.

Dakarai caught his elbow. "You're exhausted. Perhaps we should leave on the morrow."

Sharo stepped forward. "You've learned a lot, just after paying a high cost for your healing. Rest, my friend." He brushed his fingers against Jetekesh's shoulder. "Tomorrow will be soon enough."

"No." Jetekesh's voice cracked like thunder. He pulled away from Sharo; away from his guilt. "I'll leave as soon as I've assembled my company. If Amantier has been party to injustice, I'll right it." He whirled, struggling to keep his feet. The world spun around him, but he wasn't experiencing the effects of his recent healing. This was deeper, and with it, a fire kindled inside, gnawing at his bones.

Navolleth believed the royal line of Amantier unfit to rule. He believed Cavalin had been the last worthy human in Nakania. That Jetekesh's house had brought a curse on the world.

I'll prove him wrong. I'll find the rightful heir. I'll...

He froze. Seeking out the blood fountain was only one step. What came after that? He couldn't just travel around the war-torn countries looking for some pauper meant to sit upon Amantier's throne.

Dakarai was at his side again. "One step at a time, my friend."

Jetekesh craned his head to find the man's kind eyes. Nothing but patience shone there.

"Come along." The clansman tipped his head toward the clusters of tents. "We should pack and seek out our companions."

Jetekesh trailed after Dakarai, thoughts heavy as he weighed who he should bring on his quest. Anenyasha's presence was already assured. Kethalas was no doubt flying with Taregan toward the dragon lands and recovery.

What about Emerin? Would the keep lord choose open war to avenge his fallen sister, or would he want to search for the blood fountain?

Best thing to do is simply ask.

Jetekesh looked up from his feet as he approached the ring of tents beyond the council. Kajsa approached, her eyes bright in the midday sun. Should he bring her or leave her in a war camp?

Neither place is safe.

His mind stuttered on that. Who was he to demand that she stay wherever it was safest to be? He'd already determined that she wasn't his subject, nor was he her leader now that they'd accomplished what they set out to do.

"What will you choose?" he found himself asking.

"I'll come with you." She said it like there'd never been a question.

Heat climbed Jetekesh's cheeks, but he found himself smiling. "Very well. We leave as soon as everyone is packed and assembled."

Kajsa nodded, then turned and slipped off between two tents. He watched her until she was out of sight, tension bleeding from his muscles. Somehow, he was glad she was coming.

It's the sensible choice, isn't it? War will definitely be more dangerous than some quest to the backwoods of Shinac, and having a healer would be wise.

Jetekesh grimaced. "Dakarai, how do we even begin? I...I don't know the lay of Shinac at all."

Dakarai held up a scroll and joggled it. "This should help. Sharo believes the fountain is in Valliath. That is northeast of our present location. By my reckoning, we are two weeks from the gates of that realm."

More travel. "Well," said Jetekesh with a sigh, "there's no helping it. At least we have a direction."

Dakarai grunted. "And at least one river to cross."

Jetekesh bit back a groan. "Tell me Shinacians use barges or ferries."

"Often," said Thrissa, approaching with a gleam in her eye. She bowed her head, then straightened. "Marked Prince, Sharo has asked me to be your guide to Valliath."

Dakarai chuckled. "I suppose I didn't need to nick the map, then."

"No," she said. "You can return it to the table at your earliest convenience."

Dakarai offered a shallow bow, then strode off, leaving Jetekesh alone with the elven woman. He studied her ageless face, the shimmer of her silver hair. Had she really been alive long enough to remember Cavalin—and much earlier events than that?

"Did you ever speak with Cavalin the Third?" he asked.

"Yes. We were...friends." She spoke the last word like she was trying it on for the first time. Her eyes darted toward Dakarai as the clansman returned. "Cavalin was a good man. And a great one."

"So the historians say," Jetekesh said. "Three hundred years is a long time for humans."

"It can be a long time for elves, too," she said. "Especially after such losses. We of Shinac were no less heart-worn by Tallat's war—and by the sundering of our two lands. There was much we loved in Nakania." Her eyes brightened, and Jetekesh wondered if tears collected in her vision.

Thrissa twisted away, motioning to the path between the nearest tents. "Shall we?"

The three companions started toward the main area of the camp, and Jetekesh returned to his immediate need: selecting his companions. He could only offer and see who accepted. Keeping his numbers few was best, yet he struggled against the idea of leaving anyone behind. They'd traveled for so long together, faced so many travails, buried a friend...

"Your Highness!"

Jetekesh whirled toward Emerin's voice and found the man jogging toward him. The Amantieran prince waited, Dakarai and Thrissa halting beside him. Emerin arrived, panting, perspiration glittering on his brow. His hair was damp and pressed flat against his skull, like he'd slicked it back with his hands as he ran.

"Take me with you," the keep lord said, gasping for breath.

Jetekesh raised his brow as his heart throbbed with relief. "Where are you coming from, my lord?"

"Horses." Emerin stabbed a finger toward the corrals. "I just heard about the council, and what Sharo asked of you." His green eyes narrowed. "I wish to come. To help." He inhaled through his nose, casting his gaze to the ground. "To prove to you my penitence for my deception."

"That isn't necessary." Jetekesh took a step forward and rested a hand on Emerin's shoulder. "I understand why you did what you did, and I won't punish you." His throat closed before he could utter his next words, but he steeled himself and forced them out. "Losing your sister was a cruel blow. One you didn't deserve."

Emerin squeezed his eyes shut. His throat bobbed as he swallowed. "Thank you, my prince."

Prince. The word cut through Jetekesh like a butcher's blade. *Prince of what?*

He curled his fingers into fists, digging his nails deep into his palms, until the pain brightened his mind to his purpose. Truth. Wasn't that the sigil marking his soul? All truth, not only what was convenient for him.

"I'm leaving as soon as possible," Jetekesh said. "Be ready at the corrals in one hour."

"Within the hour," Emerin said, dipping his head. The man pivoted and darted off, blond hair flying out behind him.

Jetekesh moved again toward the main paths of the camp, scanning every face he passed for signs of someone familiar. Soon, he reached the healer's tent, and Thrissa slipped in ahead of him. As he entered, the same scent of herbs tickled his nose, and he sneezed.

"Saints bless you," said Dakarai, flashing him a smile.

Jetekesh grinned back, but it was a forced gesture. His soul pressed in on him, threatening to crush his bones. He gathered the few meager belongings he'd brought from the *Unsielie* fortress, then turned toward Thrissa.

"What do we do about essential supplies?"

"I'll see to them," she said. "You should rest."

"Impossible." He stared at the tent flap rippling in a breeze. "I'll seek the rest of my companions."

Dakarai went with him, and they meandered along the narrow paths, slowly making their way to the palisades jutting above the rows of tents. As Jetekesh's gaze strayed to the spiked logs, a flash of light beyond the looming wall blinded him.

"*Vashalan*!" cried a watchman. "We're under attack!"

CHAPTER 13
PARTINGS

A second voice cracked across the air, strong, commanding. "Stay your hands! The Sundered One comes as an ally."

Jetekesh's heart dropped into his stomach. Navolleth, back so quickly? He twisted away from the palisades. "We don't need to meet him again."

Dakarai's voice was quiet. "Agreed." He followed Jetekesh away from the wall, nearly silent.

"A moment, Marked Prince."

Navolleth's soft, sorrowful voice chased chills up Jetekesh's spine.

He turned toward the fallen dragon in human shape, and their eyes locked, sending a jolt through Jetekesh's body. He'd been afraid of Navolleth before. Now, he was petrified. This creature, so utterly broken, blamed Nakania for Cavalin's death.

How can Sharo trust him, even a little?

The fae prince's strategy made sense. Keeping one's enemy close was smart, especially when one could employ that enemy against another. King Aredel had made similar maneuvers during his conquering of the known world.

But it's terribly reckless.

Navolleth drifted closer, pale hair fluttering along his arms. His eyes, slitted, glittering, traveled up and down Jetekesh. "You're going." His voice was low, barely audible. "You seek the blood fountain."

Jetekesh tried and failed to read the man's emotions. "Yes."

"To prove yourself to be the rightful king?" Venom dripped from those words. "You'll fail. You'll die."

Fury kindled in Jetekesh's chest, and his jaw snapped closed. He pried his mouth open. "I'm not the king. My father is. And he's a *good* man."

"Ah," said Navolleth. "You will sentence him to death then. To drink the waters of truth unworthily has only one outcome."

Jetekesh's eyes narrowed. "Sharo asked me to seek out the blood fountain. I will do so. And whoever is meant to be king will become king—or queen—whether you or I like it."

He nearly whirled around to march away, but something inside made him stand firm. He held Navolleth's gaze for a long moment. "I know who you are. Sharo told me. And you have my deepest sympathy for your loss—but that doesn't excuse you for your actions. For unleashing a water demon upon innocent souls. For stirring up hatred and starting a war." He inhaled, and blew out his breath, letting some of his anger burn away. "I doubt Cavalin would approve of your methods. Indeed, I believe he'd be horrified by your actions."

Dipping his head, he turned and started off, Dakarai at his side.

"You will take Axel with you." Navolleth hardly raised his voice, yet it carried.

Jetekesh jerked around. "I'll take whom I please."

"Axel will come with you. He will make certain your task is accomplished, even should you fail."

"No." Jetekesh turned away and marched between the tents,

not caring where he went. His mind spun, and his heart battered his ribcage.

"You were very brave to stand against him," Dakarai said, keeping pace.

A scornful laugh escaped Jetekesh's lips. "I was scared spitless, but I will *not* let him use Cavalin's good name to burn the world, all while blaming me and my father. My father's as noble as Cavalin. Whether he should remain king or not, he doesn't deserve whatever Navolleth's broken mind plans on delivering."

They broke free of a gathering of tents, and Jetekesh dodged around a group of elven soldiers huddled close and whispering about the army of *vashalan* in the meadow.

Jetekesh shuddered but didn't slow his step. For now, the *vashalan* weren't a threat. Nor were their numbers as impressive as they appeared if Navolleth was up to his old illusory tricks.

Clutching his belongings close, Jetekesh prayed to the One God that his companions had all heard of his impending departure. Hopefully, they'd already chosen whether to stay or go. He didn't want to linger with Navolleth back in camp.

Nor did he want to bring the dragon's minion along.

Approaching the corrals, Jetekesh scanned the fences near several stables where a handful of boys mucked out manure. The heady odor filled Jetekesh's nostrils, mingled with the sweet scent of hay.

A shadow detached from the edge of the stables.

Jetekesh recoiled. Aredel's approach was like watching a mountain cat slink toward its prey. The KryTeeran's brown eyes seemed red in the sunlight, and the motes of dust around him took on a glittering quality, no longer benign. Here he was: the caged beast who'd been silent over the past year, brooding.

A few paces before Jetekesh, the Blood King halted. "You're on your way." Whether he asked a question or merely stated the obvious, Jetekesh couldn't tell from the crisp tones.

"Yes," the prince said. "No sense delaying. Once you and Sharo win this senseless war, and bring down Darint, chaos will ensue unless the rightful ruler is found." He kept a level tone, but doubt curled around the final few words. Would Aredel accept a high king over Nakania to end the curse?

The Blood King nodded. "Jinji has asked me to leave you be." He paused. "And I fully recognize you were a mere pawn in Darint's craven game. So I will let you go."

Jetekesh found himself staring at Aredel's boots. A lump swelled in his throat. "I..."

"Don't." Aredel's voice cracked like a whip. "Do not, Prince of Amantier. I do not desire your apologies, your sympathy, nor any excuses. The facts are what they are. Best to steer clear of me, and I will not lose my temper."

Shame burned Jetekesh's face. The kindling anger in his stomach flared up. He knew he must accept Aredel's censure; he'd earned it through his blindness. But it still smarted.

Hefting his chin, Jetekesh managed to capture Aredel's gaze. "If you wish me to avoid you, why are you here?"

"To wish you success," said Aredel. "Find the rightful king or queen. Succeed in this. Nakania must be ruled by one chosen through the magic of Shinac."

Jetekesh blinked at that. So, Aredel wouldn't challenge the new ruler?

"At that time," Aredel continued, "perhaps...perhaps I might be able to set aside this fury and find it in myself to forgive you." His dark eyes closed. "Gods know I will never forgive myself."

The Blood King turned and strode away, the tatters of his once-regal KryTeeran wardrobe rippling in a rising breeze. Diamonds winked in the beams of sunlight.

Jetekesh exhaled, letting his shoulders slump a little. Tension bled from every muscle, and he realized he'd been clutching his sword hilt. He pried his white knuckles loose.

"So then." Jetekesh's voice was a stranger's in his ear. "One day we may become friends again."

"It seems so," Dakarai said. "Now, let us look northeast, to Valliath."

Jetekesh let his instincts turn him in the direction Dakarai indicated. A shadow crossed the sun, and he glanced up to find a cloud. As it crept above the earth, his heart lifted a little. Hope endured, more candle than torch glow, but that was enough.

He dropped his eyes. Standing at the fence posts, his company had assembled. Including Yeshton, Song, and Rille. He moved forward to meet them.

Thrissa had provided pack horses as well as saddled mounts, along with food, bedrolls, warm cloaks, and extra weapons. She had also brought enough leather armor for each member of the company, though Rille declined hers, as did Dakarai and Anenyasha.

Jetekesh smiled faintly. Time to seek out the truth and face it, no matter what.

CHAPTER 14
THREE SIBLINGS

As he raced his borrowed horse across the open fields, the cries of the *vashalan* drew Jetekesh's head around.

He jerked his gaze back to the ground before him. His mind churned at the thought of Navolleth's hellhounds tracking the company thundering toward Valliath. Golden hair whipped in his eyes, tugging free of his new shimmering elven cloak.

Will he send Axel after us?

The possibility was strong. Navolleth didn't seem the sort to heed a firm no.

In that, I suppose we're a lot alike.

A painted mare came level with Jetekesh's mount. There hadn't been time to wait for Sharo's scouts to bring Hickory and the other horses from the *Unsielie* wetlands, though, the fae prince had turned up to bid them farewell, and he'd promised that the horses would be well cared for.

Emerin rode the mare, his elven cloak billowing behind him. He nudged the horse faster and turned his gaze on Jetekesh. "Do we ignore them?"

"Yes," said Jetekesh. "Whatever Navolleth's reasons for chasing us down, I'll not let him hinder our speed."

The keep lord nodded, then turned his attention ahead to where Thrissa led the company.

Behind them, the rest of their companions kept pace. Kajsa and Rille shared a horse in the center among the pack horses, while Dakarai and Anenyasha made up the rear. Rille had been an unexpected addition, especially without Yeshton, but she'd argued that her sight might come in handy—and Yeshton had reluctantly chosen to remain in Sharo's army, along with Lady Song, where their skills were most needed.

According to Yeshton, he intended to ask Sharo to let him ride ahead to warn the king in Amantier of all that had transpired. Bearing that in mind, it only made sense to let Rille come with Jetekesh since Yeshton wouldn't risk taking her with him across enemy lines.

As important as Jetekesh's quest was, he still felt queasy as he pushed his gray stallion farther and farther away from the growing storm of battle.

Focus. Don't be distracted.

He gritted his teeth and dug his heels into the horse's flank, eking out every burst of speed he could manage.

Howls rose higher.

Jetekesh ignored them.

NIGHT SETTLED over the world like a damp blanket. Clouds brewed above the camp. Occasional rumbles and tongues of lightning painted the sky silver, while Emerin and Rille bickered over the contents of the pot roiling on the trivet.

Dakarai sharpened his spear nearby while Anenyasha used a kind of chalk to color a braid in her coarse hair. Both still declined to wear the restrictive armor Thrissa had offered, preferring their loose, colorful clansfolk wardrobe.

The pursuing howls of the *vashalan* had faded hours before, but Jetekesh's nerves remained on edge. His good ear stretched out, trying to hear anything beyond the storm. They camped in a copse of aspen trees whose leaves clattered in the buffeting wind.

The fire guttered, coughing up smoke. Rille and Emerin kept changing where they stood while Rille challenged the keep lord's choice to add peas to his stew.

"They don't belong with beef," she said flatly.

Emerin rolled his eyes. "Every vegetable belongs with beef."

Jetekesh shook his head and returned to oiling his sword—but Kajsa caught his eye instead. The Norvian girl sat straight-backed on a fallen log near the fire, her eyes trained on the rolling hills they'd crossed before sunset. She shifted slightly, and her elven cloak shimmered. Beside her, the ghostly form of Raum sat, alert, also staring into the darkness.

"What is it?" Jetekesh asked, chills prickling his arms.

Kajsa stirred but kept her gaze riveted on the grasslands. "I think—"

Raum let out a soft whimper, then a short, sharp bark.

"Ho, the camp," called a voice. "I come in peace."

Kajsa shot to her feet with a gasp. Raum yipped.

Slipping into the firelight, a young man appeared like a specter, draped in fur, toting a bow, leading a gray gelding by the reins. His eyes flitted across the company, then fell on Kajsa.

A smile spread over his lips. "Ky."

"Xel!" She darted across the camp and flung her arms around the stranger. A sob escaped her lips.

The stranger—Axel, Jetekesh could easily surmise—drew Kajsa into a tight embrace, tucking his face against her neck. They stood there for a long moment, while Emerin slinked close to Jetekesh.

"Navolleth's man, isn't he?" asked the keep lord in low tones.

Jetekesh nodded, feeling lightheaded. He'd ridden the company hard to avoid this. The idea of Navolleth's agent coming with them was unbearable. Axel was essentially a spy, and Jetekesh wouldn't put it past the Norvian to stab everyone in the back once they located the blood fountain.

Dakarai slipped up on Jetekesh's other side and spoke in a whisper. "It cannot be helped now. Anenyasha and I will keep a close eye on him. Should he prove to be a danger, he will meet with an unfortunate accident."

Glancing at the clansman, Jetekesh read a hardness in Dakarai's visage that he rarely saw. It was the same look the man had worn when he'd dealt with the marauders within the Clans-lands. The rigidity of a blooded warrior.

"Thank you," Jetekesh whispered back.

Kajsa pulled free of her countryman and turned toward Jetekesh. "Your Highness, this is Axel, my dearest friend."

"Yes, I know."

"Axel," she said, "this is Prince Jetekesh of Amantier."

"The Marked Prince," said Axel. "I've heard of you." His pale green eyes glittered like frost, unfriendly, and his arm slithered around Kajsa's waist like an overprotective lover.

Jetekesh arched his brow. "I notice you speak without an accent."

"The explanation for that is simple." Thrissa stepped between the two clusters of people. "You were gifted to understand all mortal tongues when you entered Shinac through the Arch. While we are within the bounds of Shinac the gift will remain, but I doubt you will retain it once you step outside our old borders and enter Nakania. Fortunately, our quest requires us to travel within the fae country." She tipped her head to one side. "Have you come to aid us, Axel of Norva?"

"I have at my master's behest," replied the Norvian. He shot

Kajsa a smile. "And glad I am to be reunited with my friend." His gaze flitted to Raum standing near the fire.

The wolf's tail thumped the ground in a cheery greeting.

Darkness gathered in Axel's eyes. "A Shingese woman told me Raum was dead. Is he...a..."

"Yes, he's a ghost," whispered Kajsa. "He died saving me from *vashalan*."

"From your master's *vashalan*," Jetekesh added with vehemence.

Axel's eyebrows pulled together. He dropped his arm from Kajsa's waist and turned to face her. "I didn't know, Ky. Honestly, I had no idea he controlled the *vashalan*. But it's for the greater good. He never meant to harm any Norvians. Not once."

Kajsa's lips trembled. "His beasts killed my father."

"That was before he came through the Arch. Before he could leash them. He said it occurred because of something that happened a year ago, something outside of his control. He regrets that incident more than you'll ever know."

"They murdered Ingrid in her cottage—and killed Raum when they tried to keep me from crossing the Snowblinds."

Axel's fingers wrapped around her upper arms. "Navolleth didn't know it was you up there. They were merely protecting our borders. And as for Ingrid...he said that was most regrettable."

Jetekesh scoffed but held his tongue. Surely, Kajsa could read between the lines as well as anyone else. Regret didn't make it an accident.

"They died, Xel," she whispered.

Axel ran a hand through his platinum hair. "I know." His voice cracked. "I told Navolleth that. He—he was truly sorry. You should've seen his face. Kajsa, he's a good man. A good man betrayed by those he trusted most. He lost everything. And he's trying to avenge all those who fell in Cavalin's name." Axel glowered at Jetekesh. "He'll right all the injustices our people have faced these last three centuries."

Heat flashed over Jetekesh's bones. He took a step forward. "I intend the same. Our goals are aligned."

A sneer flickered over Axel's face, but then he smiled to belie his revulsion. "Well, that makes this all much simpler. Yet things might grow awkward if you discover that the water you seek is deadly on your lips, Crown Prince. You *might not* be the rightful heir of Nakania."

"I suspect as much myself," Jetekesh said. "Fortunately, should I lose my place as Amantier's prince, I'll lose nothing that inherently belongs to myself, or anything of which I'm most proud." His words surprised him; most of all, because he truly believed them.

He'd learned a great deal from books and tutors in Rose Palace, but he'd learned much more beyond those walls about friendship, loyalty, trust, and even hatred, grief, and guilt. Without those hard-won lessons, he'd still be a sheltered prince, spoiled and self-absorbed, like his mother intended him to be: A blind man charged with the rule of a kingdom.

Axel's sneer returned. "A pretty speech, but we in Norva are slow to forget the suffering inflicted upon us by Cavalin's son and *heir*."

Jetekesh's brows flew up. "If you refer to the Frost Exodus, scholars agree that your people left of their own accord. King Clydo didn't banish his brother or his kin."

Axel tensed, then pushed Kajsa behind him. "So your historians *would* say, but—"

"In my experience," Emerin said, stepping forward with a hand upon his sword, "truth usually falls somewhere between record and legend. There's a gray area, hard to sight with half-closed eyes. I suspect neither King Clydo nor his brother Prince Norvik was entirely wrong nor entirely right. They were grieving for their father's death, hungry for power and order, and shut out from the wisdom and magic of the fae. It was a dark time by *all* accounts. And carrying their feud into the present avails us nothing but continued mistakes and useless prejudice."

Axel's face reddened, and his clenched knuckles turned white. "Stay out of this, lapdog."

"Hold your tongue, Norvian," growled Jetekesh. "Emerin's also descended from Cavalin through Saint Vashi, daughter of light." His words gained power as he invoked the woman's sacred name.

Cavalin had sired two sons and one daughter—the youngest. Legend claimed she'd been touched by the fae, even blessed, and both of her brothers had adored her. She'd always kept the peace between them, at least, until Norvik took his family and loyal followers south beyond the mountains. Not a soul in all Nakania—and likely Shinac—had disliked the gentle, sweet Vashi. Upon her death, the church had declared her the first female saint.

Judging by his expression, Axel appeared to know the legend of Vashi too. He swallowed, and his stance relaxed. With some hesitation, he inclined his head. "And your name?"

"I'm Emerin, lord of the Keep of the Falls." His hand slid from his sword. "In a strange way, it seems those three siblings have met again through their distant kin. Let's use this opportunity to end grievances through peaceful resolutions. I'm worn out from burying the innocent."

Jetekesh's mind flashed to Tifen's and Palan's graves, to Jinji's alone in the Drifting Sands, to Mother's unmarked resting place at Keep Falcon. His shoulders drooped. Anadin, Artassa, Harn, and Emerin's sister, Saylia. Even Sir Lafe had nearly met his end in the Clanslands.

Jetekesh was tired of burying the guilty as much as the innocent.

"Agreed," he said. "Let's try suing for peace rather than war.

And, no matter who it may be, let's find the rightful ruler of Nakania."

Axel and the prince regarded each other. A darkness still lurked in Axel's eyes, an anger no speech alone could dissolve—but the Norvian nodded. "Very well."

A star fell overhead. Jetekesh watched its descent until it vanished beyond the silhouette of the trees.

Saints guide me. Help me keep my temper. Let us end this before blood dyes the fields of Nakania.

CHAPTER 15

NEVER PROMISED

Jetekesh sat at the edge of camp, watching tendrils of mist curl around the tree trunks. The last embers of the fire mingled with the golden strands of approaching dawn, mesmerizing, drawing Jetekesh into memories that danced before his vision like ghosts.

Golden days. Distant. Lost forever.

Tormented by the quest set before him, he hadn't been able to sleep. Its weight had settled on him slowly. At first glance, Sharo's request had felt like a dismissal. Jetekesh was being tucked away from the action, given a significant but out-of-the-way goal to avoid angering Navolleth. To escape open war.

To hide.

But that wasn't the case. If Darint revealed that Amantier's king wasn't the rightful ruler—that by the laws of magic, KryTeer, Shing, and even the Clanslands must bend the knee to a high king—chaos would ensue. Nakania might fall beneath its long-standing curse. The *Unsielie* would win.

Jetekesh's quest was of the utmost importance, and he had little time to succeed. Slumber was a burden.

Mist kissed his cheeks and caressed his hair. He gripped his sword, glad he'd convinced Emerin and Dakarai to let him take the last watch. He'd not slept at all. Why pretend?

With a sigh that clouded before him, he stood and moved to the fire to throw on more logs.

In the rising flames, he caught Rille staring at him from across the firepit. She sat up and offered a small smile, then slipped from her bedroll. They hadn't bothered to bring tents or padding. No wagon or awning. Time was what mattered, not comfort.

Rille shook her smudged skirts straight, then padded around the fire to stand beside her cousin. Jetekesh studied her solemn expression, then turned his gaze to the smoke curling up from the fire in a lazy dance.

"You really don't mind not becoming king?" she asked.

Jetekesh shrugged. He tried to speak, but his voice caught. He licked his lips and tried again. "Of course, I'd like to be king. It's what I've worked for all my life. I...don't know what else to be."

"How about a sailor?" Rille's eyes glittered.

Jetekesh snorted. "Oh, yes. I do so *love* to sail."

"Well, how about a storyteller."

"I lack the verbal skill to weave a proper scene."

Rille's smile softened. "Then, why not a decent human being? After that, no one really cares what else you are on the side."

Jetekesh scratched his jaw. "That's rather a high bar, you know. Few manage it."

"Few try." She shrugged. "It just takes practice, like swordplay or hunting. No one's good at first."

He considered her words. Like his quest, they grew heavier as he held them against his heart. "A worthy alternative to king, I think."

"I agree," she said, smoothing a fold in her dress.

The rustle of bedding drew Jetekesh toward a lump in the

shadows. Dakarai peeked out from under his covers. "Good morrow, fair royals. Is it dawn already?"

"'Tis," said Rille. "Time to be up, m'lord slug-a-bed."

Dakarai chuckled and crawled from his bedroll, then stretched where he knelt. "Well, I shall get our breakfast started then, hm?" He leaned over Anenyasha's bedroll and brushed his lips against her cheek, then pushed to his feet and moved to the fire.

Jetekesh sheathed his sword and crept to the pack horses. He grabbed the oats to feed the nickering animals. Rille stayed close to him, watching in silence as he moved from horse to horse with the muzzle sacks.

"You've really changed," she said as he retied the oat sack to the pack.

"Have I?" He let himself smile. "Not enough."

"No," she said. "That takes a lifetime."

THEY RODE from the aspen grove after breakfast. No one spoke much as they maintained a trot across the rolling hills, heading northeast. The sun crawled over their backs, moving the opposite direction, throwing shadows across the wild grass.

Jetekesh took the lead, and the formation fell in like it had yesterday, with the addition of Axel. The Norvian positioned himself on Emerin's other side near the front. Annoyance twisted in Jetekesh's gut, but he ignored his displeasure. Let the fool do what he liked for now.

They halted for a brief respite at lunch. Jetekesh munched on an apple and a strange, delicate, fae bread as he studied the view ahead. The grasslands would give way to forest by late afternoon, and after that, Thrissa said they would hardly see the sky until they reached the roots of the eastern mountains. Beyond those peaks, the map showed the river they would have to cross one way or another, but that was a week or more away.

Someone moved to Jetekesh's side as he considered the distant, snow-capped ridges.

"Your Highness?"

He pried his eyes away from their path and blinked at Kajsa. He smiled faintly. "It's Jetekesh, remember?"

Blushing, she ducked her head like a turtle hiding in its shell. "Yes, Jetekesh. Um. F-forgive me... Are...are you angry with me?"

"Why would I—?" His eyes snapped to Axel who stood next to his own horse, cooing in the gelding's ear. "Did someone suggest that I was?"

"N-no." Kajsa drew a long breath. "I...I didn't know about the feud between Clydo and Norvik. I..."

"I'm not Clydo." Jetekesh grimaced at his cold tones. He sighed and swept back strands of his hair. "Kajsa, that was three hundred years ago. As Emerin so eloquently put it last night, we need to set old feuds aside. I have no bone to pick with Norva, just with Navolleth. Luckily, our peoples haven't come to blows yet. There's still time to mend things before blood is shed." Razor-sharp fury shot through him like a flaming arrow, and he welcomed the reprieve from guilt. "At least, between humans. I don't mind spilling *Unsielie* blood, I confess."

"I wish we could stop the war altogether."

The flames of his anger died down a little. "That would be ideal, but impossible at this point, I think."

Kajsa kept her eyes on him. "What about Axel?"

"What about him?"

She dropped her eyes and inhaled again, fidgeting with her elven cloak. "He's not a bad person." She lifted her eyes. "I hope you can become friends."

Not likely, he nearly blurted out, but stopped himself. Pursing his lips, he let his gaze flit back to the Norvian now feeding his horse an apple. Jetekesh plastered on a smile, though he knew Kajsa could tell it was fake.

"I'll try to get to know him," he said. "But I don't like what he does to you."

Her brows pinched together. "To me?"

"This." Jetekesh waved a hand at her. "This timid thing you've reverted to. I've watched you come alive these past weeks. Yes, you're a quiet person, but you're also brave and fiercely loyal. You're not some mouse, scared of every noise. If this is what Axel's influence does, I'm tempted to—" He cut himself off as a tear slid down Kajsa's cheek. "You're crying. I—I'm sorry..."

"No," said Kajsa, swiping at her eyes. "Don't be sorry. You're right. I don't like this timid thing either. But don't blame Axel. He didn't do this. I did." She sniffed and batted away a fresh tear. "His presence took me back to my village, that's all. I'll not let it affect me, I promise. I won't slide backward." Her shoulders straightened, and she offered up a watery smile.

"Fair enough," Jetekesh said. "I well understand the inclination to backslide. I wrestle against it every single day." He scanned the mountainous horizon. "Being out here, away from pomp and peacocks, it's far easier to grow than it is at home, where I've been...lesser, for years."

"Thank you." Her tones were gentle.

He brushed his fingers against her sleeve. "I'll expect the same bluntness from you if I take a step or two backward. Deal?"

She chased off a last stray teardrop and laughed. "Deal."

"Time to go," called Emerin, swinging into his saddle.

Jetekesh caught Kajsa's fingers and squeezed them. "As my cousin Rille told me this morning, we have a lifetime to get it right."

Kajsa's smile faded. "But a lifetime is different for everyone. Tomorrow is never promised, Jetekesh."

He released her hand as she moved away. How well he understood her words. To gain the use of his arm, he'd lost a year of his life. To drink the waters at the blood fountain, he might risk much, much more.

Jetekesh set his hand against his sword hilt, glad of the familiar surface, cool and smooth against his palm. No, tomorrow was never a certainty. Better to live now, in this moment, trying to become a decent human being.

That he could control.

CHAPTER 16
FOREST AMBUSH

The march toward Nakania was a never-ending slog.

At Prince Sharo's request, Song had agreed to ride among the supply wagons as a guard, glad of something more active to do than merely cantering among the cavalries. Still, progress was slow, with the road being so bumpy. She often switched between riding her horse, and sitting alongside the lead wagoner, a fellow named Crosson, whose quiet ways were so like her grandfather's, she knew how to interact with him.

Crosson seemed to like her. During stretches of silence, as he smoked his pipe, he'd offer her a pinch of bread or a handful of nuts. Now and then, he'd point out some landmark that meant something to the fae or the few Shinacian humans, like Crosson, who had followed Sharo into battle.

The forest road the company took was the straightest shot to the northern realms of Nakania. The trouble was between these fae lands and the borders of Amantier stood the tainted country of the *Unsielie.*

Sir Yeshton had gone ahead of the company, taking three elven warriors and Ledonn of the Blood Knights with him. If luck and the good spirits attended them, they might traverse the *Unsielie* lands without being spotted. Sharo seemed to think it likely. He was convinced the dark fae forces were too intent upon his army—not to mention hungry to converge upon the fair fields and fens of the human lands.

Song had debated traveling with Yeshton, but there hadn't been any need. She was more useful with the army, especially to act as a guide once they entered Nakania. Besides herself, only Aredel and Shevek were familiar with the lay of Amantier. And she wanted to keep an eye on Aredel. His brooding manner had darkened since he'd buried his first wife and younger brother. From what Shevek had described to her during their brief imprisonment in Norva, the Blood King had lost half of Bahadronn as well.

He can't be trusted in such an emotional state.

As the wagon jostled, Song carefully slipped off the seat. She crawled into the covered space among the barrels and sacks of food, barely detecting the light fae armor she'd been gifted. It was more flexible than human steel. She settled into the nest of bedding she'd made for her respites, pulled out a rolled map, and smoothed it against the floorboards.

Her finger traced the northward trail, through the dark lands, until it met Amantier. Shinac's landmass was much larger than the cartographers of Nakania had depicted the Drifting Sands—but King Aredel had explained that easily enough when Song had brought it up. The ocean had been eating at the desert wastes for centuries, claiming bits of the shoreline until it had shrunk to its present shape and size.

Not present now, Song told herself with a grimace. *Shinac is returned.*

She studied the broad shape of the continent, largely unchanged except the Drifting Sands. Three hundred years hadn't done much to alter the higher lands. She fingered the ink lines of Shing, homesick for her sheep and pastures.

If we lose this war, those won't exist.

The wagon struck a rut and the map was flung from Song's hands, springing back into its roll. She grabbed a barrel to keep herself steady, while beans rattled and pots clanged.

A horn ahead of the train blared a warning.

"Whoa," said Crosson, in a deep rumble. "Steady, now."

Song leapt to her feet and stuck her head out of the wagon. Ahead, the line of soldiers rippled like floodwaters, drawing sword, lances, or bows.

Song's arms prickled. "We're under attack."

Crosson grunted. "Goblins, I'd wager."

Catching up her sword, Song threw herself from the wagon and landed on the rutted road. A thousand red eyes glinted in the dark treelines like wicked fireflies. She unsheathed her blade, noting the crimson flash against the steel.

A second, closer horn sang out.

The high-pitched shrieks of goblins grew like a swarm of locusts in the wind. Song let herself grin. Too long she'd held back, unable to cut loose, but now she could unchain her frustrations, her fears, her insecurities.

She positioned her blade, chose her target—a slender, bony, gray goblin with wrinkled flesh—and *danced.*

CHAPTER 17
THE UNENDING LIGHT

Aredel rode beside Sharo at the head of the army. In the forest gloom, he let his mood plunge into dark fissures until the scouts ahead thundered toward them on horseback.

"Goblins!" one shouted.

A horn blasted close by.

Shevek urged his mount up next to Aredel. "Finally, some real action."

Aredel cast him a sidelong look. "You've never fought goblins before."

"That hardly matters," the Blood Knight scoffed. "Does it?"

"Not really." Aredel drew his curved sword.

Beyond the scouts, a dark mass flowed toward them along the road and from within the thick mess of trees.

A second horn called out down the line.

Sharo drew his blade, which rang like angelic music from an Amantieran cathedral. "Their hides are thick, but their brains are small. Aim for the abdomen. It's the softest point."

"Understood." Aredel kicked his horse forward. The steed,

bred for battle, didn't flinch as it charged the surging goblin forces. Aredel swung his sword, caught a screaming goblin in the teeth, and cleaved the head in two. Black blood stained his sword and splattered his stallion.

He wheeled the horse around and sank his sword into another goblin's naked stomach. The hideous creature bared needle teeth at him, then slumped over, its leathery hide slick with its tainted blood. The creature wore nothing more than a tattered loincloth, no armor, no helmet.

Foolish, no matter how thick one's skin.

Aredel nudged his stallion on, cutting and hacking. The clash of steel rang around him, somewhat muffled under the cover of the old trees. He caught a glimpse of Sharo—no longer mounted on Amaranth—sword bright and humming, swinging at a cluster of goblins.

Aredel whirled back around to stave off a lunging creature.

The goblin teetered, then sprang for the stallion's legs. At the same moment, a second goblin jumped onto the saddle behind Aredel and sank razor claws into his borrowed armor, puncturing the metal.

The horse bucked, and Aredel crashed against the ground, crunching the goblin beneath him.

He shoved himself upright, reclaimed his feet, and stabbed a new goblin through the ribs, sinking his sword in deep. Black blood foamed between the goblin's teeth.

Nearby, Shevek struggled against a swarm of goblins, his blade dyed black with slick blood.

Aredel wrenched his own sword free and lifted his gaze to the endless flood of goblins pouring across the road. He knocked aside several more and sought out his horse. It had escaped the sea of bodies and was retreating deep into the woods.

Grimacing, Aredel spun and decapitated another goblin. Wrath surged through him, hot as magma, adding strength to his swings. He cleaved through more of the foul wretches, letting his fury guide his actions.

For Artassa. For Anadin. For Bahadronn and his people.

Gore slickened his grip, but he didn't let up, hacking, hacking, hacking. Every stroke was cathartic. Every stab promised justice.

A scream jarred him from his reverie. Aredel straightened over a heap of bodies.

The road was muddied with blood, red and black mingling among the corpses of goblins, horses, and elven soldiers.

Aredel wiped sweat from his eyes. *This isn't ending.*

He picked his way through the bodies, dispatching any creature that dared enter his path, as he made his way toward Sharo.

The fae prince's sword hummed louder as Aredel neared.

Sharo twirled, hacked, stabbed—a graceful portrait despite the splatters of black blood on his cheeks and armor. His white hair was coming loose from its high ponytail, and his blade was dark with gore, except for the hilt where a sky-blue stone shone with an uncanny light.

Aredel cut down goblins as he moved closer, his jaw set, his heart hammering. Adrenaline flooded his limbs. He kicked aside another creature, then stumbled as a goblin threw itself at his sword.

"Sharo!" he called. "They keep coming!"

The fae prince spun toward him, then kept turning, cutting into a goblin pack prowling toward him. The sword hummed a higher refrain.

"We need more light!" Sharo called back. "They cannot abide the sun!"

A band of elven soldiers screamed as goblins tore into their ranks. One elf fell, followed by another.

Aredel cast a glance at the interwoven branches above. Even if he climbed a tree and sawed the limbs down, only a patch of light might seep through. That was a fool's errand.

He glanced at his hands. His white smoke wasn't sunlight—but would it work? The *Unsielie* had burned up or fled when he'd turned it on them before.

He glanced at Sharo. "Use your sword!"

"It's not enough on its own," Sharo shouted, then stumbled back under a barrage of goblins.

"On its own, no." Aredel gritted his teeth and slammed his sword through the throat of a larger, stouter goblin. The creature gurgled and slumped back, replaced by a half dozen more. "Try!"

Did Sharo nod, or was that a mere reflex as he blocked a goblin hammer?

Aredel mustered his power, pulling it from deep inside where his anguish and guilt lived.

Harness that. Use your feelings as fuel.

He'd done so in the swamp and had thus aided the dragons against their *Unsielie* foes.

He must hurry. The goblins had moved through the entire army. The supplies might be ruined. Jinji might be wounded. Where was Shevek?

I'll lose no one else!

The white light exploded from his palms, climbed his sword, burst out between the tree trunks, answering his fury. It punched through the enemy, knocking goblins off their leathery feet. A split second later, Sharo's sword rang out, and silver light slashed through the ranks of creatures.

The combined light, though not sunshine, sent the rest of the goblin forces skittering back into the trees, screaming and shrieking, smoke rising from their hides.

Aredel funneled as much of his anger, his frustration, his guilt into his newfound power, siphoning it from his soul. Memories of Anadin, Artassa, his other wives, his fallen soldiers, the wastes of upper Bahadronn—it all ripped through him, stripping him of every last bottled emotion, purging the goblins under direct fire.

He didn't let up. He wasn't certain he could.

Sharo's blade flashed several more times somewhere on Aredel's right side. Perhaps the fae prince was picking off the goblins that escaped the Blood King's attack.

Aredel's hands began to tremble. The particles of light and smoke streamed from his palms, ceaseless, raging—yet his body quaked with the effort.

If I don't stop, this will destroy me.

His bones shook.

The wind force crafted by his light sent his hair billowing around his face.

Stop. Find a way to stop.

He ground his teeth, trying to pull the magic back inside. To stopper it. To *cease*. But the flow kept on, siphoning off more than emotions now.

Sharo shouted at him, but the words were lost in Aredel's private storm.

Someone approached, and the world dimmed. A hand caught his shoulder.

"Breathe in, Blood King." Navolleth's voice was silken, soft, calming. "Just that."

Aredel obeyed, and the twisting spiral of light slowed. He breathed in and out again. And again. As his heart slowed, so did his magic, until he had the clarity to close his palms. The light snuffed out, revealing a trail of goblin bones between the unharmed trees.

Aredel sank to his knees, shaking like he'd caught the ague.

Footfalls pounded close, and Jinji sank to his side. "Aredel, are you well?" His half-brother searched his face, then smiled faintly. "No need to answer that. You most certainly *aren't*." He turned to someone beyond Aredel's line of sight. "Please bring me a blanket and some water."

"The goblins?" Aredel's teeth chattered, so he closed his mouth.

"Dead or fled," Sharo answered, stepping into view before Aredel. He wiped a spatter of dark blood from his pale face. "What is left of them, at least. That is twice now you've demolished a dark army. It seems the tales of you are all quite true, Your Majesty."

Aredel managed a grimace. "You've implied before that tales of Nakanians exist among your people. Have you a storyteller true besides Jinji here?"

"Several," Sharo said. "But none quite so rash."

"Ah." Aredel tried to stand, but his legs refused to twitch. "It seems I'm incapacitated for the moment."

"He can take my bed in the lead wagon." The voice belonged to Song, unless Aredel missed his guess.

"That will do," Sharo said. "Rest a while, King Aredel. After that stunt, any dark entities nearby will think thrice before they approach. No one likes to be reduced to bones."

Arms lifted Aredel from the ground, and two armored elves aided him to the supply wagons at the back of the company. As they moved, he took note of the losses. Over a dozen horses dead. Four times that many soldiers. Only one wagon had been damaged, and already humans and elves were shifting supplies into the other wagons. He was certain the losses were greater than what he could spot, hampered as he was, but it could have been a massacre.

If he was unable to fight for a few days, that was a small price for victory.

Better than losing my life.

He'd thought himself prepared to die. He'd even believed he longed for an end.

Not yet, it seems. There's so much still to do. I hope Shevek is well.

His thoughts, oddly, trailed to Prince Jetekesh and the small company sent out to find the rightful high ruler. More likely than not, that king was already seated on Amantier's throne—but would the prince risk his father's life with the fatal waters of the blood fountain?

I'd wager on it, but Jetekesh might not.

The soldiers eased Aredel into the back of the lead wagon. Nearby the driver—a man someone called Crosson—soothed his harnessed horses.

Lying among Lady Song's bedding, staring at the wagon's wooden ceiling, Aredel tried to find sleep. It never came. Even several hours later, as the army finally rolled forward, their dead presumably buried under rocks along the roadside, Aredel couldn't rest.

He wasn't sure he would ever rest again.

CHAPTER 18
A FATHER'S PRIDE

King Darint crumpled up the report brought by carrier pigeon and tossed it into the bonfire like a stone into a placid lake. The parchment curled as the edges glowed, then blackened.

His lips pulled toward a grin. "It seems, Tavassed, that our enemies have combined forces."

"That was expected," the *Unsielie* replied, drawing close. His lacy wings fluttered, then drew tight at his back. His dark eyes studied the fire. "Navolleth is soft where he should be fiercest."

"Best not to underestimate him, though." Darint moved away from the glutting flames and sank into his plush throne under the awning his servants had erected for the night. So far from home, he allowed himself few comforts, as they would slow down the progress of his army. They were mere days away from the border of Amantier. A little longer and he would set foot on the fields of his ancestors.

"I do not underestimate anyone." Tavassed glided close like a ghost in his black and silver robes. His long dark hair trailed against the ground behind him. "Navolleth least of all. But I do think he is not the warlord many have assumed him to be. He remains in the clutches of Cavalin's *noble* memory."

Darint considered the *Unsielie*, then he shrugged and applied an easy smile. "Cavalin's memory is noble, like it or otherwise." He turned his gaze to the bonfire. Beyond its roar and crackle, the distant sounds of his army camp making merry filled the starlit sky. "Martyrs are like that. Best not to sully the dead. And do not forget, Cavalin is distant kin of mine as well."

"Ah, yes." The *Unsielie* positioned himself under the awning and turned toward the bonfire. "Human genealogy often escapes me."

Darint reached for a bottle of wine on the table next to his throne. He poured a little into his bronze goblet. "If we're to win, we mustn't forget what makes this war possible. You did well to manipulate the Amantieran heir, but I dislike that we've seen no sign of him."

"My scouts will locate the Marked Prince," Tavassed whispered.

"More importantly, what can we do about that Blood King from KryTeer? *He* concerns me a great deal. That power of his is potent and troubling."

Tavassed sighed, though his stoic expression remained in place, as it ever did. "An unfortunate result of his first visit to Shinac."

"Well, we can't do anything about that now." Darint sipped his wine, then set his goblet aside and leaned forward, steepling his fingers. He shook back loose strands of silver-threaded brunet hair. He'd removed his crown and left it in his tent, allowing his shoulder-length locks to blow free.

Aredel, the Blood King of KryTeer. Despite how young the man was, he'd become a legend in Shinac over the past decade. A fierce fighter and one Darint had known he must face once the seal broke.

But it seems I'll face him sooner than I'd planned, and with a power I didn't foresee.

Most troubling of all, Aredel had allied with Sharo. Darint hadn't expected that either. He'd hoped to pit the kingdoms of Nakania against each other. That would give him room to maneuver...

Yet Navolleth, too, had claimed one of those factions, and now they were part of Sharo's army as well.

Darint's smile stretched wider. Whatever he felt about his son personally, he wasn't so proud that he couldn't acknowledge Sharo's cunning.

We're more alike than he'll ever admit.

Darint rose and moved back to the bonfire, though his gaze turned inward, to memories of Sharo—and Sharo's mother. Ah, Thrissa. A rare and fierce beauty.

A family reunion is on the horizon. I can hardly wait.

The king lifted his eyes to the moon shining its cool yellow light on the shadowed world. Howls rose around them, probably *vashalan*. Navolleth was spying, was he?

Tavassed hissed out alien instructions, and several shadows detached from the rest, likely gone off to dispatch the canine scouts.

"We could draw the Blood King away from Sharo's forces," Tavassed whispered, coming up next to Darint. "Lure him back home."

Darint chuckled. "We've already tried bullying, threatening, and even rewarding Aredel. What's left? You sacrificed his wife, and your sand golem murdered his brother." The king narrowed a look on the *Unsielie*. "If I were you, I'd be searching for ways to appease the ravening beast. He's angrier with *you* than he is with me."

Tavassed's expression remained unchanged. "Humans waste energy on grudges."

"I doubt that man's energy has ever been a waste." Darint shrugged. "Find the marked boy, and watch the Blood King. I'll—"

"Sire!" A Shard knight peeled away from the darkness, dropped to one knee, and waited.

"What is it?" asked Darint in a pleasant voice.

"Word just reached us. The goblin legion was eradicated." The knight lifted grim eyes to his king. "The Blood King of KryTeer summoned that smokey light again. Only a few hundred escaped, and none will return to face Sharo's army."

Darint blinked, and his smile slanted sideways. "That's inconvenient. But it was a possibility from the start. Very well, send the goblins back into the tunnels with their kin. Keep them moving toward Amantier."

"Yes, sire." The knight rose, bowed, then sprinted off in clinking armor.

"Troubling indeed," said Tavassed.

The king grunted, then sighed and rubbed the side of his head. "We really need to find some way of stoppering that magic. Would a witch do, do you think?"

Tavassed shook his head. "Your dealings with witches in the past proved too one-sided. They will not come if you summon them."

Darint sighed through his nose. "All right. What do you suggest?"

"A demon."

The king tensed, though the *Unsielie* had spoken in mild tones. The implications trickled through him, cold, saturating. "That's a dangerous road for a mortal to take—or even a fae... How could I possibly bargain with a demon?"

The *Unsielie* turned his dark eyes skyward. “You have gained powers like none since Tallat.”

The king’s brow twitched up, half skeptical, half scornful. “It hardly served him in the end.”

“Ah, but Tallat was a mere fisherman, ambitious yes, but simple-minded. You, King Darint, are superior to him.”

“Yes,” Darint said, flashing a grin. “Enough so to see the folly in giving up my soul to a demon. My taleweaver favors Nakanian stories. She’s told me more than once about the line of KessRa rulers, not least of all Emperor Gyath. In the end, that demon abandoned him. I’ll not suffer the same indolent fate.”

The *Unsielie* offered up a graceful shrug. “Suit yourself as you always do, my king. But few things short of a demon will be enough against the powers of Valliath.”

“I’ll take my chances.” Darint’s eyes drifted to the borders of his encampment. Sharo was coming, and he brought with him allies of an impressive nature. A fresh twist of pride caught in Darint’s chest. Sharo had always been resourceful, clever, even in his early, selfish days.

Darint had since produced a new heir, but the boy was nothing like his elder half-brother in terms of his potential. Perhaps Darint had tried *too* hard to stamp out any aspects like Sharo’s. Nothing in Prince Dij spoke of cleverness or fortitude. He was as dull and uninteresting as dead brown leaves on a garden path in springtime. Not bright, effulgent, bursting with promise.

Still, Darint preferred dull and malleable to bold and unbridled.

“Blaze bright,” Darint whispered, imagining Sharo in his gleaming fae armor. “Blaze like summer before I snuff you out, my son. There’s not room for both of us in this new age.”

King Darint smiled, allowing himself to indulge in the memory of his firstborn son. Soon, they would meet upon the field, and Darint would strike Thrissa's child down once and forever.

But for now, cloaked in the darkness of night, he could remember.

He could regret.

He could dream.

CHAPTER 19
THE FAITHFUL

The roar of the falls brought Jetekesh's head up from the map perched before him on the saddle horn. Though Dakarai had returned his nicked map to Sharo's table, the fae prince had gifted Jetekesh with another before the company left the war camp. Presumably, he'd felt the need just in case anything happened to their guide.

Ahead, Thrissa directed her palomino mount around a wide bend in the forest trail where dewy moss gleamed against a stand of boulders.

As Jetekesh reached the same bend, mist brushed fingers through his golden locks. The falls were enormous, cascading from ancient cliffs into a gorge that plummeted eighty feet or more below the pathway. Jetekesh studied the churning water as the fragrance of moss and damp air stroked his senses.

"Quite a drop," said Emerin, bringing his horse up beside Jetekesh.

"It is." Fortunately, heights didn't bother Jetekesh, and he found the plunge more fascinating than anything else. "I wonder what they call these falls."

"The Faithful," Thrissa said, twisting around in her saddle. "There's a story to go with it, but you'd best let a taleweaver tell you." Her lips curved in a wry smile. "I would butcher the telling."

"I doubt that," murmured Emerin. "With her voice, she could sing the praises of dirt and I'd heartily listen."

Jetekesh chuckled and nudged his horse on. "Fancy her, do you?"

Emerin snorted. "Like I admire a cathedral, Your Highness: lovely and untouchable."

"I don't know," said Dakarai behind them. "Had my heart not already been won by my beloved"—he glanced at Anenyasha riding beside him—"I'd perhaps be tempted to woo the fair elf." His teeth flashed in a quick smile.

Jetekesh rolled up his map. "You'd not mind the age difference?"

"Or that Sharo is her son?" asked Rille.

Silence answered her words. Jetekesh blinked, but the truth settled into him like a familiar strain of music. He glanced behind him to find Dakarai's raised brows and open mouth.

"So," Emerin said, "they're not lovers."

Jetekesh laughed. "No, it seems they're not. Though I thought the same thing."

"They're nothing like lovers," Rille said.

"A man would have a chance then." Emerin rubbed his chin, then shrugged. "But war isn't the time for romance."

Jetekesh's fingers tightened around his reins. That was true. Entangling oneself in matters of the heart was foolish when pitted against the machines of war.

"I disagree," said Dakarai in his mild tones. "In times of war, as in times of peace, tomorrow is never promised. Skirmishes in the Clanslands often break out. Does that mean I should not have courted my Anenyasha? Not have fallen in love? Not have taken that risk? No, my lord Emerin. Better to love in hardships than snuff out one's feelings like a candle in the dark. Love is the light that guides our steps."

"Then are we blind, Dakarai?" asked Emerin. He dipped his head toward Jetekesh. "Do His Highness and I not see?"

Dakarai didn't hesitate. "You see because you love your country, hearth, freedom. These are things to love. Falling *in* love is no different, except perhaps deeper still. If you carry a candle, perhaps I carry a torch."

Jetekesh shifted, thinking of Father and Mother. Of their loveless marriage. "What of those who never fall in love? Do they live a half-life?"

"Nay," said Dakarai. "We can be filled by many kinds of love. But too often we shy away from any kind of deep, abiding devotion. We do not wish to carry a torch at all. Better to hold a candle, for it is less of a burden. Often, falling in love starts as a blazing torch but we find it too heavy to carry for long. We exchange it for a candle."

A frown stretched across Jetekesh's face. "If love's so wonderful, why does it become heavy?"

"Because we forget that we needn't carry it alone," Dakarai said. "Indeed, we mustn't carry it alone." The clansman hummed a few notes. "All this I say in defense of love. If we cease to embrace it for fear of losing it, we lose all. Without love, peace is impossible."

"That's beautiful," said Kajsa in soft tones from the horse she shared with Rille.

"It's silly," Axel chimed in. "And simplistic. You can't compare feelings to objects. Candles. Torches. Those are tangible things. Loyalty to country, to lovers, to goals—these aren't measurable. Nor is peace as simple as love. Love has caused wars since the dawn of life."

Jetekesh tightened his hold on the reins until his knuckles whitened.

"It isn't a perfect analogy," Dakarai agreed. "But I do not believe that love is to blame for war. Selfishness, rather, is the cause."

Axel snorted. "Isn't that what love is?"

Emerin spoke. "That's a sorry way to examine life."

"But true," Axel said. "Name one person you know who isn't selfish."

Jetekesh started to open his mouth, to throw out Jinji as the perfect example, but his jaw snapped shut. No one existed who wasn't selfish. He knew that already. Everyone had moments of greed.

"I can't," said Emerin. "We're all flawed."

"But love is what helps us overcome that." Kajsa's voice was stronger than usual and firm.

Her words brought Jetekesh's head around. His horse slowed. He found her watching him rather than Axel or Dakarai, her expression a cross between pride and terror. He smiled at her, trying to convey that he was on her side; that she was brave to say what she did. Perhaps the message came through, for Kajsa smiled back and lifted her chin higher.

Axel was studying her, a sour expression tugging against an evident desire not to argue with his childhood friend. He definitely harbored feelings deeper than friendship toward the girl, as she obviously did for him.

Jetekesh turned away, his stomach knotting. *Let it go. Don't be an utter fool.*

His gaze snared on Thrissa's. She'd halted ahead, wearing a dry smile, the cloth of her strange outfit shimmering in the shifting shadows of the path. "Ready to continue?" she asked.

He nodded. "Lead on."

"Jetekesh, wait." Rille's voice came from behind.

He turned to catch sight of where his cousin was seated before Kajsa. The girl didn't look at him; her amber eyes were trained on the shadows to the right of the trail, within the dense trees. Despite a stray breeze, Rille held still, even her hair, like the world couldn't touch her.

An instinct within Jetekesh responded to her stillness. He whipped around, heart hammering, hand falling toward his sword. He expected *vashalan*—but what swooped from the trees was made up of feathers and talons.

Emerin let out a warning cry and swung his blade.

The bird-woman dodged, spinning in flight. She snatched at Jetekesh, but he leaned sideways, sliding from his saddle as the talons closed over open air.

Screeches filled the sky. Jetekesh landed lightly on the ground, then scrambled to his feet and dragged his sword from its sheath. A flock of bird-women hissed and squawked in the sky, dodging the swords and arrows the company sent at them.

Harpies. Jetekesh had seen illustrations in ancient scrolls, and the painted battles depicted upon the holy cathedral ceiling back in Kavacos.

They're real.

Of course, they were. This was Shinac, home of magic.

Jetekesh shook himself, clutched his sword, and charged the nearest enemy. At the same moment, Kajsa's arrow pierced the creature's wing, and the harpy let out a deafening scream as she tumbled from the air.

"Decapitate them!" cried Thrissa, demonstrating with a wide, clean stroke. Blue blood sprayed the air.

Jetekesh wheeled and swung, trying to catch the closest harpy's throat.

"Look out!" shouted Rille.

Talons sank into Jetekesh's shoulders, digging in deep. He screamed and pulled against the strong grip, but the harpy lifted him into the air, her wings beating against the sky.

"Your Highness!" Emerin shouted.

An arrow hissed past, narrowly missing the harpy's wings.

The harpy carried Jetekesh over the gorge, perhaps to discourage him from struggling, but he didn't stop. He still clutched his sword, unwilling to release it. Grinding his teeth, Jetekesh swung hard, aiming for the harpy's leg. The blade sank into feathered flesh, and the harpy swerved, grip loosening.

Not enough.

Jetekesh yanked the sword free and swung again, blind but determined. It caught, and the harpy squawked, then dropped him. Jetekesh plummeted, wind streaming through his clothes and hair, sword clasped close. Streaks of blue blood stained his blade.

He squeezed his eyes shut, unwilling to watch his doom's swift approach.

Waterfall droplets kissed his face, and he found himself opening his eyes. As he did, something swooped from the cascading falls, spraying rainbows over the misty air. It caught him up, letting him spread across the firm, smooth body of a horse, and he found himself flying back toward the cliffs.

White wings sparkled like diamonds under the sun's glow. He sat upright just as his new mount landed on solid ground. A Pegasus. He sat upon a pure white Pegasus. The creature folded its wings, pawed the ground with a hoof, and let out a baying sound that sent the remaining harpies scattering. Emerin chased the creatures back into the trees.

Dakarai and Anenyasha reached the Pegasus first, followed by Thrissa, then the rest.

"Are you well, cousin?" asked Rille.

Jetekesh tried to catch his breath while he shakily sheathed his sword. "I—I—Yes. I think so...mostly..." He wiped droplets from his face, then slid from the Pegasus's back. Turning toward his rescuer, he bowed. "Thank you."

The majestic creature inclined its head, and words entered

Jetekesh's mind like orchestral music, sweet and soul-piercing. *'Art thou well, Prince of the Mark?'*

Jetekesh straightened. "Yes. Yes, I'm well."

The Pegasus held his gaze, her eyes not bestial at all, but deep and ancient, more golden than brown. *'Beware the path ahead. Darkness seeks thee.'*

"I'll be careful." Awe needled Jetekesh's flesh.

With a second bow of her head, the Pegasus adjusted her wings, then trotted up the path before taking flight. The fair creature swooped back into the falls and disappeared in a spray of prismatic colors.

Thrissa spoke into the breathless silence. "You've been blessed by the Faithful this day, Your Highness."

Jetekesh blew out a low breath. "I *feel* blessed."

Fingers probed at his shoulder, and he hissed as pain lanced down his arm. He turned, unsurprised to find Kajsa trying to examine his wounds.

"Do those blue creatures carry poison?" asked the girl.

"Not as a rule," Thrissa answered. "But infection could easily set in."

Jetekesh grimaced. "Saints know I've had enough of that. Let's cleanse the wound before we move on if it's safe enough." He cast a wary glance at the sky.

"It'll be safe," Emerin said, prowling near the trees. His blade glinted in a strand of sunlight.

Axel scoffed where he stood beside his horse. "If such dangers waylay us at every turn, this company will never reach the blood fountain alive." His pale eyes speared Jetekesh. "You're rather fragile for a prince."

Jetekesh stiffened as fire flared in his chest. "I—"

"Stop trying to pick a fight, Xel," Kajsa said. "Jetekesh's mark draws enemies to him. He can't help that. And he freed himself from that—that creature..."

"Harpy," Jetekesh supplied.

She nodded. "Yes, that. He freed himself from that harpy, didn't he?"

"And nearly fell to his death." Axel sighed and shrugged. "Sorry, Ky. I'll stop voicing my doubts." He turned to his saddle and fiddled with the straps like he was securing them.

Jetekesh shut his eyes while Kajsa dabbed at his shoulder. "He can say what he likes," he whispered. "I'll not let it get to me." He opened his eyes and found Kajsa watching him. His lips tugged upward. "If I really am a beacon to all dark things—not to mention everything else—I need to be better about watching my back. In that, Axel has a point."

Kajsa pressed a bandage to his wound. "You don't have to watch it alone. That's why we came with you."

The fury in his chest faded, and gratitude curled over him like welcome flames, glad of the company he kept.

All but one.

CHAPTER 20
MERCY

The dull thud of wood striking wood was followed by a whoosh and pop of flame. Kajsa turned over in her bedroll and blearily stared at the campfire. Emerin stirred the embers, bringing the blaze back to life. He had taken the middle watch; it must be past midnight, then.

The keep lord straightened up, pulled his cloak close against the chill, then moved away from the fire and the sleeping bodies around it. His steps grew fainter, moving away from camp.

Kajsa sat upright. Cold air slithered under her clothes, and she caught up her cloak to wrap it around her shoulders. She tracked Emerin's retreat, teetering on an impulse to follow him.

Axel shifted in his sleep nearby, and Kajsa froze.

Jetekesh's words returned to her. "*I don't like what he does to you.*"

Leveling her shoulders, Kajsa flung aside her bedding, picked her way around her sleeping companions, and followed after Emerin. Outside the fire's ring, the chill air was damp and smelled of distant rain. She plunged ahead, ignoring the cold—then halted before a fallen log where Emerin sat, hunched beneath his grief. Moonlight puddled the ground around him.

Drawing a breath, Kajsa padded forward, clutching her cloak against her chest. Every step pounded in her ears.

Was this a mistake? Perhaps Emerin didn't want company.

She dodged a twig, and made it to the log without a sound. There, she cleared her throat.

Emerin jerked his head around, blond hair falling in his face. His hand clutched his sword. His feral eyes widened. "Kajsa?"

She tried a smile, then dropped onto the log at his side. "I—I saw you leave."

He studied her.

"Do you want me to..." She started to rise.

Emerin caught her arm. "Stay. Be welcome."

Kajsa eased back onto the mossy log. Faint wisps of fog curled over the night air, taunting the trees. They sat in silence for a long while, and Kajsa was content to leave it that way.

An owl hooted in a nearby oak.

Emerin sighed, and his breath puffed before his face. "You remind me so much of her."

Kajsa tensed. "Of...your sister?"

"Yes. Her name was Saylia."

"Is that why...you've been so kind to me?" She winced. What a thoughtless question. Yet she'd wondered why he bought her threads or offered her fresh strawberries on their way to the Clanslands.

"It's the main reason, I confess," he said. "I missed her so much." His voice dropped low, turning gruff. "I still do." He turned his head away.

"You did all you could."

"She would be very disappointed in me, Kajsa. She would never have betrayed the prince for my sake."

"No?" Kajsa tipped her head to one side and leaned out, trying to catch a glimpse of Emerin's face. "Perhaps not...but I think she would have been just as desperate and scared. Even more so if she was like me."

He snorted faintly. "You're most alike in your bravery. When it really matters, you stand tall and do the right thing, no matter how hard."

"That's not true."

"I assure you it is." He twisted on the log to face her. Unshed tears shimmered in his eyes, bright in the moon's glow. "You and she—you were both born with the heart of Saint Vashi. I'm not saying that merely because you remind me of Saylia. I see it clearly in your eyes." Pain flashed over his face. "But I? I've shamed my family's name. Once we return to Nakania—once this war is over—I'll denounce my titles. My cousin Fetrik will take—"

"Don't you dare." The words spilled out of Kajsa's mouth, and panic stabbed her chest, but the damage was done. She inhaled, then held his gaze, narrowing her eyes. "If you have made a mistake, keep standing and fix it. If you run from your heritage, how does that restore your honor? Why do you travel with us now if not to make amends and right your wrong?"

He stared at her, transfixed. The faintest twitch of a smile touched his lips. "You think I can repair this?"

"Yes. Otherwise, Jetekesh wouldn't have agreed to let you come. He trusts you. And if that's so, then...then I trust you." Her cheeks warmed, and she rushed to add, "He sees truth, after all."

His snort was louder this time. "I'm sure that's the only reason."

Kajsa tore her eyes away. Her cheeks grew warmer still. "It's the most important one."

"So it is. And you're right. I mustn't let my guilt stand in the way of my atonement." He set his strong hand on her shoulder. "Kajsa, I—" He broke off, his gaze flitting to the forest floor. Then he looked at her with a brightness in his eyes. "I won't try to replace Saylia. I can't. I wouldn't ask anyone to try. But...I would like to count you as a friend."

She rested her fingers over his and squeezed. "I would be honored, Lord Emerin."

"Just Emerin."

"I— Oh, very well. Emerin the Just, then."

He blinked, then let out a rumbling laugh. "Well played, my lady."

"Just Kajsa," she said, smiling shyly.

"No. That won't do." His lopsided grin softened into a warm smile. "Kajsa the Merciful suits you much more."

Her cheeks caught fire. "I don't—"

"No arguing. It's final."

She scrambled for a compromise. "Then, can we settle on using first names only?"

That grin returned, and he extracted his hand. "If you insist."

"I do." She spoke with a firmness born from relief.

His chuckle was mischievous. "Well then, Kajsa. So it will be." He rose and offered his hand. "Shall we return?"

"Don't you want to be alone?" she asked, letting him heave her to her feet.

"Not anymore. I find I prefer the company of friends this night."

They walked back to camp in silence, and Kajsa found that her stride was long and comfortable beside her fierce companion. She returned to her bedroll, curled up, and stared into the fire for a long time. Once, she risked a glance toward Jetekesh asleep under his black cloak. If she told him what she'd done tonight, would he be proud?

Yes, she decided. He would.

She snuggled deeper into her bedding and smiled to herself. She was rather proud, too.

CHAPTER 21
SHADOWS AND SHADES

On the following day, heavy clouds stalked the company until nightfall.

Just as rain spilled over the cliffs to drench the forest, Thrissa led them to a cave. Hunching under the deluge, Jetekesh urged his gelding into the wide cavern, but the dratted beast reared up, kicking mud from a puddle across his boots and pants. The prince grimaced but ignored the mess, maintaining his grasp on the reins.

"Whoa there, easy," he soothed.

Thrissa neared, one hand raised. She spoke in soft tones that rang out like music. "Be calm, Iliarass. Be still."

The horse obeyed, the reins going slack in Jetekesh's fingers.

He eyed the elven queen. She must have spoken in her native tongue—the language of Valliath—but Shinac's magic allowed him to understand her.

"Is that his name?" asked Jetekesh. "Iliarass?"

"'Tis, or as close as I can come to it in my tongue," said Thrissa before she slipped into the cave.

Jetekesh tugged the horse after the woman, and the gelding came quietly. "What does it mean?"

"*Resilient one.* He is young and earnest. Give him patience, and he will prove himself true." She moved deeper into the cave where Dakarai and Emerin had already lit torches. Kajsa and Rille rummaged through the baggage with Raum nosing helpfully at their hands.

The rest of the horses stood near the cave entrance to Jetekesh's left, so he guided Iliarass to his fellows and proceeded to unsaddle each in turn. As he worked, he found himself smiling. Somewhere along the way, without ever realizing it, he'd come to enjoy caring for horses. After setting each saddle around the firepit Anenyasha had built with large stones, Jetekesh collected the horse brush and a drying cloth and started to groom each beast.

Anenyasha appeared at his side with a muzzle sack full of oats and fed the closest mare.

Jetekesh considered her as he wiped water from Emerin's mount. A hundred questions crowded his mind, some benign, others more pressing. He knew so little about the woman, and she could communicate now, but Dakarai had said she didn't care to speak.

"You have a question?" Anenyasha's voice was soft, low, and melodic. She didn't turn from watching the horse eat from the sack.

He offered up a motion between a nod and a shake of his head, then a smile cracked his lips. "I...don't know where to start."

"Perhaps with what matters."

Sensible. Jetekesh managed a nod, feeling strangely foolish. "You...love Dakarai. I—I already know that."

"Astute," she said with no inflection to suggest mockery or amusement.

"Well." He cleared his throat. "That's *all* I know about you. That—and I suppose—you're deadly with a spear."

A fleeting grin flashed over Anenyasha's lips. Her hand came up to stroke the horse's neck. "Is that not enough, Prince?"

He shrugged. "Is that all you want to be known for?"

"It's enough." Her brown eyes met his gaze, steady, unflinching. "I know myself, and that is all I need. Your perception of me will never be correct—even with that truth sigil."

His cheeks warmed. "Is that because I'm missing something vital or because no two humans can ever really know each other?"

"The latter. We are not meant to. We are meant only to accept who others are—and that tomorrow they will be a different creature." She frowned. "You inspire too much speech in me. Goodbye." She ducked around the horse and moved on to the next. Lightning flashed outside.

Jetekesh studied Anenyasha's back as he resumed rubbing down Emerin's horse. He was in peculiar company, which appeared to be his lot. But then, he preferred it that way.

Thunder boomed overhead. He started upright, chills skittering over his flesh like a thousand insects. Fresh lightning burst, piercing the cave's shadows. Thunder answered again, almost at once.

"We are in for quite a storm," Dakarai said mildly, coming up beside the prince. He pressed an apple into Jetekesh's palm. "Eat. Dinner will take time." He winked, then moved off toward Anenyasha.

The low voices of Emerin and Rille debating food again scratched at Jetekesh's good ear. He suppressed an eye roll and moved off to the next horse. Once he finished, he wandered to the cave entrance where rain fell in sheets. The forest beyond was shielded by shadows, the details lost in night's shades.

Closing his eyes, he listened to the *slap*, *drip*, *splash* of the deluge. The sounds of the company were faint behind him. The fragrance of fresh soil and crisp air swirled around his nose. Thunder clapped again, still close, fierce, ripping through his body like an energizing surge. His eyes snapped open, and he stared out into the blackness.

A transparent figure stared back at him.

Jetekesh had seen ghosts before in Shing's throne room. Raum was technically one, too. Yet this figure speared him with a coldness that sank razor teeth into his bones. It drifted toward him, one hand extended, its features vague in the storm—until lightning struck the ground behind the ghostly frame.

The apple dropped from Jetekesh's fingers.

It was a man standing in the storm. Tall and muscular. Imposing. Dark-haired.

Jetekesh knew him. Instinct screamed the name.

Cavalin.

The same instinct urged Jetekesh to step from the shelter of the cave. He held out his hand. His heart pounded against his ribcage like a prisoner desperate to escape. They stared at each other, the ghost trying to communicate, but seemingly unable.

Thunder drummed the heavens. Rain needled Jetekesh's scalp, frigid in the ghost's presence. The coldness swelled around Jetekesh, urgent, probing.

"What do you need?" asked the prince.

The ghost's eyes bored into him, searching. Loud. Yet no words came. The urgency encircled Jetekesh, quivering through him, chilling him to his marrow.

"Your Highness!" Emerin's shout broke the spell.

The ghost vanished, stealing the otherworldly light, leaving Jetekesh in a darkness so complete he nearly lost his balance. Lightning cracked the sky, and he whirled to find the keep lord trotting toward him from the cave.

Emerin splashed to a halt. "Are you all right?"

The prince tried to speak, but words failed. He swallowed, tried again—and finally shook his head. He trembled like a brittle leaf in a windstorm.

Emerin caught his forearm. "Come back inside, Your Highness." He tugged Jetekesh toward the cave where the rest of the company peered out, backlit by the campfire reflected off the stone walls and ceiling. Jetekesh slipped through the sheet of water at the cave's mouth.

"What was that all about?" asked Axel.

Jetekesh shuddered as the memory of the ghost's chill raked over his bones again. "I...I think I saw Cavalin."

Silence fell around him. Jetekesh resisted squirming. Instead, he shrugged off his sopping cloak, padded to the fire, flopped down on his saddle, and yanked off his boots.

Kajsa moved first, claiming a blanket from the bundle tucked to one side of the fire. She brought it over. He accepted it with murmured thanks, then wrapped himself up. His teeth started to chatter.

Emerin sat to his left on Dakarai's saddle. "Cavalin, you said." His tone was cautious.

"His ghost, yes." Jetekesh eyed the bubbling pot on the trivet. "Any chance that's water for tea?"

"It can be," Dakarai said.

Rille pushed past the clansman and hunched before Jetekesh. "You saw Cavalin's ghost?"

"I think so. That, or something very much like him."

"How do you know?" asked Dakarai.

"We have portraits in Rose Palace and the Holy Cathedral. We have one depicting his lost crown—the one he died wearing." Jetekesh rubbed his numb fingers together. "His likeness is well known to all Amantierans."

"We have paintings, too," Axel said. "In Norva. The Archon of Frostfire Canton has a portrait hanging in his dining hall."

Jetekesh eyed the Norvian young man, trying to gauge if Axel was mocking him or not. Then he rolled back his shoulders, sighed, and decided he didn't care. Cavalin's image was seared into his mind, banishing petty concerns. "I think he was trying to tell me something. Maybe warn me. Or—or ask for help. He didn't speak." Jetekesh ran a hand through his tangled wet locks. "Then he vanished."

"Was that my fault?" asked Emerin, a wince drawing lines around his mouth.

Jetekesh shook his head. "I don't know. Hopefully he'll appear again."

"Either way," said Rille, "we'll pay attention, and watch our steps, just as we did before." She stood up and shook her skirts straight. "Drink your tea."

Jetekesh almost asked what tea before Kajsa stepped around the girl, proffering a steaming clay cup. He accepted it with more earnest thanks than before, breathed in the herbal fragrance, then nursed the tea with relish as the others set about making food and arranging the bedrolls.

The sogginess in the air seeped deeper into Jetekesh's clothes. He downed the rest of his tea in a quick gulp, then rummaged through his satchel for a change of outfit while his leather armor dried. Everything was damp, but it was better than what he wore.

"Let me help," said Dakarai, holding aloft a blanket.

With a grateful smile, Jetekesh slipped behind the temporary shield, stripped down, and quickly draped himself in a tunic, hosen, and woolen socks. The borrowed apparel was plain compared to his usual wardrobe, and Jetekesh welcomed it. He was on a quest, likely to end his family's reign; he shouldn't parade around like a prince anymore.

Adjusting his tunic, Jetekesh resolved to make the change official. He stepped around the blanket. "Thank you, Dakarai."

The clansman nodded. "Next time I'm soaking wet, perhaps you can return the favor, Your Highness."

Jetekesh nodded. "Count on it. And please don't use titles any longer. It's probable that I'll not be a prince by the time we're back in cultivated lands. I should grow more accustomed to my given name well before that." He turned toward the fire and raised his voice. "That goes for all of you. Call me Jetekesh going forward. I'm no longer royalty."

"No offense"—Emerin straightened from the trivet—"but I'll not be able to heed your command, Your Highness. Not until the high king or queen is crowned. You're not deposed yet."

"Emerin's right," Rille chimed in. She sat at the fire, stirring the coals into gentle tendrils of flame. "You're still a prince, throne or no throne. Amantier can't be plunged suddenly into chaos because you feel uncomfortable with the truth."

Jetekesh blinked at that, then faintly scoffed. "It's not just about that, Rille. I realize my father's still king for now—but I feel far less like a prince and far more like a friend to everyone, and I'd prefer to have that title upon the road ahead."

She shrugged. "Then just say so."

Jetekesh rolled his eyes. "I just did." He stalked back to his saddle and flopped down, determined to appear as unprincely as possible. He caught a glimpse of Rille's smile before she turned to sprinkle salt into the roiling pot.

Once the food was ready, Rille passed out bowls of rice and roasted grouse. Despite how humble the fare was, it tasted good, and Jetekesh was too ravenous to feel picky. He ate fast enough to scald his tongue but kept eating just the same. As the wind howled outside, Dakarai took up a humming sound, then broke into song. Rather than the usual clicking noises, the lyrics were decipherable.

Dakarai sang about a forbidden love deep within the Clanslands that ended in an oath of eternal devotion before both lovers died in each other's arms. After a heartbeat, the clansman took up a fresh song about a mournful droplet of water that eventually turned into a great lake, one tear at a time. The nonsensical words, woven into a jaunty tune, warmed Jetekesh little by little.

By the time he fell asleep, his stomach full, his thoughts heavy, he'd nearly forgotten about Cavalin's ghost.

Until the man appeared above him in the gloom.

CHAPTER 22
THE FLAME IN EVERY SOUL

The Ruin.

So Sharo called it.

King Aredel studied the blasted land before him. The cracked soil was black as a raven's wings, and clouds hung low, like the sky hid itself from the broken land. Wide clusters of dead, gnarled trees stood as if the forest had been destroyed beneath a dragon's fiery breath. Perhaps that was the case. The air itself tasted of smoke and rot, worse than any battlefield Aredel had trod on the heels of victory.

As he urged his mount forward, black dust puffed up around his stallion's powerful hooves, then wisped away on a breath of wind.

Sharo trotted to Aredel's side on the back of Amaranth, and the fae prince surveyed the horizon with a deep crease in his brow. "Unpleasant, isn't it?"

Aredel nodded. "It reminds me of Peresen's fortress."

"It should," said Sharo. "That abode stands within this fell realm. My lord uncle always had a flare for the dramatic and the macabre."

Nodding again, Aredel studied the twining trees and recalled his fight against that dread lord when he'd come to Shinac the first time. The fight had been close, far closer than Aredel was accustomed to, but in the end, Peresen had died. Satisfaction trickled through the Blood King at the memory of that man's bones bleached and buried somewhere in the Drifting Sands.

He stiffened. Somewhere *here*. Shinac had returned. Now these lands were what had been the Drifting Sands for three hundred years or more.

Now war brewed in the north. Aredel could taste the bloodlust, the greed, better than he could the sulfurous air left from the long-ago scourge that had blackened this dominion. Somewhere ahead, King Darint and his *Unsielie* allies marched on Amantier.

Aredel turned in his saddle, leather creaking, to eye Sharo. "Your Highness?"

Sharo lifted a brow. "What grave question do you have for me, Blood King?"

"Your father. Is he as strong as Peresen or stronger?"

The fae prince fell still. His blue eyes skimmed the horizon again as though he sought the answer from far away. His knuckles tightened over his reins. "Stronger." His voice was a faint whisper. "But perhaps not as you imagine strength. Or...perhaps you do." He exhaled and brushed aside a stray lock of white hair. "He's cunning, not brutish. Peresen was the tough, looming giant. Darint found his strength in less...conventional paths. Both paid steep prices for long life, but Peresen relied on his body to take him far. Not so my father."

"Darint is long-lived?" Why hadn't that idea crossed Aredel's mind before?

Sharo tipped his head in a slight nod. "Indeed, he is. Darint should have been dead a hundred years now, but his alliance with the *Unsielie* won't allow it. He cannot die while the contract between them is unfulfilled—even if a sword runs him through."

Aredel's brows flew up as the ramifications swept over him. "Then what will we do? We cannot let the *Unsielie* win."

Sharo's eyes lost their focus. "We kill the single *Unsielie* who offered the contract. That is the only means to defeat Darint short of letting him first gain victory over Nakania."

"Is Tavassed the one to whom your father is bound?"

"I suspect so, but I haven't been able to confirm it." The fae prince pulled a face. "The methods one must employ to obtain such information are distasteful to me."

"Would I find those methods distasteful?"

Sharo hesitated. "That I couldn't say. But my conscience won't let me tell you how to go about seeking them."

"I see." Aredel turned his eyes on the wastes. "In KryTeer we employ many methods you'd likely find repugnant. Culture is a strange thing. One more question. What of Peresen? He had long life, yet I killed him. Did he not use an *Unsielie* contract?"

Sharo shook his head. "His was a different, less binding price. That is all I shall say about it."

Aredel nodded. "I'm not interested in immortality, or I might have allowed *Erisyrdrel*'s possession. Shall we proceed?" He nudged his horse forward.

The stallion strode into the Ruin without fear, kicking up puffs of black dust. Sharo followed. The army rolled forward at their heels, armor clinking, hooves drumming. They moved at a steady clip, despite the absence of a road.

As they crossed the dead land, Aredel stayed alert, prepared at any moment for some kind of ambush. Shinacian battles were vastly different from Nakanian wars. He couldn't merely watch the scenery around him. Anything might swoop out of the sky or break through the cracked earth.

Distant thunder rumbled. Aredel studied the clouds. He couldn't taste a storm.

Is war what bellows in my ears?

Since his skirmish against the goblins, an excitement had been building within him. A hunger. A bloodlust. Unleashing his grief and fury had calmed him a little. Had settled his restless loathing for life. Not enough, but it was a beginning.

He needed more.

Soon. War comes swiftly.

He found himself grinning.

Shevek trotted up to his left side, staring ahead. His jaw was set, eyes grim. After a moment, the knight pried his attention from the north to glance at Aredel. "I don't like it. Isn't this supposed to be the realm of the dark fae? Yet I see no fae. No structures. What do they do, build invisible cities?"

"A fair question." Aredel glanced at Sharo riding on his right. "Does the fae prince have an answer?"

Sharo crooked a smile. "Their cities are in the rocks and other formations, east and west, not so near the borders of the light fae. This used to be a road, decimated in a brutal war one hundred years ago. So many died in that conflict that few dare to cross this stretch. It is too painful for most." Sharo's eyes softened. "Ghosts still haunt the byways."

"That isn't chilling at all to think about," murmured Shevek.

"Ghosts haunt every battlefield, I should think," Aredel said. He steered his stallion around a large, blackened rock. The breeze picked up and caught his hair, brushing acrid fingers across his face. "Only a few can see them."

Shevek grunted. "Glad I'm not special."

The Blood King glanced at Sharo. "Can you see them, Your Highness?"

A frown dusted Sharo's lips. "Sometimes, from the corner of my eye. I suspect Jinji can see them always."

Aredel glanced back at the horses behind him. Among them, Jinji rode behind a bannerman he'd befriended en route. The storyteller preferred walking, but he'd agreed to ride so he wouldn't hinder the army.

It did Aredel's heart good to see his elder half-brother whole again, though not technically alive. Jinji hadn't changed, except that he wasn't bone thin and nearly dead. He was much as he had been when they'd first met in Shing seven years ago—except for the snowy locks that matched Sharo's so well.

Several times during the past few days, Aredel had nearly probed Jinji for information on Shinac's True King, Ehrikai of Valliath, but resentment toward that ethereal being had been growing inside the Blood King. He didn't want to hate the man more because Jinji was so fiercely loyal to him. Loyal enough to return for Ehrikai's sake, but not for Aredel.

That's just like him. Selfless. It's not meant to slight our own bonds.

Yet Aredel couldn't bring himself to dismiss the twinge of jealousy that stabbed his insides when he observed his brother. Jinji was content with death, content to be away from Nakania, content to serve Ehrikai somewhere far away. He would return to that distant realm when all was settled—no matter whether Aredel, Sharo, Jetekesh, and all their armies won or failed.

His struggles in death are far different from yours. That's to be expected.

Aredel wouldn't discuss Ehrikai with the storyteller, but he could converse about ghosts. Wheeling his horse around, he cantered to the bannerman's horse and met Jinji's turquoise eyes, so vivid and knowing.

"Ho, Aredel," Jinji greeted with his warmest smile.

"Jinji. Are you surviving the ride all right?"

"Quite," replied the storyteller. "Grivin and I have been discussing the merits of song these past hours. He wishes to be a bard once this danger passes."

"And will it pass?" Aredel glanced at the youthful bannerman, barely a man at all. Grivin wouldn't meet his eyes.

"All dangers pass, just as all trials," Jinji said. "But that isn't what you came to ask me."

Aredel scowled. "A mind reader now, are you?"

Jinji shrugged. "Some are easier for me to read than others."

The Blood King lifted an eyebrow while annoyance squeezed his chest. "Well then, what have I come about, Storyteller True?"

The Shingese man only chuckled. "Do not be offended. I don't read you so well as that, my brother."

The annoyance eased and fondness settled in. Aredel let his shoulders loosen. "It's about this place. The Ruin. Sharo says ghosts linger here. Do you see them?"

The sparkle in Jinji's eye dimmed. "Yes, I do. There are many; dark and light fae, humans, and dragons alike. Some are from the Flame War one hundred years ago, but many more are from the age of Cavalin and Tallat. These spirits have been waiting for Nakania and Shinac to reunite. They would not rest until the two worlds joined together anew."

"Yet they remain, even now?"

"Indeed. They wait for peace. Most wish to return to their homes, but they cannot rest until justice and mercy meet."

Aredel scoffed. "Is such a thing possible?"

The storyteller tipped his head to one side. "After all you've seen, you remain so cynical?"

Aredel steered his stallion around a gnarled tree stump. "After all *you* have witnessed, Jinji, how do you keep your faith in people?"

"Easily." Jinji's expression softened to an almost sorrowful smile. "I believe people are inherently good, Aredel. We are foolish only when we are ignorant. We hate when we are ignorant. We judge when we are ignorant. And we are ignorant because we are afraid of what we do not know."

"I know learned men who fear and hate."

Jinji shook his head, sighing softly. "They aren't learned. Not where it counts. They know letters, warcraft, manipulation. But they do not know people. Hearts. Feelings. They learned poor lessons from ignorant people who were afraid."

"Then I have known many ignorant people."

"Yes." Jinji's faint smile faded more. "*That* is the true war of any age, Aredel. The fight against ignorance. The fight to teach man the right lessons: to love and to respect others."

Aredel shook his head. "I can't love people like Gyath or Peresen or Darint. I can't love the *Unsielie* for what they've robbed from me."

"No," whispered Jinji. "I understand."

"Can you love them?" asked Aredel, lifting a brow. "Can you forgive them for being murderers and tyrants?"

Jinji bowed his head. "I can love what they *could* be."

"That's a dream. A lie. Jinji, you're not a fool. You can't possibly love what is evil."

"No, I do not. And I do not love their actions, their choices. But I do love the flame of goodness that I firmly believe lies in every soul."

Aredel turned away. Disgust churned in his stomach, heavy, bitterly so. "Go on loving the soul, Jinji. It suits you. But do not ask we lesser beings to understand how."

"Aredel."

The Blood King turned to meet Jinji's eyes. Clear. Bright. Gentle.

"I believed in you when others saw only a cruel, heartless monster," Jinji said. "What I believed in was your ability, your *strength*, to change. Truly change. To become great, noble, even kind. I will not deny *anyone* that right to become better, no matter how dark their present. Some never will—I will not fool myself on that point. But so many could, and so many *shall* change. I will not condone the actions of anyone who preys upon another. But I will hope for something better. *That* is how I choose to love."

The firm, kindly tones, the luminescence of that soul, brought Aredel's eyes low. He turned away, wrestling pride and shame. How like Jinji to find the right words. The right feelings. How like him to pry open Aredel's soul, spill his sins, and tenderly sprinkle hope through him like spring rain on brittle earth.

Swallowing a lump, Aredel flicked his reins and urged his mount back to the head of the army, away from the sunlight that blinded his cankered soul. He *wanted* to believe Jinji, to take that offering of hope and fill himself with its lustrous power—but he also wanted revenge. Death. Mayhem. And he didn't fool himself into believing he could have both.

Hadn't he tried? Hadn't that been exactly his trouble these past months; giving up his conquered lands, freeing slaves, devoting himself to reformation and reconciling the traditions of KryTeer with the demands of peace-loving countries? He'd tried so *hard* to change, and in so doing, he'd lost all that mattered most.

I'm sorry, Jinji. I cannot be what you want.

Aredel was bred for war, and if he had his way, he would die upon the field to bring about the world Jinji so dearly hoped to see.

Perhaps that has been my road all along. Maybe that is how I can become what you want, my brother: through my death.

Something flickered in his vision. Aredel jerked his eyes toward it.

Did he imagine a woman standing at the edge of the road paved by Sharo's army?

The vision was gone before he could determine if he'd truly seen a ghost. It was possible. Ghosts existed. He knew that already.

Will I become one of them when I die? Will I haunt the plains for centuries as they have done?

It seemed like a fitting end.

But not until he killed Tavassed with his own hands. Nothing would stop him until then.

CHAPTER 23
A PLEA

Jetekesh shot upright. His heart collided with his ribcage. Cavalin's ghost stood serenely beside his bedroll, watching him with eyes that could pierce thick armor with a glance. The faint sounds of breathing around Jetekesh stilled his quaking bones while his mind processed the specter before him.

Steeling himself, he met the ghostly eyes, translucent and luminous in the semi-darkness of the cave. They were the same green color as Emerin's.

The prince said nothing. Words wouldn't come. He merely waited.

Cavalin reached out a transparent hand. That urgency flooded the Amantieran prince's veins again.

Drawing a deep breath, Jetekesh reached out. Raum was solid despite being dead. Perhaps Cavalin was too. Their fingers met. Cavalin's were frigid as ice—cold, but tangible. He tugged, prompting Jetekesh to gain his feet.

'Come,' Cavalin's expression seemed to say.

Jetekesh nodded, then stooped to claim the still-damp cloak

spread out beside his bedroll. He threw it over his shoulders with a faint shiver.

Cavalin drifted toward the cave entrance. Moonlight cascaded outside the wide maw, and relief rushed over Jetekesh. The storm had moved on. He wouldn't soak himself through again.

The ghost reached the entrance, and Jetekesh caught up with him to stare out into the moonlit world. Everything seemed ethereal, like a silver film had coated the trees and rocks, the moss and tendrils of fog.

The dead king's gaze sliced through Jetekesh, sparking that same sense of urgency. He didn't speak, but his message was plain: Follow.

"Lead on," Jetekesh said.

Cavalin moved into the remnants of fog under a sky riddled with stars that sparkled and hummed. Jetekesh shadowed the ghostly figure up a ravine wending away from the path the company trekked. His legs burned as he trailed the tireless specter for what felt like hours. Pebbles skittered and bounced down the path behind him.

At last, Jetekesh crested the narrow trail on Cavalin's heels. The ravine gave way to a sudden drop overlooking a valley that had been torched years before. Strange scrubs and young trees grew up around the blackened bones of ancient redwoods. The husk of an old fortress and the surrounding remains of a city scarred the ground.

His breath caught. Among the broken stones and jutting tree trunks, distant lights wandered the valley. Not a few, but hundreds—no, thousands. Under the waxing moon, they glowed like distant fairies, but Jetekesh's instinct called them what they were: ghosts.

He glanced at Cavalin. "What does it mean?"

The dead king considered him, then nodded toward the distant valley. No words escaped his lips. Instead, images poured into Jetekesh's mind like Jinji's stories—but these were sudden, convoluted, hammering into him like he was steel under a smithy's hammer.

He fell to his knees, covering his head with both arms, trying not to drown in the deluge of memories.

War. Destruction. The sundering of two lands torn apart for what seemed forever.

The ghosts of both lands, caught between Nakania and Shinac, unable to move on.

When there was room enough in Jetekesh's mind for his own thoughts, he lifted his head and drew a shuddering breath. He couldn't stop himself from shaking.

"But the two lands are reunited now," he whispered. "Why can't you all move on?"

The onslaught of memories was expected this time, but as each image slammed into Jetekesh, he flinched and curled into himself. Navolleth. He saw the mighty dragon, a pure white shade, wheeling over the battlefield as Tallat and Cavalin dueled near the borders of Shinac. And then Cavalin fell.

The dragon screamed, and ice filled the heavens. The images that followed were mere fragments of Navolleth tumbling from the air as though he, too, had been struck down. Perhaps, bonded as they'd been, that was true.

The war surged toward the boundary of Shinac, but Navolleth, changed into human form, knelt before the fallen king and wept. Dark tendrils wrapped around his body, dripping with grief and hatred, tainting the very ground he touched. From the droplets sprang the *vashalan*.

And into the ground poured his curse. The dragon, broken in his grief, had unleashed a dragon curse upon the field. Upon the living and the dead. Trapping the ghosts of the fallen, including his own bonded.

The memories rolled away, and Jetekesh stared into the valley below where the dead roamed, awaiting freedom, longing for it.

Two curses. One from the fountain, and one from a fallen dragon.

He sucked in rattling breaths, trying to compose himself. Setting his jaw, he heaved to his feet and turned to Cavalin. "How do I break Navolleth's curse? I—I haven't the power." Panic swelled up his throat, closing it, but he corrected his posture and forced himself to breathe. "You've come to me because I can help, right? Tell me how."

Cavalin the Third met his eyes. They stared at each other as fog curled around their ankles and stars winked overhead.

In the stillness, words came as though the air itself spoke. "*Save him.*"

Jetekesh flinched. "I don't think I can. He hates me."

"*Save him. Please.*"

The prince of Amantier bowed his head. This was Cavalin, the hero of stories and legends that believers and heathens alike embraced. Sainted, immortalized. Jetekesh's ancestor. The last true king of Nakania.

I'll not deny him this request.

"You believe I can," Jetekesh said aloud. "I will try."

The ghost faded into something like the memory of moonlight. Words whispered on the wind: "*Thank you.*"

Cavalin vanished. The ghosts below disappeared in the next breath.

The stars winked out, and rain fell from the heavens in a ceaseless barrage. Jetekesh pulled his cowl up over his head, though he was already soaked through, like he'd been standing in the rain for hours.

Shivering, he moved back down the ravine as quickly as he dared in the slick conditions. He stumbled once and caught himself on the natural wall to his left. Mud stained his fingers, but he wiped it against his cloak and kept going.

At the bottom of the ravine, lights bobbed in the storm. Torches, probably.

Guilt needled Jetekesh's insides. He quickened his pace on the even ground. He approached the closest blob of light. It was Kajsa, with Raum at her heels.

The girl whirled toward him and shouted "Found him!" as she raced to his side. Axel was right behind her. The torch Kajsa was clutching sputtered but didn't die. "What happened?"

"We've been looking for you for ages," Axel added with heat.

Jetekesh managed a weak smile. "I took a walk with Cavalin." He turned and pointed toward the ravine, but it was gone. Solid rock and moss stared back at him, slick and glittering in the storm.

Turning back, his smile faded. "It's a long, sad story."

CHAPTER 24
STARDUST STONES

"I'd yell at you," Emerin said, as he helped Jetekesh change into apparel Axel had grudgingly lent to him. "But I'm certain it would do no good." The keep lord sounded shockingly like Sir Lafe, Jetekesh's protector.

The shivers wouldn't stop. Jetekesh worried he'd caught a cold, but there wasn't anything he could do about it now. Slipping Axel's fur-lined cloak around his shoulders, he welcomed the blanketing warmth. He shuffled to the fire. His limbs were stiff, and his fingers and toes burned as they thawed. His nose still felt numb.

"I realize I should have awakened someone, but..." Jetekesh hesitated. "Who was supposed to be standing watch?"

"I was," Axel growled from where he sat at the fire under his second fur cloak.

"I didn't see you."

"Nor did I see *you*," Axel said. "Which makes no sense."

"You dozed off," Emerin said. "Understandable but unfortunate."

Axel's face colored. "I *didn't* doze off. I'd never do so on watch."

"He might not have," Jetekesh said. He eased onto his saddle, half-expecting his limbs to shatter like ice. "The world wasn't... well, normal, when Cavalin came for me. It wasn't storming."

Emerin glanced at the sodden world beyond the cave. "The storm hasn't let up."

"No," said Dakarai. "It hasn't." The clansman offered Jetekesh his second cup of tea this night, then sat beside him. "Was your venture worthwhile?"

Jetekesh stared into the clay cup, drinking in the minty scent. Steam curled around his face. He finally nodded. "Who discovered I was gone?"

"I did," Kajsa answered as she brushed out her sodden hair. "I woke up because I was chilled, and I thought you might be more so, since you'd gotten soaked. You weren't in your bedroll, and so I alerted Lord Emerin."

Jetekesh glanced around the cave. "Where's Thrissa?"

"She went looking for you farther out than the rest of us," Emerin said. "But she promised to return soon to see if you'd been found." The keep lord sighed. "We wondered if Cavalin had anything to do with it."

Lifting the cup, Jetekesh took a sip. "I'll explain what happened when she returns."

"That is reasonable," Dakarai said.

Something moved near the cave entrance. It was Anenyasha, standing guard, clutching her spear, barely more than a shadow against the stormlight. Her presence was reassuring. After the chilling vision of that valley of ghosts, he was glad to be surrounded by friends—and even Axel, since the Norvian could fight.

Moments stretched on in silence. Jetekesh drank his tea and let his body thaw. Halfway through his cup, Thrissa stepped inside the cave and shed her shimmering cloak. She wasn't wet at all.

"Where were you, Your Highness?" asked the elven queen.

Jetekesh set his cup aside and imparted his experience with Cavalin in as few words as possible. The company probed him for the details he'd overlooked. Silence resumed its reign. Jetekesh retrieved his cup and let the rest of them absorb what he'd said.

"Who did he mean?" asked Axel. "Save whom?"

"That's obvious enough," Dakarai said. "He meant Navolleth."

Jetekesh nodded. "So he did."

Axel's face darkened. "*You*, save Lord Navolleth? How? And why? He's fine as he is, and far more powerful than you. Than any of you."

"Take it easy," Emerin growled. "You hardly know the man. Did you even know he's a dragon?"

Axel stood up straight. "He showed me his true form. He trusts me. I'll hear no disrespect concerning my lord." He turned a sneer on Jetekesh. "And he needs no saving—especially from the likes of you."

"Xel," said Kajsa in a low, fierce voice. "Sit down. You're behaving like a pompous snake."

No one moved. Every eye turned to her. Kajsa ducked her head, her cheeks flushed.

Perhaps Axel was more stunned than the rest, for he sat as though she'd slapped him.

"Well," said Emerin, "if we're quite done posturing, we need to decide our next move. Go on to the blood fountain, or turn around and see about fulfilling Cavalin's desire."

No one spoke.

The fire popped, drawing Jetekesh's gaze. Orange light dyed the stones around the flames. Finally, he stirred. "I think we can accomplish both objectives at once."

Emerin's eyes, so much like Cavalin's, sliced into him. "Go on, Your Highness."

"It's a feeling—an instinct—I think." Jetekesh rubbed his thumb along the rim of his cup, weighing his emotions against the brightness in his heart. "If Cavalin has called on me—on *us*, really—it must be because we're on the right track. The blood fountain is crucial to ending Nakania's curse. But the waters of truth do more than simply reveal a worthy king or queen. That was just one instance. Isn't it possible they would reveal the truth of matters from long ago? And wouldn't that...allow Navolleth to witness what really happened? To know who's truly responsible for Cavalin's end—and—and break that curse too?"

"Do you think that's the answer?" asked Dakarai. "Showing Navolleth the truth will save him?"

"The truth is supposed to set one free," Jetekesh said with a shrug. "Don't the philosophers say as much?"

A new voice spoke from the cave entrance. "I think you're right. The fountain should be able to heal a dragon's curse." Lightning seared the sky behind the newcomer, highlighting Kethalas's features. The dragon in human shape moved deeper into the cave. Raindrops had frozen against his skin, his clothes, and hair, and they sparkled in the firelight as he strode closer.

Jetekesh jumped to his feet and rounded the fire to greet Kethalas. He caught the dragon's arms and grinned. "Welcome back. I didn't expect you to join us."

Kethalas's fangs showed in his own wide grin. "I wouldn't let you find the blood fountain without me. It's legendary among the dragon clans. I'm among those who've never seen it. Elder Taregan gave me permission to seek you out."

"Were we that easy to find?" Emerin stepped up to Jetekesh's side and folded his arms.

The dragon tipped his head sideways. "Did you forget you ride with a beacon?" His slitted silver eyes darted to Jetekesh. "I had a difficult time breaking through a mass of nasty winged things as I headed this way. Harpies, among other less savory creatures." He held out his closed fist, then opened it for a split second—long enough to reveal a blinding flash of light—before he closed his fist again, leaving the company blinking in the relative gloom.

"What is that?" asked Jetekesh, releasing Kethalas's arms.

"It's called a stardust stone, but for our purposes I'll call it bait. Taregan's idea. It's a special gemstone that shines as bright as a meteor if cut right. I've been releasing dozens of these at different places across Shinac, hoping they'll distract the enemy. False beacons, you see?"

"That's brilliant," said Jetekesh, eyeing the dragon's closed hand. "Will it work?"

"It seems to have. When I met that winged army, I led them back to one I'd already dropped, and they abandoned me at once to seek it out. I spotted your light earlier, Your Highness, and made my way northward to leave a false trail or ten. We should be safe for a few days. After their merry chase, those creatures won't trust any light for a bit."

Emerin grunted his approval. "How does the light of these gemstones compare to our prince's?"

"Up close, it's the difference between a candle and a forest fire." Kethalas pocketed his gem. Somehow, it didn't glow through his clothing. "But from the air, it's harder to tell unless one knows what one is looking for. Stardust stones glow white. Jetekesh here is more silvery."

Dakarai slipped up to join the cluster. "That's excellent news, even if it buys us only a little time. It's good to have you back, Lord Dragon. Are you all healed up?"

Jetekesh's stomach prickled with guilt. How could he have forgotten to ask? "Yes. Are you fit enough to travel with us?"

"Not quite as good as new, but much, much better than I was." Kethalas's eyes sparkled. "I can fly now within limits. I would have been here sooner if not for that." He rolled his shoulder. "The wound is closed and well-sealed. Only very foolish actions on my part will pry it open once more."

"I'm glad." Jetekesh caught Kethalas's arm again. "I've missed you. And we've all been worried." His voice lowered. "What of your clan? Were you welcomed back?"

The dragon's cheeks flushed. "Indeed, I was. Most warmly. It seems my shame is remembered only by myself. They were appalled to think I'd deemed myself unworthy to stand among them. They'd perceived my gatekeeping status as an honor rather than a punishment." He ran a finger under his nose. "Seems you were right, princeling."

Jetekesh batted that away with a hand. "I'm happy for you, Kethalas. Truly. And I'm so glad you've returned. We need you."

"More than you know," Kethalas said with a firm nod. "According to Taregan, the blood fountain was removed from the dragon lands at the same time that Valliath closed its gates. Few may enter that realm, but all dragons feel certain that's where it now resides." His eyes flicked to something behind Jetekesh. "Lady Thrissa understands, I'm sure, how difficult it is to enter Valliath now. Taregan said that even beyond that challenge, approaching the blood fountain without a dragon is tantamount to death."

A shiver slithered up Jetekesh's spine. "Then be doubly welcome, good dragon."

"I thank ye." Kethalas turned grim. "We should leave at once, my friends. Dawn approaches, and an early start will serve us well. Besides, your scent is all over this cave. Better to use the cover of rain and approaching daylight to hide it along with my own arrival."

Emerin stooped to pick up his saddle. “Agreed. We’ve certainly chatted enough.” He straightened up and shifted the saddle in his arms. “Any arguments, Your Highness?”

Jetekesh shook his head. “None. Let’s be underway.”

CHAPTER 25
RACING NORTH

Goblins.

Yeshton ducked back behind the mound of stone and broken trees, his hand caught on his sword pommel. Beside him, Ledonn slid an arrow from the quiver at his back. Yeshton quickly shook his head. The Blood Knight halted, offering up a questioning look.

Beyond their hiding place, another goblin appeared beside the first in the evening gloom, under the shelter of the scant forest canopy. Yeshton eyed the short, thick-skinned creatures, instinct screaming at him to wait and watch. A half dozen gray goblins joined the first two, then a dozen more.

"There must be a tunnel close by," murmured Dejani, one of the elven warriors crouching on Yeshton's other side. "If they discover us, we are worse off than dead."

Ledonn huffed but slid his arrow back into the quiver. "Fine."

Even more goblins appeared among the trees. They were near the borders of Amantier—or so Yeshton assumed from the green forest that crept into the blackened wastes. Watching a host of goblins appear made his nerves hum. He must reach Kavacos and warn King Jetekesh before these leathery creatures swarmed the farms and villages of Southern Amantier.

How, by all the saints, am I supposed to manage that?

He scowled. Kavacos was still weeks away, and here he was, hiding from a growing mass of monsters in loincloths. Yes, he could send a messenger pigeon, but who in the north would believe anything about Shinac's return written in a hasty note?

His fingers tightened against his sword. He needed to speak to the king personally. Soon.

"Wait," whispered Dejani, perhaps sensing his tension.

Yeshton did wait, though he hated every lost second as goblin after goblin marched north—hundreds of them, each wielding ugly short swords, staves, cudgels, or hammers. So many instruments of death.

At last, as a few stray goblins moved ahead under the shroud of night, Dejani stood. The other two elves—a female named Lunalere and a male named Maccus—joined him.

"We should circle wide to the east," Dejani said. "We can meet the river there and cover our scent. You have barges in Amantier, I understand."

Yeshton rose and hope lit in his chest. "We do, yes." Of course, that was the answer. Hadn't Aredel used a barge to reach Keep Falcon ahead of Jinji's company when last they'd traveled south? Going upstream would be slower than coming down, but not by much. It wouldn't stop the carnage in the south, but the warning was vital just the same.

"Good." Ledonn unsheathed his curved blade. "I appreciate a sensible plan."

They moved to their hidden horses and mounted to start east. Night owls hooted in the boughs. As they moved among the widespread trees, Yeshton felt a growing sense of coming home. The moment he stepped across the true border into Amantier, he knew it deep in his bones. Though the lay of the land had changed drastically, it couldn't trick Yeshton's instinct.

Grueling days and sleepless nights had brought them this far. By barge, they could cover ground twice as fast as on horses—which meant they might reach Kavacos in one week's time.

It was small comfort, but comfort nonetheless.

In the middle hours of night, they reached the flowing river. Before the joining of the two lands, the water hadn't flowed quite so far south, ending near Keep Falcon. Yet now it glistened, almost overflowing, seeming to carry on far into southern lands.

Yeshton shook off the wonder of it as he forded the river at a shallow place, along with the others, cutting off their traceable trail. They tracked the river northward for several leagues before Yeshton spied the southern Amantieran keep, with its torches and parapets. A kind of bittersweet attachment settled inside him as he neared it.

There, within Keep Falcon, Jetekesh's mother had died. Jinji's friendship with King Aredel had been revealed. Yeshton had spent a night in a dungeon, alongside Rille and the rest of their company.

After that, Yeshton's world had changed forever.

Grief lanced his chest as he urged his horse a little faster. He'd met Prince Anadin shortly after that and had supported Rille as she'd won the hardened man over. Now, Anadin was dead. The world was upside-down. Nothing would go back to what it was.

Does it ever?

He meant to head straight for the dock, but something made him switch directions.

"Where are you going?" asked Ledonn.

"Pay the dockmaster. Ready the barge." Yeshton didn't look over his shoulder. "I need to warn Keep Falcon."

While he was at it, he would try sending a pigeon on to Kavacos with news of the invasion. Whether or not the king believed him, Yeshton would do anything he could to stave off unnecessary bloodshed.

Anything.

It was worth a short detour, and then he would be on his way upstream.

One week. Yeshton ached to reach Kavacos sooner.

So much could happen in one week.

CHAPTER 26
STORM OF FAE

A ferry.

Jetekesh eyed the contraption with a critical eye, noting the moss that grew on the weathered wood. It wasn't well cared for, but then, by Thrissa's report no one came this close to the Hold of Valliath. Why should they? No trade existed here. No wide plains or valleys for growing crops. He supposed, in this rocky terrain where trees and mountains held dominance, one might be able to mine. Surely, ore riddled these peaks if not gold.

Yet no one lived this far east. Not that he could tell.

The river cut north to south through a wide, green canyon, roaring like it threw an endless tantrum. Its intensity made sense, considering the season. The mountains were shedding their winter cloaks as warm weather breathed over Shinac.

Against the torrential water, the ferry looked brittle and untrustworthy.

Kethalas made fording the river unnecessary except for one important factor: the horses.

Emerin, Dakarai, Thrissa, and the dragon discussed possible solutions while Jetekesh stood apart and glowered at the rapids.

Kajsa slipped up next to the prince, Raum at her side. “We could try the ferry.”

Jetekesh dragged his gaze back to the pathetic ropes strung over the water which were meant to guide the ferry across in a straight line. But even if Kethalas flew to the far bank to tow them across, the ferryboat itself was little more than a ramshackle raft bobbing fiercely in the current.

“It’s little different than suicide.” He sighed and shook his head. “I won’t risk the horses—or any of us.” He avoided glancing at Axel. The One God decreed that one should always shun temptation. *Saints give me strength.*

“The horses will have to stay,” Emerin declared. “We can travel on foot.”

“That will slow us considerably,” Dakarai countered. “I am willing to try taking them across on the ferry.”

Anenyasha stepped forward. “No, Dakarai.”

Jetekesh grimaced and turned to face the company. “I’ve made up my mind. We’ll leave the horses. I’m sure if we leave all their feed as well, they’ll stay nearby and we can round them up on the return journey.”

“That wouldn’t be necessary,” Emerin said. “If Kethalas has a few more days to heal, he can carry us all the way to Kavacos.”

“That’s a large burden for a dragon so young, even were he fully recovered,” Thrissa said, stroking her horse’s nose.

Kethalas sighed. “She’s right. One or two of you, I could carry across long distances. More than that—I’m sorry. It’s not possible.”

“If only another dragon had come with you,” Axel said.

Kethalas shrugged. “We couldn’t spare any others. They have joined Taregan to fight for the free lands.”

Emerin scratched the side of his neck. “Then, we leave the

horses, cross using Kethalas, and carry on to Valliath. Once we collect the waters of truth, we can then return here, grab the horses, and let Kethalas carry two of us off to the warfront while the rest head north more slowly. It's our best course of action."

Dakarai grimaced. "It makes sense."

"Agreed," Thrissa said.

The others nodded or murmured assent.

Trudging to his horse, Jetekesh unstrapped the saddle and whispered reassurances to the gelding. "We'll be back as soon as we can. Don't...don't let wild cats eat you. All right?" He sighed and hefted up the saddle to lay it aside. "Will they have enough food?"

Dakarai unburdened his own mount. "Yes. There's plenty of foliage nearby as well. And horses are clever. They'll be fine, especially in each other's company."

Once the horses were freed and the feed spread, the company turned its sights on the raging river. The canyon rose before them, adorned in trees that grew out of the hard rock and glistened with wet moss. The scent of fish and watery plants filled the air, mingling with an endless mist. The view was stunning in that way nature's deadliest formations tended.

Kethalas was unable to transform into full dragon shape in the tight space between the canyon walls and the riverbank, but he pulled out his wings.

Dakarai volunteered to be flown over first.

"Can you really support him?" asked Jetekesh, weighing the tall, muscular clansman against Kethalas's more lithe shape.

"Even in this form, I'm a bit heartier than humans." Kethalas leapt into the air, scooped up Dakarai, and beat his wings across the river.

As they neared the far shore, Raum let out a sharp bark.

Jetekesh's nerves tightened. He tracked Raum's gaze toward the sky. An arrow shot from an airborne *Unsielie*'s bow. It whistled over the air, then ripped through Kethalas's wing. The dragon tumbled, taking Dakarai with him, and together they plunged into the river.

The prince cried out and bolted toward the water, but Emerin caught him from behind, yanking him back.

"Seek shelter!" the keep lord yelled.

More arrows loosed from above, raining down on the company like storming death.

Jetekesh was hauled away from the river, but his gaze never strayed from the two forms struggling in vain against the torrent dragging them downstream, away from the company. Then the river swallowed them.

"Someone stop her!" Emerin shoved Jetekesh behind a mossy boulder.

Wrenching his eyes from the place where Kethalas and Dakarai had vanished, Jetekesh found Anenyasha slicing arrows from the sky with her spear. She raced along the riverbank, chasing her beloved and the dragon. Thrissa darted after her, dancing around the arrows like they were down weeds in the wind. Anenyasha reached the water's edge farther down the canyon. As she dove into the river, an arrow struck her back.

Jetekesh started to spring over the boulder, but Emerin caught his arm and pulled him back down.

"No time to be a hero," the keep lord growled, his eyes pinned above.

With a shiver, Jetekesh lifted his gaze. A horde of *Unsielie* hummed above them, darkening the blue sky like a storm cloud laden with rain. Every dark gaze settled on the boulder, drawn by the ethereal beacon encircling Jetekesh.

He drew his sword while a wry smile played at his mouth. What could a sword do against *Unsielie*? What could any of them do against such forces? Aredel wasn't here to blast them from the heavens with his newfound magic. Taregan was off fighting with Sharo. And Kethalas was downriver, possibly drowning.

Jetekesh's throat closed and his insides writhed. What options did they have left?

The name of the True King.

He'd used it before. Against *Erisyrdrel*, he'd invoked Ehrikai's authority to banish the water demon. But this wasn't the same scenario. These were a multitude of *Unsielie*, and he wasn't certain they'd done anything to warrant the justice of the True King.

Small fingers caught his arm. Jetekesh nearly jumped from his skin and jerked his head around. Beside him, Rille crouched against the boulder, her amber eyes wide and bright.

"Cousin, go to the water's edge. Invoke the name. Call for aid." Her voice was singsong, and her eyes slid out of focus as though she'd entered a trance.

He pried her fingers loose, then turned to eye the rapids. Steeling himself, he clutched the warm metal of his hilt tighter, then dove out from behind the boulder.

Emerin called for him to return, but Jetekesh let Rille's voice ring through his mind over and over: Water's edge. Invoke the name. Call for aid.

The ground sloped down to the water line near the mooring where the moss-covered ferry ropes danced above the roaring river. Jetekesh stumbled. He righted himself and splashed into the shallows. Even here, the current snatched at him, urging him to join the ceaseless flow.

He turned his eyes skyward and lifted his chin against the hundred arrows aimed at him. "In the name of King Ehrikai, I call for aid!"

He exploded with light, like curtains flung away from his soul. Power filled him. Every nook and cranny, every thread that held him together, warming his bones, cleansing his lungs, blazing in his vision. He shivered under the glow like golden sunlight after a storm.

Gasping, his body responded to the magic. His arms lifted toward the sky, oddly heavy. At the same moment, the blinding glow dimmed enough to let him see. Above him, strange birds with giant golden wings ascended toward the *Unsielie.*

No, not birds. Gryphons.

A wild grin stretched over Jetekesh's lips. Dozens of glorious gryphons struck the *Unsielie* forces like a battering ram, scattering lacy wings, forcing arrows off course.

Emerin splashed up next to Jetekesh. The keep lord stared skyward. The clash of arms rolled like thunder in the heavens, and shadows danced over the ground.

"Never feel useless again, Your Highness," Emerin said. "I think your accoutrements are top-notch."

Jetekesh allowed himself a laugh. "It was Rille's idea. I didn't know gryphons would answer my summons."

"Well," said Emerin, "you *listened* to her, didn't you?"

True. Jetekesh wouldn't have one year ago. He shifted his feet, trying to ignore the squelch of soggy boots or his numbing toes in the icy current. Despite his momentary elation, his heart hung heavy in his chest. Had Dakarai, Anenyasha, and Kethalas survived?

"They'll keep coming after us." Emerin rubbed at his stubbled chin. "I've tried to summon fire, but it's not answering. I likely lost that gift when the *Unsielie* fortress fell." His voice trailed off, not finishing what they both knew he meant. *When his sister died.*

Jetekesh set his jaw against a jolt of guilt, determined not to wallow while the *Unsielie* remained close by. He shook his head. "If the True King sent these gryphons, it will be enough for now. And we can ride them to the gates of Valliath, I should think." His gaze flicked downstream. "We just need to find our companions."

A stray arrow struck the ground and bounced off a stone near

Jetekesh's boot. He sprang aside on instinct, nerves singing. Too close.

Emerin swore under his breath and jerked his hand toward the boulder. "Let's seek shelter until this battle concludes."

They raced back to the mossy rocks. Jetekesh flung himself to his knees beside Rille, who eyed him with her calm, grown-up smile.

"Did you know gryphons would come?" asked Jetekesh.

She offered a half-shrug. "I had an inkling. This same river flows into the southwest. I met a gryphon there recently."

He grunted and turned back to the battle. Gryphons tore off fae wings, and *Unsielie* warriors speared the lion bodies through. Allies and foes alike tumbled into the river and were swept away. Jetekesh's guts twisted. He should be out there. He should be fighting.

What good is a truth sigil if I only condemn others to fight in my stead? His hands clenched into fists. *What more can I do?*

Trying to engage an airborne enemy was ludicrous. Standing in the open, equally so.

Get to Valliath. Find the blood fountain. That's your quest.

He knew it. Knew it was the only sensible course. Yet watching the noble gryphons fall from the heights to their deaths ripped Jetekesh's grieving heart open all over again. So many good souls had died, so many more would fall. All because of Darint and Navolleth.

Save him, Cavalin's ghost had begged.

Was there anything left of the fallen dragon to save?

A cheer rolled over the heavens. Jetekesh realized he'd stopped watching. He dragged his eyes up and found the *Unsielie* in full retreat, several teetering on tattered wings. A dozen gryphons chased them, while the remainder—fifty strong at least—stayed overhead, beating the air with their impressive wings.

Three gryphons descended, touching down in front of the

boulder as Jetekesh, Emerin, and Rille emerged. Farther down river, Thrissa, Kajsa, and Axel slipped from the shelter of smaller boulders and a fallen tree trunk. Kajsa clutched her bow, but her quiver was empty.

Approaching Jetekesh, the gryphons shifted, stretching taller and shedding their lion bodies for human forms with wings—two men and one woman. Golden hair and amber eyes adorned their visages. White robes wrapped around their frames.

The middle gryphon, a man with a trimmed beard over a strong jaw, inclined his head in a respectful bow. "I give you greetings, Marked Prince. I am Garthune, first elder of the gryphania."

Jetekesh returned the nod. "You have my deepest thanks for answering my call and risking the lives of your fellows, First Elder Garthune. I lament your fallen with all my heart."

The gryphon's amber eyes flashed as he inclined his head again. "The True King has marked you. We will always come when we are able." His voice was a deep basso rumble.

"Then..." Jetekesh hesitated, but he couldn't waste time. He took a step forward, chest tight. "I have two more favors to ask of you."

"Name them," said the gryphon.

"Three of our companions were swept down river. Can you track them and bring them back?" He paused. "Whether alive or dead."

The gryphon eyed the companion to his left, and that gryphon —a slighter man, but full grown and with a similar beard— stepped to one side, spread his wings, and took to the air. He met another gryphon, and they conversed, then the latter winged off. The former returned to ground still in human skin. He reclaimed his position at the side of the other two.

Jetekesh studied the female gryphon. Though beardless, she too had strong facial features, and her frame was sturdy. She looked like she could snap Jetekesh in two. Despite that, she wore a friendly smile, almost mischievous, like she'd rather whisper a daring secret about her companions just to make you laugh.

"What is your last request?" asked Garthune.

Jetekesh pulled his eyes from the female's and gathered his thoughts. "We need transportation to the gates of Valliath. We're running out of time, and our quest is imperative."

"As you wish. We shall select gryphons enough for each of you to ride." He turned to the female. "Lerasundy, if you please?"

She answered with a graceful nod then hopped into the sky and soared toward her fellows waiting on the wind.

"Thank you," Emerin said.

"We are honored to serve the True King's chosen," said Garthune, spreading his wings wide. "Farewell, Marked Prince. May you and your companions win truth and prosperity for all realms of this world."

Jetekesh inclined his head. "We will certainly try."

The two male gryphons flew back to their companions, and the company waited. Jetekesh's mind raced downstream, praying to the One God and all His saints that the bodies returned would be breathing and hale.

Minutes passed like sludge, growing toward an hour. Eventually, Jetekesh sat, his every nerve taut and humming like a lute's strings.

The gryphons overhead stirred, wings glistening in the afternoon sun.

A second later, Kajsa jabbed a finger through the air. "There!"

CHAPTER 27
GRYPHON WINGS

Jetekesh shot to his feet, a bruise on his knee protesting. Dragging back wisps of hair, he stared hard at the river and spotted the gleam of golden feathers beating toward him. The gryphon bore three riders, all sitting upright.

Saints be praised!

He darted toward them, heart soaring.

Dakarai waved as they neared. The gryphon touched down, and all three riders slid from its back, Dakarai supporting Anenyasha. An arrow still jutted from her shoulder, and she wore a grimace.

Jetekesh turned to call for Kajsa, but she swept past him, already digging out poultices and bandages. Thrissa was right on her heels.

Kethalas left the clansfolk and healers beside the gryphon, and he limped toward Jetekesh, a grin wide on his lips. "Hail, Marked Prince. You summoned reinforcements, I see."

"Well, somehow I prefer living to dying."

Kethalas snorted. "Glad I am to hear it." His silver eyes scanned the company. "We lost no one?"

"Mercifully," said Jetekesh. "We have Rille to thank for a well-timed vision."

The dragon chuckled. "After all, what's the point of ill-timed visions, hm?"

A figure stepped toward Jetekesh, and he turned to find Dakarai approaching, dripping wet, while the healers tended to Anenyasha's shoulder. The clansman reached him and wrapped a sopping arm around Jetekesh's shoulder. Smears of colored chalk had bled down his braids.

"It's due to your gryphons that we're still alive," Dakarai said. "Thank you, Jetekesh."

A lump closed the prince's throat, and he struggled to clear it. "I'm glad I'm not as helpless as I feared."

"Not you," Dakarai said, pulling back. His dark eyes twinkled in the sunlight. "Never again, I'd wager."

Kethalas grunted his agreement.

Jetekesh shuffled his feet, cheeks blazing. "We're, uh, taking the gryphons to the gates of Valliath. They've agreed."

"Marvelous," Dakarai said. "I could get used to flying."

Kethalas laughed. "Once you do, you'll never go back." His grin weakened. "Unfortunately, my wing was struck. I'll need the gryphons' aid as well." The last word ended in a growl.

"I'm sure they'll be fine with that," Jetekesh said. "It seems my mark is rather persuasive. Now, both of you go dry off." He paused. "I'll hold a blanket up for you."

Dakarai grinned. "No need. We can stand behind the trees."

"No need." The dragon's grin stretched wider and the droplets of water running down his face cracked and hardened into pearls of ice and webs of delicate frost, glittering in the sun. Even his eyelashes sparkled. He shook his body, and the ice flecks tinkled to the ground around him like tiny diamonds, leaving him perfectly dry.

Awe skittered over Jetekesh, and he bent to pluck up a single ice pearl. The cold surface bit into the pads of his fingers, but despite its fragility, it didn't melt at his touch. "That's a handy trick."

"Isn't it?" Kethalas turned to the clansman. "Do you wish me to dry you off as well?"

Dakarai chuckled and shook his head. "I prefer to be a little damp over dry and frozen." He moved toward the nearest stand of trees.

Jetekesh excused himself and moved off to Kajsa. She'd just finished patching up Anenyasha and was tucking her herbs away. Raum stood close like a sentinel.

"Here." Jetekesh handed the girl the glittering pearl.

She took it. "Beautiful."

"Keep it. I don't think Kethalas will want it back. I'm also not sure it melts, so you'll need to let me know."

She smiled. "Thank you. I will."

"What do we do about him?" He nodded at the wolf.

Kajsa chewed her lip. "I think...if he wants to come, he can keep up. I'm not sure a river will impede him."

"I suppose we'll find out."

She bent down and looked into Raum's eyes. "Do what you must, my friend. I'll understand if it's time to say goodbye."

The wolf let out a huff, then sat on his haunches.

Thirty minutes later, the company mounted seven gryphons —Kajsa and Anenyasha rode together, as did Jetekesh and Rille— and they soared across the river, up the cliffs, and high into the sky. Dakarai let out a resounding whoop.

Jetekesh gawked at the world below while cold mountain winds stroked his hair and a thrill rushed through his blood. Rille clutched the gryphon's mane with white knuckles, her body rigid, her eyes sealed shut. The prince couldn't help but feel a prickle of satisfaction. Usually, she was the calm one, always in control, while he looked like the stumbling fool. Letting that satisfaction take root, the last tendrils of his fear fell away and Jetekesh drank in the freedom of flight, just as Kethalas had described on the plains of Amantier a few weeks and a thousand ages ago.

He let his eyes close. The crisp air sank into him, tugging at his senses with tales of far-off places, ageless memories, and a pinch of magic. Something deep in his soul responded to the pull of Shinac, and he felt the direction of Valliath like a living force beckoning him home.

Home, to the world's seat of magic. To the realm of the True King.

To the blood fountain and the end of his line's rule.

Somehow, that idea sat well inside his chest today. Not because he wanted to give up all he'd been raised to be, but because Cavalin would call it just. Because somewhere out there, the best high king or queen for Nakania would set the world to rights.

And because Jetekesh had come to love right over power.

Opening his eyes, he leaned to one side and stared out at the ground flitting by below him: the grand mountains patched with snow, the lines of rivers meandering like snakes between the crevices, the trees dotting the land between rock and water. How vast yet small it felt. A tapestry woven by divine hands.

An ache caught fire in Jetekesh's bones. This same world faced war. People and lands would perish unless Sharo's forces defeated Darint.

Also unless Jetekesh could soothe Navolleth's heartbreak, and end two curses.

Determination flooded the prince of Amantier like an unquenchable fire. Right would win. It *must*.

The gryphons dipped down, down, down, bringing their paws within reach of the tips of trees. The fragrance of sap and the spice of pine needles filled Jetekesh's senses. His boot brushed against a fir tree's crown. Then the gryphons rose again, swooping over a wide, lazy river and past a high mountain caped in thick banks of snow. The rugged terrain gave way to flat, fertile meadows and orchards, and to the south, Jetekesh glimpsed a glimmering city that rose in spires like a scape of cathedrals.

"It's fae," whispered Rille, shifting in front of him. Her eyes were fastened on the faraway sight, like she could see details Jetekesh couldn't. Likely, that was so.

The lead gryphon, carrying Thrissa, slowed until it came level with Jetekesh, and the elven woman gestured toward the city. "We could gather supplies there and treat our wounds, but we'll lose a lot of time. What say you?"

Jetekesh hesitated, glancing toward the city. They could use more food and herbs, but they weren't in dire straits. Sustenance would last, and losing time meant staying out of the fight longer. He shook his head. "We press on."

"As you will."

The gryphons maintained their northeastern flight, and the distant fae city vanished against the red-streaked horizon. The sun sank closer toward the west.

At nightfall, the winged beasts landed along the shores of a vast lake. Jetekesh slid from his mount's back, cringing as his muscles protested. Nearby, the shimmering, ghostly form of Raum wandered into sight. Kajsa raced to the wolf's side with a happy sob.

Jetekesh smiled, then helped Rille down from the gryphon, and they wandered to the bank to admire the glimmering black water under a rising moon.

As fog drifted over the bobbing water, a chill seeped into Jetekesh's limbs. He drew his black cloak tighter and pulled his cowl over his head. Behind him, the clamor of the others setting up camp came dully through the thick fabric.

For a second, he resisted the urge to help set up the bedrolls or light the fire. He knew he must, but his legs were leaden, and his bones ached. Weariness begged him to succumb to old, selfish habits. He shook himself, then started gathering up stones to ring the firepit Emerin dug.

Emerin looked up when Jetekesh dumped the first pile of rocks nearby. "You know, I got that cloak of yours when I was in Shinac before. Kethalas's too."

Jetekesh arched a brow. "I wondered about the strange material."

"I stole them." Emerin went back to digging. "I'd heard they might conceal me from fae, and I tried using them to rescue Saylia. It didn't work. But I'd hoped it might stifle your beacon glow a little."

"It does," Thrissa said, passing by with a handful of chopped vegetables. "At night, you would appear like the sun at noon if not for that cloak. Keep wearing it when you are in the open."

Jetekesh tugged it closer and wandered off for more rocks.

Once the bedrolls were laid, and the fire was crackling, with freshly caught fish roasting on sticks, Jetekesh flopped down in the spring grass and stared into the starry heavens. Nearby, the gryphons splashed in the shallows, catching raw fish for their supper. The noise lulled Jetekesh's mind into that restful stupor between daydreams and sleep. His eyelids grew heavy.

"Cousin?"

His eyes snapped open. "Yes?"

Rille shifted closer, but he didn't look up into her face. Instead, he stared at the stars again, picking out formations he knew among the strange constellations.

"How do you intend to find the rightful ruler of Nakania once we have the water from the blood fountain?"

There it was. That same problem; the one he couldn't solve.

He sighed and shook his head, the scratch of his hair against the grass filling his good ear. "Dunno."

The faint sound of crickets rose between them.

"I see," Rille said at last. "Maybe I'll have a vision."

"I'd definitely welcome that," he mumbled, letting his eyes close again.

Silence. Then, "Will *you* try to drink the water?"

His lips twitched down. "I...don't know."

"Are you frightened?"

"...Yes."

"Ah."

Grass rustled, then Rille's footsteps moved off, heading for the fire and the murmur of conversation. Jetekesh stayed still, determined not to move until supper was officially declared ready.

Cricket song rose higher and the moon tucked beams of light beneath his eyelids. Near the fire, someone laughed—probably Dakarai.

A knot tied in Jetekesh's stomach. He'd almost lost three members of his company. Three friends. Even now, Anenyasha lay upon her bedroll, resting from her wound. Kethalas seemed hale but for his torn wing, and he'd reassured Jetekesh that it would soon mend. But still...

Footsteps crunched close. Someone halted and hovered above Jetekesh. He grimaced. Why was everyone so chatty tonight?

"Can we talk?"

Every muscle in Jetekesh's body tensed. He cracked one eye open, determined to appear nonchalant.

"About what, Axel?" he asked, glad his voice held steady and calm.

"The gryphons say we'll reach the realm of Valliath in two days. After that, we must enter through the gate—no simple task, they say—and then we're on our own trying to find the blood fountain. Do you have a plan, Your Highness?" Axel's pale eyes glinted and he tipped his head in a menacing motion.

Jetekesh heaved out a breath and dragged himself upright. "With Kethalas here, seeking the fountain shouldn't be too hard.

He's confident he can sense it. As for the gate, I don't know what to expect, so no, I have no plan there. If you have suggestions, I'll listen."

The Norvian paused. He crouched down, then sat and crossed his legs before him. "According to the gryphon I rode, we'll be tested at the gate. Only honorable souls can enter."

"Ah, so that's the trick." Jetekesh plucked up blades of grass and tossed them. "We should be fine. None of us are ignoble."

"But can we pass the test?" asked Axel, impatience threading through his voice.

"I should think so if all they seek to prove is that we're honorable."

"Does that include bygone actions?" Axel canted his head. "What of your past misdeeds?"

"My..." Jetekesh stared at him. "Do you mean because I used to be a spoiled, self-centered prig, I'm not worthy *now*?" He rolled his eyes and stared into the shimmering lake. "I suppose by that reasoning we're all doomed. Saints save us from our own shortcomings." He turned back to Axel. "If you came here to pick a fight, allow me to spare us both a little time: I'll not let this conversation escalate. Say what you have to say, and let it be done."

Axel's mouth snapped open, then shut. He sniffed, then looked away, taking his turn to stare at the water. "You've stolen her from me."

Jetekesh's eyebrows shot up. "What?"

"Ky. She's different. You've bewitched her with your *beacon glow.*"

A strange, euphoric mirth swelled in Jetekesh's chest—and he burst out laughing. "Tell me you jest."

Axel flushed, ducking his head. Then he steeled himself and looked up, his eyes like flints. "I said what I said."

"I've done nothing, stolen *nothing*. Kajsa is my friend. She's entitled to more than one, you know. And if she *should* see me as more than that, if you're not just a paranoid fool, that's *her* choice. She's not yours to claim, Axel. She's her own person. And you're an idiot." Jetekesh pushed to his feet, ignoring the dull headache pounding against his skull. He glowered down at the young man. "If you really cared—if you truly understood her—you'd not feel so insecure as you do right now. Whatever strain lies between you, discuss it with Kajsa. It's none of my business."

He strode back to the fire, leaving Axel to examine his words. Heat wafted through Jetekesh's cloak, warming him. He sat on the ground, spread his fingers before the licking flames, and shook his head.

That idiot.

His gaze drifted to Kajsa chatting quietly with Rille. The two laughed at something, then Kajsa's eyes flicked to his. His breath caught, then he smiled. She replied in kind, then turned back to Rille.

Axel was a fool among fools to think anyone could steal Kajsa. She was delicate, yet strong. Clever, kind, and brave. Shy, yes, but full of courage.

Jetekesh lowered his gaze to stare into the fire. He was lucky to know her. To call her friend.

He would never ruin that—that much he could promise himself.

CHAPTER 28
RED EYES

The ghosts sang.

Each night in the Ruin, otherworldly strains drifted through Sharo's camp.

The heartrending, eldritch music was enough to drive a weak man mad. Fortunately, the fae prince's army brimmed with brave and noble souls. Only a dozen had deserted over the past several nights as they crossed the desolate country.

At dusk, two days' travel from the borders of Amantier, Aredel stood at the edge of the encampment, staring northward toward the unseen enemy. He'd never expected to march with fae folk to defend Amantier from invaders. The ironies of his life piled at his feet, intangible monuments to his failures.

Once, he'd half believed himself to be a god.

Scanning the shadowed path before him, Aredel listened to the night's growing whispers. The crackle of bonfires, the distant hammering of the army's smithies, the breath of wind that stirred parched earth up in eddies of black dust—all counterpoints to the ghostly song.

"Aredel." The calm tones belonged to Sharo.

He turned, eyeing the elven prince still clad in silver armor, a shimmering cape bright in the first sprinkle of starlight. Sharo's hair almost glowed, matching the gleam of his kind eyes. At the prince's side, Jinji stood, adorned in his simple homespun apparel, his knowing smile in place.

For a moment, Aredel resisted the pull of their dual serenity. The way they quieted fears and concerns with their very auras. He wanted no comfort. But they persisted, standing there, soaking in the healing stillness of night, the starlight, the cleansing winds, quieting the sorrow of the specters surrounding the camp.

"Do you have a moment?" asked Sharo.

Aredel glanced at the nearby sentries. They were sturdy men, alert and skilled. And somewhere beyond the firelight, Shevek lurked, hoping for enemies to strike so he could take out his restlessness on something.

"I do," Aredel conceded.

Sharo's smile brightened, then he and Jinji turned and led the way toward the eastern side of camp. The odor of iron and smoke thickened, while the ring of hammers filled Aredel's ears. Several soldiers sat near the mobile forges where a dozen blacksmiths repaired armor, horse tack, and other bits of metal.

As Sharo, Jinji, and Aredel approached, one blacksmith raised his head. His long, sleek black hair slithered back, revealing pointed ears. He lowered his hammer, rubbed his hands over his apron, and moved away from the glowing fire of his forge to bow to Sharo.

"Hail, Prince."

"Hail, Eviril."

The blacksmith's dark gaze trailed to Aredel's face. Eviril's eyes caught the firelight and seemed to glow. "It is ready, Your Highness," he said, turning back to Sharo.

"Excellent. Bring it forth."

Eviril turned back to the line of forges and slipped past the closest to grab something from a chest hunched on the ground. He stooped, then straightened, clutching a bundle in his arms. He returned, eyes still blazing with apparent pride.

Sharo took a step forward and accepted the bundle, then turned to Aredel. "I'll hold it while you unwrap it."

Aredel untied the cloth, revealing a gleaming breastplate of red steel. The design was intricate, not quite KryTeeran, not quite Shinacian, but a blending of both. Runes and swirls patterned the sleek, flawless plate.

"'Tis a gift, Aredel," Sharo said. "The light armor I lent you is fair protection, and while you may come close to immortality on the battlefield, my dear friend, I'd much rather secure your future beyond a doubt."

Aredel ran his hand over the polished metal. "It's exquisite."

"The other pieces are finished as well," Eviril said.

"Eviril is the most skilled blacksmith of my acquaintance." Sharo shifted the breastplate. "The armor will assuredly fit. Have no doubt as to that."

It looked as though it would.

Jinji stepped closer. "It is also pure fae steel. Stronger than any forgery you've known, even in KryTeer."

Aredel pried his eyes from the priceless gift. "The pauldrons. Are they—"

"Curved," Eviril said. "Per my prince's instruction. He sketched what your fierce KryTeeran armor looks like, and I took a few cues from Lord Shevek. But I hope you'll allow that I did fashion it to suit Shinac as well as your homeland."

"I do allow it," Aredel murmured, turning back to his study of the breastplate.

Sharo chuckled. "Well. Try it on, my good fellow."

Eviril gestured to the chest. "Everything is there. Allow me to aid you?"

"Thank you." Aredel hefted the breastplate, startled to find it almost weightless, despite how sturdy it felt under his fingers.

At Sharo's invitation, he strode into a nearby tent and stripped off his tunic, then slipped into an aketon provided for him. When he stepped back into the chill night air, Sharo, Jinji, and Eviril closed in like a swarm and dressed Aredel in the fae-forged armor, starting with chainmail that felt as light as the breastplate. The nearby embers cast a red sheen across the ensemble, while the featherlight steel wrapped Aredel in a strange sort of comfortable strength, like a warm cloak on a winter night. Finished, the three men stepped back.

Aredel strapped his sword around his waist, then unsheathed it with a satisfied smile. He sliced his blade across the open air in wide, deliberate strokes. He felt so light. Swift. Faster than he'd ever been in his KryTeeran armor.

Sharo drew a delicate dagger from a sheath strapped to his leg. "Observe." He threw the blade hard, and Aredel resisted his instinct to dodge. The dagger seemed to slow, to lose its thrust, and it bounced off Aredel's gauntlet, harmless.

"The magic will hold under quite a few hits before it must be renewed." Sharo rapped knuckles against his own armor. "Mine usually lasts for a full hour before I start to take damage."

An entire hour of added protection, unburdened by the weight of human steel. A grin stretched across Aredel's face. "This is a kingly gift. I thank you." He inclined his head, then turned to Eviril. "And you, Master Smith."

The elf dipped his head. "I welcomed the challenge. If you'll excuse me, I must return to my work." He glided to the forges and plucked up his hammer.

Sharo moved to claim his discarded dagger while Aredel sheathed his sword.

Jinji retrieved Aredel's tunic, then drifted away from the smoke, drawing the other two men along. Sharo fell into step beside Aredel, still appraising the Blood King's armor in the light from torches surrounding the camp proper.

"Knowing you, you'll still take a lot of damage once we engage the enemy," Sharo said. "Please avail yourself of my forges whenever you need to."

"You're very generous, Your Highness." Aredel fingered his pommel.

"We're allies." Sharo turned his eyes skyward. "I relish the chance to see you in combat once more. You're like a great beast. Not a dragon, but nothing so mundane as a tiger either."

Aredel chuckled. "A tiger is exactly what my people call me."

Sharo laughed with him. "Perhaps you're a gryphon."

The memories of the river where Aredel and Anadin had been forced into a trial flitted over the Blood King's thoughts, dampening his mood. His smile fell. His heart hollowed. His steps faltered.

Jinji turned around, his eyes lit with compassion. He strode close and caught Aredel's arm. "It's all right to grieve."

A shadow swooped from overhead. Aredel snatched Jinji's wrist and flung him aside as the *Unsielie* thrust a glaive at the storyteller. Jinji landed against the ground with a grunt.

Aredel and Sharo drew their blades. The latter sprang high into the air, slashing at the *Unsielie*.

The winged fae twirled away, glaive glinting in the torchlight. Aredel chased after it, blood warming at the prospect of dispatching the foul creature. As he chased the retreating form, a new figure moved in his periphery. He expected a second *Unsielie*, but instead, Shevek peeled away from the shadows like a wraith, still adorned in his bloodred KryTeeran armor.

Together, they raced out of camp and into the open field, dust puffing up from their feet.

"Nice armor," Shevek said.

"A gift," Aredel replied.

The Blood Knight unslung his bow, nocked an arrow, and took aim. "Shall I?"

"Please do." Aredel fell back a step but kept running, fingers tight over his sword.

The arrow struck the *Unsielie* down, but just as Aredel had expected, a half dozen more swooped into view among the stars, glaives angled at the KryTeeran men.

A voice boomed out of the darkness. "Hold!"

The Blood King slowed, then halted, Shevek staying at his side. The *Unsielie* retreated higher into the sky and hovered, still wielding their polearms.

Darkness parted to reveal a man draped in tattered robes, slightly stooped over, while a tall, willowy *Unsielie* walked at his side.

Aredel's heart slammed against his ribs. His blood blazed. Tavassed. The *Unsielie* in charge of Tarradarryn Hold, where Anadin had fallen.

The Blood King set his jaw and willed himself to stand still. Wait. Keep patient.

The stooped man lifted his head, revealing a worn, aged face behind a storm-gray beard. Bright red eyes stared out from that face in vivid contrast to his otherwise faded appearance.

"What do you want, old man?" asked Aredel.

"*You,*" the man said.

The word rolled through Aredel, lifting the fine hairs on his neck. His body locked up, unwilling to move from the plot of ground beneath his feet.

A sort of vapor rose from the old man, stretching like flexible, shimmering moonlight; a mass of substance like the incorporeal cloth of the ghosts that haunted the Ruin. Its movement was slow, laborious, as it stretched high above the tattered man.

Close by, Shevek bit out a curse, seemingly paralyzed, just like Aredel.

The vaporous mass expanded further, then—as though it snapped its bands—it shot at Aredel, swifter than an arrow. He tried to brace. Tried to lift his useless sword. The vapor enveloped him, painting the world like a watery canvas, smothering his lungs, cutting off the flow of air.

A voice boomed in his ears. *Succumb to me.*

Aredel wrestled against an urge to obey that command as he understood: Like *Erisydrel*, this was a demon.

And it had come to consume him.

CHAPTER 29
THE DEMON AND THE BLOOD KING

The vaporous magic tightened its grip on Aredel. Somewhere beyond the muffling substance, shouts rose like a distant storm.

Shevek, likely. Helpless and angry.

Succumb, boomed the voice, reverberating off Aredel's bones.

The Blood King gritted his teeth and stood firm; unwilling to writhe; unwilling to bend.

A roar filled his ears, an ageless fire, tearing at his fae armor, trying to melt it.

Aredel found himself grinning. Had Sharo sensed that a threat loomed this close, to gift him with magicked armor just now? Or had the fae prince merely been lucky?

Luck is no small thing.

Aredel strained against the vapor, his will to fight strengthening, knowing the fae steel protected him from possession, if only for mere moments. Mere moments were often enough.

"I...will...not...yield," he growled.

You will, whispered the voice. *It is your fate. You were made to be a vessel.*

How well Aredel knew what his fate should have been. As he'd witnessed his father's decline under the influence of *Erisyrdel*, his instincts had screamed at him—he'd sensed his fate without ever understanding it.

But Jinji and Sharo had rescued him from that course, and that was why he'd decided to change. Why he'd given up his empire.

To thank them.

To cave now, to succumb to this new demon, would be spitting upon the graves of all the people Aredel had lost up 'til now.

Besides, Aredel elvar Gilioth d'ara KessRa did *not* like to lose.

He reached for the white smoke deep inside his soul.

With a tug, it answered. He let out a scream as the force of power exploded from his body, warming his armor and illuminating his sword.

The light shot upward like a pillar, piercing the cluster of clouds that shrouded starlight.

The vapor retreated, and the body of the old man burst apart like sand.

Tavassed shot into the sky with a hiss, then spread his wings wide and retreated, the other *Unsielie* at his back.

Aredel's instinct yelled at him to follow, but he sank to his knees, trembling under the ceaseless force of his power. What had Navolleth said? Breathe in. He squeezed his eyes shut and inhaled, clasping his sword tight. The power pulled back inside. His body still shook, and his throat burned.

Shevek dropped beside him, the sound of his rapid breaths scratching at Aredel's ears. More distant shouts came from camp, and the thunder of running feet followed.

"My king," said Shevek.

Aredel cracked his eyes open and managed to turn his head to find the Blood Knight's face. The man eyed him with unveiled concern, his features highlighted under the starlit heavens. Torches bobbed close, painting his face orange.

"That was too close," Shevek whispered. "Are you well, my king?"

Aredel managed a dry smile. "No, Shevek. But I'm myself."

"Thank the gods of war for that," breathed the Blood Knight. "I hate that those *Unsielie* cowards escaped though."

"Their leader—the one who stood by the old man—is Tavassed. Him I will kill myself." Aredel tried to stand, but his legs wouldn't budge. "I need your help, Shevek. I cannot rise."

The Blood Knight stood, then hooked his hands under Aredel's arms and hefted him up. At the same moment, another pair of hands slipped around Aredel's back to support him. He turned, expecting Sharo or Jinji.

Navolleth met his gaze, cold and imperious. His golden eyes gleamed under the moon's glow. "Take care," he whispered. "The demon was chased away, his decrepit vessel destroyed, but he endures. Demons do not take kindly to wounds. He will try again and punish you most dearly should he succeed in possessing you."

Aredel scowled. "Let him try."

Sharo came around him, breathing heavily. "Aredel, what happened?"

"A demon ambush. Thankfully, your gifted armor bought me time."

Sharo's eyes widened, catching moonlight, then his face darkened. "Cursed *Unsielie*..." He shook his head, then stepped closer. "Best get you to a bed."

"I'll be well soon. Don't fret over me."

Aredel leaned on Shevek more than Navolleth as they guided him back to camp. Dust puffed up around him, and fae soldiers looked on, their expressions ranging from awe to worry. The Blood King ground his teeth. He hated to look weak, hated to be aided back to his tent. He must harness this power, and soon, or he would never defeat Tavassed.

And that was the one thing he must accomplish.

CHAPTER 30
THE LANGUAGE OF FAIRIES

Jetekesh jolted from sleep, drenched in sweat. He sat upright and stared out across the camp, where the silhouette of Emerin on watch was like a cutout against the glow of dawn. Somewhere, a bird trilled good morning.

Shoving aside his blankets, Jetekesh grabbed up his cloak from the top layer and wrapped it around himself to combat the shivers nibbling at his arms. He stood up and padded to Emerin's side.

The keep lord glanced down at him, offering a grim sort of smile. "Your Highness. You look a little ill."

Jetekesh sucked in a breath. "My dreams were unsettled."

Emerin rubbed his bristled jawbone. "Do you feel they were significant?"

"I..." Jetekesh tried to recall. "Perhaps. Yes, I think so."

"Can you recall what they were?"

The prince blew out a breath. "No, unfortunately. Only what they...*felt* like."

Emerin twisted to eye the bedrolls. "When Lady Thrissa awakens, perhaps you should describe your feelings to her."

"A good idea." Jetekesh drew his cloak tighter around himself. "Why is it getting *colder* as we head north?"

"Legends claim that the southlands used to be hot," Emerin said. "Before the sundering."

That was true. How had Jetekesh forgotten? Had the weather patterns readjusted when the two worlds collided again? Would Tivalt and the other island countries lose their tropical climates and become plagued with snow?

Yet another problem Jetekesh had caused by breaking the seal. He scowled and pinned his eyes on the golden horizon. The sun was peeking over the edge of the world. "Can we leave soon?"

"Yes, Your Highness. Do you want me to wake everyone?"

Jetekesh turned from the dawn glow to seek out the gryphons. They were asleep in a pile like oversized kittens, a little away from the camp. "Yes, please. I feel like we need to hurry. I know we already are—but *more* so."

Emerin moved off to wake the company while Jetekesh turned back to the northeastern horizon. Valliath. They were so close.

AT BREAKFAST, he spoke with Thrissa about his vague dream impression, and she answered that it likely had to do with the war.

"Do not let it burden you, fair prince," she said. "Your truth sigil may tap things far away, but you must bring yourself to let others handle matters beyond your control."

After the meal, the company packed up camp and headed out. Another long, arduous day's flight brought them to a great wood. Thrissa shushed them when they landed among the stately trees.

"Be respectful," said the elven woman. "These ancient souls were born when the world was first forged by the Holy Celes."

Jetekesh eyed the trees, wondering if, like dragons and

gryphons, they could take on human shapes. It seemed a ridiculous notion, but then, so had fairies not so long ago. He turned back to Thrissa. "Are the Holy Celes like Amantieran saints?"

A slight smile lightened her eyes. "Perhaps. Consider it something like a fae religion."

Emerin directed Kethalas and Axel to gather the dead wood around the campsite, then asked Kajsa and Rille to work on supper. Dakarai offered to help Emerin set up the bedrolls while Jetekesh was left to gather stones to make the fire ring. Thrissa helped him after shooing Anenyasha off to rest. The clanswoman faintly scowled, but slumped down beside a tree.

The company was quieter than usual under the hush of the ancient boughs. The gryphons, content to remain in their true forms, fluttered their wings and rummaged, perhaps looking for prey or maybe scenting their surroundings like the feral cats at Rose Palace often did near the kitchens.

As Jetekesh stooped to grasp a large rock, something glimmered in his periphery. He craned his neck. A handful of golden fairy lights bobbed toward him in the gloom of dusk. One fairy landed on the rock, her iridescent wings slowing to a lazy flutter like a butterfly. She folded into a bow, her tiny, pearlescent armor sparkling like diamond dust. Her hair, a sea foam green color, hung down her back in a delicate braid.

"Hail, Marked Prince," the fairy said in a soft, clear voice. "Welcome to the First Wood. We of the legion of Valliath's outer guard welcome you to our land. You shall reach the main gates tomorrow during the noon sun's reign."

"That's good news," Jetekesh said, bowing his head. "I thank you for the welcome and the information."

The fairy smiled. "We would be honored to escort you on the morrow."

"I accept and gladly. Have you any idea where the blood fountain stands beyond those gates?"

"Alas, we do not." The fairy glanced at her fellows hovering above the rock, then turned back to him. "We have not stepped into Valliath since it was sealed. None have. We can take you to the gate but no farther."

"I understand. Thank you."

The fairy dipped into another bow, then flitted from the rock. "Until the morrow, Your Highness." She and her companions zipped away. Jetekesh watched their departure until their faint glow was swallowed in the growing darkness.

Grasping the rock, he hefted it and turned back toward camp. Everyone in the company—except Thrissa—held still, staring at him.

Jetekesh shifted his grip on the rock. "What?"

"You understood them?" asked Emerin.

The prince blinked. "You didn't?"

"The noise was like bells," said Kajsa, the tug of a smile at her lips. "It was beautiful."

"The fairies can communicate with whom they wish," said Thrissa, positioning several of her gathered stones where the firepit had been dug. "Those living here are shy of strangers, having seen so few these past centuries."

"Ah," said Emerin.

Kethalas slipped past the others, his silver eyes twinkling. "What did she say?"

"They wish to escort us to the gates tomorrow." Jetekesh moved forward and dropped the stone beside the others. "I agreed."

"Excellent." Kethalas rubbed his hands together. "A fairy escort is considered good luck."

"We could certainly use that," said Emerin. He turned back to the bedrolls.

Jetekesh ventured off to find a few more stones, and Thrissa joined him.

"You will receive the aid of all light fae, great and small," said the elven woman. "You must merely ask."

"I didn't ask the fairies," he said.

Thrissa shrugged one shoulder. "They are whimsical, and less restricted by magical laws than most fae. Don't assume others will be so bold."

He nodded and plucked up two large rocks. "What can we expect tomorrow, my lady?"

She hefted a large stone and studied it. "Judgment. Those who are deemed unworthy will not be punished, but shall not enter Valliath."

Jetekesh frowned. "But that prince—the one in Jinji's story who escaped his brother's plots and sought out the fae—he entered Valliath, even though he pursued vengeance."

"So he did." Thrissa picked up another stone. "The gates were open then. Now, they are shut." Pain brightened her eyes. "Valliath once dared to believe in the goodness of all men, but those such as that prince and others—like the vile man who took King Ehrikai's mother as his wife—they taught the fae folk not to trust. And many humans since, men like Darint, women like your mother, have fortified that position."

Jetekesh's heart panged. He strode back to the fire and dropped the rocks into the pile with a resounding *clack*. "I struggle with trust myself." He inhaled. "But I find it sad, nonetheless." He knelt and arranged the stones into a ring.

"To be cautious is not a mistake," Thrissa said, setting her stones beside his. She knelt next to him to help finish the fire ring. "To let caution turn to paralyzing fear—that *is* a mistake."

He nodded, his mind flitting over the people he'd come to trust. Emerin had used and betrayed him, yet his reasons had been understandable. "It's hard," he said. "Hard to know when to trust my instincts."

"It takes time and pain." Thrissa rose and dusted her hosen

off. "But fear not, O Prince. There is joy in the journey, too." She moved off to where Kajsa and Rille measured out flour.

Jetekesh pushed the last stone into place and stared at the speckles in its texture. His finger brushed the cool, rough surface. When honor was weighed tomorrow, who would enter Valliath?

Will I pass? Am I honorable at last?

Tomorrow, he would know beyond a doubt whether he could trust the company and himself. Especially himself.

CHAPTER 31

A FAIRY GIFT

Kajsa chased sleep, but finally gave up. She sat near the fire, feeding logs to the flames whenever they threatened to die. A distant howl filled the air, but she was confident only wolves prowled the woods this night. Axel had assured her the *vashalan* wouldn't be a problem anymore.

That was hard to believe after everything, but she chose to trust her friend.

At least, she told herself she did.

Axel meant well. That much was obvious in the fervor in his pale green eyes. The confident timbre of his voice. The awe when he mentioned Navolleth.

Kajsa was far less certain of the future Axel foresaw, and she feared his presence in the company. He kept picking fights, and even his silence came across as sullen and discordant.

He hadn't used to be that way. Had he?

Looking back, she recalled his kindness to her and Ingrid and the way he'd urged her to speak up for herself. He'd hunted for her. Traveled with her to the nearby canton. He'd even kissed her.

Warmth spread across Kajsa's face at the last memory. His strong arms, wrapped around her, fighting off winter's chill.

She dipped her head to stare at her bare fingers. The kiss had been sweet, despite its brevity and his dismissiveness afterward. That had always been the case, too—that flippant, almost mocking attitude. Just part of what made Axel, Axel. So she'd told herself.

As a stray breeze brushed over her, she pulled her blanket closer. Her gaze wandered to the bedroll where Jetekesh slept, tucked deep into his bedding to fend off the midnight chill. A smile caught her mouth, and she wished he'd stir, sit up, and chat with her. Maybe their cozy conversation would lull her into sleepiness.

Outside of camp, Thrissa kept watch. She was too other-worldly and ancient for Kajsa to dare approach when no one else was around. The elf was pleasant enough, but more than a little intimidating, like she could read your soul when she looked at you. Raum sat near Thrissa, content to heed the night music around the encampment.

Rubbing her fingers together, Kajsa turned her thoughts to the coming day. To the gates of Valliath. They were so near. Never in her wildest dreams had she thought she would venture into the very heart of the world and with so many she called friends.

What would the gates look like? How would the lands beyond appear?

Trying to envision the fae realm, Kajsa admitted to herself that she'd never fall asleep. Not with her thoughts so active. She sighed, pulled her blanket closer, and dragged herself to her feet. Surely, she could find a project to work on until morning. Maybe prepare breakfast.

She chewed her lip. Dawn was still hours away.

The tinkle of faint bells twirled Kajsa around. She stared into the woods. There, among the branches of a wide redwood, tiny golden lights bobbed. Kajsa stepped toward them before her mind caught up with her body and she froze.

The lights chimed again.

She inched closer.

One tiny light bobbed away from the boughs, whirling a few times in its approach, and then the tiny thing drew near enough for Kajsa to see its delicate features: a male fairy with wings beating swiftly. He wore pearlescent armor, and his hair was an amethyst shade caught back in a braid.

"Greetings, Kajsa of Norva," he said in a singsong voice. "We have been waiting for you."

She blinked. "For me?"

He nodded. "Ingrid told us of your coming, and we believe you are the right one to select."

She tipped her head to one side, her heart quickening. Ingrid had? "For what?"

The fairy lifted his hands like he proffered a tray, and across his palms, a large bronze key winked into view, its design delicate and etched with swirls. "This will open the gate to Valliath."

She stared at the key sparkling in the fairy's glow. Tentative, she reached for it. "Why give this to me? Jetekesh—"

"He must play his own part," the fairy said. "This key would become a burden to him. You shall be its keeper. Only those whom you deem worthy may enter by the gate and leave by the same."

Kajsa closed her fingers over the cool metal, and as she lifted it up, the fairy vanished. Dawn rimmed the world. She blinked and lifted her head. Camp was stirring behind her, and she spun to find Thrissa at the blazing fire, her eyes intent as she studied Kajsa. The elf smiled, then turned away.

How had time flown so swiftly?

Kajsa pocketed the key. She drifted toward the campfire, and its warmth reached for her like invisible fingers, welcoming. She sat upon her bedroll and turned the fairy's words over and over in her mind.

Only those she deemed worthy could enter Valliath.

Emerin climbed from his bedroll and greeted Thrissa with questions about the watch. The keep lord had betrayed them in the swamps, but his reasons had been understandable. Surely, he was worthy to enter Valliath.

What of Axel, sworn to Navolleth? Could he be trusted to enter the true fae lands?

The others, she didn't question. Not at all. Each had proven to be above reproach.

Her hand slipped into her tunic pocket, and Kajsa fingered the heavy key. Should she tell Jetekesh about it—ask for his advice? Or would that be an added burden to him as the fairies believed?

Axel was still bundled in his bedroll, fast asleep. Once, she'd have gone to him and explained, but not anymore. She couldn't. He would sway her to give him the key...and she might listen.

Kajsa pinched her eyes shut and drew deep breaths.

Think this through.

She still had time. They weren't at the gate yet. She should use this period to deliberate on everyone's passage into Valliath, rather than try to foist her decision onto someone else. This was her task.

As Dakarai took his turn preparing breakfast, Kajsa tended to Anenyasha's shoulder, while Raum looked on. Her fingers worked mechanically, cleansing and wrapping the wound in fresh bandages, while she kept one eye on Emerin.

She had nothing but compassion for his plight—for his tireless efforts to save his sister. But he had still caused the deaths of many and forced Jetekesh into an action he could never unmake.

What if the keep lord was still under the control of the *Unsielie*? What if he'd lied...

Stop it. She tightened her fingers over the bandage knot, and Anenyasha hissed.

She released the bandage. "S-sorry."

Anenyasha shook her head. "I am well. You seem distracted."

Tears gathered in Kajsa's eyes, and she bowed her head to hide them. "I didn't sleep well, that's all."

The clanswoman caught her hand and squeezed her fingers. "Whatever is bothering you, you will sort it. You are strong."

A tear escaped Kajsa's eye and dropped onto Anenyasha's hand, but the clanswoman didn't flinch. She squeezed the girl's fingers again, then let go and pulled her colorful layered clothes back over her shoulder, hiding the bandages. "Thank you." The woman rose and moved off to help Dakarai at the fire.

As Kajsa tracked the woman's movements, her hand absently slipped into her pocket. Her fingers curled around the key.

Footsteps crunched close, and she wrenched her hand from the pocket like the key had singed her. She found Axel smiling down at her, his pale hair mussed from sleep, a dazed look in his seafoam eyes.

"Good morning, Xel," she said, trying to conquer the faint tremble in her voice.

He flopped down on her bedroll and rested his head against her shoulder. She tensed. "Morning," he mumbled. "Snowy gods above, why do we have to leave so early?"

Kajsa's cheeks burned like a bonfire. "B-because...we n-need to find the blood fountain soon."

"Why all the hurry?" He shifted his head but remained propped against her shoulder. "The war is leagues away. We'll never return in time to stop it. That's what Navolleth said."

Kajsa scowled. "Then why did he send you?"

"Because he needed someone he trusts to find the waters of truth and make certain the rightful king sits on the throne of Nakania." He lifted his head, the sleepiness gone from his eyes. "Kajsa, you know what all this means, don't you? Valliath will be opened again soon. The true king of the fae will return. We need a strong high king to represent the magicless, to keep things balanced. Navolleth agrees. He wants to prevent another Tallat from rising and destroying what's honorable."

Kajsa resisted an impulse to finger the key again. "That makes sense, Xel. But Jetekesh is an honorable prince, and his father sounds like a noble-hearted man. Nakania is in good hands. We don't need war, and we don't need to seek a new ruler. We only need the fountain to break the curse upon Nakania."

Axel sighed. "You're too trusting, Ky."

"Me?"

"Yes, you. You believe all people are good, even if they scare you. That's not how life goes, Kajsa. People are greedy, and power corrupts them. We need a proper ruler. Someone who knows what struggle is and how to protect the poor. Someone who can unite all the countries of Nakania."

Kajsa's gaze traveled across the fire. Jetekesh was up and laughing with Emerin and Dakarai while Anenyasha rolled her eyes. Nearby, Rille stirred the pot, stifling a smile, while Kethalas brushed off his hands, like he'd added something suspect to the roiling pot.

"Jetekesh can do all that," she said, pleased that her voice sounded as certain as she felt. "Look, Xel. The only major country of Nakania you don't see here is Shing, and we've allies there too —thanks to the prince of Amantier. He's the rightful king." When she turned back to Axel, she shrank back. His dark expression struck her like a physical blow.

"You're so blind," he whispered, shaking his head. "Navolleth was right. You've been bespelled. Don't worry, Ky. I'll free you of the Marked Prince's chains."

"I'm not—"

Axel stood up and stomped away.

Kajsa's heart pounded in her chest, and her ears burned. She dipped her head and the weight of the key seemed to grow in her pocket.

CHAPTER 32
A CHANGE OF PLAN

At dusk, Tavassed limped into King Darint's camp, clutching something in his hand.

From where he stood surveying maps, Darint eyed the *Unsielie* in the guttering firelight, one part curious, one part annoyed. The fae creature had left the war camp on the cusp of their invasion of Amantier, never saying a word. Now he'd returned, one lacy wing ripped and sporting a twisted ankle.

Resisting the snide comment that hung on his tongue, Darint instead donned a friendly grin as Tavassed rounded his campfire. "Do you need a healer?"

Tavassed shook his head. "No, Your Majesty. I am well enough, and I bring news." He stood straight, a portrait of regality and stoicism despite his damaged wing. "Firstly, we located Prince Jetekesh, but he summoned gryphons and chased off the *Unsielie* sent to capture him. He aims for Valliath."

Darint tensed, fear lancing through him. "For what reason?"

"I suspect he seeks the waters of truth at the blood fountain."

The king's eyes narrowed. "Does he indeed? So, the fool boy intends to find a contender for the throne."

"It would seem so. Should he succeed, your cause will be in shambles."

There was no need to state that. Darint let his annoyance fade before he spoke again. "And did gryphons rip your wing?"

"No, this is the doing of King Aredel. He fended off my... champion."

Darint's brow ticked up. "What does that mean?"

Tavassed lifted his hand and slightly uncurled his fingers to reveal a pulsing red light hovering above his palm. The very sight set Darint's teeth on edge.

"A demon, Your Majesty." Tavassed spoke above Darint's sputtered curse. "Fear not! I did not intend to attach it to you. The demon was willing to possess Aredel and consume him."

Darint took a step back. "Did you really trust a demon to fulfill his bargain? You might've given Aredel all the strength he needed to slaughter us."

"Not so," Tavassed said. "The demon cannot lie to a fae, only to humans. He would be true to our deal. But Aredel wounded him." The fae tightened his fist over the red glow. "The Blood King grows stronger. We are running out of time and options."

Darint folded his arms and fastened his gaze on the fire sparking and guttering in the growing darkness around him. The scent of burning pine filled his senses, sweet and spicy. "There must be a way. Something..." His mind caught on the demon, wounded, but still useful.

Don't. It will be your end. You're smarter than that, Darint.

He paced away from the *Unsielie.* The Marked Prince sought the blood fountain, and the Blood King tracked Darint's forces to Amantier. As far away as they were, Darint could still raze villages and towns, but eventually, Sharo's forces would catch up, and the true slaughter would commence.

Darint needed the upper hand. The dragons would no doubt side with the *Sielie* and all the other revolting fae creatures.

I need Aredel on my side.

It was the clearest path to victory. But how? Not through a demon...

His mind settled on a shadowy thought. Disturbing, but feasible.

"Tavassed."

"Yes, King Darint?"

He turned to the *Unsielie*. "Do you know how to contact a necromancer?"

The stoic fae before him fell still, utterly so, then a cruel smile stretched across Tavassed's face, revealing needle-sharp teeth. "Yes. Indeed, I do."

CHAPTER 33
THE KING'S COURT

The barge bumped up against the dock. Yeshton sprang over the side, too eager to wait for the gangplank. He tossed a coin to the dockmaster, while Ledonn and the three elves crossed the ramp, leading their horses behind them.

On the dock, Yeshton mounted his stallion. His companions shortly followed suit.

They rode hard from the river harbor of Kavacos, northward, toward Rose Palace. The sandstone structure stretched into the bright blue sky, a symbol of peace against the flames of approaching war.

The din of merchants; the odors of flourishing flowerbeds, food stalls, and horse manure; the milling crowds among the well-tended cobblestone streets, all fell away as Yeshton raced the wind for the palace gates. They arrived to the blast of horns announcing their coming, and King Jetekesh met Yeshton in the manicured courtyard.

"I received your pigeon, Sir Yeshton." The king's blue eyes flitted from face to face, lingering a heartbeat longer on the three armored elves. He motioned inside. "I presume you warned Lord Milgar at Keep Falcon about the impending attack."

"Yes, sire," Yeshton said. "Though he was already quite prepared for invasion." The old man always was, as he'd long believed fairies would invade from the desert. Perhaps Milgar wasn't the declining fool everyone thought him to be.

As they moved inside the palace, Yeshton took his place at King Jetekesh's back. From the high rafters, banners toting the Crowned Rose—Amantier's crest—fluttered in a draft from the open door. Guards saluted the king's passage.

Tapestries lined the wide-set walls of the hall, depicting the various heroic acts of past saints. The golden hair of Saint Vashi snagged Yeshton's attention, and he took in her glowing visage, haloed in fine stitching, as he pressed on. The image imprinted on his mind, conjuring up what little he knew of King Cavalin's sister. No one spoke ill of her.

But then, who would dare speak ill of any saint and risk the church's wrath?

He checked himself, scowling as he scrubbed out his heretical thought. He didn't doubt the faith of his country—but the coming battle darkened his hopes of divine aid.

The king entered the throne room whose stained-glass windows painted bright rainbows in the midafternoon light. The room was filled with courtiers and a dozen or more armored men, most of whom Yeshton recognized as high-ranking military leaders.

King Jetekesh had taken his warning seriously—and had convinced others to at least listen.

"Stand before us and report," the king said, motioning to the space in front of his throne. The monarch stepped onto his dais and claimed his seat as the first murmurs broke out. The crowd stared at the three elves with their pointed ears, long sleek hair, and foreign armor. Ledonn got his own share of the attention and more than a few glowers. Prejudice dies slowly.

"Thank you, sire." Yeshton raised his voice to cut through the din. "The long and short of it is that the fae kingdom of Shinac has returned."

The murmurs broke into cries and gasps, some excited, others skeptical, despite the fae evidence before their eyes. Dejani and his two compatriots turned to survey the room, armor glinting in the sunlight. The voices faded. Most of them.

One voice warbled high. "Saints preserve us!"

"They will," King Jetekesh said, a mild smile on his lips. "Thank you for that prayer, Lord Huith."

Grins flashed among the nobility.

"Proceed, Sir Yeshton," the king said.

Yeshton clasped his hands behind his back, keeping his feet wide apart. "While the majority of the fae kingdom wishes for peace, a dissident army of dark fae and monsters—*Unsielie*, goblins, harpies, and other unsavory souls—marches upon Southern Amantier even now. It's possible Keep Falcon has already fallen under attack by an advance force."

Silence filled the throne room. Someone coughed.

"How many?" asked the king, though he already knew from the messenger pigeon.

"We estimate the main enemy force to be six hundred thousand, with an advance force of goblins approaching three thousand on its own."

The quiet broke as voices communed with each other, heads leaning close, feathered caps bobbing.

An armored knight strode forward, the silver in his beard catching the light. Yeshton recognized Sir Tarrid from his knighting ceremony on the heels of the KryTeeran incident last year. Tarrid was a somber fellow, hard to approach, but a lion on the battlefield.

"Sir Yeshton," the knight said, inclining his head. "I believe only the foolhardiest folk in this chamber will doubt you, considering your companions, but I would ask you to bear with us as we absorb our new reality. You speak of goblins, harpies, and dark fae as though they were commonplace—and perhaps you've seen enough to accept that. The rest of us—well, the last goblin I encountered was under my sister's bed when I was nine."

A ripple of laughter cascaded over the room. Yeshton blinked. Had Sir Tarrid really jested?

He let his mouth curve up. "What's your point, Sir Tarrid?"

The man's eyes bored into Yeshton, all seriousness. "Describe them, please. We know of goblins only as myths, as childish nightmares. We must take them seriously. What are we in for, Sir Yeshton?"

No, the man hadn't been in jest. Not Sir Tarrid.

"I've seen them from afar," Yeshton said, "and I'm not eloquent in speech, but I'll try." He paused to let the horrible images of the goblins bleed into his mind, but Dejani stepped forward and brushed fingers against Yeshton's arm.

"I will tell them."

Relief cooled Yeshton's nerves. He nodded and allowed the elf to take his place. Every eye was riveted as the fae warrior spoke in carrying tones tinged with a faint accent. His descriptions, while not spellbinding like Jinji's stories, nevertheless painted a clear, foul image of the lean, short, gray brutes with their bald heads, red eyes, and wrinkled flesh. Dejani's voice was a poet's, his words articulate and fluid. Once he'd properly painted the goblins, he moved to blue-feathered harpies, then last, to the *Unsielie* with their gauzy wings, sleek darkness, and otherworldly beauty.

Chills tracked up Yeshton's arms. He'd first encountered the *Unsielie* in KryTeer. He didn't relish meeting them again. Their ways were hypnotic, and Yeshton wasn't certain he could fend them off in a one-on-one fight.

Once Dejani finished, he stepped back, leaving an echoing silence.

King Jetekesh shifted and leaned forward. "As we hold council, my knights are gathering from across Amantier. Since the fight will not be in Shing and our enemy is no longer coming from the Snow Wastes, let us turn our attention south to meet King Darint and his army of horrors. As in the days of Cavalin the Third, we fight against evil itself. Let no man here turn from the honorable path."

The assembled knights fell to their knees, and Yeshton mirrored them. A thrill raced over him, stronger than his chills. War. He'd dreaded it, and the prospect brought death, yet his desire to prove himself in combat, to fight for king and country, dampened the fear nipping at his bones like hounds on the hunt.

For King Jetekesh, for Rille, for Nakania, and for the free lands of Shinac, he would fight.

CHAPTER 34
BEYOND THE MISTS

The gate to Valliath gleamed like alabaster stone.

From atop his gryphon mount, Jetekesh stared down at the intricate, twining arch that rose before a land shrouded in mist. The sun had passed its zenith and tipped toward the western horizon, but for all its rays, the mist remained undaunted.

Following the trail of tiny fairy lights that made up their escort, Jetekesh's gryphon descended, feathered wings shining like molten gold. Rille caught Jetekesh's wrists, unwilling to trust her fate to the magical beast alone. The other gryphons swooped down on the same air current, aiming for the arch, which seemed to stretch taller during the rapid approach.

Touching down on an ancient highway with a gentle bump, Jetekesh slid from the gryphon's back, then offered his hand to Rille. She accepted it with a grimace and slid down too, using her free fingers to brush back her windblown hair.

Together, they turned to the looming archway where their fairy escort hovered. Raum stepped from the trees near the entrance.

"Welcome to the Way of Valliath, travelers." The tiny, bell-like voice belonged to the female fairy Jetekesh had spoken with before. "We leave you now to face your fate."

Without awaiting a reply, the fairy escort vanished.

No solid gate barred the way, only undulating threads of mist hovering beyond the arch. The alabaster stone shone with its own light, revealing veins of white against an almost translucent exterior carved into delicate vine-like cords. The cords weaved around themselves, twisting upward into a fine curve where an enormous diamond winked in the bright sunshine.

"It's exquisite," Rille breathed.

"It is." Jetekesh lowered his stare to the mists. "Do we just pass through?"

"No," said Kethalas from where he still sat on his gryphon. "Those mists are death to trespassers. We must first pass the trial."

Axel helped Kajsa from her gryphon, then the young man frowned at the archway. "It feels...wrong."

For once, Jetekesh agreed with the Norvian intruder. His lips tightened and he turned back to the archway. "Do we hail someone?"

Thrissa moved toward the arch. "It will respond to our approach."

Of course, the elven woman would know what to do. She positioned herself mere feet from the entrance while the others followed her lead. As they neared, the ground beneath Jetekesh quaked. Pebbles skittered around his boots. Rille stumbled toward him but caught herself.

The mists shifted, undulating faster, and the alabaster stone glowed brighter.

Thrissa turned to face them, her strange silvery eyes dancing with an otherworldly light. "You have reached Valliath, weary travelers, and now you must choose who shall enter the realm of the True King. Keeper of the Key, step forth."

The mists curled around Thrissa as the company fell into stunned silence.

Someone drew a long breath, then stepped forward. Kajsa. In her hand, she clutched something tight enough to whiten her knuckles. Dakarai gave a low whistle.

"Present thyself," said Thrissa.

Kajsa held out her palm, and Jetekesh glimpsed a bronze key. She tipped it forward for Thrissa's inspection. "I..." Kajsa's voice caught, and she cleared her throat. "I...am Kajsa of Norva, and I present this key."

Thrissa smiled warmly. "As the one found most worthy of Valliath's paths, you have been chosen to wield this key and grant entrance to all whom thou doth trust. Who dost thou elect to enter with thee?"

Kajsa trembled. Jetekesh almost moved forward to steady her, but his feet stayed stuck in place.

Silence whispered around the company.

"All," Kajsa said after a long moment. "I choose to trust all."

Did Thrissa's smile deepen? "Bring the key hither."

Kajsa strode ahead. The mists writhed around her, and the key began to hum and then to glow like a torch. The swirling vapor parted in response. Ahead, a path opened between the archway, sunlit despite the roiling mists.

Thrissa caught Jetekesh's gaze. "Enter Valliath, Marked Prince. Behold the hidden realm. Seek out the blood fountain."

He swallowed. "Aren't you coming?"

Thrissa shook her head. "I shall never set foot in the elder realm again until the True King returns at last to claim his throne."

Dakarai rested a hand on Jetekesh's shoulder. "Then we will meet you here after we've found the fountain, my lady."

The elf shook her head. "Our journey together ends here. I shall ride on the back of my gryphon friend and return to my son. I'm needed there now. Farewell." She moved toward her gryphon mount, leapt onto its back in a graceful bound, and caught the creature's mane. "May the king of Valliath attend your steps. Let us go, my friend."

The gryphon bounded into the air, leaving the rest of the fae beasts behind. Once Thrissa and her ride winged out of sight, Jetekesh turned his sights to Valliath and stepped under the archway.

A tendril of mist stroked his cheek. His companions and the gryphons stood at his back, while ahead, on the path, stood Kajsa. She watched him, waiting.

He pressed a smile onto his face. "Well, we're on our own now."

As he spoke, the last of the mists burned away, and he stared up the path toward the distant spires of the castle he'd seen before in Jinji's stories. The Hold of Valliath.

They'd made it.

CHAPTER 35
WITHIN THE REALM

The pathway was lined with trees whose bark glowed white. Round leaves clacked in the wind, reminiscent of an aspen grove, but these were golden, veined with brilliant silver.

Jetekesh took his place at the fore of the company, with Emerin on one side, Rille on the other. The rest followed close. Even the path wasn't the usual dirt or cobblestone one might expect—but then, what within the heart of Shinac did Jetekesh expect to be normal? The smooth stone beneath his boots glittered like granite, and it spread before him in a seamless slab—no notches or blocks, no chips or scuffs, flawless and glinting.

On either side of them, beyond the treelines, hills rolled across the fae countryside, dotted with trees and berry bushes. The grass was covered with meadow flowers, and birdsong poured in from all around. Bees darted past, and three large butterflies danced around a stand of bright pink flowers near the pathway. The fragrance of summer swept over the company, floral with hints of honey.

Jetekesh unlatched his cloak and draped it over one arm,

letting a warm breeze brush fingers over his leather armor. He yearned for a bath. His last had been in the lake two days ago, and that water had nearly frozen him through. He scanned the hills for any hint of a stream or pond.

"Look." Kethalas stabbed a clawed finger at the sky, and the company craned their heads.

Glimmering above, swan-like birds—strangely alien—glided over the air. The gryphons shuffled, perhaps hungry, but none pranced into the sky after the fowls. The birds' wings flashed like crushed diamonds.

"What are they?" Jetekesh asked.

"Royals, they're called," Kethalas said. "Good omens and rare even in Valliath's golden age."

Jetekesh's heart swelled. He could use all the good omens he could find.

As the company continued up the path, Jetekesh glanced back to find Kajsa and Axel almost at the rear of the line. Only Dakarai hung further back, his spear at the ready. Axel was speaking at Kajsa in low, agitated tones, his hands jerking to emphasize whatever point he was making. Kajsa's head was lowered, and Jetekesh wondered if she was crying.

"You should go back there," said Rille. "I think he's chastising her."

Jetekesh bristled. He pivoted and stalked toward them, fire searing his veins.

Axel looked up and scowled. "What is it, *Your Highness*?"

Kajsa's head shot up, and the color bled from her cheeks. Her eyes were red-rimmed, but her cheeks were dry. "Is something wrong?"

"Yes." Jetekesh reached out his hand. "It dawned on me; you shouldn't be back here. Please join me at the front, Kajsa. You're the Keeper of the Key and have every right to lead us to the castle."

Her mouth gaped and she blinked several times.

Jetekesh let his smile warm, fondness rolling through him, as welcome as the summer breeze. He kept his hand extended, waiting.

She slowly, very slowly, reached out and rested her slender fingers on his palm. He curled his hand around hers and tugged. Kajsa followed him, keeping her eyes fastened on his face. He glanced ahead only often enough to keep his feet until they reached Rille and Emerin.

Rille caught Kajsa's other hand and kept it, swinging their arms together as the company moved on again.

Jetekesh started to slip his fingers free, but Kajsa twisted her hand and caught his, never looking at him. She stared ahead, her cheeks red, a faint smile illuminating her eyes.

Jetekesh clutched her fingers and tried to relax despite his pounding heart. He turned his sights on the far-off castle spires sparkling in the bright sun. The walk was at least two hours more, and he knew they could ride gryphons to speed up their progress, yet the urgency he should feel had melted away. He found himself wanting to absorb the subtle magic of Valliath instead.

It was a quiet thing, layered under the beautiful scenery; a soundless music that thrummed within Jetekesh, like the very air caressed his soul to heal it bit by bit. His steps grew lighter, softer, and the last dregs of his tension bled away. Kajsa's hand in his felt natural, *right*.

Did the others feel this same healing glow?

He glanced at Kajsa and found her staring at him, her lips parted. "You're radiant." Her voice was a faint whisper.

He blinked, yet the word resonated. He *felt* radiant, like he fit into his skin as he never had before. He stood taller, straighter. His hair stirred around his face. It was a truer shade of gold. He was more aware of the leather of his clothing, and while it was stiff, it didn't agitate his skin.

"I feel strange," said Rille dreamily, then her step faltered as she glanced at him. Her jaw dropped. "*Cousin.*" Disbelief and awe curled over her voice.

Jetekesh halted. "What is it?"

"It's you," Emerin said, the same awe in his eyes. It also toned in his aura.

Jetekesh reached his free hand up to touch his cheek. Did he look so changed? The others appeared, perhaps, brighter, but nothing had altered in their visages. They were virtually as they'd been all along—except he could almost, not quite but nearly, read their emotions. It was like that moment when he'd first entered Shinac to join Jinji and Aredel, to meet Sharo and defeat the dread lord Peresen. At that time, his senses had opened up, giving him insight into others. Nothing intrusive, more instinctive.

This was the same—only deeper and higher and all around him.

The world's song enveloped his senses, stretching them.

"What is this?" asked Dakarai, coming forward. Behind him, Axel's scowl had darkened.

Jetekesh tore his gaze from the Norvian to meet Dakarai's wondering stare. The clansman shone like the rest, and Jetekesh read his kind, open heart, and deep, fresh pain beneath. Grief for those of his clan whom he'd lost. And deeper still, an eagerness to be of help and bring peace to the world.

"You're as noble as they come, Dakarai," Jetekesh found himself saying. He turned toward Anenyasha, reading her fierce devotion and fathomless courage; Emerin, with his broken heart and thirst to restore his honor—to prove his loyalty; Kajsa, timid yet strong, with a heart as sweet as a dove; Rille, bold and true to her course; Kethalas, clever and fearless, with a warm, giving soul.

Last, Jetekesh set his eyes on Axel. He read ambition, frustration—but also loyalty to his cause and affection for Kajsa. Conflict, guilt, and something like kindness.

Turning back to the castle, Jetekesh moved up the path, warring with himself as he pulled Kajsa and Rille along. He'd wanted to assume Axel was entirely bad, that he was merely Navolleth's weapon, then Jetekesh could dislike him outright and feel justified.

He should've known better. No one was strictly one hue.

Besides, Kajsa wouldn't care so deeply for someone who didn't have redeeming qualities.

Then can I trust him not to sabotage me after all?

That felt foolish too. He must keep his guard up, even if Kajsa had let Axel into Valliath. Worthiness in the now didn't prevent a poor choice in the future. Jetekesh couldn't afford more mistakes.

The Hold of Valliath drew closer as the hour passed away. The castle rose upon a tall hill, just as Jinji's stories had painted. Pure white walls stood smooth and straight, veined with gold, sparkling with crushed glass and diamond. A meandering path weaved up the hillside among tall, full trees crowned in the greens of summer.

Another hour might see them to the summit. Jetekesh approached the hill, his steps still light and tireless. He maintained his hold on Kajsa, unwilling to break their connection. The others followed, Rille keeping her grip on the Norvian girl as well.

The gryphons let out a roar and pounced into the air, their talons curling, their wide, strong wings glittering. They swooped toward the castle, letting out more cries—but they sounded excited, not terrifying. Jetekesh's heart panged for them. How long had the fae creatures of Shinac yearned to behold this hidden realm?

Today, at last, Valliath didn't stand empty.

The path sloped up. Nearly there. He was almost at the castle where the True King had spent his childhood. Where an ugly girl blessed by a willow fairy had become queen, and Shinac had transformed into a kingdom of magic. Where the fae and fantastic would one day bend the knee to their rightful ruler.

He rubbed his damp palm against his leg while sweat trickled down his neck. Soon.

Soon.

He eyed the distant spires, taking one step at a time.

What would he find in the castle? Would the blood fountain be near?

"Halt!" The voice tore across the air, freezing the company in place. From the trees along the path ahead stepped a handful of elves wielding bows. Arrows aimed at the company. Platinum armor winked under the sunlight. "Humans are not permitted here," said the leader in cold tones. "Turn back, or we will end your lives where you stand."

CHAPTER 36
THE CHASE

Keep Falcon had fallen.

Smoke rose from the shattered stones, scarring the sky, while embers danced upon a chill wind. Aredel scanned the carnage. Mostly human, though goblins and a few harpies littered the field. The polluted water of Lily River had turned pink in the aftermath of battle.

The acrid air carried the scent of charred flesh mingled with rot.

Sharo picked his way ahead of the army, his jaw set, his mouth a grim line. His blue eyes were dim with grief as he stooped to inspect a corpse, scaring off a nearby crow.

"Only a day old," he said, rising. "We're catching up."

So they were, though at a great price. The army had marched day and night without rest after Tavassed's attack against Aredel. The Blood King had agreed with Sharo's decision, more determined than ever to stand against the enemy.

The army had begun to flag until the scouts noticed the billowing smoke. Now every eye followed the path of destruction that led from the keep toward the village where smoke was streaming off the buildings. Beyond the village, the forest was a dark shadow.

Aredel's stallion tossed its head and nickered. The Blood King wound his hand tighter around his horse's reins to keep the charger still. "Easy. We'll be underway momentarily."

Sharo returned to Amaranth and swung into the stallion's saddle. "Let's go. Double-time!"

The forces poured out of the fortress's bones, headed north, toward Darint's army.

As they moved out, the crows circled overhead, then dove to carry on their morbid work of picking the dead clean.

CHAPTER 37
THE HOLD

Jetekesh stepped ahead of Kajsa and Rille to address the elven contingent. His hand slipped free of Kajsa's fingers to grasp his sword. "We've come at the request of Prince Sharo of the Blood of the Wood, and his mother, Lady Thrissa of the True King's line."

The elves stared at him. Several shifted, and one lowered her bow.

The leader took a step forward, his eyes narrowed. "I will not be fooled a second time by human scum, boy. I've warned you once."

Jetekesh lifted his chin. "In the name of Ehrikai, King of Valliath, I command you to stand down."

The bow slipped from the elf's fingers and fell with a clatter to the stone path.

Kethalas pushed to the fore of the company, and the elves' eyes widened more. "We've come in search of the blood fountain."

Leaves fluttered in the trees while the elves stood motionless. One elf padded forward, as ageless as the rest, with white hair and piercing eyes of midnight blue. He wore shimmering clothes, similar to Thrissa's wardrobe.

"I am of Valliath's royal line," the elf said. "Be welcome, Marked Prince. I have been expecting you for many years."

Rille gasped. "He's a seer."

Jetekesh wrenched his eyes from the elf to his cousin. "You can tell?"

"I...I can *feel* it." Her hand rested against her chest. "Like an echo."

Jetekesh turned back to the elf who wore a smile as he considered Rille.

"I have seen you in my visions, young seer," the elf said. "I am called Heyethir."

The elves glided to either side of the path, giving passage to the company. The suspicious glowers had fallen from their faces, and most wore soft, curious smiles as they studied the company with new interest.

Heyethir motioned up the path. "Please, allow us to escort you to the Hold."

Jetekesh started forward, then glanced back and met Kajsa's eyes. "Come along." He offered his hand. She took it. They walked up the hillside together.

The honey-scented air stirred around Jetekesh's face as he let his gaze rest on the spires atop the hill. Each step brought him closer. He found himself walking faster.

A question nudged to the fore of his mind. "Lord Heyethir?"

The elf glanced over his shoulder. "Yes, Marked Prince?"

"Jetekesh, please. Do you know where the blood fountain is?"

The elf's lips curved in a sly smile. "Soon, Prince Jetekesh. Let us reach the Hold first."

The last stretch of the hill was steep, yet Jetekesh still didn't tire, as though the land itself breathed energy into his frame. He welcomed it, relieved that he wasn't weary or cold—or even hungry. It was as though Valliath suspended him in a moment of full vitality, and were he to remain here, he too would become ageless.

The idea wasn't impossible, after all he'd seen.

The wending path straightened for the last several hundred paces, giving Jetekesh a full view of the gleaming castle. Jinji's stories had painted a marvelous picture, yet even he hadn't been able to offer this Hold full justice. It was exquisite. Seamless, as though no mortal hand had fashioned the castle. It had simply been magicked into being, whole and flawless. Perhaps that was so.

"I could die this moment," breathed Kethalas. "I'll see nothing greater than Valliath."

"That may be true, Lord Dragon," Heyethir said, a laugh in his voice. "Yet you are young by dragon standards, and the universe is vaster than you know. There may be other places, older or newer, that steal your heart away."

"Nay," said the dragon. "My heart belongs to Valliath from this moment, forever."

Kethalas's words resonated within Jetekesh's soul, like a sweet note of music. He said nothing, but his fingers tightened over Kajsa's, suspecting she would understand his feelings. She squeezed back.

The Hold of Valliath was enormous, standing open and undefended, despite its name. No outer walls blocked the grandeur of the castle proper. A crystal drawbridge spread across a wide, clean moat, beckoning one and all to enter.

Heyethir strode across the delicate bridge, his elf companions following. Jetekesh paused before it and gazed down into the clear water below. Golden fish darted to and fro beneath the surface, causing ripples to cascade to the shore. Valliath stood unravaged by time, by war, by travail.

He drew his gaze from the moat. "Do any others still dwell in Valliath beyond your company?"

Heyethir shook his head. "We are the last. We chose to remain here and protect the realm. All else withdrew before the seal was invoked." His midnight eyes skimmed his companions. "We were thrice this many in the beginning, but many have since chosen to give up their immortality and move on through the Veil."

Jetekesh tilted his head. "Veil?"

"The Afterlife, perhaps, is a better word in your tongue." Heyethir gestured to the grand doors behind him. They were crafted of alabaster and glowed like starlight in the shadow of the entryway. "Shall we enter, Your Highness?"

Jetekesh set one foot on the drawbridge and found it sturdy despite how thin it looked. He crossed, keeping his hold on Kajsa, who in turn kept her hold on Rille. The rest in the company followed as Heyethir and another elf pushed the castle doors inward, revealing a stately chamber five times the size of the Rose Palace throne room in Kavacos.

Marble and alabaster stone made up much of the room. Furniture carved from silver wood dotted the grand scape. Chandeliers of delicate crystal shone with flickering lights made of something other than fire, blazing as though they would never go out. Tapestries of threaded gold and silver depicted the royal line of Valliath, including a childhood portrait of the True King before he was taken by darkness. Those pale blue eyes seemed to watch the company as they passed.

The chamber whispered of a distant past, longer by far than Jetekesh could account for.

"Valliath stepped out of time," Heyethir said, striding across the chamber. "We were caught between two enemies. One such enemy came from beyond the Veil, and we hid away lest we be crushed." The elf turned to meet Jetekesh's eyes. "Even Nakania has been suspended, hidden from the timeline of Mithrinn."

Jetekesh frowned. "Mithrinn?"

"The universe has a name, just as we do." Heyethir turned his eyes toward the ceiling, a dome made up of runes that hummed with power. The elf continued. "Some beyond the Veil wished to eradicate this world, fearing our strength and influence. And so, one Celes came who had the power to shroud us. Alas, the shroud has fallen. Nakania and Shinac stand like beacons, bearing the mark of Valliath." He found Jetekesh's gaze again. "We must gain balance between our two lands. We must silence the cry of this world before they notice. Your light, O Prince, serves a great purpose, but it cannot remain so bright, or all foul things will descend upon us from beyond the stars."

Jetekesh shuddered. "That's why I've come. To find the blood fountain and end the curse. By so do, perhaps the beacon light will dim. I—I think that's my calling."

"So it may be." Heyethir turned and pointed to the far wall where a door stood. "Step beyond this chamber, and keep to the straight passage until you reach the garden. There, peer into the southern valley, and see what you will see."

The prince's heart skipped a beat. So close as that? "I thank you, Heyethir."

The elf dipped his head. "We cannot go with you. We must guard the castle. But in the company of a dragon, you shall encounter no dangers beyond your own company. Fare thee well, Marked Prince. And should you return well and whole to the battle for Amantier—greet my sister Thrissa for me. Wish her well."

Jetekesh inclined his head. "I will; I promise." He strode forward and passed the elves, his companions at his heels. The far door opened as he approached. Raum darted ahead of him and out into a wide, tapestried corridor that ran on for what seemed like ages. It eventually led the company into a garden as lush and vibrant as everything else in Valliath.

As peaceful as it was, Heyethir's words had thrown a sort of pall over its appeal. Now, Valliath felt like an illusion, a false promise of contentment and peace. This was a place of ghosts, and Jetekesh ached to return to the living.

The garden was large, and they weaved between trellises and around benches and flower beds, ignoring the teasing fragrances of wild roses and strange plants he didn't recognize. At last, the garden gave way to a hill sloping down into a far-off valley.

His heart clenched.

The valley was red, like a blanket of blood spread before him. A distant stone circle stood at the dead center of that valley surrounded by bloodred hills.

"We've found it," Kajsa whispered.

"So we have." His voice sounded far away. His insides churned with growing trepidation. The moment of truth had arrived, and the need for it had never felt greater.

Jetekesh must lay aside every mantle, from prince to mark bearer, in order to protect the world from within and without. He drew a breath, set his jaw, and started down the hill toward the fountain cradled in the center of the valley.

CHAPTER 38
TO WAR

Dawn brought the first glimpse of the enemy army camped near the dense forest.

Aredel sat upon his war horse, overlooking the valley where King Darint's army slumbered. A grim smile touched the Blood King's face, brittle as the stillness of the moment.

They had caught up.

Aredel wrapped his reins around his hands, his eyes fastened on the grand tent in the middle of the distant encampment. Beside him, Amaranth shuffled his hooves while Prince Sharo surveyed the same sight with the same sober air.

"Our men are exhausted, and our numbers are half of his," the fae prince said. "We can attack and hope the element of surprise tips the scales—or we can stall them and hope the dragons reach us soon."

Dragons would certainly help, yet Aredel resented the idea of waiting. Of *stalling*. He set his teeth and weighed their options. "If we wait, the goblins will likely tunnel around and flank us, cutting off our retreat. Then they'll pick us off while we wait. We cannot afford to lose any men before the true battle begins."

Sharo sighed. “Agreed. And yet...” He shook his head. “I feel unsettled, like this is one of my father’s traps.”

That matched Aredel’s own feelings. He grimaced. “Spring a trap or await a trap. Neither sounds appealing.”

“Indeed not.” Sharo fluted out another sigh. “Very well. We spring the trap and trust Taregan to arrive soon.”

“He shall.” Navolleth’s voice was as chill as the morning breeze.

Aredel craned his head to eye the pale man cloaked in deep blue. Navolleth’s golden eyes, slitted, sparkling, met Aredel’s stare with mild indifference.

“I feel the dragons behind us,” the man continued. “They will come by nightfall.”

Soon, yet too far off. So much could happen in one day upon the battlefield.

Sharo nodded at the news, taking it in stride. “So, we spring the trap, fight like wolves, and let our reinforcements arrive at the perfect moment to spare us from the slaughter.” He massaged the bridge of his nose. “I wish we’d been allowed one night’s reprieve, but that could spell our doom.” He lowered his hand, took up his reins, and nudged Amaranth toward the waiting ranks of soldiers.

Aredel wheeled his stallion around and followed, Navolleth taking up position beside him. Shevek approached and flanked his other side.

“Prepare yourselves!” Sharo called. “This is the moment we ride to war!”

No cheers welled up. The army knew better than to raise a ruckus so close to the enemy camp. But every eye was pinned on Sharo as he rode up and down the front line, offering encouragement, stirring them up for the conflict.

Aredel watched the fae prince with respect. This gentle soul rode to war against his own kin, not because he craved power but because he resisted evil. Jetekesh had once compared Sharo to

Jinji, and Aredel could see the comparison. But Jinji resisted fighting at all, and Sharo took up arms to defend right.

In a better world, perhaps I might have been like Sharo.

Perhaps, he thought with a sudden thrill, Sharo was the blending of Jinji and Aredel. The answer to his question: What could Aredel become?

After a few last heartfelt words, Sharo unsheathed his magic sword. It flashed and sparked as he wheeled Amaranth around, then ordered the charge. Aredel took his place at Sharo's back, and they galloped down the hillside toward Darint's army.

Behind Aredel the hooves of the cavalry horses thundered over the ground. Alongside the horses raced hundreds of *vashalan* under Navolleth's command. The wind whistled in the Blood King's ears, while his hair streamed behind him. He drew his sword, already tasting blood.

Just as dawn spread fingers of gold across the valley, the tents collapsed, and thousands of Darint's horsemen streamed forth, ready for combat. Swarms of *Unsielie* took to the air, bows and arrows letting loose. Airborne *Sielie* answered them in a clash of glaives. Below, knights held up fae-charmed shields to fend off stray arrows.

Aredel steeled himself. His blood ran hot and wild. This was it. The day he could exact revenge.

The day he would destroy Tavassed and end Darint's reign forever.

For Anadin. For Artassa. For Bahadronn.

An armored man charged him. Aredel urged his horse on faster, and their swords met with the sound of steel. White smoke curled up Aredel's sword, and he set his teeth, resisting the pull of his magic. If he used it now, he'd be useless when it counted most.

The smoke faded, and Aredel let his body fall into its instinctive dance. He'd ridden his horse long enough, they'd grown used to each other's motions. The beast moved with the Blood King, prancing and wheeling around the attacker, while the din of battle around them fell from Aredel's conscious mind.

He entered his frenzy—the perfect state where fear and indecision fell away. His movements quickened. His eyesight sharpened. He swung and hacked, forcing his opponent backward on his steed. The man tried to gain an advantage, to force Aredel back, but the Blood King charged ahead, striking, striking, striking, until the man's sword flew loose of his grip and landed with a thud to the ground.

Without hesitation, Aredel plunged his sword into the man's gorget, puncturing his throat. He wrenched it free, then rode on. No sign of Shevek or Sharo. No glimpse of Navolleth. He aimed for the center of the conflict, where battle fever pitched high and bodies lay strewn across the ground already. As he approached, he cut down several would-be attackers, disinterested in common riffraff.

He scoured the field, seeking Tavassed or any other *Unsielie*. Most remained airborne, fending off *Sielie*, though over a dozen dark fae lay among the dead. He turned his eyes back to the sky, slid his spear from a sheath at his back, and took careful aim.

The spear flew true. It plunged into the chest of one *Unsielie*, who screamed, then toppled onto the field. Aredel nudged his stallion toward the body, dancing around skirmishes. He reclaimed his spear, noting the hole in the dark fae's body with grim satisfaction.

Not Tavassed, but a start, nonetheless.

His instinct tingled.

Aredel wheeled and knocked an arrow off course with his spear haft. A cluster of *Unsielie* swooped down upon him, their dark eyes blazing with unholy light, their lacy wings beating the air in a blur.

He'd gotten their attention. *Good.*

Aredel charged to meet them, swinging his spear.

They met—spear against glaives, horse against wings. Aredel allowed the white smoke to pour forth, careful not to let it consume his body and tax him. The blinding light sent the *Unsielie* backward, hissing and baring needle teeth.

The smoke curled up his spear, and he hurled it at the closest *Unsielie*, then drew his sword while the others scattered. The punctured fae fell hard to the ground, writhing under the magic's potent light.

Galloping hooves approached. Aredel risked a glance over his shoulder to find a handful of enemy soldiers rushing him. He grinned, wheeled around, and allowed his magic full rein. It burst from him, and the *Unsielie* retreated in a flurry of wings and cries.

Satisfied he wouldn't be stabbed in the back, Aredel urged his stallion forward, charging the knot of soldiers. They veered off, likely too petrified of the white smoke to stay the course. Aredel bore down on the nearest soldier, reached him, caught his shoulder, and drove him sideways in his saddle. The man slipped off, and the horse sped away.

Aredel wheeled, his frenzy growing hotter and brighter. He let his magic die down. He needed to preserve it.

Swiping droplets of sweat from his chin, he surveyed the field and spotted an assault against a band of Sharo's elves. Aredel prodded his horse into motion and galloped at the enemy. His sword flashed as he lifted it. He cut and hacked his way toward the elves under fire, sparing no thought for the enemies who fell from their saddles.

Aredel hadn't counted his kills in years.

He lopped off a head. The spray of blood tasted metallic on his lips.

He won free of the pressing enemy and joined Sharo's knights. They cheered and gained new strength to overwhelm the enemy. As they plunged away from the center of Darint's camp, a handful of *vashalan* joined them to tear into the enemy. Satisfied, Aredel left the knights, determined to make his way to the heart of the engagement.

Wherever Darint was, Tavassed would be close.

No doubt, Sharo was aiming for the same goal.

Aredel dragged threads of damp hair from his face, then pierced through the throat of another enemy with his sword. The man gurgled and fell while Aredel moved on. Three more fell in seconds. Aredel's sword gleamed with blood as he aimed for another soldier.

The man lifted his helmed head, his eyes wide. He wheeled his horse and ran.

Aredel gave chase.

No coward shall live. The KryTeeran scripture rolled through the Blood King's head, as much a part of his philosophy as bathing in the blood of his strongest foes.

Tavassed would have that morbid honor once Aredel removed his head and wings from his corpse.

A glimmer snagged his eye. Aredel caught the fleeing soldier, swung hard, and took his head. Then he wheeled his stallion around. There, before the rising sun, Tavassed hung suspended as though he stood upon solid ground rather than air.

The Blood King allowed himself a grin as fury boiled up. White smoke leaked from his fingertips.

The *Unsielie* dipped his head, greeting Aredel. Then the dark fae lifted his hands as though they held strings.

Aredel's heart told him to run. The unfamiliar sensation made him hesitate, and he dropped his gaze to the ground before Tavassed. A path stretched between them, free of fighting soldiers, as though Tavassed had thrown up invisible walls to create a corridor.

And there, at the end of that corridor, stood Anadin.

CHAPTER 39
RED ON RED

The grass changed from green to red in a single step, like Jetekesh had crossed the borders of reality and into a dream.

Ahead, the long wild grass swayed in a breeze, reminding the prince of his favorite crimson velvet cloak back home in his wardrobe. He wore it only at balls and high court functions and always found himself rubbing the material back and forth, fascinated by the light and dark effect depending on how he brushed it.

Kajsa tugged against his grip, and Jetekesh glanced back to meet her ice-blue eyes. Fear framed them.

"What is it?" he asked.

She shook her head as Raum padded to her side. "Just a feeling..."

His chest tightened. "Do you want to stay here and wait for us?"

The girl hesitated, then shook her head. "I want to stay near you."

Despite himself, Jetekesh smiled, and his chest loosened. "Come along, then. We'll face the truth together."

Kajsa searched his face, perhaps seeking reassurance, or perhaps reading between his words and finding the fear he, too, harbored. After a heartbeat, she nodded. "All right."

They carried on down the hill, leading the company along. The wind rose, snatching at Jetekesh's hair, tossing it into his face and mouth. He dragged his hair to one shoulder and held his tresses in place, unwilling to relinquish his hold on Kajsa's hand.

The hills seemed endless, but progress was steady, and the constant downhill motion kept Jetekesh going despite a weariness that seeped into his bones. Here, it seemed, the energy of Valliath couldn't sustain him.

He found himself puffing for breath as he crested another slight hill and stared down into the heart of the valley. He could make out the blood fountain now. Smooth crimson stones formed three bowled tiers. Under the influence of the red stone, the cascading water appeared like blood, and Jetekesh's insides chilled at the idea of drinking it.

Didn't the dragon present the water as wine to the king in Jinji's story?

Perhaps the water *was* red like blood.

Kajsa squeezed his fingers. He squeezed back, then started down the final hill.

Soon, we'll have what we need.

Even so, the impossibility of finding the true ruler dragged him toward despair. Had Sharo and Jinji sent him on this quest just to keep him out of danger after all? Was the curse even real?

Don't think like that. Perhaps they suspect my father is *the rightful king, and—and maybe I won't risk his life if I bring him the waters of truth.*

Fear stabbed at Jetekesh's gut, and he swallowed a lump in his throat.

He pressed on.

The sun sank toward the western mountains, streaking the sky gold and scarlet. Jetekesh conquered the last stretch of red grass and approached the burbling fountain. The air smelled sweet and clean, nothing like iron or metal to suggest actual blood.

A single step up gave him access to the flowing, red-tinged liquid. Jetekesh stared into the shimmering depths. Apart from its pinkish hue, the water was clean. No algae or scum edged the water, no plant life had taken it over. Lifting his gaze, he stared at the topmost bowl-like tier of the tall fountain far above his head. At its narrow peak, a burnished silver goblet stood, winking with garnets edging its brim.

He drew a breath.

"So," Emerin whispered, "we've found it."

Jetekesh nodded, keeping his eyes on the goblet. "Can we... touch the water, do you think?"

Silence answered.

"Probably," Emerin said. "We just can't drink it." He gestured to the fountain. "Shall I fetch the goblet, Your Highness?"

Before Jetekesh could answer, Anenyasha plunged her feet into the fountain and splashed toward the higher tiers. With agile motions, she conquered two tiers before she reached up and plucked the goblet from the peak, then she returned, holding out the prize.

Jetekesh accepted it with a grimace. "That was reckless, Anenyasha."

She shrugged. "Why are we here if not to help you succeed at any cost?" She sat on the fountain rim, swung her legs out, and let them hang, dripping into the grass.

Dakarai set a hand on her shoulder. "My heart nearly gave out, my love."

She shrugged, saying nothing.

Jetekesh studied the goblet in his hands. The burnished metal was cool, and droplets of water sparkled on the silvery etchings. The design was intricate, beautiful, and sleek. Each garnet was cut into flawless gems, catching the glow of sunset as he turned the piece over and over in his hands.

"It'll be a pain to transport," Emerin said, studying it over Jetekesh's shoulder. "Is the goblet necessary, or can we pour the water into a flask?"

"I don't..." Jetekesh paused. "The goblet is part of the ritual." He could see the vision clearly in the facets of the gems. "I think we can store the water in a flask and pour it into the goblet when we locate the rightful ruler." He frowned. "If we ever manage that." Another fleeting image flickered over his mind. "We'll need some of this water for Navolleth as well."

Kethalas inched closer, his eyes riveted on the goblet. "Surely, there's a way to divine the direction we must go to find the true ruler—or—or something."

Jetekesh glanced heavenward, wondering if the gryphons would help them in their search—but he saw no sign of the mythical beasts against the ruddy sky. "There must be some way or Jinji wouldn't have sent us here."

"Could it be that he believes you're the rightful king?" Emerin asked, folding his arms.

Jetekesh frowned. "I think he'd have told me if he believed that." He stared at the goblet. "I won't risk it. I won't let my vanity cause my end."

The keep lord grunted. "Is that your vice, Your Highness? Vanity?"

Jetekesh shifted to sit on the fountain's edge. "I thought of taking it to my father. He's a good man. Surely..."

"Don't be so coy." Axel stalked forward, his pale green eyes flecked with gold in the sun's glow. "Give me the goblet, Jetekesh. Navolleth sent me to claim Nakania. I'm the rightful ruler."

Jetekesh blinked up at the Norvian. "Is *that* what you want? To rule Nakania only to destroy her people and let Norva take over?"

Axel's lips lifted in a sneer. "I'll repair the injustice done in the past. Navolleth was bonded to Cavalin. He knows what the great hero would desire. I'm of his blood, his kin, same as you—but your line has failed to protect Nakania. You yourself caused this war through your blindness and your ambition. Your ancestor stole the throne and brought a curse upon the world. Give me the goblet."

Horror ripped through Jetekesh's frame. He stood up, gripping the goblet tight. "Did Navolleth also explain what happens if you drink the water and you're *not* the rightful ruler of Nakania?"

Axel held out his hand. "He chose me. I'll survive. Give me the goblet."

Jetekesh stared into the young man's confident gaze. The hairs on his arms rose, but he drew a breath and hefted the goblet, then offered it to Axel. "If you *are* meant to rule Nakania, let me be the first to show you good faith. I hope you survive—and I pray you'll treat every nation within her boundaries with mercy and benevolence."

Axel snatched the goblet, but Kajsa moved from the fountain's brink. "Don't, Axel. You'll die."

He froze, then scowled. "Do you doubt me so much, Ky?"

She took a shaking breath. "I...I'm afraid for you. Axel, you're my dearest friend, but you're not suited to rule Nakania. The waters will destroy you. Please don't let Navolleth lead you to death."

Axel's knuckles tightened over the goblet's stem. "I thought to make you my queen, Ky. We'd rule together. Imagine it: Bringing our people over the Snowblinds, bringing them into Shing and Amantier to experience true warmth. To see the blossoms. We deserve that!"

"Not at the cost of human lives," Kajsa said, leveling her shoulders. "Give me the goblet, Xel. It's not for you to drink from."

He pressed the glittering dish to his chest. "I've as much right to try as *he* does. We're both descended from Cavalin the Great." A fervor burned in his eyes, widening them until he looked almost deranged.

Jetekesh cast around in his mind for some argument—anything to stay the young man's hand. *What if...?* The voice of doubt filled his mind. *What if he* is *the rightful king?*

Dakarai's voice chimed in, clear yet soft. "What did Lord Navolleth tell you, *exactly,* Lord Axel? What were his words?"

Axel hesitated, some of his vehemence bleeding away. "He said I must come with you. That I must be certain you didn't break the old oaths and *pretend* you drank the water. He told me to seek out the rightful ruler, and just as I was leaving, he smiled and said, 'Perhaps you are the worthy heir of Cavalin. Partake if the waters call to you.'" Axel thumbed the goblet. "They do call. They *do*. I can hear them."

Kethalas rolled his eyes. "We can *all* hear the waters. They're right here."

Dakarai shot the man-dragon a warning glance, then stepped forward. "It's possible you are worthy of the throne, Axel. With or without Cavalin's blood, someone is. And that someone must take on a heavy burden. They must rule, not one, but all the countries of Nakania—equally, justly—with no prejudice against race, creed, or status. So Cavalin did, insofar as each country allowed—and he never overstepped himself. He governed the great matters while allowing each country to maintain its own identity. He never usurped authority where it was unwanted and unnecessary. He settled the hard matters and left the rudimentary things to the people."

The clansman took another step forward. "Can you—would you—do this, Axel? If so, if this resonates in your soul, then drink the waters. Become our high king, and we will answer the waters' will."

The Norvian's hands trembled. He lowered his eyes to stare into the empty goblet. "My people need good land. They need to escape the cold of Norva...to know true summer."

"They will," said Jetekesh. "The world has changed with Shinac's return. The very seasons will alter. It's possible Norva is already melting." He winced at the ramifications. Mass flooding was likely. Jetekesh braved a step forward. "Axel, I won't speak as a prince. I've laid that title aside. But as—as your friend, I promise to aid your people. If Norva isn't habitable, I'll help you petition the high ruler for land. The rolling hills of Eastern Amantier are fair and unoccupied. We'll find them a place where four seasons thrive."

Axel stared into his eyes, probing. Then he scowled. "You're not my friend."

"I'd like to be." Jetekesh inhaled. "I've had few and little practice. But I'm learning how to be a good friend. Kajsa has helped me a great deal with that. I should like—"

"Don't." Axel drew back a pace. "You're just trying to gain allies for your dictatorship. Navolleth told me all about you. He knows your history. You're responsible for the death of the storyteller true. For the honorable knight Palan. For the women sacrificed in that *Unsielie* fortress—and who knows how many others —because of your spoiled upbringing and deplorable mother."

Jetekesh froze. Bile climbed his throat, and his eyes misted over. No one could have aimed better. He curled his hands into fists, wrestling to regain his composure, to not allow guilt back in.

"You're right," he whispered. "I *am* responsible for the deaths of good men and women. I will bear that weight all my life." His eyes cleared, and he seized Axel's gaze. "But I'll not let it cripple me, or their deaths will have no meaning. Instead, I'll strive to atone, to build a better world, where spoiled princes can't wreck lives. Where ambitious fools don't win out. Where storytellers are heralded as much as knights. Where tyrants fear to walk abroad." His eyes narrowed. "And I dare any man to fault or hinder me."

Did Axel shudder, or did Jetekesh only imagine it?

Drawing back his shoulders, Jetekesh nodded toward the goblet. "What is your answer, Axel? Will you risk drinking the waters of truth?"

The young man rubbed the goblet, garnets sparkling in the flushed sunset. He pulled in a breath, his eyes darting between the dish and the tinkling fountain. "I...I believe in Navolleth. He said I could rule."

"Do you want to?" asked Kajsa.

Axel tensed. "Why wouldn't I?"

"It is a great burden," Dakarai answered.

"I'd hate it," said Rille, stirring the water in the fountain base with one finger. "Better to travel light and freely."

Jetekesh understood that sentiment, but his heart clenched just the same. He'd always seen himself on Amantier's throne, ruling as justly as his father before him. Yes, not long ago, he'd only envisioned what *he* would gain from that crown. From commanding a vast army and indulging in strong drink as he pleased. Not answering to anyone, least of all Mother.

So much had changed since that small-minded boy fled Kavacos alongside a storyteller, a pretend knight, his strong-willed cousin, and his loyal protector.

Now, he ached to rule as he never had before. To offer up land to the Norvians. To welcome Shinac and broker a treaty between fae and humans before war rolled over the entire world. To maintain the infant treaties between KryTeer and Shing. To find out all he could about each nation and culture, to learn from them. To find true paths to peace forever or die in the effort.

Crownless, titleless, Jetekesh understood at last what being a ruler was, and he would never again have the power to use it.

Had Jinji ever felt this helpless? *Probably every day of his life.*

Axel let out a frustrated growl. "I'm right." He gripped the goblet tighter. "I hear the waters."

"What do they say?" asked Dakarai, maintaining the same patient tones.

The young man hesitated. "...Come. They say to come. To drink."

"He's lying." Kethalas's fangs flashed as he bared his teeth. "Are you so desperate to rule, you'll risk your very life, you fool?"

Axel's cheeks colored. "I'm not a fool. I do hear them!"

Jetekesh studied the Norvian's face, trying to find truth. Shouldn't he be able to read it? If Jinji had sent him to the blood fountain because he could somehow sense the true ruler of Nakania, shouldn't he be able to tell if Axel *was* that ruler?

Frustration bubbled up, warming Jetekesh's chest, closing his throat. He swallowed hard, pressing against those feelings. They served no one.

Guide me, Jinji.

A chime filled his ears, and with it, a flood of images poured into his mind's eye. The moment he'd stood in Shing's throne room, fending off *Erisyrdrel*'s attacks, formed into an almost solid memory. Though he held no crest now, Jetekesh lifted his hand. "By the might and power of the True King, I call upon truth to light the path to peace." The words struck like chords of music, humming with power. A breeze rushed through Jetekesh's hair, tossing it.

Axel screamed. The goblet glowed white-hot in his hands. He flung it away, then hugged his hands to his chest. Kajsa raced to his side, while the goblet rolled across the red grass, no longer glowing. It halted near Jetekesh's boots.

The Norvian sank to his knees with a sob. "Curse you, Marked Prince! Why do you bring woe and destruction wherever you go?"

Kajsa pried Axel's fingers from his chest. Jetekesh expected to find puckered flesh, but Axel's hands appeared whole. Kajsa turned Axel's hands over and over, seeking some hint of a wound while the latter sat in stunned silence.

Jetekesh lowered his arm, then stooped to pick up the goblet. "It seems," he said softly, "you're not the chosen high king." Jetekesh turned toward Rille. "Will you keep this for now?"

She nodded and accepted it with a sober expression. "Gladly."

Turning to the fountain, Jetekesh pulled his water flask from his satchel and dumped his drinking water in the grass. Then he bent before the fountain rim and plunged his flask into the shimmering depths. Water bubbled as he filled it. His mind gnawed on Axel's question.

Why do you bring woe and destruction wherever you go?

His hand shook, and he drew a bolstering breath. Once the flask was full, Jetekesh extracted and capped it, then turned to his companions. "We've got what we came for. Let's—"

Axel flung his knife over the air, aiming for Jetekesh. Kajsa let out a scream.

CHAPTER 40
TOO MUCH

Dakarai threw himself in front of Jetekesh. The knife plunged into his back. The clansman's eyes widened. Anenyasha bolted to his side with a cry.

Jetekesh reached out and caught Dakarai as the man stumbled. They staggered backward, and Jetekesh struck the fountain, then collapsed, clutching his friend.

"Hold on." His words sounded far away against the beating waves of panic.

Anenyasha caught Dakarai's arm. Her eyes shimmered.

The clansman gasped, and flecks of blood stained his mouth. "M-my beloved Anen..." He reached for her face, cupped her cheek, and smiled. "Long live the...high king..." His hand slipped from her grasp and fell like lead against Jetekesh's leg.

"No, Dakarai," Jetekesh whispered. "No. No! Please, not you. Please." He caught the man's arm and squeezed, willing his life force into Dakarai's. He'd given up a year of his life already, take the rest... Take it...

His vision blurred, and he slumped against the body, burying his head in the familiar scent of his friend and confidant. Dakarai. Gone. So much loss.

Too much.

He screamed. And screamed.

And screamed.

CHAPTER 41
THREE TEARS

Clutching a shepherd's crook, Jinji Wanderlust overlooked the battle on the southern plains of Amantier.

Two tears slid down his cheeks. His heart quaked for the losses below...and those far away. In his mind's eye, he saw Jetekesh slumped over the body of brave Dakarai, surrounded by companions equally bereft.

Lord Emerin gripped Axel in his arms, a knife to the boy's throat, while Kajsa sobbed beside them.

The waters of truth hummed a song of sorrow as they turned a darker shade of red for another fallen soul lying at their heart.

He lifted his eyes from the carnage in the valley as another tear slipped free.

"Do not reject this grief or call it pointless, my dearest friends," he whispered. "It serves a great purpose, greater than you know." The sky shimmered, giving Jinji a glimpse of a faraway spell and the ever-approaching Meridian.

He closed his eyes, and let the grief enfold him.

Let it pour through him.

Saturate his soul.

"Dakarai, you will not be forgotten, just as Cavalin of old. No hero who dies for the cause of right will ever be forsaken. Rest, brave warrior, and enter your repose."

CHAPTER 42
LIKE A MARIONETTE

Thunder rumbled. Aredel barely heard it.

His attention was squarely upon his brother as Anadin approached, his movements as lithe and loose as they'd ever been.

But I buried you.

Aredel's sword shook. His insides tightened.

This must be a trick. It *must.*

Anadin clutched a sword—*his* sword—the one Aredel had buried with him. As he neared, the prince of KryTeer lifted his eyes and smiled his most winsome smile. "*Shaqin*, I am returned!"

The stallion beneath Aredel backed up, snorting a soft, concerned sound. Aredel nearly let the beast continue retreating. Something in his heart urged him to flee this wondrous horror.

Anadin canted his head, silken hair slipping down his shoulder, black clothes torn and scuffed from the fights within the *Unsielie* swamp. It was as though Anadin had awakened, crawled from his grave, and traveled straight here within a single instant.

"What devilry is this?" Aredel dredged up every ounce of

strength to keep his voice even. "What manner of creature are you?"

The prince laughed, that clear, pure sound. "Ah, Aredel. Has no one told you the battlefield is a poor place for jests?"

Aredel's eyes narrowed. "My brother is dead. I buried him myself."

"So you did," said a singsong voice from above.

The Blood King jerked his eyes skyward to find Tavassed hovering above Anadin. Robed in black, haloed by wings, the *Unsielie* resembled an unholy priest.

"Which is an unfortunate tragedy," Tavassed continued. "Had you not betrayed us, there would have been no need for his end." He tipped his head, and eerily, Anadin mimicked the gesture. "Alas," the *Unsielie* said, "now he is reanimated, brought back by the art of necromancy. And he will remain under my power unless you surrender to our will and submit your skills to our use in this war."

Every word the *Unsielie* spoke was a hammer blow to Aredel's soul. Red bled into the edges of his sight, and his fingers tightened around his sword. As Tavassed's speech wound down, the Blood King tested the weight of his weapon and calculated the distance between his horse and the winged fae above him.

"You have tested my patience for the last time," he said between gritted teeth. "Enough of your cowardice. Come down here, and let us fight!"

Tavassed's wings hummed a different pitch as he lifted himself a little higher. "Do not forget that I hold your brother hostage."

The *Unsielie* made a strange gesture with his fingers. Anadin set his blade against his own arm.

Tavassed spoke again. "Shall I have him cut it off?"

"Ta-va-ssed." Each syllable scraped over Aredel's lips. Smoke gathered around his clenched fists, but he resisted the magic's pull. What would it do to Anadin?

Should I spare him, or cleanse him?

Aredel had no priests nearby to consult. Jinji had remained behind the army, up the hill, and Shevek was nowhere in the vicinity.

What should I do?

He longed to slice Tavassed up. To grind him into bone powder and force Darint to drink the powder in a mixture before the tyrant king died a slow, painful death. But he forced himself to meet the *Unsielie's* gaze and offered him a feral smile.

"I'll say it once more, Tavassed: Come down here."

The *Unsielie*'s face darkened, and his fingers jerked before him.

Anadin charged, sword flashing in a beam of sunshine. Aredel reacted, bringing his blade up to block the blow. Steel met steel with a song, then Aredel drew his horse back, disengaging. The stallion tossed his head and stomped while Anadin checked his stance, then charged again.

Agreeing to the *Unsielie*'s terms was out of the question. Anadin was already dead, and besmirching his memory to spare his corpse was ludicrous.

Even so...

Aredel angled his sword down to catch Anadin's jab. He twisted his wrist, throwing Anadin off.

Even so, he couldn't bear to desecrate his brother's body, alive or dead.

"Anadin. Forgive me." He wheeled his mount around, swung his leg, and kicked Anadin in the chin. The prince stumbled backward, losing his grip. Aredel turned a glare on Tavassed as white smoke wisped off his shoulders.

The *Unsielie* flinched back. "Unleash your power at the cost of Anadin's soul, Blood King."

Aredel set his teeth and nudged his stallion forward. "Wherever Anadin's soul ends up, it will not be in the same place you and I go after this life, you maggot." He prodded the horse's flank, and the stallion broke into a canter. The Blood King aimed and threw his sword with all his strength.

At the same moment, he released the full fury of his power. White light blazed across the field; tendrils of smoke curled around skirmishes, broken tents, and oozing corpses.

The scores of *Unsielie* above screamed and fled the explosion of light.

Tavassed took the sword in the chest and lurched backward. His tattered wings beat the air in a mad attempt to regain height. He crashed into a tent, snapping poles and tearing canvas. Aredel urged his stallion toward the wreckage as his fingers dug for a dagger at his bootstrap. Grabbing it, he straightened, never letting his eyes leave the place where Tavassed had landed.

He halted a few paces off, swung from his saddle, and approached the heap of tent cloth. "Tavassed, stand if you still live. Let us end this."

A tingle whispered at his neck. He pivoted and caught Anadin's strike with his dagger mere inches from his neck. The prince pitched back, aligned his feet, and stood in a defensive pose with both hands clasping his sword. His skin was too pale, his eyes slightly sunken in the light that flamed around Aredel.

"My *shaqel*," the Blood King whispered. "To see you like this splinters my heart."

Anadin's smile was lopsided. "Resist them no more, *shaqin*, and we will have no need to duel." He adjusted his grip. "Surrender, and my soul will be freed." Something like pain caught in his eyes, burning, and his voice dropped. "Please, Aredel. I cannot endure this torment."

The Blood King's heart twisted. "Dear brother, how deep my remorse penetrates I cannot say in words. You will be avenged, make no mistake."

"Not if you value the state of his soul." Tavassed stood up from the wreckage, sword still sticking through his chest. He jerked his fingers upward, and Anadin let out a scream that ripped through Aredel.

"Enough!" Aredel flung out his hands. "Enough. I yield." The words tasted heavy on his lips. Heavy and false.

Anadin sank to his knees, gasping. Relief trickled through the Blood King while his mind raced. Ignoring the *Unsielie*'s faint smile, he moved, though his legs were leaden; knelt before his brother's panting corpse; wrapped an arm around Anadin's shoulders.

"I'm sorry, *shaqel*."

Anadin shook his head. "Not your fault. World's...gone... mad..." He laughed. "Nearly as mad...as us..."

Kicking aside debris, Tavassed drifted toward them. He latched both hands onto the sword in his chest and yanked it loose. Blood gushed down his front, darkening his black robes. He didn't seem to notice. "That was a near thing, Blood King, and for that, I must commend you. But you risked your brother in the attempt. I suggest you refrain from another such stunt."

Aredel rose and pinned a glare on the *Unsielie*. "I have already surrendered to you, *filth*. What now?"

Tavassed's lips twitched up again. "We wish the same thing as before: Sharo's death."

The words sank in, and Aredel nodded once. "Then take me to King Darint."

The *Unsielie*'s wings fluttered. "Why?"

"Because that is where I'll find Sharo." Aredel took a step toward the dark fae. "Once I've accomplished this task, you will free Anadin's soul without harming it in any way, correct?"

The creature offered Aredel his sword, then pressed a swath of robe against his chest, his stoic expression never faltering. "Accomplish your task, and I will let you loose on the necromancer who brought Anadin here. Convince him at your leisure, O King." He turned in a fluid motion. "This way."

Aredel cleaned and sheathed his sword, then retrieved his stallion and helped Anadin to climb into the saddle. He mounted in front of his brother and guided the stallion after Tavassed who glided amidst the carnage like a being beyond feeling. Perhaps that was so.

Clouds settled over the sun, threatening rain. Already the ground was broken and muddy in places from the bodies strewn across the field. Aredel weaved around patches of carnage, indifferent to the casualties. The time to mourn was after victory.

Anadin rested his head against Aredel's shoulder blades. "*Shaqin*, it hurts everywhere."

"I know. Hold tight to me. I will free you from this prison soon."

Tavassed fluttered above the ground, rising higher, higher, until he lifted a hand and pointed. "Behold, Blood King."

Aredel lowered his gaze and found Sharo astride Amaranth, facing off against a man in gold-plated armor and a helm that resembled a crown. King Darint, unless Aredel was sorely mistaken. The Blood King's lips curled up. At last, Tavassed and Darint in the same place, and presumably, the necromancer nearby.

The final engagement was at hand.

CHAPTER 43
A QUIET THOUGHT

Raum's howl rose into the night sky, carrying Jetekesh's broken hopes with it.

He hunched beside the gurgling fountain, still clutching Dakarai, though Emerin and Kethalas had thrice urged him to let go. Stars winked in the hazy heavens, distorted in the endless mist above the churning waters.

Nearby, Axel sat, gagged and bound. Kajsa paced between them, wringing her hands, tears slipping down her face. Raum sat on his haunches nearby and howled again.

Jetekesh curved forward, taking in the fire Emerin had built, its woody scent curling around his face. He knew he must move—that something important needed to be done—but his mind refused to align with his tattered heart. Nothing mattered.

After all he'd done, it just didn't matter.

Footsteps rustled close. Rille knelt before him, and he tried to brace for her lecture. The little girl tacked on a smile, but it wobbled at the edges. She lifted a hand and brushed his hair from his cheeks.

"I didn't know him well," she whispered. "But I could tell he was the very best of men. Your loss is deeper than oceans and greater than the sky." Rille drew a breath. "It's all right, Kesh. Grieve. We can leave tomorrow."

Leave. Leave where? Jetekesh tried to form the question, but his tongue wouldn't move. His eyes slid shut and fresh tears spilled down his cheeks. Why go anywhere else when this pain would simply follow him?

Rille tucked his hair behind his ear, then smoothed it with a few strokes before she stood up and shook her skirts straight. The girl padded off to the blazing fire.

Jetekesh turned his face from the warmth. How did he still have tears to shed? How did he still breathe? The wound in his heart was too deep to survive, surely...

Raum's next howl tore through him. Jetekesh curled forward more, gasping as his heart throbbed.

"Hush, Raum. Shhh," whispered Kajsa, and her movement caught Jetekesh's eye.

He clutched at his chest while Kajsa wrapped her arms around the ghostly wolf and whispered soothing words to him while she silently cried.

She's hurting, too.

They all were, not just him.

I'm still so selfish.

He grimaced as he shifted, relinquishing his hold on Dakarai with great care. Anenyasha slipped up next to him, then knelt, and tenderly rested her fiancé's head in her lap.

Jetekesh climbed to his feet and padded to Kajsa's side. His fingers brushed her shoulder, and she jerked her head around. Their eyes met. With a sob, she sprang up and threw her arms around his neck. He wrapped his arms around her waist and held her.

As Jetekesh stood at the blood fountain and wept with Kajsa for their fallen companion, time lost the last shreds of meaning.

Finally, Kajsa stirred and pulled back, revealing a puffy face and swollen eyes. "Thank you," she whispered. "I'm sorry."

"Don't be." He wiped a stray tear from her eye. "Dak—" Jetekesh's voice cracked. He swallowed and tried again. "He'd not fault us for crying."

Kajsa nodded and swiped at her eyes again. "No, he wouldn't."

Footfalls sounded behind Jetekesh, and he angled to face the fire as Emerin approached. The keep lord tried a smile but it dropped halfway to a grimace.

"Come, Your Highness, Lady Kajsa. Sit with us. Try to eat." Emerin gestured to the crackling flames.

Jetekesh reached for Kajsa's hand. She slipped her fingers between his, and together they walked to the fire where the rest sat cross-legged. The two knelt side by side, with Kethalas on Jetekesh's left and Rille on Kajsa's right. Kethalas dished up stew for the two newcomers, and Jetekesh ate without tasting anything. Kajsa ate with wooden motions, as disinterested in the fare as he was.

"We'll need to bury Dakarai," Emerin said.

Jetekesh's spoon froze halfway to his mouth. A lump swelled in his throat.

The keep lord rubbed his neck. "I've already started digging a hole. Anenyasha agrees it's best to leave him here, rather than try to take him with us back to Amantier."

The words stirred Jetekesh from the lethargy of grief. Amantier. War. King Darint and his army of dark horrors. He sat straighter, pushing aside the pieces of his shattered heart to count later. "I agree." He set aside his bowl and took Kajsa's hand again. "Let's give Dakarai as decent a burial as possible, in the way of his clan, then be on our way. Time is running out for our people back home."

His eyes skimmed over Anenyasha still seated at the fountain, cradling her fallen lover. As if she sensed his gaze, the clanswoman looked up. A grim line stretched across her lips, and she nodded as though to give permission to do what he must.

Jetekesh steeled himself, turning his mind to hard thoughts. "First, there's the matter of Axel."

Kajsa stiffened, her fingers twitching in his clasp. She turned her blue eyes on him, probing.

Jetekesh resisted returning her stare. Instead, he glanced between his other companions. "What should be done?"

"I say pour the dratted water down his throat," Kethalas said. "It feels just to me. The waters will judge him."

Emerin grunted. "That's better than my suggestion, I think. I'd just drown the murderer outright."

Rille shifted in her place near Kajsa. "Perhaps that *is* the best course—not the drowning—Kethalas's idea. That, or we bring him back for a trial among his people."

Jetekesh turned his focus to the fountain, letting the burbling sound grow in his ears as he listened, as though the waters would answer his silent question: Did Axel deserve death? Would the waters judge him justly?

Could Jetekesh bring himself to pronounce that punishment upon the young man?

A quiet thought stole across his mind. Jetekesh pulled free of Kajsa's hands, stood, and moved to the fountain where the goblet rested on the rim, presumably placed there by Rille in the aftermath of Dakarai's death. The prince caught it up. The cool metal felt soothing beneath his fingertips.

Jetekesh stooped and filled the goblet to its brim. Turning, he padded to Axel and set the goblet before the captive. Axel didn't look up. The rippling water caught a glimpse of moonlight and seemed to glow.

"At sunrise, I'll loose your bonds," Jetekesh said. "You have until then to decide your fate: Drink the waters of truth or don't.

What happens after that is upon your head alone. Consider carefully."

He rose and moved back to the fire. Taking his place beside Kajsa, he felt the weight of every eye in the company. Glancing up, he saw Emerin nod his approval. Jetekesh dropped his gaze. He felt no sense of satisfaction or relief; only a sort of quiet that had settled into his heart to cradle his broken pieces.

For now, that was enough.

CHAPTER 44
TRUE STRENGTH OF RULERS

As Aredel urged his stallion forward, every nerve hummed within him. He was so close to Darint—so near he could behead him in an instant—but the king couldn't be killed until Tavassed was dead. And Tavassed still held Anadin captive.

The Blood King's best hope was to locate the necromancer. His eyes flitted from skirmish to skirmish, from broken tent to broken tent, seeking anyone who stood out against the clashing soldiers.

Someone screamed, and Anadin flinched against Aredel's back.

"Be still, my *shaqel*," Aredel whispered.

"It's burns," whispered his brother.

"Not for long."

The clash of swords brought Aredel's attention to the fight between Darint and Sharo on horseback. Both men wore full armor, both held themselves well, yet exhaustion poured off them like steam from a cauldron. Sharo had lost his shield. Dents shaded Darint's armor.

Tavassed turned his dark eyes on Aredel. "See that this fight ends well."

Aredel grimaced, then reined in his stallion. "Climb down, Anadin."

The prince clambered down and turned his black eyes toward Aredel. "Be safe, *shaqin*."

"Always, *shaqel*." He sank his heels into the stallion's flank and took off at a canter while he slid his sword free.

Father and son faltered and turned. Within his helm, Sharo's eyes brightened, then widened as Aredel swung his blade at him. The fae prince and his horse pranced backward, narrowly dodging the attack. Darint moved in with a laugh. Both kings forced Sharo into retreat. The fae prince pulled a short sword from his saddle.

They moved in a slow dance, swinging and stabbing, while Sharo backed Amaranth toward a section of burning tents, barely catching their blows in time. Above, the beat of wings assured Aredel that Tavassed witnessed the fight.

Where is the necromancer? Aredel needed to buy time or both Anadin and Sharo would pay the steepest of prices.

A horn sounded nearby. Not one of Sharo's war calls.

Darint's attacks grew more aggressive, and Aredel fell deeper into the fray, keeping the tyrant king on his toes, forced to maneuver around the Blood King's stallion. As Aredel wheeled the horse to one side, his eye caught Sharo's, and he gave the faintest shake of his head.

Sharo dipped his own head, perhaps to acknowledge that he understood Aredel had no choice.

Their broadswords met, then Sharo whipped around and caught Darint's sword with his shorter blade.

The horn sounded again. Shrieks rose from somewhere to the west. Had Darint's side called in reinforcements? Had the light fae army fought fiercely enough to make the other side afraid, or were

Darint's generals superfluous enough to waste their trump card so early?

The shrieks grew louder, closer. Aredel risked a glance over his shoulder, the red of his armor glinting. A pack of goblins burst into view around a section of intact tents. A handful of Sharo's men scrambled before them, but the goblins were faster, and they slammed into the soldiers with the force of a tidal wave.

Goblins. Thousands. They poured into the crevices of the field, filling up the spaces, tearing down the fae in silver armor. Phoenix banners toppled. Shouts changed to screams.

Aredel's veins filled with fire. A mad desire to unleash his power clawed at his mind, but he resisted. He couldn't risk Anadin's soul. Not that. It would be too much—he'd never recover from the guilt.

Find the necromancer.

Surely, no matter how foul, the necromancer wouldn't be able to handle himself in a sea of filthy goblins. To keep Anadin upright, he would have to stay near but well-hidden from the creatures running rampant.

The Blood King's eyes roved over the scenery. Shattered tents. Corpses. Smoldering fires.

Fool. He needn't be earthbound.

Aredel lifted his eyes. Most *Unsielie* clashed against the fair *Sielie* winging across the cloudy heavens. Glaives and swords smashed into each other, ringing long and loud. Winged beings tumbled from the air as victors moved on to their next opponents.

Tavassed hovered nearby. And there, farther in the sky, drifted a second lacy winged figure cloaked in tattered grays and blacks. The *Unsielie* hung back, keeping his gaze on the fight between three royals.

I've found you.

Nearby, among a cluster of corpses, a spear jutted up.

Aredel increased the speed of his attacks, trusting his body to anticipate Darint's and Sharo's movements. The fae prince answered him blow for blow. Aredel found himself grinning. He should have trained more with his fae friend.

Did he catch the flash of a grin behind Sharo's helm?

As Sharo met his advance, Aredel let his fingers slip—and the sword careened out of his hands. He pulled back, swung out of his saddle, and took up his sword. Then he caught up the jutting spear in the next motion, aimed, and threw it hard at the necromancer.

His aim was slightly left, but true enough. The spear pierced the *Unsielie*'s wing, and the necromancer plunged groundward. Aredel mounted his horse, and raced toward the necromancer. Tavassed cried out a warning.

Heedless, Aredel reached the necromancer's side and unleashed billowing tendrils of white smoke. The fae creature writhed before the stallion.

Aredel dismounted in a breath, pinned the *Unsielie*'s wounded wing with one boot, and slashed his sword across the creature's throat. The necromancer gurgled and thrashed, then fell still.

Heart pounding, Aredel spun in time to watch Anadin's corpse topple. Threads of pain cut across Aredel's soul. Twice, he'd lost his brother. Twice, he'd not said farewell.

Tavassed shot toward the Blood King. Aredel lifted his head, tempted to let the *Unsielie* run him through and end his agony.

Not yet. The war isn't won.

White smoke exploded from Aredel's body, pouring forth with an unrelenting force that flung the dark fae backward, feet over head. Aredel swung into his saddle, then whipped his reins and sent his stallion racing forth, fingers tingling as he gripped his sword tight.

Tavassed landed among a pile of debris and broken tents and a toppled supply wagon. Aredel was upon him in the next moment, sword raised.

"Do not!" cried the *Unsielie*, throwing his hand over his face.

"Or what?" snarled the Blood King. His sword slashed across Tavassed's arms, then he rammed the blade through the fae's face—and twisted his grip. When Tavassed ceased to twitch, Aredel beheaded the creature with a thrill of satisfaction.

Now, Darint could die.

The Blood King swung into his saddle. The stallion marched back to where Sharo dueled the tyrant king—but as they neared, Aredel's gaze fell on Sharo kneeling beside his horse, helmless, supported by his glowing sword piercing the earth.

No sign of Darint or his steed.

Aredel dismounted and trotted to Sharo's side. "Are you wounded?"

"Y-yes." He pressed his gauntleted hand against a gash across the back of his thigh where the armor ended. "Goblins came. Seized my attention. Father got me from behind."

The wound was bleeding badly. Aredel trotted back to his saddle bag and pulled out bandages, along with a length of rope. When he returned to Sharo's side, he knelt and shoved a wad of cloth against the gash.

"Where is Darint?"

"Escaped." Sharo winced, catching his lower lip between his teeth. Threads of snowy hair clung to his sweat-soaked face. "Once you took down the first *Unsielie*, he panicked. That's w-when the goblins appeared. He was gone after your flash of light." Aredel tugged off Sharo's cuisse to get to the leg, and the fae prince hissed. "Got Tavassed, did you?"

"He's dead." Aredel wrapped the rope around the leg several times. "This needs to be cauterized."

Sharo managed a shaky nod. "Find someone to help...then seek out Darint."

"You needn't tell me twice." Aredel used a sheathed dagger to wind the rope tighter, creating a tourniquet. He secured it and stood. "You need to come with me. Can you stand on your own?"

Sharo pulled himself upright, leaning heavily on his sword.

Aredel led his stallion closer, then helped Sharo up behind the saddle. He mounted in front of the prince, then cast a last glance at the spot where Anadin lay among the dead. Heavy-hearted, Aredel wheeled the horse around and started across the carnage toward the hills where Jinji watched. Amaranth followed, content to let Aredel maintain the lead.

The cries of death, the streams of dark smoke, and the clamber of battle were dim in Aredel's ears. Darint had gotten away, and the goblins were overrunning Sharo's forces. If the dragons failed to arrive soon, the war was as good as over.

Sharo slumped against Aredel, his breaths ragged. He shifted, and his voice drifted toward the Blood King. "We'll win... Watch..."

Aredel grimaced. Everything indicated otherwise. No reinforcements had come from Kavacos or any closer keeps. Shing was silent. KryTeer couldn't answer.

"Yes," he said anyway. "We will."

A goblin raced into their path, needle teeth wide and grinning, red eyes like coals. The creature clutched a glaive twice its height, probably stolen from a fallen *Unsielie*. With a screech, it hurtled toward Aredel, weapon raised.

The Blood King danced his horse around the glaive and lopped off the creature's head without a backward glance.

Three more monsters tumbled into their path from the north, and Aredel dispatched them with no feeling. He didn't have time for these delays. Sharo was still bleeding. He wouldn't let the fae prince die. Shinac needed him. Nakania needed him.

"Hold on a little longer."

Sharo grunted.

A handful of goblins met them. Aredel plowed through them

with growing irritation. He swiped his sword across the air, sending black droplets flying, as he trotted on.

"Where would Darint flee?" He needed a starting point to hunt down the cowardly king, but more than that, he needed Sharo to stay alert.

The prince took a moment to answer. "He...he needs *Unsielie* cover. The goblins aren't enough. And he doesn't...trust...his human soldiers."

"Would they take him into the sky?"

"Possibly. It's safest there."

Aredel scowled. Hunting an airborne man would be tricky. "Will they still follow him, despite Tavassed's death? The contract is broken."

"Only the life contract is broken." As the horse jumped over a pile of corpses, Sharo sucked in a breath. "The rest will remain with him until this battle is decided or my father...draws his last breath."

Then Darint must be taken down, or Nakania would be overrun by evil.

Aredel's lips twisted in a dry smile. He'd never believed in evil; all growing up, his father—the tyrant Gyath—had taught Aredel that war was won by the strong. That if one had such strength, they must use it to conquer and control, for the weak were incapable of governing themselves.

Ruling by force was a responsibility as much as a reward.

But then Aredel had met Jinji, and the humble storyteller had proven that strength could lay in places other than brawn or brain. That a strong heart mattered most. That perhaps the meek were more suited to governing than any tyrant king with his mighty armies.

I want to see that kind of world. Could I help to carve it out?

Aredel cleaved through a goblin before the creature swung its mace.

Jinji, can I use my strength to that end?

He couldn't stop fighting. It was all he knew.

But perhaps, for Anadin, Artassa, and great Bahadronn, he could put his skill to better use.

For the shepherds, farmers, poets, and cobblers.

For the children alive and yet unborn.

I hate ruling.

He'd never wanted KryTeer's crown. And if Jetekesh succeeded in finding the rightful ruler of Nakania, perhaps Aredel would never need to put it on again.

He set his jaw and rammed his sword through the leather hide of another grotesque creature. At the same moment, an arrow lodged into another goblin's eye socket. The foul thing toppled backward with a grunt and, a moment later, Song rode into view, her black hair streaming free, her helm missing.

She nocked her bow. "Allow me to escort you and Prince Sharo from the field, Blood King."

Aredel inclined his head. "I welcome your aid, Lady Song."

They rode toward the hills, Song staying beside Aredel's stallion, clearing the path ahead with her arrows. Soon, the battlefield gave way to the hills, and the Blood King guided his steed toward Jinji at the tor of the highest slope.

There he was, the storyteller true. Jinji stood with a shepherd's crook in his hand, white hair streaming in a stiff spring breeze. His eyes lit with concern as he glimpsed Sharo.

Aredel pulled up the stallion and swung from the saddle. "He needs immediate attention."

Jinji turned and waved at the supply train. "Bring a healer!"

Aredel and Song guided the fae prince to the ground, then the Blood King caught up his stallion's reins. "I'm off to find Darint."

"I'll stay here and protect Prince Sharo," Song said. "He's too tempting a target in this state."

"I thank you, Lady Song." Aredel inclined his head.

"To find Darint, go northwest," Jinji said. "And stay safe, my brother."

The Blood King allowed himself a grin. "Fear not, Jinji Wanderlust. I'm not quite ready to die."

Jinji's eyes caught fire as a proud smile appeared. Aredel carried that image like a torch as he galloped downhill and back into the fray, aiming north and west toward a swarm of *Unsielie* in the sky.

One king would die this day upon the field—and it would not be Aredel of KryTeer.

CHAPTER 45

THE CHOICE OF DESIRE

Dawn cracked the black sky, spilling gold and pink and slate gray across the eastern hills. Jetekesh sat in silence upon the fountain's rim, watching the slow ascent of morning. Dakarai's grave had been dug, and his remains were covered now by fresh soil. Dew sprinkled the grass at the grave's head like a crown to mark the hero's passing.

Anenyasha knelt at the graveside, weaving back and forth, singing a Zindwéan song whose words were too muted to understand.

Jetekesh imbibed the woman's grief, determined never to let the memory dim in his mind. He wished to treasure every moment he'd known Dakarai. Every conversation, no matter how brief. If only he could pluck out the memories and keep them in a decanter, keep them fresh and whole, untattered by time.

Emerin strode up to him, a smudge of dirt darkening his cheek like a bruise. "The rest of us are ready whenever you are." His green eyes flicked over his shoulder to Axel. "It's time to let him choose his fate."

Jetekesh heaved a sigh. "I know." He turned his gaze back to the scaling light of dawn.

"His choices aren't your fault."

A nod was all the answer Jetekesh could give to that. He *knew* as much, deep down. And really, his regret stemmed not from Dakarai's death, but from the events leading up to it—and so many deaths before. But he wouldn't let the feeling paralyze him.

He turned back to Emerin. "You're blaming yourself, too. Don't deny it."

"I won't." The man shrugged. "I keep wishing I'd moved first, faster. Taken the knife instead. It...doesn't help, bearing this guilt, but it's there." He tipped his head back to study the fading stars. "I deserve death far more than he did."

"Who judges that?" whispered Jetekesh. "We deal in death like it's a punishment, and maybe it is for some. But I doubt Dakarai dwells in one of the two hells. He's likely standing with the saints, equal in stature and—" His voice caught. Jetekesh closed his mouth, letting his unspoken words hang between them.

"You're right." Emerin shifted his feet. "I know you're right. But..." he angled toward Anenyasha "...it's still so cruel to the living."

So it was, every time. Jetekesh released another sigh, unwilling to travel down the paths of sorrow any longer. He pushed up from the fountain and set his eyes on Axel. "Time for the verdict."

Emerin walked beside him as Jetekesh strode to the prisoner. Axel lifted his head, shadows cast across his face like he'd aged a hundred years.

Jetekesh drew the dagger at his hip and held it up. "I'm going to cut you free to make your choice. If you try to harm anyone here for any reason, I'll let Emerin and Kethalas have at you in whatever way pleases them. Do I make myself clear?"

Axel seemed to wrestle with himself; his eyes darted away, then back. He finally nodded.

"Good." Jetekesh moved around the captive, knelt, and untied the gag. He dropped the handkerchief aside, then cut through the ropes, releasing Axel. The Norvian slumped forward and dragged his arms around to rub his wrists.

Stepping back to Emerin's side, Jetekesh studied Axel. Kajsa came up beside Jetekesh, her face set in a grim frown, her eyes pinned on Axel like she was about to watch his execution.

That was possible, Jetekesh supposed.

Several heartbeats passed, then Axel hoisted his chin, adopting a little of the haughtiness he wore so well. His gaze slid to Kajsa, and his mouth stretched taut. "Ky."

She pursed her lips, then whispered, "Yes, Axel?"

"I didn't mean to kill him."

Kethalas crept up behind the young man in the grass, silver eyes bright and feral. "That doesn't change the fact that you did."

Axel jumped and jerked his head around to stare up into the dragon's face. Still kneeling, he had to feel utterly helpless under Kethalas's condemning gaze, and to his credit, remorse burned away some of Axel's arrogance.

"No," he whispered. "It doesn't."

"And," the dragon said, "you *were* trying to kill Prince Jetekesh. Do you deny that?"

"No." Heat curled around Axel's tones. "He's doomed to destroy the world. He can't stay alive."

The two prophecies. So, Navolleth had explained them to Axel, and the young man had decided to eliminate the potential problem. Jetekesh couldn't blame him for the temptation, but knowing himself, had their roles been reversed, he couldn't have followed through without proof.

"What's done is done," Jetekesh found himself saying. "Choose your course, Axel. Will you tempt the waters of truth?"

The young man's expression turned steely, hiding any guilt, remorse, or hatred. He dropped his seafoam eyes to the goblet resting before him. What must be going through his head? What visions of a kingly future enticed him to partake of the deadly drink? How well Jetekesh could imagine them, even ache for them; for the comfort and familiarity; for the power to control the destiny of Nakania and protect its people.

Emerin's hand fell to his sword. Kethalas's clawed fingers twitched like he would strike the Norvian down at the slightest motion.

Kajsa took a step forward. "Xel, you don't need the world."

The young man held utterly still, staring, as though he knew nothing of his surroundings. As though he couldn't hear his friend's pleas.

Perhaps he couldn't.

No one moved. They hardly dared to breathe. Dawn slid tendrils of light between each member of the company, burning the dew off the red grass, spraying cascades of light through the pouring water in the fountain.

Overhead, a gryphon soared, wheeling through the air as though to bathe its mighty wings in the glow of sunrise.

Axel plucked up the goblet.

Kajsa inhaled a sharp breath.

The young Norvian tipped the water into the grass, dropped the goblet from limp fingers, then curled forward and sobbed.

In a flurry, Kajsa ran to Axel's side, embraced him, and pulled him close.

Cool relief flooded Jetekesh's chest, easing his heart back from his ribs, slowing its rhythm. With it came a twinge of jealousy, but he shoved that down and bent to claim the goblet.

Straightening, he padded to Kethalas's side and held the jeweled cup aloft. "Hold on to this, will you? I think it's safest with a dragon."

Kethalas studied it. "If you're certain..."

"I'm certain." Jetekesh started to walk back to the campfire.

"You won't drink the waters?"

He froze, then turned back to the man-dragon. "Me? I'm not ready to die just yet."

The dragon canted his head. "You really think you would?"

Jetekesh arched his brow. "Yes. I'm not the rightful king. I'm of the line that called down Nakania's curse. To tempt the waters would be folly."

"You sound so sure." Emerin strode closer, folding his arms. "You think your father's house was unworthy of taking the throne?"

"The fountain didn't choose my family, it only chose Cavalin," Jetekesh said.

"Sure. But after Cavalin fell, and Shinac vanished, you *couldn't* drink from the blood fountain." Emerin smirked. "A tad difficult when you can't even reach it. But your ancestor chose to claim the throne to prevent *worse* chaos on the heels of his father's death."

Jetekesh scowled. "It doesn't change the fact that we conveniently forgot the story of the blood fountain. That we don't even have legends about it, despite stories of Sharo predating even Jinji."

"True, that." Emerin rubbed his chin. "My family line definitely held to the old traditions more than yours."

Jetekesh perked up. "Then...*you* might be the rightful king, my lord." He turned to Kethalas. "Give him the goblet."

Emerin threw up his hands. "No. Not a chance. I won't risk it, not after everything. Your Highness, my house is content to keep the northern passes safe. To rule within our province. I'll not be tied down to a throne, no thank you."

"Emerin, you'd make a wonderful king," Jetekesh said.

"Once, perhaps." The man shook his head. "I'll not hold that power after what I've been forced—" he grimaced "—what I *chose* to do. My hands are too bloody."

"But don't you see?" Jetekesh said. "Your hesitancy, your humility, and your past errors will all make you a better king. It's not what you've done; it's what you'll do *now*."

"Exactly!" Rille's voice cut across the chill morning hair, her eyes a bright, glowing amber. "Well said, cousin. The same is true of you, don't you see?" She stalked from the fireside. "You're terrified to drink the waters. You think you can't be high king because of what's happened in the past—both the *distant* and the *recent* past, to be clear. You genuinely believe you have no right to your throne, yet who has spent his entire life training to take it?"

"I—"

She cut him off. "Exactly. *You*." Her hands flew to her hips. "And, while I admit I've had severe doubts about your capability to be as noble-hearted as your father, those doubts have since flown."

"But—"

"I'm not finished." Rille stomped her foot for emphasis. "Bless you, cousin, but you're terribly thick-skulled."

A smile skittered over Emerin's lips before he could stifle it.

Jetekesh flushed until his cheeks caught fire. "Rille—"

She held up a finger. "What did I say?" Her hand dropped, and her eyes sparked brighter. "Listen to me: You're a good person, and you're becoming a better person every single day. Not passively either. You're striving to overcome a lifetime of privilege, pomp, and over-indulgence, and *you're succeeding*. Do you have any idea how incredible that is?"

He stared, half fascinated, half mortified. Was this really Rille talking to him? Doling out praise? To *him*?

Rille's stern expression softened. "You want to be king, don't you?"

He hesitated, then exhaled. "Yes. I confess I do."

"Why?"

His cheeks burned hotter. "I...just want to put things right. I worry about Amantier—and all of Nakania—in someone else's hands. My father's the better candidate. I know that. And I've thought of giving him the waters—thus proving his worthiness—but I'm terrified..."

"Jetekesh." Rille's voice was just above a whisper. "Do you think there's only one right ruler in all of Nakania?"

He ducked his head. "No, o-of course not. I didn't mean to suggest—"

"Hush, cousin." She moved forward and caught his hands in hers, the warmth of her fingers shocking to his chilled flesh. "If you would make a good high king, then why not drink the waters of truth? If you won't make a mess of things, and you intend only good for Nakania, then *why not you*?

He blinked twice, trying to assimilate her argument. His ear rang as he stared into her eyes, unable to swallow her words. Did Rille really believe he could drink the waters and live? He pulled free of her grasp and dragged a hand over his face. "If you're wrong..."

"Only you can know if I'm wrong," she said. "Jinji's story didn't say *anyone* who drank the water would die. Only those seeking power unworthily. Do you want to be a tyrant, Jetekesh?"

He lowered his hand, curling his fingers into a fist. "No."

"Do you intend to wrest power from all countries, enslave foreigners, and denounce Shinac?"

"Certainly not."

"Do you think you'll become arrogant with that big heavy crown on your head?"

He hesitated. "I...I hope not."

Rille tilted her head and a smile slid over her lips. "Then what's to be afraid of?"

His limbs shook. His gaze wandered to the burbling fountain, then away, like it might strike him down for even considering.

Cool fingers slipped into his, and he startled, turning to face Kajsa at his side.

"I believe in you," she whispered.

Searching her calm blue eyes, something in him settled down; something that had been raging, storming, screaming against fear and confusion. They were right. He didn't have to scour every countryside in Nakania, seeking out the purest, meekest child to raise up to become a monarch. He only needed a good person, not the best person. Someone who cared; someone who wanted to do the right thing.

He drew breath, filling his lungs with air and purpose. With renewed hope.

Kethalas moved around him, caught his wrist, and pressed the goblet into his palm. "Take it, Your Highness. Choose to become a worthy king if that is your wish."

A smile dangled at the edges of Jetekesh's mouth. He curled his fingers over the cool metal, then tugged Kajsa along as he stared at the waters flowing into the fountain.

If I'm wrong, if something inside me yearns for power to elevate myself above everyone else, then I deserve whatever the waters do to me. This is it, Kesh. The ultimate test. Are you worthy?

He reached the brimming waters. They shimmered before his eyes, dazzling, casting light against the garnets set into the goblet. Did he imagine a voiceless call from the flowing fountain? Did the waters beckon to him? Inhaling, he released Kajsa's hand, stooped, filled the goblet, and turned from the frothing pool.

His eyes collided with Axel's. The Norvian still knelt where he'd been set free, eyes red-rimmed, cheeks stained with tears. Jetekesh expected to read hatred there, but all he saw was resignation.

May God and all his saints guide my path from here, Jetekesh prayed, too afraid to speak aloud.

He lifted the goblet. Paused. Steeled himself for whatever truth he met—and set the cup to his lips. The waters poured down his throat, clear, cold, sweeter than a high mountain stream. He drained the goblet dry.

Lowering the empty vessel, he waited.

Nothing changed. Breath still came. His heart still beat. Blood flowed through his veins.

Everyone standing before him sank to their knees.

"Hail, High King of Nakania," Emerin said in a clear, rumbling voice. "Long live King Jetekesh, fifth of his name!"

CHAPTER 46
A STOLEN MOMENT

Dewdrops sparkled around his kneeling companions, vivid against the mist in Jetekesh's eyes. He squeezed the goblet, cleared his throat, and issued his first command. "Rise, my friends."

They moved to their feet, then rolled inward like a wave to offer congratulations.

"I think you're the only one here who doubted how this would go." Emerin's grin was wide and proud.

"You're the stuff of kings," Kethalas added. "Dakarai would agree."

That last sobered Jetekesh, pulling him from the heights of wonder and relief. "But how do we know it worked?" he asked. "Rille said the waters might not actually kill me either way."

"Oh, it worked," said the little girl. "How can you not *feel* that crown upon your head, you goose?"

His hand shot up until his fingers struck the cold points of a crown. He yanked it off and stared. It was stunning; a work of intricate artistry, forged by a master, all points and swirls etched into a white gold circlet set with rubies and diamonds.

"It's dragon forged," Kethalas said. "No doubt of it."

A memory tugged at Jetekesh's mind. A tapestry within the cathedral at Kavacos featuring Cavalin, crowned, wielding a sword and scepter. This matched exactly.

Cavalin's lost crown.

Jetekesh's heart swelled.

"Well," said Emerin. "We have what we came for." He set his hand on Jetekesh's shoulder. "We should head out."

Jetekesh's mind spun as he contemplated his next move. He'd been so certain they'd need to search every inch of the continent to find the high king or queen, but now...nothing had changed.

He stared at the crown again. No, *he* had changed. Proven to himself that he wasn't an imposter, no matter whose blood, no matter which lineage, no matter what sins...he was enough.

And the curse was broken.

A grin spread wide over his face. "Well, then. Let's return to Prince Sharo and King Aredel. We've a war to win—and I need to show Navolleth my new crown."

After a quick breakfast of bread and cheese, Jetekesh placed the goblet atop the blood fountain. Then the company left the red valley and started up the hills for the Hold of Valliath, Jetekesh in the lead with Kajsa in hand and Raum near her heels. Kethalas was in the rear, leading Axel along.

Once at the castle, they planned to ask the gryphons for aid to reach Amantier—hopefully before the opposing forces engaged, though Jetekesh doubted it. They'd taken so long to reach Valliath.

As they crested the third rise along the hills, Kajsa spoke, her voice quiet but strong. "Now that you're the high king I won't see you often."

He stumbled but caught himself. “Why ever not?”

“Well.” Her cheeks were a bright pink hue. “Kings don’t have much time for commoners.”

He tugged her closer on a whim. “This king does—especially for *this* commoner.” The words were out before he could chase them back down his throat. He wished a hole would open up and swallow him on the spot.

Kajsa jerked to a halt, forcing the company to stop.

With burning ears, Jetekesh risked a glance at her. She stood frozen in place, blue eyes wide, face a brilliant red. He tugged on her hand, and she thawed, following at an even pace.

Neither spoke for a long time.

“Why?” Kajsa’s question was a faint squeak.

He could pretend not to understand, but that was stupid. Staring straight ahead, he willed his nerves to sustain him. “Because...” He pulled in a steadying breath. “Because I care about you. Because...” *Say it.* He fumbled for the words. “...You’re strong, kind, and—and beautiful. And I’m very fond of you.” The last came in a rush.

Somewhere in the back of his mind, something screamed at him. Mortification, perhaps. Or could it be his irrational fear of falling in love with a woman like his mother?

Kajsa wasn't like that. Not at all. She was goodness incarnate, wrapped in a shy exterior that he’d begun to see through to her warmth and compassion. He started to smile, but it toppled as he remembered Axel. Her best friend. Her protector for years.

Clearing his throat, Jetekesh pinned his eyes on the distant spires of the fae castle. “That doesn’t mean I expect anything of you. Your feelings are as valid as my own. If you feel more strongly for someone else, for instance, I’ll not behave like a brute and assert my authority to steal you away...”

Tempting as it may be, he finished in his mind.

“Jetekesh?”

He glanced at her, finding a shy smile. “Yes?”

“Are you saying...?”

“I’m asking if you’ll let me court you, yes.” The heat in his ears died, as though saying the words—really spelling them out—snuffed out his uncertainties. It was up to her now; he’d done what he could and must accept her decision with whatever grace was required.

“Yes.” The word was spoken in a breathless rush.

He kept walking but he didn’t know how. Sneaking a glance at her, he found her eyes glittering with welling tears. “Yes?”

She nodded, meeting his gaze with her startling, clear eyes. “Yes. I—I’ll let you court me. Please.”

His heart stuttered. “What about Axel?” Stupid, insubordinate mouth.

“Axel? Oh.” She paused, perhaps questioning her decision. “I thought he was what I wanted. I fully expected...” She laughed. “But I don’t want what I expected. I...I want you.” Her gaze darted away, then returned with a look of defiance that was clearly directed inward.

He grinned, laughed, and pulled her close until their sides touched. “When we reach the garden, remind me to kiss you.”

“I will,” she said with a soft giggle. “I promise.”

Perhaps it was the magic of Valliath falling upon them again, but Jetekesh suspected the reason he conquered the remaining hills with a tirelessness he’d never known was the thought that carried him forth: He was going to kiss Kajsa.

THE CASTLE SPARKLED like stardust in the high morning sunlight. In the garden, Jetekesh pulled away from Kajsa and fell back to Emerin’s side. “Could you take the company ahead? I’ll join you in a few moments.”

The keep lord nodded, his face strangely blank.

Kajsa hung back as the others followed Emerin's call to 'come along.' No one so much as glanced back. Not even Axel, his head bowed low.

They know. Jetekesh thought embarrassment would stab him again, but he only found himself grinning. Perhaps it was foolish to steal this moment in the midst of war, yet he couldn't bring himself to feel a modicum of guilt.

Catching Kajsa's hands, he pulled her toward an arched arbor where wild yellow roses climbed—the one variety Mother had hated, claiming they were weeds disguised as flowers. Their fragrance washed over Jetekesh, sweet, vibrant. His stomach flipped and butterflies tickled his ribcage.

He reached up, stroked Kajsa's cheek, then caught a strand of her platinum hair and looped it behind her ear. Her lips lifted into a smile both shy and happy, and she pulled closer, setting her hands on his chest.

They stepped closer still, and Jetekesh grew lightheaded. His lips met Kajsa's, tentative, uncertain. He'd never kissed anyone before. Would he do it wrong?

It was awkward for a moment, but Kajsa answered him, and heat poured over Jetekesh's frame in a pleasant way he could never have imagined. Kajsa fit against him like they'd been made exactly right for each other. They melted into each other's arms as their lips lingered. Then with supreme reluctance, Jetekesh pulled back.

Kajsa's eyes were bluer than the sky, and she beamed like she'd swallowed the sun. A tear rolled down her cheek, and he caught it on the pad of his finger.

"Thank you," he said. "For letting me do that."

Kajsa inhaled. "Thank you." Her lips stretched higher. "For doing that."

They laughed, then clasped hands, and entered the Hold of Valliath together.

CHAPTER 47
BETWEEN THE HOLLY TREES

The contingent of elves stood with the company inside the Great Hall of the Hold. Upon entering Jetekesh glanced around. Emerin was eyeing his and Kajsa's radiant faces, and the keep lord couldn't quite contain a grin before he turned to the elven seer called Heyethir.

"We're ready now," Emerin said.

Heyethir turned his gaze upon Jetekesh. "Nakania is whole once more, I see. Hail, High King Jetekesh."

"Thank you." Jetekesh dipped his head. He was glad his crown seemed content not to fall off. He hadn't known whether to wear or carry it, but Emerin had insisted he leave it on his head for the time being.

"Get used to the feeling," the keep lord had said.

Jetekesh couldn't quite explain its weightlessness, nor had there been time to discuss the fact. *No,* he chided himself. *Only to kiss a girl.* His lips quirked up.

"Lord Emerin has explained your urgent need to return to Amantier," Heyethir said. "I believe we may grant permission for Nakania's high king to use the elder paths."

"That would be tremendously obliging of you." Jetekesh had used the elder paths once before to reach Peresen's dread fortress and stop the man from breaching the boundary of Nakania. Once again, it would prove pivotal in stopping evil.

"The hour when the paths open is soon at hand." Heyethir motioned to the Hall's doors. "We shall lead you to the entrance."

The elves moved in a perfect row toward the outside world. The company followed. The scent of trees and brush and loam rolled over the new king, and he drank it in, glad to be on his way to his home country despite the beauty of the fae realm.

He'd not rest until he could confirm that his father, his people, and his allies were well.

Heyethir took a different path from the downhill road they'd traversed to reach the Hold. This one veered right and led into a thick stand of trees. As they entered the shade of the ancient forest, Jetekesh spotted two holly trees with pointed leaves and bright red berries.

His step quickened.

"Oh," breathed Rille. "The magic is thick here."

So it was, practically singing on the wind. Jetekesh could already hear the music of the elder paths calling to him. He longed to race into the ancient wood, but courtesy held him back. He turned to Heyethir. "You have our deepest gratitude for your aid, my lord."

Heyethir inclined his head. "Be aware, Your Majesty: The Realm of Valliath is separate from the world's time. The paths will take you as close to the proper time as possible, but days, weeks, or even years may pass. Do not become heedless or you may come out into Amantier one hundred years from now."

Jetekesh blinked at that, then smiled. "We'll not heed the fairy song."

"Should any of you choose to remain in Valliath," Heyethir said, "you are welcome. Otherwise, walk between the holly trees and enter the elder paths. Fare thee well, High King of Nakania." He inclined his head to each member of the company, and the other elves mirrored his actions.

Jetekesh squeezed Kajsa's fingers. "Ready?"

She started to nod, but Raum's whine drew her attention.

The ghostly wolf sat before Heyethir, his outline more faded than before. Kajsa tensed, then slipped free of Jetekesh's hold to approach Raum. "Is this where we part, my dear friend?"

The wolf tilted his head and huffed out an answer.

Kajsa knelt, her shoulders trembling. "How I'll miss you. You've been so faithful."

Axel strode forward. "He can't go."

"He must," answered Heyethir. "The Veil of Valliath gave him leave to walk with you only until the prophecy was fulfilled and Cavalin's heir was found. This has been accomplished. Once the war is decided, and one last curse lifted, the remaining ghosts caught between two worlds will be free to depart as well."

Jetekesh swallowed, thinking of Cavalin's ghost—and of Jinji. His heartbeat faltered. "Will that include the storyteller true?"

Heyethir shook his head. "His call lies beyond the bounds of this world. He answers to the True King of Shinac alone."

Jetekesh's chest tightened. The True King of Shinac, just as he himself was the high king of Nakania. How strange that he stood, if not equal, then still nearer to the height of that illustrious man than he'd ever thought possible.

Kajsa swallowed Raum in a hug, and the wolf nudged her neck.

When they parted, Jetekesh reached out to brush his fingers against the transparent fur. "Thank you for all you've done, little fellow."

The wolf inclined his head like he understood perfectly, then the canine stood, backed up, and settled beside Heyethir's feet.

Axel took one halting step toward the ghost wolf. His hand

started to rise, but he forced his arm back to his side, curling his fingers into fists. "Goodbye, Raum." He turned away.

Raum let out a bark.

"I too shall remain here." Anenyasha's voice startled Jetekesh, and he whirled, blinking at the tall clanswoman.

She wore a quiet, sorrowful smile. "I cannot leave my beloved in a strange land, utterly alone. Our clan is scattered. The world is changing. I am no longer part of it."

"But..." Jetekesh hesitated. "You're my friend."

"And when the True King returns," she said, "we shall meet again, I think."

"That could be centuries from now," Jetekesh whispered.

"Not so." Heyethir's voice was calm and soothing. "We shall soon enter the Meridian—the age of Serepoints. You are likely among them, fair king. You may be called beyond this world to answer King Ehrikai's summons. But first, you must answer the needs of this world. Once the Meridian opens, the True King may return to Valliath, and we shall then enter the proper flow of time, just as Nakania and Shinac have done. Despair not."

Jetekesh swallowed hard, unable to comprehend all that the elf declared. He set his jaw, then turned back to Anenyasha. "Farewell for now, then, my friend. May the saints and good spirits attend you in your new journey."

She tapped her fingers to her throat, then spread her hand before her. "And may the rays of the sun light your path to faithful friends."

"I—" His voice caught. He tried again. "I'll not forget you or Dakarai. Not ever."

Anenyasha's smile widened. "Nor shall we forget you."

For a fleeting moment, Jetekesh thought he saw Dakarai standing at her side, and he didn't doubt his eyes. His smile deepened as Kajsa and Rille each hugged Anenyasha. As Kajsa stepped back, wiping at her eyes, he reached for her hand instinctively.

Her fingers reached back, and he guided her toward the holly trees.

Apart from Raum and Anenyasha, the rest of the company followed, stepping between the holly trees to find two rows of berry-laden trees beyond, leading into darkness.

Jetekesh took the path with confident steps, and soon huge redwoods rose before him, widespread and lit with golden light. The trees here were watchful, but not malevolent. Simply ancient, perhaps ageless, knowing more than Jetekesh could ever dream of learning.

Kajsa fell still at his side, staring up into the canopy of boughs. Her lips parted like she might speak, but the stillness settled around them, and she remained silent.

The others in the company appeared at their backs, one by one, and each fell into the same quiet, to study the fae paths.

"Where do we go?" asked Emerin after several moments.

Kethalas strode forward. "This way." He moved straight ahead between the trees.

Jetekesh grinned. "Follow the dragon." He tugged Kajsa on, and they walked together behind Kethalas with Rille next, then Emerin beside Axel, likely to keep an eye on him.

"How close will this path bring us to Amantier?" asked Emerin.

"Hopefully it will take us to the very edge of the battlefield," Kethalas answered without looking back. "Some elder paths still remain in Nakania—they've just been inaccessible until now."

That made sense, Jetekesh supposed. "Do you know the way by instinct, or have you trod these paths before?"

Kethalas chuckled. "A dragon rarely gets lost. Our instincts are honed to magic, and our sense of smell is more refined than the finest hounds."

"What scent are you following?" Rille asked.

The dragon hesitated. "Blood, my lady. The blood of *Sielie* and

Unsielie, of goblins and humans, all at the battlefield we seek, I suspect."

Silence filled in the spaces around the company after that. Jetekesh wished the path would end and he could reach the other side, though his stomach churned at the thought. Were Sharo and Aredel all right? Had Thrissa reached them? What of Yeshton and Song? Had Navolleth remained true to his alliance with Sharo, or would the fallen dragon betray them?

Patience, Kesh. Soon, we'll learn all.

The hand clutching his satchel twitched with an urge to grasp his sword hilt and run his thumb over the gemstone set into the pommel. He resisted, clasping Kajsa's hand a little tighter. *Soon* became his mantra as they navigated the elder paths until the golden light gave way to the blue hues of evening.

Kethalas halted. "We're losing the light. We'll find no way into Amantier until morning." He turned to face the company. "That means we should rest. If we're about to enter the fray, that's best anyway." His silver eyes settled on Jetekesh. "Agreed?"

Jetekesh's heart plummeted. "Agreed." He slid his satchel off his shoulder and plopped it to the ground. "Though I hate the thought of waiting."

He pulled the crown from his head, sat beside Kajsa beneath a redwood tree, and kept his fingers wrapped around hers. She shifted close, then rested her head on his shoulder, fitting just right.

He tried to rest as the hours crawled by, but in his head, he heard the distant cry of battle, the clash of arms, the moans of the dying—and he prayed the proper path would open soon.

CHAPTER 48
RIDE ON

Yeshton maintained a steady pace, guiding his horse ahead of King Jetekesh's army. Ledonn rode with him. Both had eagerly volunteered as scouts to pick out the path toward the distant battle.

"I hate not knowing what's going on ahead of us," muttered the Blood Knight.

"You know enough," Yeshton said.

The KryTeeran sighed. "Yes, the war has started without me. I despise that."

Yeshton rolled his eyes. He would never understand the hunger for battle professed by the Blood Knights, though he suspected that it wasn't a lust for killing as much as a show of bravery and honor. He'd come to respect Ledonn and Shevek too much to think they were warmongers.

Well, not in all things.

Each day, as they rode, both knights kept their eyes on the horizon, seeking any sign of the approaching enemy. King Jetekesh had sent a messenger pigeon ahead, informing Prince Sharo and King Aredel of their march south—but Yeshton knew the truth as well as the Amantieran king or any other soldier marching from Kavacos: They would never arrive in time.

The war would be decided long before they reached the battlefield.

An image welled up in Yeshton's mind of the Lady of Crimson Lilies riding into the fray with her Shingese blade, her eyes bright as burning coals. *I hope Song is well. I'd have liked to know her better.*

He urged his horse into a faster pace. Too late or not, he'd reach Southern Amantier as quickly as possible and learn the fate of Nakania. He must.

CHAPTER 49
WINGS OF ICE

Carving his way on horseback across the battlefield, Aredel fell into an old, familiar dance. Every enemy who engaged him fell by the wayside as he made his way toward the swarm of *Unsielie* on the far side of the field.

He had no time for goblins—not with Darint on the run, perhaps about to bind himself to another *Unsielie* to extend his life.

Aredel pierced a goblin's heart, wrenched his sword free, kicked the creature aside, then cantered on. Another goblin raced into his path. He angled his blade to lop off the monster's head, and moved on before the body had even fallen.

No time for this.

A humming noise approached, and he drew his eyes up in time to find a half dozen *Unsielie* warriors swooping toward him.

Darint is trying to buy time, is he?

Light burst from Aredel's body, pulling from his soul. He wondered how long he could keep up the use of his power but didn't linger on it. He'd find out the moment it petered out. He must simply use it as needed until then.

He held his sword high, ready to engage with any remaining *Unsielie* as he drew in his light—but a roaring cry tore across the air as the white smoke faded. Golden wings collided with the airborne force. A gryphon.

Aredel tensed, pulling his stallion to a halt. A figure rode on the gryphon's back, long silvery hair streaming behind her.

He found himself grinning. Lady Thrissa of the Wood had returned.

Did that mean Jetekesh was back? Wasn't it too soon?

Did he fail?

That wasn't the only possibility where magic was concerned. Perhaps the boy had found the rightful ruler en route or the fountain had been nearer than presumed. Perhaps he'd gotten a ride back, something swift—like a gryphon.

"Go on your way, Blood King!" Thrissa called, then crashed her sword against an *Unsielie* glaive. "Find the tyrant!"

Her words startled him—she must have spoken with Jinji before she came here.

"Much appreciated." He brought his horse to a gallop. The stallion jumped debris and galloped like the wind itself through carnage and black smoke, past clusters of soldiers locked in deadly combat, carrying Aredel northwest.

As he rode, he took in his surroundings with a critical eye. It was impossible to tell which side of the conflict had the upper hand from his vantage point, but the odds had favored Darint's forces from the start. Despite Tavassed's death and Aredel's power, he doubted that had changed.

Where are those dragons?

The stallion leapt over a shattered phoenix banner jutting up from another heap of bodies. Elves, humans, and fairies lay together in their new, eternal rest. So many lost. Gone forever, their spirits roaming the fens of Amantier.

Would they be trapped like the ghosts haunting the Ruin? Did Anadin's soul dwell there too?

The swarming force of *Unsielie* was closer now, and Aredel's mind switched tracks. How could he gain the sky to challenge Darint? Thrissa's gryphon would have come in handy.

A familiar figure stood in the path ahead. Aredel slowed, lifting a brow. Navolleth was clad in his customary blue cloak, but was otherwise as pale as a specter.

"I've been waiting for you, Your Majesty." Navolleth turned his gaze skyward. "Darint is not there. He fled as I approached." The man-dragon pointed a slender finger toward the forest several leagues away. "Shall we hunt him?"

A feral grin stretched over Aredel's face again. "I do enjoy a good hunt."

"As do I." Navolleth lowered his arm, then stepped back and shifted. His features stretched and grew as shimmering scales appeared on his skin, wrapping him in natural armor. Navolleth expanded, growing, growing, until he became a mighty, lithe beast: white scaled, with a long silvery mane, and reptilian eyes of molten gold. His claws were massive, sharp, glittering like diamonds.

'**Climb onto my back, Blood King**.' The dragon's voice thundered through his head, yet it still held that tinge of sorrow ever-present in Navolleth's tones.

Aredel swung from his saddle, patted the stallion's flank, and moved to the outstretched wing extended like a gangplank to the dragon's ridged back. He climbed the leathery wing, noting the pearlescent sparkle woven into the white scales, scattering rainbows across the Blood King's crimson armor.

He stood at the dragon's long neck, grasped threads of silken mane, and set his feet. "I am ready, Lord Dragon."

As the words left his lips, a mighty crash of thunder flooded the skies behind him. Aredel whipped his head around. A drive of dragons swooped toward the battlefield, spirals of fire and ice streaming from their enormous maws. They glinted like jewels of every color; some were red, others blue, green, purple, silver, pink, black, orange—all glittering and massive and terrifying. Chills prickled up Aredel's arms as he admired their fluid, powerful movements across the field.

Goblins screamed below. *Unsielie* scattered above.

Navolleth lifted himself into the air with his great beating wings, and Aredel turned his attention toward the forest.

"Don't burn the trees," he shouted above the wind noise.

Navolleth kept his reptilian face on the timberland as they started over it. **'I would never willingly wound a forest—and besides, I am an ice dragon.'**

Airborne, Aredel scanned the northern horizon, seeking any hint of the Amantieran army Yeshton had gone to fetch. They'd received a messenger pigeon the day before, but the army could only move so fast, which likely meant they would arrive too late.

A pity. The king of Amantier would have enjoyed the sight of dragons chasing down and crisping the dark creatures of Darint's forces.

We've not won yet.

Yet it seemed inevitable now. Dragons were so nearly invulnerable, from all Aredel knew from legends and Jinji's stories.

Yet you stand upon the back of one who will be a greater threat to you than Darint in the end. The alliance with Navolleth was a brittle, fleeting thing.

The Blood King drew his thoughts back to the present. One enemy at a time; that was how a man conquered the world.

Navolleth flew low over the firs, and the fragrance of sap and needles filled Aredel's senses.

'I can smell him.'

Aredel wrapped his fingers around his curved sword and

quieted his mind, dismissing all irrelevant matters. Time to kill a king.

CHAPTER 50
A NEW PACT

Darint crouched in a thicket, ignoring the bite of thorns from the wild roses and the throb in his sprained ankle. The *Unsielie* who had carried him to the forest lay dead nearby, a stray arrow lodged in her temple.

The king listened with growing frustration to the roar of the dragons. So many of them. Curse Sharo and his allies. Curse Navolleth for joining their cause.

Darint ground his teeth while he strained his ears for sounds of pursuit. Navolleth had seen him; had charged him—and the Blood King had been close behind. After the crash, Darint couldn't run properly. He was a dead man once they found him.

I must tip the scales back. But how?

He knew how. He had only one option open to him to stave off defeat, but he loathed the idea. His fingers twitched toward the pouch at his belt. Toward the gift Tavassed had given him, intended for King Aredel.

Glancing at it, the faintest glint of red flickered in the pouch, part beacon, part warning. Did he dare use Tavassed's gift?

The king chewed his lip, fingers flexing. He needed to live.

Needed to win. Needed something more powerful than an *Unsielie* contract, so easily broken by the Blood King.

You really have no choice.

He untied the pouch and loosened the cord, letting the demon's red glow stain the trees around him. The wild roses seemed to shrink back while the thorns dug deeper into the back of Darint's legs where the armor didn't protect him.

"Demon, can you hear me?"

I hear you, King of Shard Kingdom, whispered a voice, soft as silk.

Darint licked his lips, his nerves humming in his ears. "I—" He hesitated. Doubts clawed at his mind and chest. But he had no alternative. Nothing else but this would save him and his armies. "In exchange for victory and a long reign, I offer myself as host to you." The words roared through Darint's head.

Silence filled the woods. No birds chirped. No insects darted by.

The voice slithered forth again. *I was promised the body of Aredel of KryTeer.*

Darint grimaced. "Well, things have changed. The dragons are here. And I am hunted by the Blood King. If he finds me as I am, I'm dead. Not a fate I prefer, as you might imagine."

The red light pulsed. *Very well, King Darint. I shall agree to this pact: Long life for you, and victory in war. Let us unite!*

The light stretched up from the pouch, taking the shape of clawed fingers.

Darint had a moment to question himself—a moment of sheer terror—and then the light consumed him, enveloped him, penetrated every layer of his being.

CHAPTER 51
GAIN AND LOSS

In the stillness of the elder path, hidden in the silence of night, Axel sat in the torment of his thoughts.

Since Navolleth had entered his life, nothing had been the same. Half-formed dreams of glory had taken solid shape, and the white dragon's promises had soothed every doubt.

A throne—only at the cost of a few twisted lives.

New land—meant for Norva from the start.

And Kajsa as part of that future.

All Axel had to do was get his hands dirty. That should be easy for a hunter, raised to butcher animals to feed his village in the sparse winter months. What were corrupt human lives compared to the majestic creatures of the woods?

After all, Jetekesh and his ilk deserved whatever Norva gave them, didn't they?

Rubbing his wrists, Axel eyed the slumbering forms around him. A faint song hummed in the gloom of the path, tickling his ears. He ignored it.

The plan had seemed so simple. Axel would prevent Jetekesh

from stealing the crown of Nakania again. Instead, Axel would drink the water, thereby proving his worthiness as a descendant of Cavalin to rule.

How had it all gone so wrong?

Why had he tried to kill Jetekesh?

Navolleth said you might need to dirty your hands. Axel rested his head against the redwood trunk and choked back a sob.

He hadn't meant to kill an innocent man. A *good* man. Dakarai had done nothing but defend his friend.

Why? Why? Why?

It was supposed to be Jetekesh who died.

Axel cast a glare toward the new high king and found Jetekesh standing at the edge of the path, listening to the stillness of the woods. His back was to Axel. The boy king didn't know the latter was awake, or how much he was suffering.

Have you ever known true suffering, Jetekesh? Axel wondered.

Anger kindled in his chest, but sputtered and died in the waters of regret.

Axel hadn't meant to hurt Dakarai. He hadn't wanted to kill anyone.

Yet I did.

He stared down at his hands and imagined blood staining his fingertips. How could he ever touch Kajsa with these hands? How could he draw her in for a kiss or caress her hair?

His gaze fell on his childhood friend. She was curled up nearby, using Jetekesh's satchel for a pillow. Her hair glowed in the indigo hues of the elder path. She'd become more beautiful, more confident, outside the boundaries of their home. And since the events at the blood fountain, she'd become something else, too.

A woman in love.

Axel turned away, swallowing a lump. He hated that. Hated to think of it. To admit to it.

But the moment he'd thrown that knife, he'd lost...
...everything.

CHAPTER 52
GATHERING ALLIES

Jetekesh stood within the blue-tinged woods and listened.

There it was again, the faint song of the fae—but this wasn't the fairies of the elder paths taunting and luring him. This was something else. Something that flared the mark he wore.

He inched toward the sound, to the left of the path they must take in under an hour if his instinct was right.

"What is it?" he whispered.

A kind of knowing pulsed through him. Lafe, beckoning. He moved faster, ignoring someone's call behind him. Stepping among the redwoods, he made his way toward the beckoning path as a pinprick of light twinkled before him.

He reached out his arm. "Sir Lafe, grab my hand."

Through the broadening light, the knight's gauntleted hand appeared, stretching toward him through a crack of light. Jetekesh grasped the hand and pulled, dragging his protector through and into the ancient woods. The knight staggered to a halt, clasping Jetekesh's fingers, his eyes wide and wandering as he took in the redwoods. Then his gaze dropped to Jetekesh, and his eyes widened more.

The young king grinned. "Welcome to the elder paths of Shinac, Sir Knight."

Lafe fell to one knee. "Your Highness—" He winced. "Forgive me, Your *Majesty*."

Jetekesh tensed. "How did you know?"

"I dreamt it," the knight said. "I saw you partake of the waters, and then the crown appeared upon your head. A voice followed: 'Behold, the High King of Nakania has been chosen.' I awakened from my slumber within the Clanslands and cried out, begging the One God and all his saints to let me come to you—and then the light appeared, and your voice summoned me."

"I'm glad of that, Sir Lafe. I've missed you—and we'll need every sword. We march for war within the hour. Arise, my friend. Are you mended?"

Lafe stood and inclined his head. "I am, sire. Or nearly so. Well enough to fight."

"Then join us." He motioned back to the company just beyond sight, then turned and led the way.

As they entered the makeshift camp, Emerin met them wearing a scowl, but it fell as his eyes landed on Lafe. "Well met, Sir Knight." He clapped Lafe's shoulder, grinning broadly. "We have need of your blade."

"So I hear," Lafe answered with his own wolfish grin. He explained his dream again, then Emerin turned to Jetekesh with vibrant eyes.

"Well, sire, it's possible many now know of your new status."

Jetekesh shrugged. "That makes things easier for me if so." His attention strayed to the path not yet open to Amantier. "Emerin, even if word reached my father of Darint's army's approach, he won't have much time to answer. I worry about Sharo's numbers—dragons or not. I just...have a feeling."

Emerin sighed. "I know. If only we could—"

"Can't we?" Jetekesh broke in, his heart beating faster. "I pulled Lafe here, didn't I?"

"Did you *mean* to?" asked Emerin.

Jetekesh shook his head. "No, but Lafe wanted it, and his yearning reached me. What happens if *I* want to reach my father and pull his army through the elder paths?" He moved along the trees, stretching his senses.

"They need an invitation, don't they?"

Rille's voice cut in. "Wouldn't the Marked Prince's desire be enough of an invitation?" She paused. "And, come to that, the High King of Nakania?"

Jetekesh tossed her a grateful smile, and she returned it with a small one of her own.

He paced along the edge of the trees, stretching his senses further, trying to feel the source of his father…

That same tingle returned. He whirled. "I think I've found it."

If this worked, he could also reclaim the horses he'd left near Valliath, rather than leave them in the mountains to starve.

Think bigger. What of Shing's army, ready to march at any moment?

His grin stretched wide.

Kethalas was at his side in a few bounds, scenting the air. "It does smell like King Jetekesh." His lips trembled. "The elder one."

Jetekesh winced. "That will get confusing very quickly." He turned his gaze on the wooded path. "Let me just try…" He held out his arm again, fingers reaching. Another crack of light appeared at his will, broadening as he inched toward it, until he stood halfway between the redwood forest and the plains of Southern Amantier.

Before him marched an army of human soldiers glinting in their silver armor and red capes beneath a cloud-cradled sun. The red plums of their helms bobbed on their heads. The scouts in front reined in their horses, one wearing the bloodred armor of KryTeer. The second lifted his helm for a better look at the portal of light where Jetekesh stood.

Jetekesh's heart soared. "Sir Yeshton, how glad I am to see you!"

"Your Highness." Yeshton straightened. "Welcome back. Is Lady Rille—"

"She's as well as ever," Jetekesh said. "Please bring my father the king here, and I'll reunite you with my cousin post haste."

Yeshton wheeled his steed around and galloped back to the main forces with all speed.

Jetekesh didn't dare step from the portal, worried he would lose the path if he did. Instead, he waited in silence until the knight returned, bringing a bannerman, an elf, and Father. The king of Amantier was clad in ornate armor, with a red cape edged in gold which flowed down his back, and a helm with a red and gold plume atop. He clutched a shield bearing the Crowned Rose of Amantier.

"Kesh!" Father called as he approached on his cantering horse. He passed his shield to his bannerman, flung himself from his horse with a clatter of armor, and raced through the tall grass until he could throw his arms around his son.

Jetekesh welcomed the embrace, despite Father's armor biting into him. "Hello, Father."

The king pulled back to study Jetekesh. "You look very well, saints be praised."

"I am well, and I'm on my way to the battleground now. I wish to take your army with me." He gestured to the portal. "It's a shortcut."

Father's eyes sparkled as he peered into the forest beyond. "I won't attempt to fathom all that this means, my son, but I'll come along anywhere you choose to take us."

Jetekesh grinned. “Then let’s be on our way. We’ve one more army to claim, horses to retrieve, and a victory to seize!”

CHAPTER 53

THE DREAD ENEMY

Red light enveloped the trees, and then a pulse of black smoke poured over the forest, shriveling all it touched. Navolleth pulled higher into the sky, taking Aredel from the center of the tainted magic.

The Blood King frowned at the shrinking view. "What is that?"

'A demon pact.' The dragon wheeled, turning southeast. **'It seems we backed Darint into too tight a space.'**

Aredel's chest tightened. "He let a demon possess him?"

'The same demon who attempted recently to claim you unless I am much mistaken. The tables are turned yet again.'

Aredel set his teeth. He'd spent years under the thumb of *Erisyrdrel*, watching as KryTeer changed from a thriving kingdom to an overreaching, bloodthirsty empire, while the demon feasted upon Gyath's sickening body.

Now, a new demon would emerge within a host perhaps more prepared for the demands of evil. Darint was no fool.

At least, until this moment he wasn't.

What manner of greed or fear drove a man to shed his freedom in favor of false power?

"Navolleth." Aredel leaned against the cool scales of the dragon's neck. "We must face him."

'Demons cannot easily be killed, Blood King. We will die instead.'

"Better to die fighting than live under a demon's reign," Aredel replied. "Take me to him, and then do as you please."

Navolleth circled again in the sky, great wings glittering in the dappled sunlight. Aredel leaned out, seeking the area of the forest now blackened like a fire had swept over it. A crater stood at the center of the dead trees, and there, Aredel spotted a single figure among the blasted fir trunks.

King Darint was engulfed by an eerie red glow that flamed against his head and shoulders. If *Erisyrdrel* was a water demon, this was an entity of fire. Heat rose in waves before the possessed king, and Aredel's instincts, usually fine-tuned for any challenge, insisted he run.

Instead, the Blood King grinned. If this was his final battle, his last duel, so be it. He couldn't hope for a better death than at the hands of such a foe.

But he'd not make the matter an easy one.

'Landing within that crater will be difficult.'

"Bring me lower, and I will leap down—" Aredel cut off as the fiery figure below spread wings of flames. His grin deepened. "It seems he will be meeting us."

As the words left Aredel's lips, the possessed king lifted himself into the air, where his wings expanded further and further, and his body transformed, like Kethalas or Navolleth shifting into their true dragon forms—but this was no dragon.

Darint had become a gigantic creature of nightmares and flame—a demon true. As he conquered the air, he swung enormous claws at Navolleth. The dragon veered left, forcing Aredel to clutch Navolleth's mane as he dangled, desperate not to fall. His sword flung away. Navolleth righted himself, and Aredel staggered back into a standing position, heart pounding in his throat.

He reached for his short sword, drew it, and steeled his nerves as Navolleth made a charge at the demon.

How do I best such a beast?

Smoke curled from the demon's nostrils; from its strange, skull-like head; from its wings and long, barbed tail.

Aredel reached for his power; it felt tired, worn down, and he grimaced as he drew from the last dregs of its strength. White smoke climbed his short, curved blade, shimmering like tiny fairy lights.

The beast opened its maw.

'Brace, Blood King,' Navolleth said.

He did—as much as he could.

Fire streamed over the dragon, singeing the air. Aredel held aloft his sword and clenched his jaw. The assault roared like an inferno in his ears, deafening, all-encompassing.

CHAPTER 54
ERSULTUR

Jetekesh rode on horseback from the elder path, onto the southern hills of Amantier. Two armies emerged behind him while the young high king surveyed the fields below. Carnage, debris, and flames marred the once-green sweep where two armies still clashed. *Vashalan* darted among goblins, elves, and humans. Meanwhile, dragons, *Sielie*, fairies, and gryphons fought off *Unsielie* and harpies overhead.

Father guided his horse to Jetekesh's left side, along with Prince Liu and a Shingese general leading the armed forces of Shing, while Emerin and Kethalas observed the field to Jetekesh's right.

"We came just in time," Father said.

"So we did," whispered Liu, his attention snared on the dragons. "The emperor will never believe..." He shook himself. "You were right, Your Highness." He glanced at Jetekesh. "The world *has* changed forever."

Jetekesh had appeared within the Shingese court, declared Shinac's return, as well as his need of their armies to fend off Darint's invasion, then he'd offered up access to the elder paths.

The new emperor had agreed without hesitation, eager to repay his debt to the prince of Amantier.

With Amantier and Shing at his back, Jetekesh considered the field where so many elves, fairies, and humans had already fallen.

We can turn the tide now. It's not too late.

Strange red flames exploded over the forest on the far side of the field. Jetekesh flinched, then caught sight of a white dragon wheeling around, perhaps investigating the explosion.

"That's Navolleth," said Kethalas.

Jetekesh glanced at the man-dragon. "Did he cause that?"

"No. That wasn't dragon fire—"

Jinji's voice cut in. "It was a demon's flame." He strode toward the company, clutching a shepherd's staff, his face grim. "Darint has bargained with a demon to win this war."

The words sank in like ice, chilling Jetekesh deeper than bone. "What demon?"

"*Ersultur*," Jinji said. "A fire demon. The greatest of his kin."

"Can Sharo banish him?" Jetekesh asked, recalling Jinji's summons of the prince in Emperor Gyath's court. The elven prince had appeared, run Gyath through, and commanded the water demon back into her ocean prison.

Jinji shook his head. "*Erisyrdrel* was a lesser demon, and Sharo had permission to banish her from Lord Ehrikai himself. And even should he have permission now, he's badly wounded."

Jetekesh's heart stuttered. "How badly?"

"He'll live and wholly mend, do not fear." Jinji managed a fleeting smile. "But he will fight no more in this battle."

Too late. Jetekesh had come too late. He ground his teeth as fury licked at his insides like the two hells' flames. "What can we do—"

A great black beast rose from the distant trees, arresting Jetekesh's full attention. His mouth gaped as the beast grew to enormous proportions—larger than Navolleth—with terrible flaming wings.

Kethalas whispered what might've been a Shinacian curse.

"Blessed Cavalin and all the holy saints," Father whispered in more understandable terms.

The demon and dragon charged each other, and fire bloomed across the sky, engulfing Navolleth.

"Aredel is out there," Jinji said, standing closer.

Jetekesh whirled on him. "In the forest?"

"He rides upon Navolleth." The storyteller turned his gaze on Jetekesh. "You must go to them. You alone have the authority to use the True King's power. It may be enough if you also use Sharo's sword."

A shudder tremored up Jetekesh's frame. "I? But I'm not—"

"Will you try?" Jinji spoke in calm, soft tones. It wasn't really a question. They both knew he would.

"Where is his sword?" asked Jetekesh.

"Here," said Song, marching toward them from beyond Jinji. She wore elven armor, light and delicate, gleaming silver and gold under the weak sunlight. "Sharo asked me to give it to you. He said the blade will heed your music." The Shingese woman held the sheathed sword up, spread across both palms.

Prince Sharo's magic blade. The *sword of a thousand lights*; a legend across Nakania, where every child dreamed of being Sharo, of slaying goblins and harpies, of rescuing young dragons and returning them to their kin. Jetekesh dismounted and accepted the sword reverently. A gentle tingle ran up his arm. The hilt fit in his hand like it was crafted for him; the balance of the blade, even in its sheath, was perfect.

Song spoke again. "Prince Sharo asked me to tell you this as well: 'Save my father's body, and end his reign of terror.'"

Jetekesh stared at her, trying to comprehend those words. How could he purge the demon, somehow rescue Darint, yet keep the tyrant from fighting on? Drawing a breath, he nodded. "I will try."

"Good luck, cousin," said Rille from Yeshton's horse.

Jetekesh offered her a crooked smile. "I'll need a profound amount of it." His eyes skimmed the sky. "And I'll need a gryphon."

"Not so," said Kethalas. "My wing is sufficiently healed, sire. I'd be honored to take you into battle."

"I thank you, Kethalas. And I accept." He turned to Kajsa, who stood between Emerin and Axel, each standing beside their horses. "I'll return as soon as possible."

"I know," she said. "I have no doubt of it."

Jetekesh glanced at Axel. "Emerin, will you escort our prisoner to Sharo? Perhaps the prince and Jinji can best decide his fate."

"With pleasure," said Emerin.

Axel took a halting step forward. "Save Navolleth...if you can. Please."

"I will." Insides squirming, Jetekesh eyed his protector. "Sir Lafe, will you remain here and protect Lady Kajsa? Please."

The knight opened his mouth, brow pinching, then he paused. "As you command, Your Majesty."

"Thank you, Lafe." Jetekesh turned to Father, who had also dismounted. "And you?"

"I will lead my army into the fray," Father said. "Saints willing, we'll reunite at the end of all this." He rested a hand on Jetekesh's shoulder. "Whatever happens, know that I'm prouder of you than words can state. God go with you, my son."

Jetekesh's chest warmed. "Thank you, Father. And with you." He strapped Sharo's blade on in place of his own, then turned to Kethalas. "I'm ready."

The dragon had moved away from the army, and he shifted—stretched—altered until he became the full, pale blue, sparkling dragon Jetekesh had seen twice before. The Amantieran and

Shingese armies stirred, gasps and shouts rippling through the ranks. But no one ran. After all, this was just one of the hundreds of dragons soaring over the battleground, belching flame and ice and wind upon the goblin hordes and *Unsielie* overseers.

Jetekesh jogged to Kethalas's side, climbed the glittering wing, and stood at the dragon's neck. He took up the silky mane, checked his footing, and found himself grinning. "Let's go, my friend."

Kethalas shot into the sky like gravity had no hold on him. The young dragon weaved and bobbed between his fellows, a sleek, majestic behemoth. Jetekesh let out a whoop as wind snatched at his hair and cloak.

They soared toward the forest, where Aredel and Navolleth wheeled and snapped at the demonic horror giving chase. Aredel's strange power bloomed over the charred trees like clouds of white dust, flashing and flickering while the possessed king dodged. Despite the demon's bulk, he moved with great agility, spraying flames from his mouth even as he batted aside Navolleth's blizzarding breaths of sleet and ice.

Kethalas aimed for the fight head-on. Jetekesh's hands turned cold as a film of ice collected along his friend's scales.

Two ice dragons against one fire demon.

He pried the frigid fingers of his right hand loose from Kethalas's mane, caught Sharo's sword hilt—and gasped as the warmth of springtime flooded his body, thawing him. His breaths evened. His limbs loosened. Anxiety and fear bled away, leaving his mind clear.

He pulled the sword from its sheath, and the blade sang a melody that carried across the wind. He held it aloft. Light refracted off the steel blade, and its tip gleamed brighter, brighter, until the sword pulsated in Jetekesh's hand.

"Get as close to Aredel and Navolleth as you can," Jetekesh shouted above the wind.

Kethalas swooped lower, then angled southeast, his wings adjusting to the currents. In minutes, Kethalas came up on Navolleth from behind, and Jetekesh was dazzled by the sheen of sparkling white scales.

As he and Kethalas came level with the ancient ice dragon, Jetekesh's gaze struck Aredel's. The Blood King wore a grim smile, but none of his former hostility shone through.

"Welcome back, Your Highness," Aredel called. His dark eyes landed on Sharo's blade. "I see you brought reinforcements."

Jetekesh started to answer, but a torrent of fire poured out from the demon's mouth, and Kethalas veered aside. Navolleth spun in the opposite direction. Gripping the mane tight, Jetekesh let his nerves settle while Kethalas straightened up and glided into a gradual turn, bringing him behind the demon, then charging fast.

'**Get ready**." Kethalas's voice swept over Jetekesh's thoughts like heavy snow, cold, crisp, enlivening.

Jetekesh brought up his borrowed blade again. The sword's hum grew louder.

"By the will and might—"

The demon spun. Fire poured forth from maw and flaming wings, painting the sky red and orange. Kethalas dropped his back legs and brought up his wings like a shield as he fell toward the distant ground.

Grasping desperately at Kethalas's mane, Jetekesh squeezed his eyes shut. Heat stroked his cheeks even through the ice dragon's shield. The sensation of falling flipped his stomach, and his heart landed in his throat—but he maintained his hold on the fae sword.

Kethalas drew up his wings, jerking Jetekesh's neck back. He winced, then cracked his eyes open. The dragon's tail brushed the treetops as he maneuvered beneath the demon, dodging a fresh plume of fire.

'Persistent, this one,' Kethalas grumbled.

"We need to work with Aredel," Jetekesh said. "If his power and this sword strike at once, it's our best chance."

'Right you are.'

The dragon flew upward, veering away from the demon—but *Ersultur* winged after him, discharging fire across the air. Embers fell over the battlefield. *Unsielie* and *Sielie* outliers dove away, lacy wings singed.

Jetekesh clutched his sword tighter, his mind racing.

I've got to get close.

He craned his neck, ignoring the twinge in his spine. As the demon gave chase, Aredel and the white dragon followed.

Jetekesh blinked. *Two dragons aren't enough. But hundreds might be.*

"Kethalas!" He stabbed a finger toward the fray in the field beyond the trees. "Take me to Taregan!"

Kethalas increased his speed, and Jetekesh jerked backward, barely keeping hold of the mane. The dragon ducked under a new barrage of flame, and heat curled against Jetekesh's back. Then the flames stopped, and he looked back to find Aredel drawing the demon off.

The forest beneath Kethalas gave way to the battlefield. A wave of Amantieran and Shingese soldiers poured over the sweep, joining the remnants of Norvians and the light-armored elves to push the goblins back. More corpses littered the ground. The young king wrenched his gaze from the scene, searching instead for Taregan among the dragons clawing and blasting the elements at the winged enemy force.

There. The great silver dragon ripped the wings from an *Unsielie* and tossed the creature aside, already intent upon his next opponent. A flock of *Unsielie* raced after him, glaives flashing, while one dove to catch the wingless victim.

"Taregan!" Jetekesh shouted. "I need you!"

The dragon slammed his tail into the chasing band of dark fae, and they tumbled like meteors from the sky. His flame-filled eyes lit on Jetekesh. '**What does the High King of Nakania require of me?**'

"I need you to help me distract a demon."

Taregan's eyes flicked past him. '**We are no match for one of his caliber, young king**.'

"I understand," Jetekesh said. "I only need to gain a few moments."

'**You ask a great price, but this you already know**.' The silver dragon spread his wings and issued a deafening roar that rang out for leagues.

Jetekesh winced as his good ear throbbed.

'**Steldrayss, Eatheyre, bring your clans hither**!' the dragon elder commanded. '**We fly against the fire demon**!'

Two sinewy dragons, one black and glittering like starlight, the other pale green, sent up an echoing roar. At once, a stream of dragons charged the demon, who in turn chased Aredel and Navolleth toward the clouds.

"Let's go, Kethalas." Jetekesh tightened his hold on the dragon's mane, ignoring his aching fingers. They shot after the score of dragons converging on the demon. Jetekesh leaned over to watch and braced himself for the impending clash.

The demon spread his wings, throwing out torrential flames. Dragons reeled back. The demon caught one and ripped claws across its neck. Blood sprayed the air. The dragon fell.

Dragon hides were considered impenetrable, yet *Ersultur* tore through the creature like it was parchment.

"Hurry, Kethalas."

The dragon was already beating the air at his fastest speed; Jetekesh knew that. Yet the young king's heart swelled in his throat, choking him, and the sword in his hand hummed a despairing note.

Navolleth winged up beside Kethalas, and Aredel shouted, "What is your plan?"

"Use your light"—Jetekesh sliced Sharo's blade across the air—"while I use this. In unison. You take his left side."

"I'm nearly out of power."

"Now's the time to pour out every last drop." Jetekesh's stomach plummeted as another dragon tumbled to the ground in two halves. He looked away, unwilling to think about anything but his next action.

Kethalas and Navolleth synchronized their movements, wings beating as one, throwing the wind behind them. Kethalas weaved between slicing, clutching dragons.

Jetekesh squeezed the fae blade, and his mind cleared. As though the sword resonated with the mark inside him, a clear picture cut across his view.

The two dragons broke through as the mass of reptilian forms gave way, letting them pass. They reached the demon as it sank enormous fangs into the hide of a crimson dragon. The dragon let out a pain-filled death cry.

The demon's brimstone gaze met Jetekesh's eyes and he released the dying creature. Hatred burned within those depths, searing the young king's soul. Driodere, Death himself, stared out at Jetekesh, beckoning.

Aredel's white smoke slammed into the demon's skull from behind, while Navolleth's tail smashed into the Ersultur's wing. Meanwhile, Taregan latched onto the demon's leathery neck, sinking in his fangs. *Ersultur* roared. The demon's claws slashed across the dragon elder's flank.

Words tumbled from Jetekesh's lips. "By the light of Ehrikai and the soul of Valliath, I banish thee, *Ersultur*!" He swiped his sword across the air, and a film of white smoke cut over the sky and through the demon.

Not enough.

"Closer, Kethalas!"

The dragon obeyed, and Jetekesh flung himself from the scaled back, threads of mane slithering from his grasp. He rammed the sword into one blazing demon eye, calling on Ehrikai with a ragged breath. In his hand, the True King's crest appeared. He held it aloft. Its magic twined with the sword's.

The odor of fire filled his nose.

He pulled the sword free. The crest vanished from his free hand.

A tolling note sounded in his mind, reverberating down to the core of his soul. Demonic fire rolled across his frame. He wouldn't survive this. No one could. This was his final moment—a last stand against evil.

So be it.

The world fell dark. He smiled.

What was it Jinji had said just before he died? *'I have done all that a man can do.'*

Is this enough? Have I atoned for the deaths of those I unwittingly killed?

He fell—wind whistling in his ear, his body writhing, nothing but a burning husk.

Enough or not, this was the end.

CHAPTER 55
THE YOUNG AND THE BOLD

The very last dregs of power sputtered in Aredel's hand. He clenched his fist, eyes riveted on Jetekesh leaping from the ice dragon's back to skewer Darint's eye. The possessed king let out a bloodcurdling scream and flames engulfed the boy.

The demon toppled backward, taking Jetekesh and Taregan with him, blood spraying the air in their wake.

"After them, Navolleth!" Aredel's voice cracked. A strange desperation filled him to catch Jetekesh, to rescue him from a broken end.

He's already dead.

Another soul fallen in this mad conflict. Yet Aredel urged Navolleth on.

Beside them, the blue ice dragon—Kethalas, Aredel guessed—also spiraled toward the ground, clawed hand reaching out. Navolleth passed the younger dragon, and closed his scaled hands around Jetekesh. The young ice dragon kept winging downward, presumably going after Taregan.

The demon shrank, shaping back into the mortal shell that

belonged to King Darint, before he crashed to the ground near the dragon elder's scaled body. Flames consumed the trees around the fallen figure, curling pine needles, throwing out the scent of fir and sap. Smoke crested the sky.

Kethalas reached Taregan where the dragon elder lay bleeding among the broken firs. Navolleth, still clutching Jetekesh, swooped low over the bodies. Aredel nearly jumped off to offer Kethalas help tending Taregan—but Jetekesh needed immediate attention if any chance of saving him remained.

Perhaps Navolleth had the same thought; the white dragon flew across the silent field where the four armies had paused to watch the demon fall, and he didn't stop until he reached the hill. There he gently laid Jetekesh's remains near the supply wagons before swooping to an open space and landing.

Aredel leapt from the dragon's back and raced toward the wagons, his mind darting between doubts and reality. Certainly, Jetekesh was dead—yet the boy had so much to live for.

He's better off dead, after that attack. He would have no life at all, as burnt as he is.

Weariness pressed against Aredel, but he ignored it, taking long, swift strides until he crested the next hill where Jinji knelt beside the prince's body. The young Norvian girl knelt on Jetekesh's other side, quietly crying, while the prince's protector stood above her, his face buried in one hand.

Then, he's truly dead. Somehow the Blood King had still harbored hope.

Aredel slowed his pace and moved to the prince's feet. Despite the fire, Jetekesh wasn't a charred husk. Burns marred his face and hands, but his clothes had largely been spared. Perhaps that was thanks to the strange black cloak he wore. Sharo's sword was clutched in one blistered hand.

Jinji looked up, his eyes shimmering with unshed tears. "Aredel, I'm glad you're well."

He didn't respond but moved around the still body and crouched beside the storyteller. "There's no hope, then?" Claws of guilt raked at his stomach. He remembered his anger at the young prince—his refusal to forgive Jetekesh for something far beyond the boy's control. He'd nearly run Jetekesh through himself. How stupid it all seemed now.

Jinji didn't answer. He turned back to study the sprawled form. "Is Darint dead?"

Aredel shook his head. "I'm not certain. The dragon Kethalas remained behind to aid Taregan. He will check, I've no doubt."

"Darint lives." Navolleth's voice drifted from behind the Blood King, then he moved up to Aredel's side, wearing his human skin. "But his body is broken. He will never stand again."

Aredel considered Jetekesh's corpse. "You succeeded, Your Highness. The day is won."

"So it is." Navolleth inched forward. "I would never have guessed it so."

The Norvian girl rose, her blue eyes shimmering with tears. "No, you doubted him, Navolleth. You besmirched him without ever knowing him." She shifted a satchel hanging from her shoulder and dug inside, extracting a magnificent crown whose rubies gleamed and flashed in the sunlight. "He was the rightful king of Nakania. The waters of truth confirmed it." She dug out a flask next. "He also brought this for you to drink. To heal your dragon curse."

Navolleth stared at the crown. "Then...he was Cavalin's heir?" He reached out a hand, fingers stroking the air, too far from the crown to touch it. "It appears...I was mistaken."

"Yes," she whispered. "You were. About everything."

Navolleth retracted his hand like the air had burned him, and his head bowed. "And Cavalin's heir falls like that great hero, dying to preserve life. The broken heir did indeed spill blood upon the fields of harvest...to spare us."

"To save Nakania and Shinac alike," Aredel said. "To liberate humanity as well as the fae."

"Just so." Navolleth lifted his eyes skyward. "Then let his sacrifice be the uniting banner between our two lands as Cavalin would will it. O, Shinac, thou shalt indeed rise." He lifted his hands again and took the flask. Unstoppered it. Drank deeply. Then he looked up again.

The Blood King tracked the man's gaze. The *vashalan* had all vanished. The swarms of *Unsielie* were in full retreat, and below, the combined armies of Shinac, Amantier, Norva, and Shing pursued the goblin forces, hacking and slicing at their leather hides. Hopefully, they would eradicate the vile things long before the goblins escaped the fields of Southern Amantier.

The war was over, though the loss of life had been steep.

Yet I live on.

Aredel should have been the one to give his life destroying the fire demon. It would have been appropriate—even welcome.

Why did the young die instead? Always, the young and the bold; those most enthusiastic to live and change the world.

Because they are not yet tainted, not yet turned cynical. They hope, and they strive unceasingly to learn. To grow. To love.

Jinji stood. "Aredel, look."

CHAPTER 56
A FINAL PRICE

He stood within a wide, dim space, his senses sketching the vague outline of a marble chamber lined with pillars. The outline of a throne rose before him.

"Ah," said a deep voice, strangely familiar. "This is your moment, Jetekesh of Amantier."

He straightened up. "Are you Driodere?"

"Am I Death?" asked the voice with a chuckle. "No, not quite." The shadows around the throne shifted, and one separated into the figure of a tall, lean man.

Jetekesh's eyes widened. A memory tickled his mind and instinct whispered the truth: This was Ehrikai, the True King of Shinac. He fell to one knee. "Your Majesty."

"Ah, so you do remember our meeting." The figure stepped down from the dais with a click of his boots. "You fought bravely, and you succeeded in sending me that second demon. I'm appreciative. I needed another demon for something. *Ersultur* will do nicely." He took another step, revealing fragments of his face.

Jetekesh had met this man once before in the Drifting Sands. Ehrikai had saved Jinji from an untimely death, so the storyteller could face Gyath in KryTeer. At the time, Jetekesh had been furious and screamed his displeasure at the True King for not healing Jinji of his illness. Fortunately, this powerful, imposing figure had chosen not to take offense.

"Your body is ruined," Ehrikai said.

Jetekesh bowed his head. "I know."

"You're dying."

He swallowed and looked up. "I thought I was already dead."

"No, you're merely in between." Ehrikai took a last step into a shred of light that illuminated his piercing ice-blue eyes. He was a beautiful man, fair like Sharo, with platinum hair so much like Kajsa's. "Do you wish to live?"

Jetekesh wrestled down a lump in his throat. "I do, but not if I'm crippled beyond the capacity to lead my people."

"Is that your single stipulation? What if your face is marred beyond recognition? And your hands, what if you can never use them again?"

A knot formed in Jetekesh's stomach, but with it bloomed a modicum of hope. "If…if that's the price to return, I'll accept it."

The True King smiled. "So changed. It seems Jinji's faith in you has been warranted—not that I'm especially surprised. My storyteller is exceptionally clear-sighted. Rise, High King Jetekesh of Nakania."

Jetekesh obeyed. He was glad that, in his present state, his body moved as it should with no hint of pain. He met the king's eyes steadily.

"You have undertaken a bold and difficult task," Ehrikai said, "and exceeded the expectations of all who have witnessed your rise. You will be granted new life and an opportunity to stand as Cavalin's undisputed successor. Return, Jetekesh the True, with my blessing and the Mark of Valliath evermore, though it will be much less of a beacon until it's needed again." He lifted a hand

and waggled his fingers, like a dismissal. No fanfare, no bright lights.

Jetekesh blinked, and the strange dark chamber was replaced by a fierce blue sky. He lay in the tall grass, surrounded by weeping faces.

"Aredel, look," Jinji said somewhere out of sight.

Kajsa knelt nearby, and she gasped as her stunning eyes met Jetekesh's.

"Hello," he said in a whisper.

Lafe slumped to his knees and pulled Jetekesh into an embrace that drove the air from his lungs. No pain afflicted his body.

Have I been healed?

"May God and all his saints be praised forever for this miracle." Lafe's voice quavered. "Welcome back, my king."

CHAPTER 57
HER NEW HOME

The sun stretched its long fingers across the somber field where soldiers searched the fallen for any who might still breathe. Kajsa averted her gaze from the field and ducked between tents upon the eastern foothills, seeking the area where prisoners of war were kept.

Guards eyed her with mixed curiosity and concern, probably recognizing her Norvian roots. Stories she'd overheard as she made her way across camp suggested that a burgeoning camaraderie existed between the fae and Norvian soldiers, but the Amantierans were still understandably wary.

The Crowned Rose insignia of an Amantieran knight drew her eye, and she steeled herself before walking up to the brawny man and dipping into a curtsy. "Sir?"

The knight turned a questioning gaze on her. "What is it, lass?"

Kajsa held up Prince Sharo's letter, stamped with his seal: a delicate depiction of a phoenix. "I have the prince's permission to visit the Norvian prisoner, Axel."

The knight accepted the letter, read it, then passed it back. "As you wish, lass. He's safe enough. Mellow as a fish, that one. This way, please."

She winced. If only Axel had been mellow before, instead of willing to kill for his ambition. She followed the knight past several tents to one with a single elven guard posted before the flap. The guard tipped his head, revealing a pointed ear beneath long, sleek amber hair, then he moved aside at the knight's murmured word.

Kajsa ducked into the tent on the knight's heels and blinked to adjust her eyes to the dim interior. Axel sat upon a bedroll, the solitary prisoner within. That surprised Kajsa—but then, he was the only Norvian prisoner she knew of. Perhaps Prince Sharo had been afraid he might come to harm among the others.

The young man stared at the ground before him, oblivious to her presence until she stepped closer.

"Xel?"

He jerked his gaze up. "Ky?" His eyes brightened, then dimmed. He ducked his head. "What are you doing here?"

She ignored the knight looking on, and knelt before Axel. "I spoke with Prince Sharo. He's agreed to let you return to Norva in company with Navolleth."

He blinked at that. "But...after Dakarai..."

Kajsa's heart twisted. "I won't pretend that doesn't anger me—and everyone else. While killing Dakarai was an accident, you still meant to kill Jetekesh. I can't..." Water filled her vision, and she squeezed her eyes shut until the tears spilled down her cheeks.

"I can't believe it either." Axel's voice was a faint murmur. "It was as though...every fiber within me demanded I end his life. To—to..." His voice broke. "Kajsa, I deserve to die."

She swiped at her tears to clear her vision, then studied his face. Anguish carved deep grooves around his eyes and mouth, and he looked vastly older than he was. She tried to find words, but no sound met her tongue.

Axel let out a small sob, and a tear rolled down his face. "I could hear voices. Not—not crazy voices, Ky. It was like a compulsion. Like Navolleth was inside my head, spurring me on. He wanted me to kill Jetekesh. I wanted to please him—and—and to claim the throne for myself. Navolleth said I was worthy...but after I threw that knife— No. As I threw that knife, before Dakarai even jumped in the way...I knew I'd failed already. That I'd forsaken any possible right to *anything*." His gaze steadied on her. "Especially to you."

She lowered her head and threaded her fingers together. "That's true, Xel. I don't love you. I'm not sure I ever really did. You were good to me, and I'll cherish the friendship we had. But..." She rose and brushed back her hair. "Prince Sharo said your punishment will be living with what you've done. With killing a great and innocent man. Navolleth has promised not to let you bring anyone else to harm. He spoke for you. Begged for you to be spared, claiming his curse had influenced you. And Prince Sharo relented to both our requests."

Kajsa drew a long breath, settling her writhing nerves. "I came to say goodbye, Xel. I think we'll never meet again."

His face pinched. "Ky...please."

"No, Axel." She shook her head. "That's my wish, and I'll ask you to respect it. Please. I'd rather remember you as you were, not...not this." She gestured to his prison. "Not as a murderer." The words stung her tongue. She knew they were harsh—but they were also true. She turned away. "Goodbye, Axel."

As she started for the flap and the knight waiting in silence, Axel called out, "Wait, Ky."

She halted but didn't look back.

"You won't return to Norva?"

"I won't," she whispered. "I'm going home."

"I don't understand."

"No, Axel." She glanced over her shoulder. "You never did." She tried a smile to soften her words. "You see, home is where your loved ones dwell. Land has little to do with it. I've found my home, after all these years, and it's not in Norva."

"Where, Ky?" His voice broke. "Where will you live?"

"In Amantier. The land I helped to rescue from Navolleth...and from you." She turned away and slipped from the tent, the knight on her heels.

"Well said, lass," the knight murmured, then motioned the elven guard back to his post.

Kajsa didn't reply. She rested a hand over her cracked heart, inhaled, then turned her gaze north toward far-off Kavacos. Toward her new home.

A chime like bells sounded near her ear. She whirled and found a tiny fairy bobbing before her vision. It was a woman, slim, dressed in similar armor to the other fairies Kajsa had seen.

"Greetings, Lady Kajsa," said the tiny female. "I have come to claim what you keep."

An ache settled in Kajsa's throat at the idea of giving up the skeleton key, though she couldn't say why. Drawing it from her pocket, she rubbed her thumb over the cool burnished metal.

The fairy touched a delicate hand to the bronze key, and it vanished, leaving a hollow place against Kajsa's hand. The tiny fairy bobbed a curtsy. "You are to be commended for safeguarding the key. If ever you have need of it again, we will answer."

Kajsa tensed. "You mean, I may return to Valliath if—if I must?"

The fairy tinkled a laugh. "Of course. Once a keeper of the key, always a keeper of the key, unless you use your authority unworthily. I bid you a fine day." The fairy winked into nothing.

"Well, saints keep us," said the knight. "That was a first."

Kajsa turned a smile on him. “The first of many, I think. Shinac has returned.”

“So it has.” He scratched his cheek. “Well, why not? I always wanted to ride a dragon.” He grinned, then bowed and walked off with a simple “good day, lass.”

Kajsa stood still for a moment, then clutched Prince Sharo’s letter tight in her hand and moved off to find the healers’ tents.

There was still a lot to do.

CHAPTER 58
CAVALIN'S SUCCESSOR

Crickets sang across the hills. Jetekesh sat within his tent, listening to the music of approaching night, his hand resting on the parchment he was attempting to write on.

Father glanced up from his work nearby. "Son?"

Jetekesh shook himself. "Sorry. I'm just weary." He set aside his quill and rubbed his fingers, still in awe that he'd awakened from death without a mar on his body.

Father set a palm on his shoulder, smiling gently. "Rest. Tomorrow will come swiftly as it is."

"I need to finish—" Jetekesh stopped when he heard the crunch of footsteps and the command to halt from the guard outside the tent.

Voices rose and fell, then Sir Lafe poked his head through the tent flap. "Sires, Navolleth has come to speak with..." He hesitated. "With the new king."

A fleeting smile whispered across Jetekesh's lips as he stood from his chair. "Let him enter."

He'd expected this exchange since the afternoon when the

formal surrender of the dark fae had been signaled. Jinji had immediately declared Jetekesh's right to rule Nakania as High King, then placed Cavalin's crown upon his head before witnesses. With the next breath of wind, Jinji had disappeared, perhaps forever. Amid the sounds of surprise and celebration, Navolleth too had vanished—though Sharo had told Jetekesh later that the dragon had gone to visit him.

Now the white dragon entered on silent human feet, his movements wraithlike in the gloom of dusk. Navolleth bowed his head to both kings, then straightened to his full height. "I wish to extend my heartfelt apologies for my actions. It seems I was dearly mistaken in my judgments." His eyes narrowed. "Many lamentable deaths have occurred due to my blindness, and I shall bear that guilt for the remainder of my days."

Jetekesh stared. Was the dragon so quick to change his view?

Navolleth drifted across the tent and, with a murmured "may I," he plucked Cavalin's crown off the table where it sparkled in the candle glow. "This crown." He held it high and turned it in his fingers, casting rainbows across the canvas walls. "It was the symbol of long peace between Nakania and Shinac. Those who saw it felt its weight. Cavalin's rule was a compassionate one, as were those who came before him. The waters of truth do not mistake hearts."

He lowered the crown and set it on the table with great reverence. His fingers stroked the gems. "My grandsire forged this crown for the rulers of Nakania. It...healed something inside me... seeing it again. I also drank your waters."

Navolleth sucked in air, then turned his golden gaze on Jetekesh. "I shall stay within the boundaries of Norva, as I've promised Sharo. I will make certain the people there thrive and none grow anxious to cross the mountain and invade these lands. I hope peace will be obtained and trade begun between Amantier and the Cantons."

"As do I." Jetekesh squared his shoulders. "Navolleth, I intend to reign, not as an overlord, but as a peacekeeper. I'll not interfere in the countries of Nakania unless called upon. I'll seek guidance from those wiser than myself and pay no heed to those who whisper silken promises. This is my vow—not to you, but to myself. Will you witness it?"

The dragon fell still. After several heartbeats, he nodded. "I so witness, High King of Nakania."

"Thank you." Jetekesh smiled. "Should I break this vow, I expect to find you at my doorstep, ready to mete out justice."

"And you shall."

The young king's smile faded. "I met Cavalin near Valliath. His ghost spoke to me. He urged me to aid you. I hope I have."

Navolleth bowed his head. "Indeed, Your Majesty. You have." His head rose, and Jetekesh caught a glimpse of tears before the dragon turned away. Navolleth moved to the tent flap, then spoke without turning around. "If Cavalin's successor requires aid in return, he has but to call. I shall hear him from anywhere in this wide world."

The dragon slipped into the darkness, leaving Jetekesh standing in the stillness, his heart full, his soul strangely unburdened.

He picked up his quill, dipped it in ink, and sat to his work.

There was still a lot to do.

EPILOGUE

Daylight folded to night's supremacy as Jetekesh stood upon the large palace balcony overlooking Kavacos. The city torches guttered and sparked in a chill winter breeze while the fragrance of woodsmoke and pine boughs curled over the air, musky and comforting. Snow dusted the rooftops across the wide city, glittering, familiar. Peaceful.

Four months had passed since the Battle of Firefall. The berries had shriveled, the wood was stacked, and the harvest was in.

In the ballroom below, laughter and music permeated the air, mingling with the spicy fragrances of the Holy Nocturne. Jetekesh had attended the holy celebration for as long as he could, indulging in several dances with Kajsa. He could have gotten lost in her eyes and the rustle of her deep green gown twinkling with seed pearls.

He could have gotten lost in the festive music and the fanfare.

But he chose to slip away. To have a moment to himself. To breathe.

He caught up the corner of his red cape, running his finger up and down the soft velvet material. The motion was relaxing, and some of his tension bled away.

His reprieve wouldn't last. The dignitaries from KryTeer, Shing, and the Clanslands would wish to discuss the state of affairs soon. Father remained the king of Amantier and would assist Jetekesh as he stepped into his role as the sovereign High King of Nakania at the commencement of the Holy Season.

This time had been selected for his official coronation ceremony as a symbol of peace sanctioned by the One God and his holy saints.

In the spring, he would move his residence to Southern Amantier. Father had granted him the ground where Keep Falcon had once stood. There, the elves of Shinac had already begun erecting a new castle for the High King—their way of thanking Jetekesh for uniting the two lands against Darint's greed. From that warm clime, Jetekesh would watch over the kingdoms of Nakania.

Meanwhile, Rille had agreed to become Father's heir. One day, she would rule as queen of Amantier, keeping the Crowned Rose and all her subjects safe and sensible.

King Aredel had quietly abdicated his throne in KryTeer in recent weeks, ending the long reign of the House of KessRa in that arid country, naming a distant cousin as his successor.

The new emperor of Shing had agreed to defer to Jetekesh in the weightiest of matters, after Jetekesh had promised Shing could keep its ancient customs, without interference from foreign powers.

The Clanslands were less receptive, but that was to be expected of a country teeming with warring clans. Someday, another sensible man like Dakarai would stand up to bring order to those beautiful, untamed jungles.

Ambassadors from Norva attended the coronation ball. They

were much more receptive to peace now that their lands were milder.

A ripple of bitter wind tossed Jetekesh's hair, and he looked up as he drew his cape close. Three dragons swept across the snowy sky, heading south toward Shinac. Sharo was now the steward of that fae land. He refused to accept a king's crown, choosing instead to wait for his lord cousin's return and the opening of Valliath.

Peace existed across the continent. Nakanian emissaries had recently sailed to Tivalt, Vylam, Neminar, and even Lormenway, carrying tidings of the new high ruler of the mainland. What would come of that remained to be seen.

Jetekesh didn't want to rule as a tyrant, even accidentally, and he'd already penned several new laws to keep his power in check. The countries surrounding him would largely rule themselves, but all were united under a new banner: The Crown and Quill, representing peace and order above war.

"Escaping your own celebration?"

Jetekesh whirled, heart leaping into his throat. He spied Aredel standing in the shadows near a trellis of dead roses. "I was told you weren't coming tonight, my lord."

Aredel pushed off the sandstone wall and strode closer, a second figure right behind him. Lady Thrissa. Jetekesh smiled at her, glad to see Sharo's mother after all these months.

The former Blood King shrugged. "I'm leaving tonight, but I wished to say farewell."

"Heading back to KryTeer?"

"No, not for a long time." Aredel glanced at Thrissa. "Her ladyship has agreed to be my guide as I travel across Shinac. I've had my fill of politics and strife. I'd much rather view the world through new eyes and support this change in governance." His lips quirked up. "Though Shevek and Ledonn are unconvinced of my intentions. They're coming along to persuade me back onto the throne."

Jetekesh chuckled. "Personally, I think this new path suits you. I hope you'll not be a stranger in Nakania, however."

"You won't see me for a long while," Aredel said. "I intend to keep out of sight."

The young king's smile faltered. "Do you plan to find Jinji?"

"No. He will come back if he wishes. I'll not keep him bound to this world."

"No, that would be unwise." The spirits caught in the Ruin and along the mountains of Shinac had moved beyond the Veil. Jetekesh had felt their absence at the moment they vanished from the living world. Cavalin and all his faithful, fallen soldiers were free at last.

"That reminds me." Jetekesh shifted his gaze to Thrissa. "I never got the chance to tell you in the commotion after Darint's fall before you slipped away—I encountered Heyethir within Valliath. He bade me to bring you his good wishes."

Aredel glanced at her. "Who is that?"

Thrissa's eyes twinkled. "My brother. I've not seen him since the Hold was sealed." She dipped her head toward Jetekesh. "I thank you for your kind gift. It heals a fracture in my heart."

He nodded back, glad to lift the weight of that task from his shoulders at last.

"I came for one other matter," Aredel said after a heartbeat or two. "It pertains to Artassa."

The young king caught the inside of his lip between his teeth. He couldn't find any words to say. Fresh guilt welled up, threatening to swallow him.

Aredel grimaced. "I couldn't say it before. Apologies for taking so much time." He considered the snow drifting down toward Kavacos, glowing against the night sky. "You were as much a victim as those sacrificed within that dungeon." He took a step forward. "You should let go of your guilt, Your Majesty. After all you've done, all you've sacrificed, the debt is paid if debt there ever was. I forgive you."

The words settled over Jetekesh like the gradual warmth of a growing flame. His lips trembled, but he stifled the tears that welled up. Instead, he inhaled and lifted his chin. "And you, Aredel? Have you forgiven yourself?"

The KryTeeran man turned his eyes away. "No. Not yet. I have much to atone for, and I go now to seek my true path. Perhaps someday..." He shifted, meeting Jetekesh's gaze again. "Ah, yes. Tell Sir Yeshton I've brought Kyella back to Amantier. She no longer wishes to remain in a place with so many memories of Anadin. Perhaps someday in her homeland, she will find healing. She dwells at the Thorny Rose Inn in Kavacos."

Jetekesh's heart pinched. "I'll tell him."

Footsteps sounded near the balcony.

Aredel glanced at the entrance, then turned to Thrissa. "Ready?"

She nodded. "Our rides are waiting."

Gryphons, Jetekesh guessed. They'd taken a strong liking to the elven woman.

"Farewell, Your Majesty." Aredel dipped his head, then slipped back into the shadows.

"Goodbye, Aredel." Jetekesh stepped toward the darkness. "May you find your peace."

In the next second, Kethalas strode onto the balcony in human form.

"Ah, here you are." The man-dragon flashed a fanged smile as bright as the diamond bangles he wore on his fingers. Dragons, Jetekesh had learned, liked their gems as much as their gold. Kethalas turned, his white tunic winking with sewn gems, and called inside, "He's out here, Ky."

Kajsa trotted outside, her ice-blue eyes catching the glint of the balcony torches. “Thank you, Kethalas.” She was breathless as she reached Jetekesh’s side and caught his hand. “You left me...in there...with all those people.” She wore a smile that belied the chastisement in her voice. “Lord Emerin arrived ten minutes ago. Apparently, the snows are what delayed him. And he’s not alone. Prince Sharo and Taregan have also come.”

Jetekesh grinned. They hadn’t been expected until tomorrow.

“Oh,” Kajsa said, “and Princess Rille demands you come and rescue her from watching Sir Yeshton attempt to woo Lady Song.” Kajsa laughed. “I thought the knight was doing rather well. He dances admirably.”

Jetekesh grinned. “We’ll go down in a moment.” He tucked a strand of loose hair behind her ear. The rest of her tresses were coiffed on her head, emphasizing her long neck and slender form. He drew close, caught her chin, and extended a kiss as a peace offering. She accepted it with a return kiss that deepened into something sweet and lingering.

They parted, and Jetekesh offered Kethalas an apologetic smile.

The man-dragon shrugged. “Love comes with peace, my king. And both suit you beautifully well.”

The words struck a melodious note in Jetekesh’s chest. Once, he’d feared love as he’d feared his overbearing mother. But now, in the stillness of the night, with splendor surrounding him and peace tingeing the air, he drank it in and cradled it close.

Love was something he’d won, something he’d earned—and he would fight for it every day as he fought for harmony across Nakania.

Because anything worth keeping was worth the battle and the cost.

EPILOGUE II

The golden castle spires gleamed under the full sun. Standing at the fore of the barge's deck, Kajsa leaned over the bow to study the magnificent, graceful, white-stoned High Castle in the lush valley beyond the shoreline. Where once Keep Falcon had stood near Lily River, now the fae-built structure rose like a beacon for the humans in the north and the magical folk of the south.

Kajsa's heart warmed, and she smiled, happy to be here at long last. After Jetekesh's coronation, he'd come to the High Castle ahead of her, then traveled to KryTeer, Shinac, Shing, then finally Norva. He'd been working endlessly with rulers, stewards, and magistrates to pen treaties and solve border disputes. In company with him were Prince Sharo, Kethalas, Prince Liu, Princess Rille, and a KryTeeran ambassador named...something. Kajsa couldn't remember if Jetekesh had mentioned the ambassador's name in their correspondence.

Brushing her fingers against the handbag dangling on her wrist, Kajsa resisted an urge to dig out her stack of letters and read them. She hadn't seen Jetekesh in six months. Before that, they'd spent every spare moment together in Kavacos, or in a village near the High Castle while it was under construction, whenever she could travel this way.

A year had passed since the Battle of Firefall. The summer celebrations were in full bloom, just like the wild roses near the banks of the river. Her smile deepened. Their fragrance stirred memories of the first kiss she'd shared with Jetekesh in Valliath.

The barge bumped against shore, and the clamor of the crew preparing to unload commenced. Kajsa stayed near the bow, keeping out of the way. Though she'd spent the last year undergoing her own battle—that of becoming a proper lady—she still struggled with crowds.

Averting her eyes, she focused on keeping her shoulders squared and her chin up. No one had pressed her into learning court decorum and etiquette. King Jetekesh of Amantier was too benevolent to suggest she attempt to refine herself, though his son was courting her, which meant she might one day become High Queen. Rille had only dropped a hint once, meant kindly, suggesting Kajsa might do well to feel more comfortable in social settings, so she didn't faint.

When Kajsa had confided in Kethalas that she was terrified of failing Jetekesh, the dragon had assured her that she could become a hermit in the woods and High King Jetekesh the Just—as he was now known—would still worship the ground she walked on.

Despite that, Kajsa had submitted herself to the ladies of Rose Palace in Kavacos. The court women had been pleased to discover Kajsa's skill with needlework and her good taste in wardrobe. They'd outfitted her appropriately, taught her the latest hair fashions, then taken her underwing to learn the nitty-gritty of table etiquette, court dances, and the subtle art of flirtation.

She'd also learned the nuances of gossip and polite backstabbing, though she prayed fervently not to fall under their spell. Instead, she aimed to dodge both like the diseases they were.

Footsteps approached the bow, turning Kajsa from her introspection. She beamed at her lady-in-waiting, Kyella. The young woman had lost her beloved, Prince Anadin of KryTeer, during the struggle last year. Jetekesh had found her and offered her a place at Kajsa's side. Though Kyella still cradled a broken heart, the two women had become good friends. They'd learned about court life together over the last year, and Kajsa felt less lonely in Jetekesh's long absences.

"Ready when you are, Lady Kajsa," Kyella said, dipping into a curtsy.

Fiddling with her handbag, Kajsa nodded. "Let's be on our way, then. I'm eager to see the High King."

They disembarked and found a carriage waiting at the end of the pier. It bore the royal mark of Jetekesh's newly founded House, and the interior was draped in red satin. A wild rose lay upon the cushioned seat. Kajsa plucked it up and drank in the sweet fragrance, her ache for Jetekesh deepening. Once their luggage was tied behind the carriage, they started on their way to the High Castle along a smooth road. The clop of hooves and the twitter of birds along the tree-lined lane settled Kajsa's nerves. Soon. She would see Jetekesh soon.

When he'd become her entire world, she wasn't certain. Somewhere in their journey together, he'd gone from intimidating stranger to welcome friend, and then...to something so much more. His earnestness, his passion, his self-reproach, and his inner strength endeared him to her, and inspired her to be braver and bolder. To speak her heart when she felt she should.

But he also made her feel comfortable even when she was quiet and shy. He didn't try to make her talk. He didn't insist she work harder to be heard or seen. When she froze up, he drew attention from her, quietly, carefully. When she stumbled to find words, he took her hand and waited with infinite patience for her to recollect her thoughts.

Somehow, he always knew when she needed encouragement and when she needed rescue.

How she loved him.

How she missed him.

The drive was short. Soon the carriage rolled across cobblestones, then lurched to a stop outside the High Castle's front doors. Servants stood waiting in two columns. The footman opened the carriage door and helped Kajsa step down, then did the same for Kyella. An elegant woman with silver threads in her dark hair approached between the column of servants and offered Kajsa a graceful bow.

"Welcome to the High Castle of Nakania, my lady. We're delighted that you've arrived safely. I'm the head matron, Deleen. If you require anything during your stay, you have but to ask." The woman proffered a sealed letter. "This arrived for you this morning."

Kajsa's name was scrawled across the front in Jetekesh's neat hand. Perplexed, she broke the seal and read the brief message:

Dearest Ky,

I've been delayed in returning to High Castle, but I won't be parted from you much longer. Please know that I yearn to see you as soon as possible.

Yours affectionately,

Kesh

Kajsa's heart throbbed, but she kept the disappointment from her face. He couldn't help being delayed. She'd just have to make the most of it. Folding the letter, she offered Deleen a shy smile.

"Please show me to my room. I'd like to wash up."

"Certainly," Deleen said, waving toward the stairs. "This way, please. Princess Rille arrived only an hour ago. She'll be delighted to see you."

THREE DAYS PASSED without any word from Jetekesh. A storm rolled in and stayed, turning the grounds a vibrant green beneath a silvery sky.

Rille remained at the High Castle for two days before traveling on to Kavacos to report to her uncle. She'd lingered, awaiting any word from Jetekesh, since she had no idea why he'd been delayed either. "Last I saw him, he was flying on ahead to greet you," the crown princess said more than once. Before she left, Rille looked Kajsa squarely in the eyes and said, "When you do see him, kick him for me."

Kajsa hadn't promise any such thing.

The castle felt quieter once Rille left. To avoid the human residents of the High Castle as much as possible, Kajsa spent her afternoons wandering the extensive gardens with Kyella at her side. There they discovered that fairies had also moved onto the estate, helping it to thrive. The little beings flitted among the flower beds, tending to the plant life, their wings humming a musical tune in the faint sprinkle of rain.

"Perhaps here, my lady?" asked Kyella, eyeing a patch of grass beneath a sheltering beech tree. Kajsa nodded, shifting her embroidery bag from one arm to the other. Kyella spread a blanket out over the damp grass, then the ladies sat together and started their needlework.

Despite the familiar rhythm of the needle—usually so

calming—Kajsa couldn't focus. Soon she rested her embroidery hoop on her lap and watched the fairies flitting about. Their iridescent wings glittered in the gray afternoon light.

"He'll return soon," Kyella said gently, pulling red thread through her white handkerchief. "I'm certain of it."

Kajsa nodded and rolled her needle between her finger and thumb. "He's with Kethalas. Nothing bad—" Shouts rose from the castle walls. Kajsa leapt to her feet, sending her hoop and threads flying into the grass. She spun toward the southern wall, heart in her throat, pink skirts swishing. There. Something flew in the air. It must be—

Oh. Gryphons. A flock of them soared across the sky, dozens, their golden wings shining even in the dull daylight. More and more of them had been migrating from Shinac, seeking new heights to build their nests and increase their territory. None of the human kingdoms had rejected the idea—it seemed all wanted a piece of Shinac's magic in whatever form it took.

Kyella climbed to her feet, sighing faintly. "Anadin would've loved to see this."

Glancing at her friend, Kajsa's chest panged. She stepped closer to the woman, wrapped an arm around Kyella's waist, and drew her into a side hug. They stood together, watching the gryphons flying by, soaking in each other's comfort.

Jetekesh will be fine. He's not doing anything dangerous.

Kajsa repeated the words in her mind over and over, but they felt discordant, like a lie. Somehow, she knew he'd done something reckless. Her first thought had been that things in Norva had gone badly. But Rille had assured her everything had been smooth there.

Perhaps he'd fallen from Kethalas's back...

Stop that. Stop it! She shook herself.

"Oh. Look!" Kyella slipped from Kajsa's grasp, darting out from under the beech tree. Sprinkling rain dotted her cheeks, glistening, as she pointed beyond the gryphons. Kajsa tracked the woman's finger—and her heart nearly burst with happiness. It was Kethalas! The gleaming dragon glided through the air, ice-blue scales rippling and winking with light.

"Thank the gods," Kajsa gasped, then remembered she'd forsaken the Mountain Gods for the faith of her ancestors. Tripping over her own feet, she joined Kyella in the open and waved her hands even before she spotted Jetekesh seated on the dragon's back. She didn't know if he would notice her but it hardly mattered. He was back! He was safe!

The dragon reached the castle grounds and raced over them, wings sending volleys of wind at the two women. Their handkerchiefs, threads, hoops, and blanket all blew away. Kyella chased them down, but Kajsa remained where she stood, loose hair whipping free, skirts lashing out. Praying that somehow Jetekesh would know to land nearby, she kept on waving.

Kethalas's great, gleaming body flashed and sparkled, turning in a wide circle above the castle turrets. Jetekesh had abandoned his clever saddle to stand. He was waving back at her. Kajsa waved harder.

The dragon swooped low. Kajsa laughed, then inhaled sharply. Jetekesh sprang from Kethalas's back, plunging thirty feet toward the soaked earth only a dozen yards away. Kajsa raced toward him—but a gryphon caught him first with its great talons and gently guided Jetekesh to the ground before Kajsa arrived.

The High King of Nakania was disheveled, smudged with dirt, his clothes ripped in places, his hair windswept and tangled. Despite that, he wore a broad grin and caught Kajsa up in an embrace that nearly squeezed the life from her.

"Kesh—w-what are you—?" she squeaked.

"I missed you!" He pulled back, studied her like a man who'd been starved, then showered her with kisses. Laughing, Kajsa kissed him back, just as fervently. After a moment, she found her senses and pushed away from him to look the High King up and down.

"What's happened to you?"

"Oh. I had an adventure." He shrugged. "I'm exhausted, of course, but it was worth it."

"Worth what?" she asked.

"There's a legend in Shinac—well, not a legend. It's real." Jetekesh laughed, then glanced beyond Kajsa. His grin softened slightly. "How are you, Kyella?"

"Well, Your Majesty." She stepped to Kajsa's side, then dipped into a curtsy.

"I'm very glad." He turned back to Kajsa. "I was on my way back from Norva when I saw a signal fire within the borders of Shinac. Kethalas agreed we should check it out—though he saw nothing—and that's when it all began. The signal fire is part of the legend. Only those who—well, only certain people can see it. And I could."

"Why?" asked Kajsa, intrigued.

"I'll get to that in a minute." Jetekesh chuckled. "I'd had something on my mind for weeks, and the signal fire confirmed what I'd been wondering. The watcher at the fire issued a challenge, which I accepted. That was five days ago, which is when I sent you my note and sent Deleen my instructions about how to treat you in my absence. Have you been comfortable? Did you get my rose?"

"I—yes. Yes, thank you." Kajsa felt more bewildered by the second. "What sort of challenge did you accept to look like this?"

Jetekesh glanced at his tattered wardrobe. "Isn't it wonderful? I don't even care!"

"Maybe you should, Your Highness," Kyella said. "You're soaked to the bone."

Kajsa brushed her fingers against his damp sleeve. "You must be cold."

"I don't feel cold," he said, then drew her in for a long, breathtaking kiss. She nearly melted into his arms, but the cool of his body snapped her back to herself again. Kajsa pushed away. "I want to hear your story, Kesh, but let's head for the castle while you speak. I think you should take a hot bath and eat something warm before you catch your death."

He shrugged that off. "Not yet, Ky. I want—I want to talk to you."

"We can on the way—"

"Please." He looped his arm around hers. "Kyella, will you give us a moment? It won't take long."

The woman hesitated, but at Kajsa's nod she curtsied and started toward the castle, her arms full of blanket and embroidery items.

Jetekesh tugged Kajsa away from the castle, past the flower beds, toward an arbor where wild roses grew.

"My tale is a long one—and I'm no good at tales," he said, glancing between Kajsa and the path ahead. "Suffice it to say, I had to accept the watcher's challenge. It was what I'd been looking for."

"You mean it answered whatever had been on your mind?"

"Yes," he said. "Exactly." He pulled Kajsa beneath the arbor, then softly kissed her lips. "At the end of my adventure—if I was successful—I would earn what I needed. The answer and the proof. So, I accepted."

Kajsa laughed faintly. "You're not making any sense, Kesh."

"I know. I..." He exhaled, then took her hands in his icy fingers. "It's this, Kajsa: I love you. Dearly. Deeply. You're what I want and need in equal measures, and I'm not certain how I can ever really deserve you—but the watcher said that if I faced the trials of the challenge and earned the reward at the end, then my love was true and would never die. Only those in love can see the signal fire, don't you see?"

He pressed his lips together, fear flashing in his eyes. "But all of this only matters if you want the same thing." He released her hand and dug into his pocket until he drew out a large, colorless diamond. "Kajsa, I love all that you are, and all that you will be. I want to marry you if you'll have me. I want to cherish and treasure you for the rest of our days. Will you let me?"

She stared at the diamond. Her heart drummed in her ears, and his words penetrated slowly. Tears gathered in her eyes. She dragged her stare up until she met his loving gaze. Kajsa rested a hand on his damp cheek and nodded.

"Yes, Kesh. I will let you—if you'll let me cherish you forever in return. I—I want to be your wife."

He huffed out a laugh, then caught her in a hug, twirling her around. "Now I'm the happiest man living or dead!" Laughing, he placed her on her feet, and they shared a deep kiss. When at last he drew back, he pressed the diamond into her hand. "This will be set in your crown, my queen. The watcher told me it would protect you. He also said that so long as we're faithful to each other, it will shield our love from the storms that come our way."

She pressed the diamond against her heart. "I knew you were doing something dangerous. Thank you for coming home."

He shrugged. "I'd face death a thousand times for you, Ky."

"I would rather we faced it together. Better still..." She took his hand. "Let us face *life* together."

His smile softened. "That's an even better idea, my beloved." Stooping, he kissed her hand, then turned his face up until their eyes met. "Kajsa, I love you."

"And I love you, High King of Nakania. More than crowns or jewels. More than rivers or mountains. More than my own soul—I love you and the good man that you've become."

He straightened and they came together for a sweet, lingering kiss beneath the wild roses, just as sunlight broke through the storm clouds and painted the world in hues of gold.

DEAR READER

And so, the chronicles of Jetekesh, High King of Nakania, have come to a close. That doesn't mean he and his companions, including Kajsa, Aredel, Emerin, Kethalas, Rille, Sharo, and all the rest will be gone forever. (I suspect I left enough hints that greater dangers await the denizens of Mithrinn down the line.)

But certainly, they deserve a long respite to bring proper order to the realms of Nakania and Shinac. I kinda put them through a fair bit, eh?

Thank you, dear friend, for reading this installment in the Mark of Valliath series. I sincerely hope you found the climax as fulfilling and exciting as I did!

If you've enjoyed this book—and this series—please consider leaving a review online. It would mean the world to me!

Stay magical,

—M. H. W.

GLOSSARY

PEOPLE

Anadin [ANN-uh-din] — Prince of KryTeer and Aredel's younger brother.

Anenyasha [ON-enn-YAW-shuh] — A female warrior from the Clanslands.

Aredel [AIR-uh-dell] — Blood King of KryTeer.

Artassa [Ar-TASS-uh] — Queen of Kryteer. First Wife of Blood King Aredel.

Axel [axle] — A village hunter in Tuksa within Norva.

Bareene [buh-REEN] — Prince Jetekesh's mother and former queen of Amantier. Deceased.

Cavalin [CAV-uh-linn] — Once High King of Nakania, he died defending his lands from a demon-possessed tyrant. He is the ancestor of Prince Jetekesh.

Clydo [klai-do] — Cavalin's eldest son and heir.

Crosson [cross-uhn] — A wagoner in Sharo's army.

Dakarai [daw-kaw-rye] — A male warrior from the Clanslands.

Dejani [day-tson-ee] — An elven scout.

Dij [dee-tsj] — King Darint's second son and heir to Shard Kingdom.

Driodere [dree-oo-deer] — Grim Death Himself.

Eatheyre [eeth-AIR] — A dragon.

Ehrikai [AIR-ihk-EYE] — The True King of Shinac.

Emerin [EM-er-inn] — The Lord of the Keep of the Falls of Moss Province in Amantier.

Erisyrdrel [eer-iss-SEER-drel] — A water demon who possessesed Emperor Gyath of KryTeer until she was banished by Prince Sharo.

Ersultur [eer-sool-turr] — A great fire demon.

Eviril [eh-vee-rill] — An elven blacksmith.

Fetrik [fet-rick] — Emerin's distant cousin.

Garthune [gar-thoon] — A gryphon.

Grivin [griv-in] — A bannerman in Sharo's army.

Gyath [GYE-uth] — The deceased Emperor of KryTeer. Father of Aredel and Anadin.

Heyethir — An elven seer.

Huith [hyu-ith] — An Amantieran nobleman.

Hyuen [hee-oon] - The new emperor of Shing.

Hickory — Prince Jetekesh's buckskin stallion.

Iliarass [eli-AYE-russ] — Jetekesh's borrowed horse.

Ingrid — The wise woman of Tuksa Village within Norva.

Jetekesh [JET-eh-kesh] — The Crown Prince of Amantier.

Jetekesh the Fourth [JET-eh-kesh] — Reigning King of Amantier.

Jinji [JIN-jee] — A storyteller from Shing.

Kajsa [k-EYE-suh] — A village healer-in-training in Tuksa Village within Norva.

Kethalas [KETH-uh-LASS] — A dragon from Shinac.

Kyella [k-EYE-ell-uh] — A farmer's daughter from Amantier. Engaged to Prince Anadin of KryTeer.

Lafe [lay-f] — Prince Jetekesh's protector.

Lerasundy [leer-uh-SOON-dee] — A gryphon.

Liu [lee-YEW] — A prince of Shing.

Lunalere [loon-uh-leer] — An elven scout.

Maccus — An elven scout.

Navolleth [nuh-VOLL-eth] — A stranger who appears in Norva.

Norvik — Second son of Cavalin the Great.

Obscure One, The — A dread specter who stole the True King of Shinac in his youth.

Peresin [pal-inn] — A dread lord Shinac. Brother to Darint and uncle to Sharo. Deceased.

Bennin [ben-inn] — A knight at the Keep of the Falls.

Raum [r-ow-m] — Axel's tame wolf within Norva. Deceased.

Rille [rill] — Prince Jetekesh's cousin. She is a seer.

Saylia [say-LEE-uh] — Emerin's sister.

Sharo [SHAWR-oh] — A fae prince of Shinac. Also called Sharovyr.

Song — The Lady of Crimson Lilies from Shing.

Steldrayss [stell-DRAY-ss] — A dragon.

Tallat [tuh-LOT] — A KryTeeran fisherman-turned-tyrant. He allowed Erisyrdrel to possess him in order to gain power. Ultimately he killed High King Cavalin in combat.

Taregan [tare-uh-gan] — The Dragon Elder of Shinac.

Tarrid [tarr-idd] — A knight of Amantier.

Tavassed [TAW-vuh-sed] — An Unsielie in Shinac.

Thrissa — A fae queen in Shinac.

Tifen [TEE-fin] — Prince Jetekesh's former protector. Deceased.

Vashi [VAH-shee] — An Amantieran saint and High King Cavalin's daughter.

Yeshton [YESH-tun] — A knight of Amantier. Rille's protector.

FAE RACES

Dusk Pixies — Tiny pixies that appear at twilight in Shinac.

Fae — A blanket term for magical races and magical abilities. Often refers specifically to the Sielie and Unsielie of Shinac.

Ice Folk – An elusive type of fae in Shinac. They can transform into two-tailed ice foxes.

Sielie — Light elven-like fae of Shinac.

Unsielie — Dark elven-like fae of Shinac.

Vashalan [vash-uh-lawn] — Wolf-like canines made from dark Shinacian magic. They carry a deadly venom in their teeth, and similar poison in their long claws.

PLACES

Alasiilay [alla-SEE-lay] — Sacred waters flowing through Shinac.

Amantier [ah-mawn-teer] — The country where Prince Jetekesh lives. Its people are the Amantierans.

Arch — A magical portal into Shinac.

Bahadronn [baw-hah-dron] — The capital city of KryTeer.

Blood Fountain — Located somewhere in Shinac, it contains the waters of truth.

Clanslands — A jungle country with many tribes. Few outsiders venture there due to its many dangers. Also called Zindwéa.

Cragen Swamplands — A swamp within Shinac.

First Wood — The oldest forest of the world where the elder paths dwell.

Flute Mountains — The northernmost mountains of Amantier.

Frostfire Canton — A city-state in Norva.

Karanki [kaw-ron-kee] — Dakarai's tribe in the Clanslands.

Kavacos [kav-uh-koh-ss] — The Rose City. Capital of Amantier.

Keep of the Falls — Lord Emerin's keep in Moss Province of Amantier.

KriShen Bay [kr-EYE shen] — A large bay between Shing and the Clanslands.

KryTeer [kr-EYE-teer] — An arid western country ruled by Blood King Aredel. Its people are the KryTeerans.

Kyon Taro [kee-on tar-oh] — The capital city of Shing.

Mahadri River [maw-HA-dree] — The oldest river in KryTeer. It runs north to south.

Mithrinn [mith-rin] — The Universe.

Moss Province — The northernmost province of Amantier. Lord Emerin's duchy.

Nagali River [nuh-GALL-ee] — It runs from the Clanslands, through the Flute Mountains, and into Amantier.

Nakania [nuh-KAWN-ee-uh] — The mundane world.

Norva [NOR-vuh] — A country hidden in the Snow Wastes south of Shing. Its people are the Norvians.

Purple River — A river running through Shing.

Rabahan Oasis [ruh-BAH-hawn] — An oasis north of Bahadronn in KryTeer.

Ruin, The — A desolate land in Shinac where the dark fae dwell.

Sage Province — A western province in Amantier. Lady Rille's duchy.

Shard Kingdom — The human realm within Shinac. Ruled by King Darint, Prince Sharo's father.

Shinac [shee-NOCK] — The realm of the fae and magical. To most, it's only a legend. Prince Jetekesh knows better.

Shing — An eastern country, considered the oldest known civilization outside of Shinac's borders. Jinji's homeland. Its people are called the Shingese.

Snowblinds — The mountains between Norva and Shing. Also called Bird Haven.

Snow Wastes — See *Norva.*

Tarradarryn, Hold of [taw-ruh-DAWR-uh] — The fortress in the swamplands of Shinac

Tild — The common name of the city-state proper of Frostfire Canton.

Tindo River [tin-doh] — A river running through Shing.

Tuksa [took-suh] — Kajsa's mountain village.

Valley of Litwathe [lit-wayth] — A hidden valley somewhere in Shinac.

Valliath [VAL-ee-oth] — The Hold of Valliath is the realm within Shinac where the True King was born. Also called the Veils of Valliath. Also see *Ehrikai.*

Valliath, Light of — The brightest star in Shinac.

Zindwéa [zin-DWAY-uh] — The native name for the Clanslands.

TERMS

Archon [ark-on] — The ruler of each Canton within Norva.

Dawn Light of Valliath — The source of Aredel's newfound power.

Driodere's Wake — The night before the Holy Nocturne's commencement.

Flame War — A century-old war in Shinac.

Frost Exodus — When Prince Norvik and his kin vanished into the Snow Wastes.

Gryphania — The highest order of gryphon warriors.

Holy Celes — A reference to a fae religion.

Holy Nocturne — A festive Amantieran holiday that takes place at the Winter Solstice.

Meridian — Details unknown.

Sahala [suh-HALL-uh] — An old KryTeeran word meaning 'sparrow.' Anadin's term of affection for Rille.

Serepoints — Details unknown.

Shaqel [shaw-KEL] — A KryTeeran term of affection meaning 'younger brother.'

Shaqin [shaw-KEEN] — A KryTeeran term of affection meaning 'older brother.'

Stardust Stone — Stones that give up tremendous light like stars. Favored by dragon clans.

Watchwoman — A seer within the Clanslands.

Wisewoman — The village healer in Norva. She is a seer.

Acknowledgments

Thank you from the depths of my soul to each reader, early and otherwise, for embracing this story and helping to make it heard.

Special thanks to Beba Andric, Laura A. Barton, R. K. Goff, Mandi Oyster, and Heidi Wadsworth for your immense efforts to tackle the messy drafts and help this thing sing! Thank you to my ARC readers for taking a chance, leaving a review, and catching some pesky last minute typos!

I also acknowledge my Kickstarter backers for believing in this story and helping to bring it to life. Special appreciation to my Dragon, Elf, and Gryphon backers for naming several of the characters in this particular book. Your skills are topnotch!

Colossal thanks to Sara B. for prodding at the full potential of this trilogy and helping me see a clearer vision. You're a phenomenal editor!

Thank you to my wonderful family, in particular, my parents, as well as Heidi and Tawnee. Your patience, support, and love mean absolutely everything!

To my beautiful Lost River readers, stay the amazing and lovely beings that you are!

And to my Father in Heaven, thank you for constantly dropping this story into my head until I realized it *needed* to be told.

—M. H. W.

Special Acknowledgments

To my Kickstarter backers who brought the special editions for this series to life—you're the best of the best!

My heartfelt gratitude to:

A, Abigail, Adriana Loughridge, ALB, Alexander Edwards, Amelia Anastasi, Amena Jamali, Amy Murdock, Andrew B, Andy F, Andy99000, Angela Morse, Ashley Bathory Araujo, Astridd, B.A. Williamson, Barbara Meijsen, Billye Herndon, Bradley Hamm, Brandon Blayney, Bree Moore, Brian Bondurant, Cam Inglis, Cathryn deVries, Charity Martin, Charles Williams, Cheyenne Thompson, Chris Edgerly, Christa Niehot, Christy, Clarissa Gosling, Danae, Dudley Pajela, Elizabeth Kiefer, Ellen Pilcher, Ellysa Hermanson, Emily Link, Emma Adams, Eric Vilbert, Erin DeBiase, Erynn M Flaherty, Faye Quinn, Felicitas Odemer, Francesco Tehrani, Franchesca Caram, Gerald P. McDaniel, Gina Mistura, Giselle Jeffries Schneider, Greg Levick, Ian Brown, H Anderson, HCM, Heidi Wadsworth, Helen Febrie, Hope Terrell, ianna C., Irinel, inco, J & G Sugden, J Mills, Jacob Kirby, James Lagos-Antonakos, James R McGinnis Jr, Jamie Dockendorff, Janice Muehle, Jennifer Klütsch, Jared Crowley, Jayme Waltz, Jenny Trevor, Julianne, K. Hendrick, Kaleigh Smith, Karyne Norton, Katherine Leslie, Katherine Malloy, Katherine Shipman, Katie Cherry, Kenyon Wensing, Kristopher Ecklof, Laura A. Barton, Laura Jacobs-Finch, Lea W Padgett, Leslie Twitchell, Liliyana S, LJF, LnL, Logan Kallander, Lucas C. Kascher, lulu,

Madge Watson, Mandi Oyster, Marshall, Matthian, Megan Kell, Meredith Carstens, Merrie Destefano, Michael Johnson, Mistril Merendras, Morgan G., Nicholas Paynter, Nicolas Breton, Nolan Barrett, OriginPlays, Peter Younghusband, phoenix17, Rebecca Hill, Rebecca L. Garcia, Renee, Ricardo E. Rubio, Robert Zangari, Rosa Thill, Sara, Sarah B, SARLE, Scott Casey, Seamus Sands, Sean Brady, Serena, Shabana, Sheldon Albertson, Silvia Morris, Sonya Bramwell, Stephanie Schwab, Steven and Scott Sobotta, T Haykus, Tawnee Wadsworth, Terry M Hulett, Tessa, Thann Shira, Thomas Bull, Tiger Hebert, Tim, Travis Schirpke, Tyler Cheek, Vannessa Goodwin, Vickie Grider, W. Roongkham, Xolotl & Yael Levy.

About the Author

Writer of fantasy, magic weaver, dragon rider! Having spent the past two decades devotedly writing fantasy, it's safe to say M. H. Woodscourt is now more fae than human.

All of her fantasy worlds connect with each other in the Mithrinn Universe, forged with great love and no small measure of blood, sweat, and tears. When she's not writing, she's napping or reading a book with a mug of hot cocoa close at hand, while her quirky cat Wynter nibbles her nose.

Learn more at www.mhwoodscourt.com

 facebook.com/mhwoodscourt

 x.com/woodscourtbooks

 instagram.com/woodscourtbooks

Also by M. H. Woodscourt

Mark of Valliath

High Fantasy/Young Adult

The Storyteller True

The Shattered Arch

The Marked Prince

The Blood Fountain

Record of the Sentinel Seer

Science-Fantasy/New Adult

Prince of the Fallen

Rule of the Night

Song of the Lost

Paths of the Broken

Heart of the Sentinel

Wintervale Duology

High Fantasy/Young Adult

The Crow King

The Winter King

Paradise Trilogy

Portal Fantasy/Humor/Young Adult

A Liar in Paradise

Key of Paradise

Beyond Paradise

www.ingramcontent.com/pod-product-compliance
Lightning Source LLC
Chambersburg PA
CBHW020307030826
48979CB00029B/2280/J

* 9 7 8 1 9 5 9 6 1 9 1 2 3 *